THE FORGOTTEN PALACE

ALEXANDRA WALSH

Boldwood

First published in Great Britain in 2023 by Boldwood Books Ltd. This paperback edition published in 2024.

I

A CIP catalogue record for this book is available from the British Library.

Paperback ISBN 978-1-83561-899-8

Large Print ISBN 978-1-80415-942-2

Hardback ISBN 978-1-80415-941-5

Ebook ISBN 978-1-80415-939-2

Kindle ISBN 978-1-80415-940-8

Audio CD ISBN 978-1-80415-947-7

MP3 CD ISBN 978-1-80415-944-6

Digital audio download ISBN 978-1-80415-938-5

Boldwood Books Ltd
23 Bowerdean Street
London SW6 3TN
www.boldwoodbooks.com

To Rosie and Jonathan.

To sleep, perchance to dream. Ay, there's the rub;

— WILLIAM SHAKESPEARE, *HAMLET*, III. I

There are more things in heaven and earth, Horatio,
Than are dreamt of in your philosophy.

— WLLIAM SHAKESPEARE, *HAMLET*, I. V

DRAMATIS PERSONAE

Present Day Characters

Dr Eloise De'Ath – a medically trained doctor who now works in research
Joshua Winter – Eloise's late husband, a barrister
Rose Hay – Eloise's best friend, a barrister
Leon Hay – Rose's husband, an artist
Sean and Marcus Hay – Rose and Leon's identical twin sons. Eloise's godsons
The Four Musketeers – a.k.a. The Four Horsemen of the Apocalypse
Claud Willoughby – Josh's best friend (1)
Davina Lawson – Claud's long-term partner
Nahjib Virk – Josh's best friend (2)
Marcella Jones – Nahjib's girlfriend
Martin Culshaw – Josh's best friend (3)

The De'Ath Family

Eric De'Ath – Eloise's father, an undertaker
Marissa De'Ath – Eloise's mother, a florist
Gareth De'Ath – Eloise's older brother, works with their father
Jessica Jenkins née De'Ath – Eloise's sister, works with their mother
Lee Jenkins – Jessica's husband
Jayden and Bella Jenkins – Jessica and Lee's children
Nadine Woodford – Gareth's wife
Ivy De'Ath – Gareth and Nadine's daughter

The Winter Family

Quinn Winter (deceased) – Josh's father
Ethelwyn Winter – Josh's mother
Gladys Draye – Josh's aunt who lives with Ethelwyn, separated from her husband

Other Characters

Faye Mostin (Auntie Faye) – Claud's godmother
Reuben Mostin (Uncle Reuben) – married to Faye
Steve Lester and John Lowdon – owners of the Brewery Taverna, a restaurant and bar in Crete
Marina and Yiannis Fourakis – friends of Eloise in Crete
Tobias and Thea Fourakis – Marina and Yiannis's children
Nikos Fourakis – Yiannis's younger brother
Michaelas and Donna – Marina's parents
Christos and Nina – Marina's brother and sister-in-law
Ezio and Selene – work colleagues of Marina
Cosmo – Marina's assistant at the Heraklion Museum

Victorian Characters
The Webster Family and Friends

Alice Webster –the youngest of four children
Norman Webster – Alice's father, a wealthy businessman
Adela Webster – Alice's mother, very progressive for a Victorian woman
Benedict Webster (Ben) – Alice's eldest brother, married to Anna Miston
Petronella Webster (Petra) – Alice's sister
Hugo Webster – Alice's brother, eighteen months older than Alice
Agatha, Lady Hope née Webster – Norman's younger sister, widow of Sir Barnaby Hope
Andrew and Robert Hope – Agatha's sons
Juliet Fraser-Price – Alice's best friend
Sir Jolyon Fraser-Price – Juliet's father
Lady Fraser-Price – Juliet's mother
Tybalt Fraser-Price – Juliet's older brother
Ross Montrose – Hugo's best friend, heir to the dukedom of Arkaig
Bernadette – a friend of Alice's from Newnham

Travelling with Lady Hope, Alice, Robert and Andrew

John Wendbury – Lady Hope's butler
Nancy Eagles – Lady Hope's lady's maid
Florence Parker – trainee lady's maid who attends Alice
Miriam Ipswich – nanny to Robert and Andrew

The Lockwood Family

Ephraim Lockwood – a business associate of Norman Webster
The Earl of Bentree – father of Ephraim

The Countess of Bentree – mother of Ephraim
Ernest Lockwood – Ephraim's son
Patrick Lockwood – elder son of Lord and Lady Bentree
Flora Lockwood – wife of Patrick
Deuteronomy Pepworth – father of Esther, the Countess of Bentree

The Perrin Family

George Asterion Perrin – travelling to Crete with his parents
Augustus Perrin (Gus) – George's father
Elaine Perrin – George's mother
William Perrin – George's elder brother
Eliza Perrin – William's wife
Charles and Irene Perrin – William and Eliza's children
Clara Thorsson née Perrin – George's younger sister, who is pregnant with Louis
Timothy Thorsson – Clara's husband
Clementine Thorsson – Clara and Timothy's daughter

The Knossos Dig

Arthur Evans – Keeper of the Ashmolean Museum, Oxford and a keen archaeologist
Duncan Mackenzie – Arthur's assistant
David Hogarth – friend of Arthur Evans and another keen archaeologist
Theodore Fyfe – architect and archaeologist
Harriet Boyd – running a dig in Gournia
Angeliki – Alice's friend
Maria – Alice's friend
Mani – Angeliki's cousin and a friend of Alice and Hugo
Vassilis – Hugo and George's friend

PROLOGUE

Do not die waiting
Live each day with love
Savour every moment
For each day may be an ending
As each ending is a new beginning

Forget sorrows, allow grief to heal
Hold your head high and do not let fear weaken your
    resolve
Every step is a complete journey
A moment in time, in truth
Where love is perfect and your heart is strong

Let the purity of the words cleanse you
Leave you washed afresh with each new morning
Close your eyes and allow instinct to be your guide
As you walk your chosen path

Be strong in the moments of darkness

These too will pass
For without the dark, there can be no light
As without evil, there can be no good

Allow the good to flow
And the rewards will be great

But remember, above all, to live each day with love

— ALICE WEBSTER, 1900

1

LONDON, PRESENT DAY

'I love you.'

The words hung in the air between the two women.

'Are you sure?'

'Yes, they were the last words.'

Rain streaked the windows, the grey sky lowering with each clap of thunder as Eloise De'Ath moved away from her friend, Rose Hay, to take a final glance in the mirror. Her long blonde hair was swept up in a style of old-fashioned elegance, her make-up was subtle, applied with help from Rose. Turning from side to side, she checked nothing marred her appearance.

'Should I change my shoes?' she said, looking down at her expensive satin stilettos.

'We have umbrellas,' said Rose. 'You don't have to walk far. The car will park outside the church.'

The two women stared at their reflections in the mirror.

'You don't have to do this, Lo,' Rose continued, slipping into Eloise's childhood nickname. 'If you've changed your mind, I can tell your dad. He'll handle any difficulties.'

Eloise reached for her friend's hand and squeezed it.

'It's come too far—' Eloise began, but a knock on the door halted the discussion.

'The cars are here,' called her father. 'Are you decent? May I come in?'

Rose gathered her handbag, gloves and coat, opening the door to admit Eric De'Ath.

'You and Leon are in the third car with Claud, Nahjib and Martin,' Eric murmured to Rose as she slipped past to hurry down the stairs. 'Everyone is being shown into the vehicles now.'

Eloise waited for her father's reaction.

'My darling, you look beautiful,' he said, tears welling in his eyes.

'Thank you, Dad,' she whispered, fighting the lump in her throat. She reached for her long black cashmere coat, and shrugged on its swirling, enveloping warmth, before easing her leather gloves over the clean white bandage that was wrapped across her right palm. 'Shall we do this?'

'Yes, my dear, we can't leave it much longer. We don't want to be late.'

Taking her father's arm, she allowed him to lead her down the wide staircase, draped with swags of white lilies. Extravagant, she thought, but everything about the service had taken on epic proportions.

Her mother, Marissa, waited in the doorway.

'We'll see you there, darling,' she said, her eyes shining with unshed tears.

Marissa's heels clicked on the mosaic-tiled path as she hurried towards Eloise's elder brother, Gareth, who helped her into the black limousine. Eloise waited on the pavement with her father, aware that several of her neighbours, people she knew only in passing, were standing at their gates, watching the spectacle. The couple from the house opposite nodded their respects and Eloise wondered whether she had ever known their names. Mr and Mrs 29 was how she had always thought of them.

'In here, lovey,' her father said, opening the door of the car immediately behind the hearse.

'Hurry up, do,' came a sharp voice from the gloomy interior, 'the weather is against us and it would be a disaster if Gladys catches a cold.'

Lowering herself into the seat beside the two old women, Eloise did not respond. Her father closed the door and, after a brief word with the driver, hurried to the car behind, joining Marissa, Gareth and Eloise's sister, Jessica. A moment later, the driver clicked his indicator and the funeral cortège of Joshua Winter, Eloise's husband, pulled away from the kerb and made its slow way through the rain to the church where, four years earlier, Eloise and Josh had been married.

'Are her shoes red?'

Eloise felt her mouth twitch in irritation as Aunt Gladys's whisper filled the car.

'Scarlet,' muttered Josh's mother, Ethelwyn Winter. 'Shameless hussy.'

'Red shoes, no knickers,' countered Aunt Gladys.

'I am here,' said Eloise, turning for the first time to observe her mother-in-law and aunt-by-marriage. 'I can hear you.'

'You should be ashamed of yourself,' snapped Ethelwyn, 'wearing those shoes.'

'They were the last present Josh gave me,' Eloise replied, watching the older woman's pale complexion tinge pink.

'Expensive, were they?' asked Gladys.

'Yes.'

'My son was always generous, with excellent taste,' said Ethelwyn.

Eloise turned away, feeling no pang at having lied. Josh had not bought the shoes; they were her choice. Glancing down, she noticed the rain had left a small tear-drop-shaped, darker red stain on the satin. Blood red, she thought, and the words *I love you* danced before her eyes as though painted on the cream panel dividing the passenger seats of the car from the driver.

'Her father has done Joshua proud,' the muttered conversation beside her continued. 'Four cars, including the hearse.'

'We always thought it would be useful to have an undertaker in the family,' Gladys muttered, rummaging in her handbag for a tin of mint humbugs, which she offered to her sister before taking one herself.

Eloise knew the sweets would not be passed to her and she did not care. Another hour and this would be over. Her gaze returned to the mark on her shoe. She wondered if it would fade away when it dried, or whether the shoes were indelibly stained, scarred by the funeral, never to be perfect again. The cortège paused at a red traffic light and, as Ethelwyn and Gladys compared the extravagance of this funeral with others they had attended, Eloise's mind wandered.

Four cars, including the hearse, was a sign of prestige to Ethelwyn; a royal procession for her little prince. Joshua led, his coffin – tasteful, expensive, provided free of charge by De'Ath's Fine Funeral Services – was adorned with a vast flower arrangement prepared by Eloise's mother and sister, who owned the florist beside her father's funeral parlour. White lilies, orange crocosmia Lucifer, also known as Falling Stars, a row of strelitzia, the extravagant Birds of Paradise standing proud in the centre, while tiny begonias and white, orange and the palest of peach roses were woven with shiny rhododendron leaves, ivy and delicate ferns, reminding Eloise of a tapestry.

The car behind the hearse was theirs, the three women in Joshua's life: his wife – widow, Eloise corrected herself – his mother and his aunt. Joshua's father, Quinn Winter, had died eighteen months ago. There were no other Winter family members to mourn

Joshua. Leon, Rose's husband, had suggested Rose ride with Eloise for moral support but Ethelwyn and Gladys had objected.

'Family are in the first car,' Ethelwyn had spluttered when it was suggested at a dinner given at Eloise's parents' house when the funeral arrangements were being made.

Eloise had wondered for a moment if she was going to suggest Eloise ride in a separate car. Perhaps if her parents were not paying for the funeral, Ethelwyn would have suggested this physical split, another manoeuvre in her silently waged war against her daughter-in-law. Throughout her relationship with Josh, the older woman had pitched every battle, while Eloise parried, defended and attempted peace talks.

Travelling in the car behind them were Eloise's parents, accompanied by her brother and sister and their spouses. For a moment, her mind flitted to her unpredictable brother-in-law, Lee, the love of her sister's life, and she wondered how he would behave at the wake. The last funeral they had attended had been of a family friend and Lee had tried to organise an impromptu karaoke before Jessica removed the pint from his hand and led him away.

Rose and Leon had laughed when, earlier in the week, Eloise had informed them that Lee would be taking a day off work in order to honour them with his presence at Josh's funeral.

'He's always such fun,' Leon had grinned, topping up their wine glasses. 'Remember the Christmas when he climbed on the dining-room table and started to strip...'

'Or the year he peed in the kitchen sink because he was too drunk to climb the stairs...' Rose had added.

'Or the time he farted the National Anthem?'

'Oh, happy days,' Eloise had sighed, but now, with a sideways glance at Ethelwyn and Gladys, a small part of her hoped for Lee to misbehave on a grand scale.

In the final car with Rose and Leon were Josh's three best

friends, Claud Willoughby, Nahjib Virk and Martin Culshaw. Eloise wondered how Rose and Leon were coping in such close confinement with these men. She recalled the night she had been introduced to Josh's three bosom buddies when the four men had explained they liked to style themselves 'The Four Musketeers', a name Eloise and Rose had changed to 'The Four Horsemen of the Apocalypse' after a New Year spent in a castle in Scotland with them. Eloise remembered standing outside as the New Year was rung in, toasting everyone with the ice-cold Champagne, and Josh dragging Claud's girlfriend, Davina, under the mistletoe.

'We'll be arriving in a moment,' Aunt Gladys murmured, nudging Eloise and bringing her back to the present.

'Thank you,' she replied, checking her hair and lipstick in her compact mirror.

* * *

The car swept to a halt outside the church and the door opened. Her father reached in, helping her out first, as etiquette required, his actions a subtle rebuke to Ethelwyn, who narrowed her eyes in dislike. Gladys fussed with her dress and grumbled about her shoes. Eloise ignored them both, moving towards Rose, Leon and her family.

Three generations of De'Aths had been funeral directors. Eric was currently training Eloise's brother, Gareth, who would one day be the fourth generation. When Eloise had suggested to her family she would like to be a doctor, her father had laughed, his eyes brimming with pride, even while he said, 'Does this mean we'll be in competition? You'll be saving my potential clients?'

'Or I could distribute your leaflets around the wards,' she had responded.

Throughout her years of study, Eloise had worked part time in the back room of the funeral parlour, helping with the preparation of the corpses. It was then she realised her training would never lead her to a place on the wards, but would take her into research as she tried to preserve life in newer, better ways.

Now, behind her, Josh's three friends hovered near the hearse. They had spent the past two weeks being trained by Gareth on the correct way to carry a coffin. Despite television dramas and films showing friends and family members shouldering the coffin for its final journey, the task was difficult and usually best left to the professionals. Depending on the layout of the church, chapel or crematorium, the heavy coffin was often placed in position before the mourners entered, avoiding the difficulty of manhandling it into place in front of grieving loved ones. Today, though, Josh's three friends were intent on doing things in a traditional manner.

This was their final farewell to their fallen comrade. Eric and Gareth had listened to their impassioned pleas and had agreed to the request for them to carry Josh's coffin. Eloise glanced over to where the men had gathered, sombre, their voices low, serious, eyes downcast; each man wearing an expensive black suit with a tie in black shot silk. The tributes surrounding the coffin were being moved aside, the ostentatious pillow display of yellow and white blooms from Claud Willoughby, Nahjib Virk and Martin Culshaw, followed by the wreath of red roses from Eloise. It was then Eloise noticed it: a tasteful wreath of white arum lilies and lilies of the valley. She did not recognise the description of this wreath from the list prepared by her mother and sister.

A lump formed in her throat as she stared at the tiny white flowers. Lilies of the valley. *I love you.* The perfume. Fury spiked in her like a snake and she turned, scanning the assembled mourners. A sea of black coats, crow-like umbrellas flapping in the squalls of wind, sombre faces, all laughter lost with the passing of Josh Winter.

The ashen faces gazed towards her, moving inexorably forward on a wave of pity and curiosity at an unexpected death. How does a fit young man drop dead in his kitchen? Especially when his wife is a doctor. She was there – couldn't she have saved him? And, the gossips murmured, his wife was questioned by the police. *All routine, it's usual in cases like this, but...*

'We should go in, darling.' Her mother's voice cut through the buzzing in Eloise's ears. 'Ethelwyn and Gladys are waiting.'

Allowing herself to be guided, Eloise walked up the five steps to the entrance of the church, hoping Claud, Nahjib and Martin would cope with those. Gareth and the other members of the De'Ath team would help take the weight.

At the church doors, Eloise took one last searching look at the crowd, but there was no one she could think would be the sender of the lilies of the valley. Claud caught her eye and gave a nod of acknowledgement, increasing her anger. Taking her father's proffered arm, Eloise began the long walk down the aisle at his side. Tears sprang into her eyes as she remembered the last time they had made the same journey, she in white, her father beaming with pride. Now here they were again, in a parody of the wedding, as this time her father delivered her to the front pew for her to wait for Josh.

With a look of malevolence, Ethelwyn steered Gladys towards the opposite side of the aisle. Rose and Leon sat beside Eloise, while her family filed into the pew behind. The 'Adagietto' from Gustav Mahler's *Fifth Symphony* filled the church as the remaining mourners filed in. The church was overflowing, with people sitting in the choir stalls above, gazing down on the black and white tiles of the aisle as the eight men shuffled forward, Josh Winter held aloft on his final journey.

Under Gareth's muttered instructions, the coffin was lowered into place. The men bowed to the altar, the undertakers melted away into the shadows, while Gareth took his place beside their father. Nahjib and Martin joined Ethelwyn and Gladys, as Claud slid into the pew with Eloise, Rose and Leon.

There was the occasional sniffle but otherwise the church was silent as the vicar began the service. Eloise gazed at the coffin, wondering still about the lily of the valley arrangement. A eulogy was said, words of love and regret cast over the congregation like pebbles on a glassy lake, creating ripple upon ripple of grief, shock and loss.

A hand under her elbow brought Eloise to her feet, and Rose pushed a hymn book into her hands. Music echoed through the chapel and, when it ended, Claud, Nahjib and Martin walked forward, ready to celebrate the life of their fourth musketeer with a touching but amusing series of tales – Josh at school, Josh at work, Josh as their friend and brother. Tears and laughter mingled as the three men resumed their seats.

As the service drew to an end, the vicar glanced at her with unease but Eloise turned away and refused to meet his eye. The final song was her tribute to her late husband, Josh Winter, the barrister, aspiring KC, who had died at the age of thirty-six, his life snuffed out as he suffered a massive heart attack on their kitchen floor. *I love you.*

With great reluctance the vicar nodded to his curate, announcing the final song. After a deep and profound silence, the music burst into life filling the church with Judy Garland's timeless voice as she belted out the show tune 'Get Happy' with its exhortation to prepare for Judgement Day.

Around her, the rest of the congregation was unsure whether to laugh or cry as the music filled the vast space. The words, sung in jaunty innocence by a long-dead and tragic star, took on a macabre intensity.

'What have you done?' muttered Claud, his liquid brown eyes swimming with angry tears.

As the song drew to a close, Eloise gathered her handbag, crumpled the handkerchief in her gloved hand and as she stood she gave one final defiant look towards the coffin before unbuttoning her sensible black coat to reveal a shimmering red dress, low cut at both the front and back, split up the sides. Handing her coat to Rose, who winked, she walked down the aisle, looking neither left nor right. Pausing at the final pew, she glanced at a tear-stained woman, a look of distain curling Eloise's lip. Lily of the valley.

Outside, a car waited, driven by Serjit, one of the De'Ath team who had earlier carried the coffin.

'Not waiting for the burial, Lo?' he asked, as he eased the car into the afternoon traffic.

'No, there are plenty of other people who can witness him being put in the ground. You know I hate that part. It's gruesome.'

'Heathrow, then?' he confirmed, glancing towards the luggage her father had placed in the car earlier in the day, piled up beside her.

'Yes,' she replied as she turned to see Claud emerge from the church, his face shocked and angry. 'Heathrow, as fast as you can, please.'

2

DIBDEN PURLIEU, HAMPSHIRE, JANUARY 1900

'Let me out!'

Alice Webster hammered on the door, rattling the doorknob as her father's footsteps retreated down the hallway. Screaming in frustration, Alice bent down, scooped up her Jack Russell terrier, Dotty, who had followed her into the bedroom, and flopped down onto the four-poster bed with Dotty in her arms.

'Oh, Dotty, what am I going to do without him?' she whispered, burying her face in the dog's wiry fur.

She jumped to her feet and hurried to the window as an idea struck her, but when she threw the window open, considered how difficult it would be to climb down the drainpipe, and looked at the gravel drive below, she shuddered. The drop was too far and she had no desire to break her legs. She ran back to the door and rattled it again, shouting for her father, but the only response was the grandfather clock chiming midday. As the twelve measured notes echoed through the house, pain seared across her heart.

The ship from Southampton was sailing with the noonday tide, steaming across the Atlantic towards her lost future. Tears welled in her eyes, which she scrubbed away in fury. Crying solved nothing, she admonished herself. She was an intellectual, preferring to apply logic, not emotion, to difficult situations. Yet, even as she tried to reason her way through her despair, she knew it was impossible – these feelings were too intense to control – and involuntary tears spilled across her cheeks.

Alice slumped back onto the bed, where Dotty licked her face before settling into the crook of her arm, mistress and dog forming a familiar curve on the buttercup-yellow counterpane in the large bedroom. Drawing a shuddering breath, Alice buried her face in her pillows, overwhelmed with unhappiness as Ephraim's face swam into her mind: his smile, the pop of the Champagne cork, their laughter, his hand on hers, then the pounding on the door and the devastating telegram, followed by the shocked white faces of her father, Norman, and her eldest brother, Benedict.

The scene that followed had left Alice reeling. Her father, Norman Webster, a quiet man, had lost his temper in a way she had never witnessed before. His cheeks scarlet with wrath and his voice laced with ice, he had demanded an explanation. Ephraim had not spoken, but had turned away, ignoring the Websters as Benedict had gathered Alice's trunks and bags, shouting for a porter to assist them. Instead, Ephraim had instructed his valet to organise his own luggage, the telegram clutched in his hand like a trophy.

As her father had dragged Alice down the corridor towards the gangplank and the shortest route off the ship, Alice had shouted for Ephraim, begging for his help, but her final glimpse of his face had chilled her heart: the mask of cruel satisfaction as he reread the telegram and the smile of triumph. For Alice, he had not spared a glance. When he slammed the cabin door shut, eager to disembark, Alice had felt her heart would break. Ordering his man to inform the captain of a change of plan, Ephraim had turned as though to hail her father but then Benedict had stepped between them and Alice had lost sight of him.

'We have tried to be kind and understanding parents,' her father had shouted as they returned to the family home of Webster House, in the village of Dibden Purlieu, in Hampshire. 'We have encouraged a progressive attitude towards your education, to your way of life. We allowed you to study at Newnham College, to have freedoms that many of our friends believed unseemly. We trusted you, Alice, yet this is how you behave. You betray us for what you laughingly call "love".'

Dotty whimpered in her sleep and Alice hugged her solid warmth. The soothing sensation of the simple love of her loyal pet, with its innocence and joy, was a stark contrast to the bitterness of the emotion Ephraim had called love.

Love, thought Alice. One word, multiple meanings. Love for her friends, love for her family and love for her pets. It was true love, her love for Ephraim – intense, passionate, dizzying her with its unexpectedness – that had corrupted her.

'*Do not die waiting, Live each day in love...*' she murmured. '*For as night is an ending, Sleep a small death, The morning is a beginning, A dawning of hope...*'

Choking on the word 'hope', Alice could see no beauty in this pain. Poetry, novels, plays – they all spoke of the exquisite agony of lost love. They were wrong, she thought, there is no divine glory in this misery, there is only grief, heartbreak and despair.

'Oh, Dotty, I'm a fool,' she sighed. 'I've ruined it all.'

Rain lashed the windows and Alice shivered, pulling a thick blanket – a product from one of the family's mills – over herself and Dotty before falling into a restless sleep.

* * *

'Alice, wake up.'

'Mother...'

The gauzy curtains whipped in the wind from the open window, ghosts in the gathering gloom of the freezing bedroom. There was a clatter as Alice's mother, Adela, slammed the window shut. Dotty bounced off the bed and hurried through the open door, her claws clicking as she disappeared in search of food and her canine friends. Within the Webster household there were numerous dogs, ranging in size from a Great Dane down to Dotty.

'It's freezing in here. Why is the window open?'

'I don't know. Maybe I didn't close it—' Alice began before her mother continued, speaking over her.

'I have instructed Mrs Green to light a fire and send up a supper tray.'

Alice tried to lift her head from the pillow but it throbbed. Lights flashed before her eyes and she wondered if she might be sick from the pain, although whether it was physical or emotional, she could not tell. Every inch of her ached, her grief went bone deep and her heart was shattered glass, shards digging into her soul. Her agile mind was blank, unable to comprehend the events of the day.

'Foolish, foolish girl,' Adela muttered, sitting on the bed and taking Alice's icy hand, but there was no anger in her words.

'I know, I'm sorry,' Alice whispered.

'My darling, you're in shock,' said Adela, gathering Alice into her arms. Alice did not protest, drawing comfort from her mother's embrace, breathing in the familiar scent of lavender eau-de-Cologne. 'The pain consuming you feels as though it can end in one place: death.'

'Yes,' she whispered into Adela's light brown hair, wondering how her mother could know this was what she had been thinking. 'It hurts more than words can describe.'

'Oh, my darling girl, the loss of your first love is a devastating blow.'

'It can't be over; he loves me.'

'Did he tell you so?'

'Yes...'

'Alice,' Adela said, her tone firm, 'he might love you but this is an impossible situation and, painful though it is, your father and your brother's actions were correct.'

'I know, and it was never my intention to upset Father. How is he?'

'Shaken, but recovering,' Adela said. 'For this evening, it has been decided that you will remain here. Tomorrow is a bright new day and we will discuss what happens next.'

'But, Mother—' Alice tried to interrupt, but Adela shook her head.

'We have encouraged your independence, we have always trusted your judgement, but it is clear we have failed in our duties in some way. When a choice was presented to you, the decision you made didn't guide you towards a safe or wise conclusion.'

Alice did not respond.

'Tonight, you must eat and sleep, then in the morning we will decide how to help you through this pain.'

Alice took the handkerchief her mother offered and wiped away the tears.

'Why are you being so kind?' she asked, her voice hoarse with crying. 'I have behaved abominably.'

'You followed your heart, you behaved in the manner we have always encouraged. We are to blame, not you. Your father and I must explain ourselves...'

A knock on the door interrupted the conversation. The house-keeper, Mrs Green, entered, followed by two maids, one carrying a tray of food, the other the coal skuttle.

'Thank you, Sylvia,' said Adela as the housemaid knelt by the fire, lighting the kindling and encouraging it to a healthy blaze. She bobbed a curtsy.

Alice gave her a watery smile when Sylvia cast her a sympathetic glance. The second maid, Brunella, gave a shy smile, too. Then the two girls departed, leaving Mrs Green to bustle around, murmuring to Adela as the two women arranged the food on a small table near the fire.

Despite thinking she would never want to eat again, the warming, fragrant smell of tomato soup, slices of freshly baked bread beside it on a plate, made Alice's mouth water. Next to these, covered with a linen cloth, was a pile of neat sandwiches, chicken and ham, with delicate salad leaves. A selection of cakes and, to Alice's delight, a steaming jug of hot chocolate, stood to one side.

'We shall leave you to eat, Alice, my dear,' said Adela. 'When you have finished, ring for Sylvia and she will draw you a bath. Then you must try to sleep. We shall speak in the morning but you must not fret. We are not angry.'

With a sad smile, her mother left the room, followed by Mrs Green. Alice heard the click as the key turned in the lock. Swinging her legs off the bed, she walked to the door and pressed her ear against it. She heard her mother's voice.

'If she's well enough to eat your soup, she will survive.'

'Poor Miss Alice,' said Mrs Green, 'a broken heart is nasty.'

'Indeed, but it does make the heart more cautious and, with luck, next time she will choose with knowledge and wisdom.'

'Next time,' muttered Alice in a moment of defiance. 'There will be no next time. I will always love him.'

3

'As you are aware, I'm travelling to Europe with the boys soon,' Agatha, Lady Hope stated two days after Alice's ignominious return to the family home.

Alice, seated between her brothers, Hugo and Benedict, lifted her teacup, relieved at the brief reprieve from the ongoing incarceration in her bedroom. Her parents were on a love-seat opposite, while Aunt Agatha reclined in a wing-backed armchair upholstered in vibrant pink velvet, which her mother said reminded her of her childhood in the Punjab.

'Barnaby and I had always planned to take the boys abroad but, when he died, things were postponed,' Agatha continued.

'Where are you planning to travel?' Adela asked.

'France, Italy, Germany, Austria – perhaps to Venice, then on to Athens, Constantinople, a tour of the Greek islands before sailing to Egypt and a trip down the Nile. The boys have been through a great deal since their father died. This was his dream, so I have decided to take them on the trip in his memory.'

The family were in the small sitting room, which Alice's mother preferred for informal or family gatherings. When they entertained on a grander scale, the drawing room, known as the Red Room, was preferred. With its dashing red wallpaper, exotic fruitwood cabinets and her father's collection of artefacts from around the world, it provided an elegant and interesting backdrop. The Small Room, as the family called it, was, in contrast, a cosy space with a variety of chairs in a range of colours, each one chosen by a family member, with a few extras for guests.

Alice and her brothers were on the pale yellow damask sofa, with wide seats and high sides to keep out the draughts. Alice always felt as though she were in a den, hidden away from the rest of the world, when she sank into its welcoming depths. The only member of the family absent was her elder sister, Petronella, who had returned to her London home with her young son and husband to deal with family business of their own.

'I do love to travel,' Adela said, smiling at her husband, who took her hand.

'Perhaps we could meet Agatha *en route*,' he suggested.

Alice watched her parents. Her father was quiet, gentle and calm, with a shock of dark hair and deep green eyes, a man who had never understood his own attractiveness. To Alice, her mother was the most beautiful woman imaginable. With her light brown hair, hazel eyes and natural elegance, she commanded the attention of any room she entered, turning the heads of both men and women. Her ready laughter and innate kindness won her many admirers, and she was in constant demand for committees, boards and at prestigious social events.

'It would be wonderful,' Adela said. 'Father adored to travel. Whenever he could push us all onto a boat or train, or into the carriage, we were away on another adventure. It was a magical childhood.'

Alice's grandfather had worked for the East India Railway Company and, having made his fortune through the supplying of steel, he had taken every opportunity to travel around India with his family, his excuse being he must oversee the works. In reality, he just loved the country and its people.

Tales of the family's travels had filled Alice's childhood, and she would imagine herself living in marble palaces, wearing jewel-coloured silks as she rode across deserts lit by a million stars. Her father had fuelled her imagination further by telling stories of the Greek pantheon of gods, of heroes and monsters, his excitement enthusing all four of his children. Whenever they had stayed in London, at their townhouse in Bloomsbury, her father had taken them to the British Museum to see the Elgin marbles.

Alice had wandered for hours, gazing at the collections. She was entranced by the Rosetta Stone and the mysterious hieroglyphics from Ancient Egypt, and had begged her father to take the family on a cruise along the River Nile. Each strand of history had woven together in her mind, and as she had learned about these past civilisations, her desire to know more had grown with each passing year. She had persuaded her parents to send her to Newnham College, Cambridge, a five-minute cycle ride from where Hugo would be attending Peterhouse. There she had studied the classical civilisations, their myths and history, revelling in the knowledge she gained.

'I feel a few terms away from Winchester for Andrew and Robert won't do them any harm, but I wouldn't want them to fall too far behind,' Agatha continued. 'The young scholar I had engaged as a tutor has caught the measles and we have been left in the lurch. It occurs to me that Alice is a bright girl; she can tutor the boys in his place and I will be able to watch over her. As you say, Norman, it's better she is absent until the shock recedes.'

Alice stared at her aunt in surprise.

'I'm sorry, Auntie, but I think I misunderstood. Are you suggesting I accompany you and the boys on your Grand Tour?'

'Yes, my dear,' said Agatha, her grey eyes twinkling.

Alice did not respond but instead looked at her parents.

'It seems a wonderful solution,' said Adela, adding sugar to her husband's teacup. 'What do you think, Norman?'

Norman Webster looked at his younger sister, Agatha, and Alice thought she saw him wink but could have been mistaken.

'For everyone's sake it would be better for Alice to be away from the glare of the scandal, so I think this is an excellent idea,' he said. 'It will mean giving up her place at Newnham, but she will learn a huge amount touring. Teaching the boys will give her a chance to put her academic skills to use.'

Alice felt a bitter blow at the thought of losing her hard-won university place, but as she had been willing to sacrifice it to run away to America with Ephraim, she could hardly complain.

'What do you think, Alice?' asked her father.

'It would be a wonderful opportunity,' she said. 'A dream come true.'

'Well, that's settled then,' said Agatha, with a smile. 'We shall be leaving in the middle of February, which will give you a month to assemble all you will need. I shall be travelling with John Wendbury, my butler. Nanny Ipswich will share the responsibility of the boys with you, Alice, and I suggest you bring your maid, Florence Parker. My lady, Eagles, will be able to continue Parker's training.'

Hugo squeezed her hand as Alice stared at her parents and aunt in astonishment.

'It'll be a good thing,' whispered Benedict on her other side. 'By the time you're home, everyone will have forgotten what happened.'

Alice did not know how to reply. Excitement was her overriding emotion, but it was tinged with panic. This tour was an amazing opportunity, but the reality was that it would remove her from even the smallest chance of seeing Ephraim. She knew he was lost to her, but that did not stop her feelings of loss and pain. At present, even a glimpse of him would have sustained her through her heartbreak. She would never love another man with the intensity she felt for him. This gift was a double-edged sword.

However, as her mind whirred at these potential losses, another, happier thought occurred to her: the possibility that she might be able to meet her best friend, Juliet Fraser-Price. The daughter of a baronet, Juliet had embarked on a tour of Europe the previous week with her family.

'Ma and Pa are desperate for me to see the Uffizi this spring,' Juliet had said when they had seen each other at Christmas, 'followed by a trip to Paris, then Spain. They're considering a sojourn to Belgium and Holland, too. Pa wants to study the works of Vermeer. As Ma says, the turning point of a new century is the right time to introduce me to the sophistication of Europe. Anyway, Tybalt will be in Italy by then, so it will be a family reunion.'

Tybalt was Juliet's older brother. He was living in Bohemia with a friend of their father's, learning sculpture. Blessed with an eagerness for life that spilled out in good-natured delight, Tybalt threw himself into each new passion, usually connected with the arts. What he lacked in artistic talent, he made up for in enthusiasm, and he was at present claiming to be the greatest sculptor who had ever lived.

'You're right,' Alice had agreed, 'This is a unique moment in history. Two years ago, we saw the Queen's Diamond Jubilee: sixty years on the throne. Can you imagine anyone ever reigning so long again?'

'If anyone ever does, I'll wager it's another woman,' Juliet had laughed. 'It's so exciting, Alice.'

When Juliet had told her about their plans, Alice had struggled to conceal her envy. Now, however, despite her disgraceful behaviour, she was about to follow in her friend's footsteps.

'Juliet and her family set off on a tour of Europe last week,' she said. 'Her parents believe the new century should be celebrated with the embracing of knowledge of other countries.'

Adela and Agatha exchanged amused glances.

'Fenella and Jolyon have always had rather radical ideas,' laughed Adela.

'But, Mother, how can you deny it?' spluttered Alice. 'We are entering the twentieth century – who knows what changes await?'

'Alice is quite right,' said Norman. 'No doubt, we shall witness events we could never imagine.'

Agatha smiled at Alice. 'Do you know, my dear, this wasn't something I'd considered before but, you're right, it makes the idea of travel even more potent.'

'Where will you begin, Aunt Agatha?' asked Benedict.

'Paris,' she replied, 'and from there we shall decide on our next destination. The boys will help me to plan each step of the journey, within reason, as I want this to be a journey for us all to treasure. You're included in that, Alice.'

As tea was finished, Norman, Hugo and Benedict excused themselves and, to her surprise, Alice was not ordered back to her room. Instead, her mother and aunt began to discuss the clothing she would require. Allowing the conversation to wash over her, Alice could not wait to write to Juliet and plan where they could meet. Her mind flew to Ephraim and she allowed herself a flutter of illicit pleasure at the thought of him. Then she remembered the distress she had caused and, once again, she felt the prickling of shame. Forcing her mind away from him, she focused her attention on her mother and aunt, wondering at their generosity and how her rashness had led, not to a long punishment, but to this wonderful opportunity.

4

The moon shone pearly white, matching the colour of the bones that lay scattered on the floor in the twisting passages from which she had emerged. He stood, his face grotesque in the flickering torchlight. Shadows danced with deft steps across the sky, the slope of his shoulders huge against the night. In his hand a weapon; on his face, triumph. She reached out to him, shaking with sorrow. Blood was smeared across his cheek, and his voice rang with disdain as he whispered in her ear:

'Did you think I loved you?'

5

The taxi drew up at the padlocked gates of Sfragida House and Eloise let out a breath she had not realised she was holding. Through the white-painted metal swirls on the gate, Quinn Winter's battered red Citroën 2CV could be seen in its usual place under the vast lemon tree. The shaded square driveway at the front of the property was swept clean and the ceramic pots overflowed with an array of herbs and bright flowers. Tantalisingly, a grove of citrus trees hid the majority of the house from view, so that only a little of its red roof could be glimpsed through the shimmering leaves.

'Are you here on holiday?' the driver asked as he helped her to unload her two large suitcases.

'For the summer,' she said, 'maybe longer.'

'You're renting the house?' He nodded towards the gates. 'The owner, he was a good man, he died.'

'He was my father-in-law,' Eloise said, handing the driver the fare plus a tip. 'He left me the house.'

A smile of such joy spread across the face of the plump middle-aged man, it was as though she had given him the answer to the meaning of life. Rummaging in his pocket, he pulled out a business card and thrust it into her hand.

'Welcome,' he said. 'You are welcome to Crete, to our island. Quinn Winter was my friend. If you need anything, you ring me.'

To Eloise's surprise, he wrapped her in an enormous hug before climbing back into the car and driving away in a swirl of dust and a tooting of his horn. Her late father-in-law, Quinn, had explained about the Greek tradition of xenia, the welcoming of guests and strangers, but Eloise had never experienced it before, and she laughed at the unexpected burst of affection. Unlocking the gates, she wheeled her suitcases inside, following the path towards the archway that led to the vast front door of Sfragida House.

Quinn had told her the door was of Turkish design and the rumour was that it had once belonged to a mosque. Huge metal hinges and studs held the ancient wood together, and Eloise felt a sense of history as she slotted the heavy black metal key into the lock. When she had seen the long, low, stone-built house, with its uneven sloping tiled roof, for the first time, Eloise had thought it was all on one level, until she had been ushered into its cool interior and realised it was built into the side of the mountain, as were all the houses in the small community. Looking at the venerable property, Eloise could not believe it now belonged to her.

Sfragida House sat in a large plot that meandered down the mountainside. An olive grove stretched away to one side, while orange, lemon and mandarin trees grew closer to the house. In the distant were the endless vines of the Perrin vineyard, which created award-winning wines.

Plants in brilliant-coloured pots were scattered at random around the inner courtyard. A trailing vine, complete with tiny bunches of grapes, wound its way up one side of the off-white walls, while the pink-red tiles of the roof glowed like polished gems. A terrace ran along the front, supported by an imposing portico

formed by two sweeping arches. Several outbuildings, which, over
the years, had been absorbed into the house, made up the square of
the courtyard, but as Eloise entered the house, its true magic was
revealed.

A vast airy kitchen-cum-living room looked out over terraced
gardens to the rear, each level brimming with plants and ancient
trees. Two stone spiral staircases mirrored each other at the corners
of the room, reminding Eloise of the long, pointed auger shells she
and Jessica had gathered as children on beach holidays. These led
to the lower floors. Quinn's vast study occupied the largest room on
the floor below. This had been his sanctuary, the place where he
had toiled on his masterwork, an account of the archaeological dig
of the Knossos complex that had taken place in the early 1900s not
far from Sfragida House. The room was crammed with books,
maps and journals, and, with two sets of double doors opening
onto the terrace and pool area, it offered the best view of the
gardens.

Beside the study, a second door led to his bedroom and en suite,
and beside this, was a storage room, which Quinn had hoped to
turn into a library but had never managed to complete. Another
short flight of stairs led to two more bedrooms with views of a
second secluded courtyard. A shared bathroom nestled between
the two. An old barn was attached to this level and had been
converted into two further guest rooms. The original mismatched
floorboards had been polished to a soft sheen, and, with a crooked
ceiling with exposed beams and arched windows in the walls remi-
niscent of another era, the room had a fairy-tale feel. Josh had
turned his nose up at it, insisting they sleep in one of the more
modern rooms.

On the other side of the courtyard was a second outbuilding,
which Quinn had begun converting into a bedroom with en suite
but, like the library, had never completed. Prior to this, the barn had

been used for storage. It was water-tight, and Eloise had plans to finish what her father-in-law had begun.

Standing in the combined kitchen and living room, her suit-cases either side of her, Eloise stared around, revelling in the smell of old books, olive-wood furniture and the bowl of fresh lavender and Bougainvillea on the table. Nothing had changed in the house since her last visit. The room was spotless and Eloise guessed this was thanks to Marina and Yiannis Fourakis, who had looked after the house ever since she had inherited it. No doubt they were also responsible for the immaculate nature of the exterior, the healthy plants in the pots and the garden, Quinn's shining car, which was, she realised, her car now, and the shimmering blue of the swimming pool.

On the walls, framed antique maps were tranquil pockets of calm among the many bright paintings by local artists, whom Quinn had supported. Ceramics, ornaments, curios and artefacts were crammed onto shelves and in cabinets, each one a testament to Quinn's love of Crete and its vast history.

* * *

The previous night, aware she would be landing late, Eloise had stayed at a hotel not far from the airport in Heraklion. Now, as she stared around the silent house, she realised this was the first time she had visited the house alone and as its owner. Before this, her few other visits had been with Josh. The first time had been to meet his father, for whom Josh rarely had a good word, the second had been to tell him of their engagement, and the third, during their honeymoon. Quinn had been too unwell to travel to the UK for their wedding.

When Quinn had died, eighteen months ago, Josh, as an only child, had been in a state of high expectation, calculating the value of his inheritance from his father. His plans to sell the house and its large plot to a developer had been shattered when the solicitor revealed that, while Quinn had left Josh a lump sum of £30,000, the house and its contents had been left to Eloise. The codicil in the will explained he felt it was safer in her hands and would be an ideal place for her to bring his grandchildren, should they ever have a family.

Josh had slammed through their house in west London, screaming every cruel and abusive taunt in his repertoire, accusing her of stealing his inheritance. During his rampage he had smashed a mirror, two vases, and the large glass bowl that had belonged to Eloise's grandmother and which she had treasured, before storming out of the house. He had returned three hours later, contrite and apologetic, asking for forgiveness, which Eloise had given, relieved his mood was calmer. But Sfragida House had remained a difficult subject between them and they had never visited it again.

* * *

Now, throwing open the curtains and gazing down at the terraced garden, Eloise shivered at the memory of Josh's anger. Her bandaged hand throbbed from towing the suitcases over the uneven ground. Clicking open the locked doors, she stepped out onto the balcony that ran along the back of the house. Another ornate staircase ran from this down to the large paved terrace below where much of Quinn's life had been spent. Under an arch of Bougainvillea, a long table with a huge umbrella dominated one side. On the other was the rectangular pool with sunloungers and chairs positioned in shady spots.

A profusion of flowers tumbled from raised flowerbeds, vines crept up the walls and citrus trees stood at irregular intervals around the gardens. There were numerous hidden courtyards and shaded areas holding chairs and benches. It reminded Elosie of a maze spread over many levels and she could not wait to share it with the people she loved. Breathing in the fragrant air, listening to the birds as they sang to welcome in the early days of summer, she felt herself relax for the first time since the funeral.

As she gazed down, she imagined Quinn had just stepped away from the table and disappeared into his study. Smiling, Eloise remembered the first time she had met him: the tall, gentle, bookish man, who had welcomed her with warmth.

'There is a great deal of Venetian influence in the architecture of Crete,' Quinn had explained on the first evening as they had sat outside eating barbecued fish. 'The Venetians were followed by the Ottomans, hence the number of mosques and the Turkish designs in many of the older buildings. There are, of course, traditional Cretan villages in the hills, but the endless occupation of this island has given it a rich architectural heritage.'

Josh had sighed, wandering away to fetch more wine, while Eloise apologised for his childish behaviour.

'He's my son, so to me he'll always be a child,' Quinn had replied, his gentle eyes twinkling. 'He's heard me talking about Crete's history too often to be interested. This house was once a collection of smaller dwellings in the Turkish style, an idea that excited me for a long time.'

'Why? Is it a style you admire?'

'No, I was hoping I might be able to prove that Arthur Evans stayed here.'

'Who is Arthur Evans?'

'The man who discovered the palace at Knossos,' he had explained. 'The site that he believed was home to the legendary labyrinth of King Minos and his son, the Minotaur.'

'The Minotaur,' Eloise had breathed. 'Asterion, the starry one.'

'I'm impressed. Very few people know his name,' Quinn had said in surprise. 'Are you interested in mythology?'

'Yes, but it's a neglected hobby.'

Her comment had made Quinn narrow his eyes with a flash of understanding. 'Don't give up on the things that make you happy,' he had said. 'You are entitled to have a voice.' Eloise had looked at him but had not replied.

Quinn continued, 'Evans's biography states he lived in a house of Turkish design in the valley below Knossos near the Kairatos stream. Knossos isn't far from here, and when I first bought the house and discovered a long-forgotten water course at the bottom of the garden, I hoped I'd found the foundations of his home, but further investigation proved this was not the case.'

He had laughed, leaning back with his glass in his hand, the ruby-red wine gathering moonbeams as he held it aloft, his eyes sweeping the glittering stars as though they held the answers to his questions. The conversation had ceased upon Josh's return with more wine, but Eloise remembered their discussion, the connectedness she had felt to the past, time winding its way through the stars, drawing her to the present moment, the whispers of ghosts in the trees, and Quinn's unexpected comment.

Her phone buzzed.

This is your fault!

The message was from Rose and was accompanied by a photograph of Rose's bedroom, heaving with clothes and a row of four suitcases.

Eloise replied,

See you tomorrow night!

and a moment later a string of alcohol-related emojis arrived.

Rose, Leon and their twin sons, Sean and Marcus, would be arriving the following evening, ostensibly to help her sort out the house but really to look after her and, if need be, persuade her to return home with them. Eloise knew they had her best interests at heart, but they would not be able to persuade her to leave. Sfragida House was her sanctuary and she intended to remain in its welcoming embrace for as long as she felt was necessary.

Home, thought Eloise. This is my home now.

Her mind flickered to the Edwardian house she and Josh had owned in west London. She would never return. When probate was complete, she would sell it. Eloise pushed the thoughts of her old house away. No doubt, Josh's mother would make a fuss, Eloise thought, as she dragged her suitcases down to the bedroom, but then her mother-in-law, Ethelwyn Winter, complained about everything.

6

Catching a glimpse of herself in the large square mirror, Eloise grimaced at her drawn face. Releasing her blonde hair from its restricting plait, she let it tumble to her shoulders. The white jeans and long-sleeved top she had chosen when she had dressed in the air-conditioned hotel earlier were far too warm for the May sunshine.

She kicked off her shoes, then dragged one of her suitcases onto the bed and rummaged inside, feeling her way through the layers of clothes until she encountered a cotton skater dress with thin straps and a flared skirt. As she pulled it from under the pile of clothes, she dislodged the soft jewellery roll she had hidden. She placed it on the bed beside the case before peeling off her jeans and top, allowing the cool lemon dress to slither over her head. The relief was instant in the growing heat.

'Better,' she said to her reflection, then reached for the jewellery roll and flipped it open. From among her pendants, she selected a glistening crystal and fastened it around her neck. Oval in shape, and with ancient markings of a labyrinth, it fell heavy against her skin. This, too, had been a gift from her late father-in-law, a wedding present.

'It's a sealstone from the dig at Knossos,' he had explained, when she and Josh had visited on their honeymoon. 'The stones were the clues that led to the site being discovered. Arthur Evans was a typical wealthy Victorian gentleman-archaeologist. He funded the dig himself because he was convinced these carved symbols represented writing. He had found them in places all across the Mediterranean, and by the 1900s they were being used as amulets. However, Evans realised they had once been used as seal-stones to mark goods and documents.'

When Josh had first seen it, he had been convinced it was a diamond and had insisted it was valued by an expert. However, the jeweller in Hatton Garden had explained that, while it was ancient and, therefore, of historical interest, as zircon, not diamond, it was worth just a few hundred pounds. Eloise did not mind. She had never been interested in the monetary value. For her, the stone was a thoughtful gift from a kind man and, as such, she treasured it.

'Hello,' called a voice, and Eloise jumped. 'It's Marina and Yiannis...'

'Hello,' she shouted back and, grabbing a pair of flip-flops, she ran up the twisting staircase to the living room.

'Eloise,' exclaimed Marina, pulling Eloise into a crushing hug. 'How are you? Was the funeral very difficult?'

Before she could reply, Marina's husband, Yiannis, had joined the hug, squeezing both women with intensity before disappearing out of the front door, returning moments later with a collection of bulging shopping bags hanging from his arms.

'You are too young to be a widow,' said Marina as she released Eloise, tears streaming down her face, a stark contrast to Eloise's dry eyes and pinched face. 'I said to Yiannis, she is coming here to recover. We will care for her like she is family. In fact, you are family. Quinn was family and, therefore, so are you. Not to mention, we are friends.'

As Marina wiped her eyes, Eloise glanced over at Yiannis, who was loading her fridge with vast amounts of food.

'Eloise,' he said, his voice muffled as he crammed items into the vegetable drawer. 'You are safe. We shall hold you tight to our bosom. You will recover in Crete, where the air is pure, where we are here to look after you.'

Eloise smiled, touched by this sentiment. Yiannis's pronouncement reminded her of her own family and their desire to draw everyone in, to protect and care for them. It was a trait Josh had, at first, loved about their marriage and his relationship with the De'Ath family. She had always felt blessed to be surrounded by people who cared about her, but now her family understood her desire to flee, even them, and to spend time alone in the secluded sunshine of the house in Crete rather than be surrounded by memories of her marriage and her husband's death.

'I have made you iced tea,' Marina declared as though it were an elixir from the gods to heal her sorrow. 'Whatever you need, you call us, yes?' She squeezed Eloise's hands.

'Of course. Thank you, Marina, but I don't want to be a burden.'

'You would never be a burden. Quinn was a good man. He helped Yiannis and me, as well as our families, many times over the years. The least we can do is look after you while you recover.'

'Anything you need – anything – we shall provide,' Yiannis continued. 'We are family. As Marina said, Quinn was a good man, and you are his daughter-in-law. He loved you very much and we will love you and protect you in the same way he would have done.'

'There are several months of my sabbatical left,' Marina said, 'so I'm available. You're not alone in your grief, Eloise.'

Marina was on a year-long sabbatical from her position as a Senior Curator at the Heraklion Museum. The time off was for her to complete her PhD. Yiannis worked for the vineyard, winery and guest house owned by Marina's family, which could be seen from the front of Sfragida House.

'We have spoken to John and Steve at the Brewery Taverna,' continued Yiannis, continuing to stock the fridge. 'They have said the same: whatever you need, they will help. You are one of us now, Eloise, and you will heal in the hot Cretan sun.'

Marina looked at her husband with immense pride. The couple were a few years older than Eloise, with two young children, Tobias and Thea, and Marina had endless energy. Now she moved around the big room, straightening cushions, dead-heading a plant, her brown eyes continuing to swim with unshed tears, her high pony-tail swinging from side to side.

'We have kept the house clean,' Marina said, spreading her hands. 'Quinn continues to pay us from a bequest in his will and one of our team will come in once a week to clean for you too. They take care of our guesthouse and the apartments, as well as our house at the vineyard; this is easy to fit into their routine.'

Eloise was about to protest, aware Marina and Yiannis and the extended family owned several businesses, all connected to the vast and successful vineyard, but then changed her mind. Being alone had been her salvation when her life in London had been endlessly busy but, in her present state of mind, grieving and shocked as she was, total isolation was unhealthy. Eloise knew that too much time on her own would leave her with many dark moments to brood, which was dangerous. A visit from one of Marina's cheery team once a week over the coming months would be helpful.

'Thank you,' she said, 'but I'm willing to pay.'

'No!' said Yiannis, his voice floating up from behind the fridge door where he was crouched, loading bottles of water, soft drinks, beer and wine from the family vineyard. As he began sliding bottles of red wine into an elaborate wrought-iron wine rack decorated with flowing metal vines and bunches of grapes, he continued in a firm tone, 'Quinn has left you in our care and this will not change.'

'Thank you,' said Eloise, 'but, please, tell me if I become—'

'Enough with the talk of burdens,' said Marina. Her tone held a hint of humour but her eyes flashed with determination as she cut off Eloise's sentence. 'And no, you can't pay us for the groceries, either. They're our gift while you settle in. Now, we will leave you in peace. Our phone numbers are on the fridge. There are takeaway menus, too, but I made you a fish stew and there is fresh bread for your supper. Tomorrow, we shall walk you around the village so you know everyone and they know you. Then you are family.'

Marina beamed and, as Yiannis finished gathering up the shopping bags in which he had brought Eloise's supplies, she rummaged in her vast woven handbag.

'Quinn asked me to give you this,' Marina said, placing an envelope on the kitchen counter, straightening it with reverential hands. 'He said, it is to help you move forward.'

She wiped her eyes, then hugged Eloise again before she and Yiannis disappeared in a flurry of '*Ta lémes*', leaving Eloise feeling as though she had been engulfed by a well-meaning but unnerving hurricane. As Marina and Yiannis drove away, waving from their 4x4, a void of silence hovered in their wake. Eloise stared around the room before slumping onto one of the pale lemon sofas.

* * *

Reaching for the iced mint tea Marina had left – a concoction of her own creation, she had explained to Eloise, a version of a non-alcoholic mojito, which she had drunk during her pregnancy with Thea – Eloise understood why Marina called it an elixir from the gods. She wondered whether the vineyard would ever think to manufacture it.

Stretching out on the sofa, she considered these people. Marina and Yiannis were behaving with more compassion than Josh's family and friends in the aftermath of her husband's shocking and unexpected death. Despite her best efforts, she heard the echo of Josh's best friend, Claud Willoughby, shouting, maddened by grief after he had been told about Josh's heart attack.

'You're a doctor,' Claud had raged. 'You should have saved him.'

But Eloise had knelt beside her husband's prone figure on the kitchen floor, trying to revive him, her phone open to the ambulance service as she worked. Now, anger bubbled inside her, volcanic, destructive, as she thought of Claud. Tall, handsome, successful, interfering, pompous – everything about the man made her cringe.

How dare he try to lay the blame for Josh's death at her feet? Claud was a doctor, too, although he had an expensive Harley Street practice and a lifestyle to match. He should have understood the difficulties of saving a life. Despite her best efforts, Eloise knew there was nothing she could have done to save Josh.

Realising such introspection was foolish, Eloise wandered over to the kitchen and opened the fridge. The contents pushed all thoughts of Claud from her mind, and she let out her first genuine laugh in weeks. It was doubtful Yiannis could have squeezed anything else inside. Tomatoes, cheeses, salad, yogurts, treats cooked by Marina, pre-prepared *souvlaki*, dishes of olives and, to her delight, a few home comforts including peanut butter, filled every shelf.

Inspecting a few of the packages, she saw a box of the Cretan *kalitsounia* – the local delicacy of sweet mini cheese pies, which Eloise had discovered on her first visit to Crete – made by Marina's mother, Donna. Groaning with pleasure, she reached for these, a dish of olives and a bottle of water, before picking up the letter Marina had left and letting herself outside to read Quinn's final message in his favourite spot in the garden.

7

There was a knock on the cabin door.

'Alice, my dear,' came her aunt's voice, 'we shall be disembarking in a few minutes. Ensure you have your valise and reticule. The remainder of the luggage will be dealt with by Wendbury and the porter. We must disembark together as we shall be shown on to the correct train for the journey to Paris by a representative of the Grand Hôtel d'Angleterre.'

'Yes, Aunt Agatha,' Alice responded, closing the lid of her inkwell with care and folding away the leather writing chest her parents had given her as a going-away present. Leaving it beside her trunk, she moved across the small private cabin her aunt had rented for their journey on the South Eastern and Continental Steam Packet, and checked her reflection in the sliver of mirror in the compact bathroom. Having smoothed her red-gold hair, she pinned her hat on at a jaunty angle before picking up her overnight bag and looping the handle of her reticule around her wrist. Checking she had left nothing behind but her luggage, she exited into the corridor, which was beginning to fill with eager travellers.

The journey had taken them by train from London Bridge to

Dover before they crossed the Channel to Calais, where a further train would now take them on to Paris. Allowing the flow of people to sweep her forward, Alice was soon clear of the narrow passageways on the lower deck and was pushing her way through the crowd onto the main deck where her aunt, Lady Hope, awaited her with Alice's two young cousins, Andrew and Robert. Andrew was thirteen and beginning to develop an awkwardness as his limbs grew and his voice deepened. Robert was two years younger and obsessed with all things to do with sport.

A few paces away, Agatha's lady's maid, Nancy Eagles, was waiting with bored impatience, while beside her was Florence Parker, who was being trained to become Alice's lady's maid. Florence stared around with eager eyes, her excitement palpable. The tall, wiry frame of Nanny Miriam Ipswich, purse-mouthed and nervous, stood nearby. With an alert air, as though danger were possible with every step, Agatha's butler, John Wendbury, who was travelling with them in the combined role of steward and chaperone, was searching the approaching quayside for the porter he had hired to ensure the smoothness of their onward journey.

'There you are, my dear,' said Agatha as Alice joined them. 'Isn't the sea air bracing?'

'Yes, Auntie,' she replied, remembering the last time she had been on a boat.

Again, the confusing cocktail of emotions slewed through her mind: shame at the pain she had inflicted upon her family, mixed with an illicit feeling of raw grief for the loss of Ephraim.

'Alice, dear,' said her aunt in a low voice to ensure no one would overhear, 'we shall shortly be boarding a train for Paris. I believe it is time you began to control your behaviour.'

Alice gave her aunt a guilty look, then her pride surfaced.

'What do you mean, Auntie?'

'You drift away at the most inopportune moments, losing

yourself in a world of self-indulgence,' said Agatha as Alice blushed. She had hoped these transgressions had been undetectable, but it appeared not. 'You're not the first person to suffer from a broken heart and, I can assure you, there is no likelihood that you will be the last. I have indulged you thus far and I will, for a short while, continue to make allowances for your emotional state, but there must come a time when you realise what you did was wrong – very wrong – and your behaviour has hurt many people.'

'Yes, Auntie, I am aware of the pain my actions have caused,' Alice said, her teeth gritted. 'I shall try, but these waves of despair overwhelm me and—'

Alice halted, cutting the sentence short at the expression on her aunt's face. They would be travelling together for the foreseeable future and Alice was sensible enough to understand her aunt's patience was wearing thin. Her mind flashed to her sister, Petronella, and their brief encounter before Alice set off on her journey. The disappointment in her sister's eyes had left Alice haunted.

'M'lady, our escort is here,' announced Wendbury.

Forcing her thoughts away from her sister, Alice turned her attention to her young cousins, ensuring they did not wander away and disappear into the crowd. As she chivvied them forward, she heard Wendbury continue, 'Shall we entrain, m'lady?'

'Thank you, Wendbury. Andrew, Robert, this way, please. Alice, are you there?'

Alice shepherded her cousins towards their mother, as Wendbury raised his umbrella in the manner of a sword and began to cut a swathe through the docile crowd as though they were hordes of marauding soldiers. Wincing at the abruptness of his behaviour, Alice offered apologetic smiles to their fellow travellers as they passed. She was intrigued to be on foreign soil for the first time and, as they wended their way down the gangplank, natural curiosity made her look around, her misery of earlier forgotten.

'This way, m'lady,' said Wendbury, ushering them towards the terminal where the train would take them first to Lille, then Arras, Amiens, Creil and on to Paris. His eyes fixed on the porter wearing the uniform of the Grand Hôtel d'Angleterre, who was corralling other travellers towards the first-class compartments of the train.

'London to Paris in twelve and a half hours,' said Florence as they entered Agatha's carriage. 'Whoever would have thought it possible? We live in a wondrous age.'

'Wondrous,' Alice echoed, grinning.

Agatha, Alice, Andrew and Robert would travel in First Class, while Nanny, Eagles, Florence and Wendbury would be in Third Class, attending the family when necessary. As Wendbury set off to check on their enormous amounts of baggage, Alice and Agatha settled into their seats. The two ladies' maids and Nanny disappeared down the train in search of their own accommodation.

With a shrill scream, the engine puffed clouds of smoke and the train edged forward, causing the boys to whoop with excitement.

'We're off,' shouted Andrew, leaning out of the window as the train gathered speed. Alice joined him, as eager for her first glimpse of France as her cousin, while Robert announced he was hungry.

'There is a restaurant car,' said Agatha. 'It will be serving breakfast in a few minutes but—'

'Can we go, Mama?' interrupted Robert, his hands held together in an exaggerated stance of pleading. 'It will be more fun than eating in here.'

Alice knew her aunt abhorred eating in public, believing it to be common, but she watched as Agatha wavered, staring down at her younger son's beguiling face. Her stern expression and the armour she wore of prim Victorian dowager hid a well of natural maternal instinct and a kind heart. As Robert whispered, 'Please, please,

please...' backed up by Andrew aping his hand-clasped praying gesture, Agatha laughed.

'Of course, Robbie,' she said, her smile lighting up her face and making her look years younger. 'We're on an adventure. I, too, should do things I would not consider doing at home. Alice, will you join us?'

'Or will you be wasting away here, writing bad love poetry in desolate isolation? A bit like the Lady of Shalott,' asked Andrew, causing both Robert and Agatha to stifle laughter.

'Who said it was bad poetry?' countered Alice, taken aback that her young cousins had noticed her misery. 'I spent two years at Newnham – I write good poetry.'

'Perhaps you could recite some of it over breakfast,' suggested Andrew, and Agatha smothered another laugh.

'Please, no,' said Robbie, hopping on one leg, while pushing his brother. 'It would give us terrible indigestion.'

Alice stared after her young cousins. Did no one understand her misery? Then a thought entered her head, one spoken in her usual rational voice rather than her recent tear-soaked breathy unhappiness: *Is this misery or self-indulgence?*

Heat tinged her cheeks into a blotchy pink as she contemplated her own traitorous thought. It is heartbreak, she assured herself, but the protest sounded hollow, causing her to squirm with embarrassment at the behaviour that her love for Ephraim and their subsequent parting was causing. *Perhaps if he had contacted me...* she thought, but she knew this was impossible. Recollection of the look of triumph on his face when he had received the telegram crept into Alice's mind. For the first time she realised the strangeness of his reaction. He should have displayed grief or despair, yet neither had been apparent. Perhaps I misunderstood, she thought, before exclaiming in pain as Robert landed on her foot.

'Sorry, Ally,' he laughed. 'I'm hopping all the way to the dining car.'

Behind him, Andrew was listing all his favourite breakfast foods, while trying to trip his brother.

'Boys, enough,' said Agatha, as they reached the coupling between two carriages. 'Walk properly, Robert, and, Andrew, stop pushing him or shall I advise Wendbury to lock you both in the baggage car until we reach Paris.'

Alice wagged her finger and said in mock-sternness,

'As your governess, I shall have to start thinking of some strict rules in order to keep you two in line.'

She took Robert's hand as he wobbled with the movement of the train and he grinned up at her.

'You've already threatened us with your terrible poetry – isn't that scary enough?' he said, and despite herself, Alice giggled as they entered the dining car.

Agatha followed the waiter to a table, where the boys wriggled in their seats until freed to make merry at the buffet. Alice sat opposite her aunt, gazing out across the enormous flat fields of France.

'I shall order tea. Please do not suggest coffee; we might be on the Continent but we are British,' said Agatha.

'Tea would be wonderful, Auntie,' Alice replied. Then, glancing over at her cousins, who were piling food on their plates, she continued, 'Would you like me to fetch your breakfast before the boys devour the entire buffet?'

'A kipper would be most acceptable, if they have such a thing.'

Having squeezed out of the narrow seats, Alice walked the length of the dining car. Her eyes darting around as she took in her surroundings, glancing at their fellow passengers, she felt a thrill of excitement running through her as she recognised French, Italian and German being spoken. The food, too, was a mix of traditional British fare, combined with pastries, platters of cold meats, cheeses and fruits she did not recognise. She selected a kipper for her aunt, which the waiter hurried to deliver to the table, then she loaded her own plate with the unfamiliar pastries and cheeses, joining her cousins, who were battling over the final rasher of bacon.

'You have three slices each,' she scolded, staring at their towering plates. 'Eat what you have first, and when the stewards refill the serving dishes you may be allowed more.'

Back at the table, Agatha inspected their choices, raising her eyebrows at Alice's selection before the boys fell on their food. Alice had eaten a few mouthfuls when her attention was caught by the steward, who was showing a tired-looking middle-aged couple to a table for two further along the carriage.

'*Monsieur, madame...*' he bowed them towards it, and the woman bit her lip and shot her husband an anxious look.

'*Trois*,' explained the man. 'My son...' he continued.

'*Mon fils*,' supplied Andrew through a mouthful of toast.

'Thank you,' the man said with a smile, his Devonian vowels soft and warm, a sound of home among the Europeans. The steward pointed to the table across the carriage from their group. 'I'd quite forgotten we were in France,' the man continued with a cheery wink at Andrew.

In contrast, his wife looked distressed, and as they took their seat, she gripped her husband's hand.

'Where is he?' she hissed. 'Did he miss the train...?'

'Don't worry, Elaine,' he reassured her. 'He'll be here. He's probably putting his bag in his cabin.'

As he spoke, the door to the dining car opened and Alice looked up. The croissant she was eating remained halfway to her mouth as she stared at the young man who was framed in the doorway. In his early twenties, he was of medium height, with dark hair, brushed back and worn long to the collar. His face was flushed and his manner flustered, his piercing brown eyes with their thick, dark

lashes scoured the carriage until his gaze fell on the couple oppo-
site the Hope party. Alice felt a thrill of unease at the look of intense
anger on his face. Despite this, his high-cheekboned face was of
such extreme beauty that, had he had not been dressed in a well-
cut woollen suit, Alice would have been reminded of the statues of
the Greek gods she so admired in the British Museum.

'Mother, Father, apologies,' the man said, seating himself with
his parents. 'It was imperative to send Millicent a telegram before
we departed.'

'It could have waited until Paris,' said the older man. His tone
was mild but the reprimand was unmistakable. 'Your mother was
worried you had missed the train.'

'As you can see, Mother, I did not,' the young man said, his voice
clipped, and Alice noticed his knuckles were white as he balled
them into fists in his lap.

'George, you have to stop this—' his mother began, reaching out
to squeeze his hand, but the rest of her sentence was drowned out
as an ear-splitting whistle sounded and the train plunged them into
a tunnel.

'Are we nearly there?' exclaimed Robert, and Andrew
pushed him.

'Of course not, halfwit!'

'Enough rowdiness, boys,' said their mother.

Alice's breakfast finished, she returned to watching the French
countryside flash past, half listening to her cousins as they
discussed their plans for when they arrived in Paris.

'We must visit the Tour Eiffel,' said Andrew, showing off his
French accent again. 'It took two years to build. It was begun in 1887
and when it was finished it was the centrepiece of the 1899 *Exposi-
tion Universelle*.'

'The what, dear?' asked Agatha.

'The Paris Exposition,' said Andrew, 'and there's another one this year. It begins in April. And in the summer, Paris is hosting the second modern Olympic Games.'

'Can we go?,' asked Robert, spearing his last piece of bacon. 'At the last Olympic Games in Athens, Launceston Elliott won a gold medal for the Heavyweight One-Arm Lift.'

'Perhaps...' demurred his mother.

'Britain won two Gold medals in Athens, but we shall win more medals this time,' Andrew said. 'These will be the first Olympic Games ever to be held outside Greece. If ever there is one in London, I'm going to enter.'

'Doing what?' sneered Robert.

'Sword fighting or horse riding.'

'I'd win the running races,' said Robert.

'You're too young.'

'I'm only two years younger than you.'

'There is no lower age limit,' said the young man from the table opposite, and the two boys turned to stare at him in surprise.

'Are you sure?' asked Robert, his face alive with excitement.

'Quite sure,' the young man replied. 'We live on one of the Greek islands and we were lucky enough to visit Athens to see the First Modern Olympiad. There were some competitors who were younger than you'd expect.'

Alice glanced over, intrigued by his claim to live on a Greek island. His parents looked the height of respectability and, from their flustered behaviour earlier, she had assumed they were inexperienced travellers, but now she viewed them with different eyes.

'My apologies,' he said, as Agatha raised her eyebrows. 'I shouldn't have interrupted.'

'Not at all, but I do hope you realise what you've done, young man. These two will pester you between here and Paris to hear more about your Greek island and the Olympic Games.'

'It would be a delight to discuss it,' he said. 'I am Mr George

Perrin and these are my parents, Mr Augustus Perrin, known to his friends as Gus, and Mrs Elaine Perrin.'

'Lady Hope, my sons, Robert and Andrew Hope, and my niece, Miss Alice Webster.'

There was a flurry of 'How do you dos'.

'Do you really live on an island?' asked Robert.

'We do,' said Gus Perrin, his broad sun-tanned face breaking into a delighted smile at Robert's wide-eyed enthusiasm. 'It's an island called Crete, where we own lots of land and are planting vines to make wine.'

'The birthplace of Zeus!' exclaimed Andrew.

'Correct,' said Elaine Perrin. 'He was said to have been born in the mountains not far from where we live.'

Alice could not help grinning at the looks of astonishment on her cousins' faces.

'I'm glad to see you've been paying attention in class,' said Agatha.

'What else is supposed to have happened on Crete?' asked Alice, feeling this was a good time to test their knowledge. Both boys stared at her and she whispered, 'The Minotaur,' as a prompt.

'Theseus and Poseidon and King Minos,' said Andrew.

'The Minotaur ate people,' said Robert. 'Every year people went into his labyrinth and he ate them.'

'Until Theseus killed him,' interjected Andrew, making stabbing motions towards his brother.

'He would have failed if Ariadne hadn't helped him,' said Alice, and George Perrin caught her eye.

'You're a scholar of Greek mythology?' he asked, and she was certain she detected the hint of a sneer.

'I studied Classics at Newnham,' she retorted.

'My niece is an exceptional scholar,' said Agatha, with a stern glance towards George.

'Sincere apologies,' he murmured, but Alice felt her face flush at the insincerity of his comment.

'We've been home to visit our daughter, Clara,' Mrs Perrin explained, 'but there is a great deal to do at the vineyard, which is why we've persuaded George to join us for the summer. We're hoping he will stay and help us in our venture.'

George did not respond, and an uncomfortable silence fell over the Perrins' table. Alice and her aunt exchanged a complicit glance. Agatha replaced her teacup in its saucer.

'We shall retire,' she announced. 'It has been a long journey for the boys and I would like them to rest before we arrive in Paris. Good day,' she said as she swept her sons before her. Alice gave a polite smile to Mr and Mrs Perrin, ignored George, and followed her aunt and cousins, relieved to return to their cabin, where she would, once again, be able to brood.

8

The door creaked and Nanny Ipswich entered, her mouth pursed in disapproval at the three of them sprawled on the bed as they read *Hamlet*. Alice had appointed them characters and when the scenes became very dramatic, the boys would re-enact sections, especially parts involving pushing each other or pretending to have sword fights. Alice had cast herself as Hamlet, and when she read his famous soliloquy beginning 'To be or not to be...' her rendition even impressed her cousins.

'It is time for your walk,' said Nanny Ipswich, and the two boys exchanged resigned looks, causing Alice to stifle a grin.

Neither of her cousins appreciated the fact that their mother had insisted on bringing their nanny along on the trip. Both believed they were too old for a nanny and Alice would suffice as tutor and chaperone, as well as favourite cousin.

'Lady Hope requests your presence in her drawing room,' Nanny Ipswich finished with a glare at Alice, her entire demeanour expressing her disgust at being treated as a messenger. 'She also wishes me to remind you that you must change into suitable attire before your appointment.'

'Thank you, Miriam,' said Alice, clambering off the bed and straightening her skirt, which was creased and had an ink stain over the pocket where her pen had leaked when they were on the train to Paris. 'Be good, boys,' she said, ruining the sternness of her tone with a wink.

Leaving the small suite of rooms shared by the boys and Nanny Ipswich, Alice made her way down the corridor of the Grand Hôtel d'Angleterre. At present, her aunt was considering where the next step of their journey would take them, a destination, she had declared, that would be selected by them all. Despite her conventional appearance, Alice was beginning to understand that, at heart, her aunt was an eager adventurer.

The previous evening, Alice and Aunt Agatha had discussed potential destinations and they were all very taken with the idea of abandoning their trip to Germany in favour of Greece and the Greek islands. During dinner, the boys had expressed a desire to visit Athens to discover more about the Olympiads, both old and new. Owing to the meeting with the Perrins on the train, the other place that had captured their imaginations was Crete.

'We might find the Minotaur's skeleton,' Robert had said, while Andrew jeered at his brother's naïvety.

Although the next leg of their journey had not been decided, the one decision Agatha had made was to leave Paris as soon as possible because no rooms had been available at the Ritz. She had been furious that this new and fashionable hotel had been fully booked, and even her influence with the British Consul had been to no avail in securing suites. Alice was unconcerned. She liked it where they were, enjoying the easy charm, elegant style and the well-established gardens that made her feel as though she were in the countryside. The gentle atmosphere of the hotel provided a relaxing contrast to the vivid and dynamic City of Lights that buzzed around her each day.

'Ah, there you are, my dear,' smiled Aunt Agatha as Alice entered the drawing room. 'We have received an invitation to a drinks and musical soirée tomorrow evening.'

'How wonderful,' said Alice, although her heart sank at the prospect of a dull evening surrounded by pompous old men and timorous women. 'Who are our hosts?'

'Do you remember the family on the train?'

'The Perrins?'

Her initial assessment of the evening changed to apprehension as she remembered the handsome but angry George Perrin and the manner in which he had interrupted their conversation. As the son of the hosts, it was inevitable he would be in attendance and Alice was disturbed by the thought of being in close proximity to him again.

'Yes, it transpires they are very well connected. Mr Augustus Perrin is one of the most sought-after wine importers in Europe and his venture of opening a winery in Crete is gaining a great deal of interest. In fact, Crete itself is becoming a place of some importance. Have you ever come across Sir John Evans and his son, Arthur?' said Agatha, as she sat down opposite her niece.

'Of course,' replied Alice, accepting the cup of tea her aunt offered. 'Sir John owns a paper mill and Arthur's a correspondent for the *Manchester Guardian*, as well as Keeper of the Ashmolean Museum in Oxford. He and his father are both keen coin collectors. Father, Hugo and I have always read up on Arthur Evans's views and his many discoveries.'

'Quite so,' replied Agatha. 'Were you aware Arthur has long been interested in Crete, believing the island to be the seat of an ancient civilisation?'

'Father said Mr Evans was organising an archaeological dig in Crete,' said Alice. 'It's been Mr Evans's ambition for years, ever since the German archaeologist Heinrich Schliemann and his wife,

Sophia, discovered the remains of the City of Troy several years ago. Evans has been keen to discover a huge complex of his own and father said, he is hoping to find the fabled home of King Minos: the lost Palace of Knossos.'

'Quite right,' said Agatha her voice as excited and enthusiastic as Alice's. 'When I was speaking to Mr and Mrs Perrin earlier, they explained that Arthur Evans has bought a vast tract of land not far from their own property and, since the unrest in Crete has abated, he's planning to excavate this year. It seems he is convinced Crete, and the area around Heraklion in particular, could hold the answers to many questions we have about antiquity.'

Alice listened in surprise, realising again how much she had underestimated her aunt. Before their trip, she had enjoyed her aunt's company but had viewed her as a stuffy adult who was preoccupied with the dull day-to-day details of life. Agatha's excitement at delivering this information to Alice made her look years younger, and, quickly calculating, Alice realised her aunt was forty years old, ten years younger than Alice's father, Norman.

'I believe the dig will begin in a few days,' continued Agatha. 'Mr Perrin explained that another reason they were able to persuade his son to accompany them is because he will be helping with the excavations. George studied at Brasenose College, Oxford, the alma mater of Arthur Evans, and the two men are friends.'

Alice was impressed, but before she could comment, the elaborate carriage clock on the mantelpiece chimed.

'Auntie, I'm sorry to halt you, but you requested I change before meeting Juliet.'

'Of course, my dear. Have a pleasant afternoon at the Ritz. Please ensure you return by five o'clock as I would like you to rest before dinner this evening.' Alice was halfway across the room when her aunt called, 'Do give the idea of a trip to Crete some thought, too. It might be interesting for the boys to witness an archaeological dig.'

Alice bobbed a small curtsy and hurried from the drawing room into her bedroom, wondering about her aunt and the glow of excitement the suggestion of the dig at Crete had created. Opening the door, she was so lost in thought, she started when her lady's maid, Florence Parker, appeared from behind the dressing screen, shaking out the pale green afternoon dress, a new purchase from one of the salons recommended by Juliet's mother, Lady Fraser-Price. As Florence helped Alice to dress, a wave of relief swept over her at the prospect of her imminent meeting with her friend. There had not yet been a moment for the two girls to speak alone. When they had met earlier in the week at the dress salon, Lady Hope and Lady Fraser-Price had accompanied them making it impossible for them to discuss Ephraim and Alice's disgrace. Alice was in desperate need of Juliet's support and advice.

'Sorry, miss, I forgot to say, a letter arrived for you an hour ago. It's on your dressing table,' said Florence as she gathered Alice's discarded garments together.

Alice's heart pounded. Had Ephraim found her at last? Was he here? He had always promised they would see Paris together. An image of them walking through the streets of Bloomsbury to have tea at a nearby hotel returned to her. As they had hurried through the grey London rain, Alice had been transported by his vivid description of the Champs-Élysées at night in the snow. Despite the heartache, a small part of her hoped the letter was from him...

'Is there anything else you'd like me to do?' asked Florence, interrupting Alice's thoughts.

'No, thank you, Florence,' she replied, colour staining her cheeks as though Florence had walked in to find her in a compromising position, such was the intensity of her recollection.

'Mr Wendbury will be waiting outside with the carriage in ten minutes.'

Florence departed and Alice flew to the letter, but her heart crashed with disappointment. She had convinced herself it was from Ephraim, so to see her brother Hugo's untidy scrawl was a let-down. Pushing the envelope into her reticule to read later, she forced back the tears that threatened to surface as her hopes were dashed. She pinned on her new spring bonnet, straightened her skirts and, with sadness weighing her down like a stone shroud, she headed to the Ritz.

* * *

The coach shuddered to a halt and Wendbury, who was sitting opposite Alice, released his white-knuckled grip on his umbrella and ceased his mutterings about French drivers in order to announce, 'We've arrived, Miss Alice.'

Alice smiled at her aunt's butler and gathered her reticule and gloves. Throughout the short journey, she had used the cocooned safety of the carriage, and the knowledge Wendbury would not wish to indulge in idle chit-chat when there were foreign drivers to criticise, to allow herself to fall into thoughts of her lost love.

During her daily routine, when she was tutoring her cousins or enjoying the distractions of shopping and sight-seeing, she managed to keep thoughts of Ephraim at bay. However, as soon as she was alone, his face would appear, as though summoned by a djinn from a fairy tale, to torture her shattered heart. He was forever out of reach, yet he remained locked in her heart. Swallowing the unexpected lump in her throat, she forced herself to concentrate as Wendbury assured her he would wait at the hotel and bring the carriage around to collect her at half past four.

'On the dot, miss,' he added with a reassuring smile, and Alice responded in kind.

Wendbury took his role as protector of Lady Hope's party with great seriousness, and Alice liked him for his care and sense of honour. He was a quiet man, widowed young, who, during his period of mourning, had been supported by Agatha and Barnaby Hope. As such, he was devoted to the family and would do his utmost to ensure their wellbeing.

'Thank you,' she murmured, as he handed her into the safe hands of the Ritz doorman.

'Alice, at last!' Juliet exclaimed as Alice was shown into the sophisticated bar and restaurant where she had arranged to meet her friend.

Breaking all protocol, Juliet hugged Alice in a bone-crushing embrace, much to the mingled horror and amusement of the fashionable clientele. Alice squeezed back with all her might.

'Oh, Alice, what a difficult time for you,' said Juliet,

'You don't think I'm awful?' she murmured in response and Juliet shook her head.

'No, you were misled,' she said and with a reassuring smile, she tucked Alice's hand under her arm. 'Come, let's discuss the terrible man. I insisted Pa book a booth for us as it has more privacy. He's said we may order anything we choose so I thought Champagne might cheer us up.'

'Why do you need cheering up? I thought we were indulging my misery,' said Alice in mock indignation. Being with Juliet was the tonic she had needed, no matter how serious the situation, her friend could always be relied upon to help Alice find a way through it, usually with laughter.

'I have to go to a dreary soirée tomorrow evening given by some wine expert. It's making me very sad.'

'The Perrins?' asked Alice, and Juliet shrugged in true Parisian style. 'We've been invited, too. We met them on the train.'

'Alice, this is the best news I've heard today,' declared Juliet. 'If we're both in attendance, the evening might be fun.'

'It can't be worse than some of the parties we attended during our début,' replied Alice, and the two girls rolled their eyes in droll fashion.

Two years earlier, when she and Juliet had both been eighteen, they had been presented at court and had spent a year as débutantes. Both had found the process a strange mixture of fun and tedium as neither had been interested in securing any of the eager crop of young men who arrived at the many parties, picnics and balls. After their début, Alice had headed off to Cambridge, while Juliet had thrown herself into her studies with the English branch of the Theosophical Society, alongside her increasing interest in the growing suffrage movement. Both believed there was plenty of time to find a husband.

Alice watched in amusement as Juliet summoned a waiter and in assured French ordered caviar and Champagne.

'Are you sure?' she asked, raising her eyebrows.

'Yes. As I came in, I saw two women, who must have been native Parisians because they were so chic, ordering the same thing. We don't want to look like gauche schoolgirls. We are young ladies of refinement and sophistication.'

Alice could not help laughing at Juliet's extravagant manner, making Juliet giggle, too. They had been friends since they were babies. Alice's mother, Adela, and Juliet's mother, Fenella, had met at Lady Palmer's Finishing School in Switzerland and had remained close ever since. They had been delighted when their daughters were born two months apart and, in childhood, had become inseparable. The daughter of a baronet, Juliet exuded a confidence and elegance

Alice had never been able to emulate, but just as Alice envied Juliet's poise, so Juliet was in awe of Alice's intellect. Each was proud of the other's achievements and they trusted each other implicitly.

Both young women were keen on the modern world and eager to be a part of the burgeoning developments of the *fin de siècle*, in particular, the new movement formed by Emmeline Pankhurst and her cause to bring women the vote. Before Alice's disgrace, they had accompanied their mothers to several talks concerning the changing role of women in society. It was a passion they all continued to share.

'How's Tybalt?' asked Alice as they waited for the Champagne.

'In his most recent letter, my brother claimed he would soon be a master sculptor,' said Juliet, rolling her eyes.

'As last year, he planned to write the perfect novel?' responded Alice with a grin.

'Exactly, and probably next year he'll be an inventor. You know Tybalt, always the dreamer. Have you heard from Hugo?'

'A letter arrived before I left. It'll no doubt be another request to help him with an essay,' said Alice, wrinkling her nose in sympathy. 'Poor Hugo, he's never going to be able to cope without me. He tries his hardest but, for him, the alphabet is a mystery, incomprehensible. He says the letters seem to move around, presenting themselves in a backwards position.'

'When is he going to tell your father?'

Alice shrugged. 'Father will understand and try to help, but Hugo says it makes him feel like a failure, especially when Ben excels at everything.'

When Alice had asked to follow her brother Hugo to Cambridge to read Classics, her father, with persuasion from her mother and Aunt Agatha, had agreed. Hugo had promised to chaperone her, but with Alice at Newnham and Hugo at Peterhouse, they had lived very different undergraduate lives.

Hugo had thrown himself into the excesses of the university, enjoying Champagne, punting on the River Cam and a riotous nightlife. Alice, however, had pushed herself to excel and embraced her studies with enthusiasm. It was at the end of their first term, when Hugo had asked for Alice's assistance, explaining his difficulties, that their secret pact had begun with Alice agreeing to help Hugo with his essays. Thanks to Alice's skills, Hugo was on track to gain a degree, despite the fact that Alice herself, as a woman, would not be allowed to receive this accolade.

'How did Hugo cope at Winchester?' asked Juliet.

Hugo, like every Webster man, had attended Winchester College prior to Cambridge, while Alice had been educated at home.

'His friend Ross Montrose helped him.'

'Ah, the dashing Ross with his dark hair and smouldering eyes,' laughed Juliet, although her eyes twinkled, in contrast to her flippant tone.

'The very same,' sighed Alice, pretending to swoon. 'He's returned to his uncle's castle in Scotland. There was a discussion that he would join Hugo at Cambridge, but his family has always attended St Andrews. Ross has no choice but to comply, especially as his uncle is paying and Ross is his heir.'

'Poor Hugo,' said Juliet.

'He sent me his most recent assignment. It was waiting when I arrived in Paris. I returned it to him yesterday and I received another letter from him today.'

She paused as the waiters arrived. With a flurry, two uniformed staff arranged an ice bucket, Champagne and small dishes of caviar on ice accompanied by Melba toast. The waiters retreated and Juliet raised a glass of Champagne to Alice.

'To us and the adventures we shall encounter during our travels. May we both marry dukes.'

Alice touched her glass to her friend's, sipping the ice-cold bubbles and feeling overawed by the refinement of her afternoon. The toast was one they had been making for years and, while Alice had no desire to marry a duke, she was aware Juliet was intent on marrying a title.

'What's happened about your place at Newnham?' Juliet asked.

'Mother and Father have declined it,' Alice's voice held a trace of bitterness, as she helped herself to the caviar. Crunching the Melba toast, she felt the smallest *frisson* as the salty taste hit her tongue, followed by the delicious sensation of the explosion of each tiny egg as she swallowed.

'Oh, Alice, how awful.'

'It's no more than I deserve,' she said, feeling her façade of serenity crumbling.

'Have you heard from him?' asked Juliet, lowering her voice to a whisper.

'No. When the letter from Hugo arrived today, I hoped it might be from him, but it was a foolish, thoughtless emotion. What we did was wrong and I am embarrassed to think I considered fleeing with him to America.'

'Will he return?'

'No,' Alice replied. 'Mother explained that with the unexpected death of his elder brother, Patrick, who died with no heir, Ephraim becomes the heir to the Earl of Bentree and, as such, must take on the responsibilities of the estate.'

'With his wife,' added Juliet, but there was no judgement in her voice. Alice dropped her head to hide the tears welling in their blue depths.

'Yes,' she agreed, 'with his wife, son, and the child his wife is expecting.'

Juliet winced, a sympathetic expression on her face. Picking up the tiny spoon on the white plate in front of her, she selected a piece of Melba toast and topped it with caviar, passing it to Alice, who accepted it with a trembling hand.

'What about the vast American holdings?' continued Juliet. 'His mother is American, isn't she?'

'Yes, and wealthy beyond belief. Her father is a Texas oil baron and he's planning to expand the holdings into Australia. Perhaps one of Ephraim's children will one day take over the American concern. It's a sad twist of fate. He had always been told this was to be his path and he was excited by the thought of starting such an adventure.'

'What about his wife?'

'Less so, which was why he was going on ahead.'

'Alice, I don't want to upset you, but I heard they've moved to Bentree House and his wife is due to deliver the child soon.'

'I know,' she whispered. 'They are said to be happier than ever. She has forgiven him his transgressions...'

Tears of despair filled Alice's eyes.

'Oh, my sweet friend,' murmured Juliet, as Alice mopped her eyes with a delicate embroidered handkerchief. '"To everything there is a season,"' she added.

Alice dabbed her nose. 'Are you quoting the Bible at me, Juliet Fraser-Price?' she said, attempting to laugh through her tears.

'Indeed I am, *Ecclesiastes*, chapter three, verse one.'

'I believe within that chapter the Bible also claims, there is "A time to love..."'

'"And a time to dance..."'

'Although, I'm less sure of the time to gather stones,' interrupted a male voice, and both young women looked up in surprise as Alice felt the full force of George Perrin's piercing brown eyes.

He gave a polite bow.

'Is this a hobby of yours, Mr Perrin?' snapped Alice, annoyed to have been caught in such emotional turmoil. 'Interrupting conversations that are none of your concern.'

'Miss Webster, a delight to see you again, too,' he said in a serious voice. Juliet snorted as she tried to suppress a laugh. 'It is hard to resist a biblical quotation and it was a relief to see a familiar face.'

Alice glared at George.

'We met a handful of times on the train,' she retorted, 'hardly familiar.'

'Yet, for a man who has been trapped between his loving and well-meaning parents for ten days, your challenging demeanour is like the first breath of air for a drowning man.'

Alice glared at him, then winced as Juliet kicked her under the table, her eyes wide with curiosity.

'Mr George Perrin, may I introduce my friend, Miss Juliet Fraser-Price.'

'How do you do?' said George, taking the hand Juliet extended towards him. In response, Juliet fluttered her eyes, which irritated Alice. 'I believe you are joining us tomorrow evening at my parents' soirée.'

'It was kind of your parents to invite us,' Juliet said.

'You will also be attending the soirée?' asked George, directing the question at Alice.

'My aunt and I are looking forward to it,' she replied.

Glancing at Juliet, who was gazing at George in awe, Alice nudged her friend on the shin with her foot, bringing Juliet out of her trance.

'I believe your parents own a vineyard,' said Juliet. 'Wine has always been a passion of mine.'

Alice stifled a laugh at Juliet's blatant attempt at flirting. Despite this afternoon's choice of Champagne, Juliet did not drink wine often, claiming it ruined her delicate pale pink and white complexion.

'Perhaps you would care to join us,' Juliet continued, sweeping her hand towards the ice bucket. 'You will be able to explain whether we have chosen well or whether the waiter has taken advantage of our naïvety.'

Alice was confident the uptight Mr Perrin would refuse, but it seemed either under Juliet's wide-eyed gaze, or driven by the desire for company of people his own age, he was unable to resist.

'It would be my pleasure,' he said.

Wondering whether to gather her belongings and leave, Alice found herself being shunted along the velvet banquette to make room for George before he waved to the waiter and began issuing instructions in imperious French. More Champagne arrived, accompanied by canapés and additional caviar. The clock on the mantelpiece at the other end of the sumptuous bar and dining room gave four chimes.

Half an hour, thought Alice, then I can escape. Unsure why he irritated her, she sipped the new glass of Champagne he had placed in front of her, half listening as he explained the differing grape varieties to Juliet.

Alice's mind wandered to the last time she had sipped Champagne. Ephraim had taken huge pleasure in popping the cork on the bottle in their stateroom, sending a showering arc of golden foam into the air, causing Alice to laugh with both delight and a tinge of fear. Despite weeks of careful planning, she had never thought beyond the stealthy journey they had planned to deliver them to the ship. However, as the reality of the situation had hit her, she had begun to feel overwhelmed with all she had agreed to.

Taking the Champagne flute, she had enjoyed the sensation of his fingers stroking hers before they clinked glasses. His toast to her had promised eternal love and her heart had pounded in excitement. When their eyes locked and she realised he was going to kiss her, a rush of unease had replaced her giddy excitement. For the first time the gravity of her situation occurred to her. She was alone with an older and experienced man with nowhere to flee if she should change her mind about their relationship. He had bent to kiss her with slow deliberation until, to her relief, they had been halted by the frantic knocking on the door.

Juliet laughed and turned to Alice. 'Don't you agree?' she said, her eyes sparkling, her cheeks flushed as she flirted with George Perrin.

'Sorry, I was distracted,' said Alice, and George gave her a considered look.

'George was saying how lucky we are to be living through such an historically important time, the turn of a century.'

'Yes,' agreed Alice as she gathered herself. 'What do you think will happen in the next hundred years, Mr Perrin?'

'I would hope that women will be given the vote,' he said.

'The sooner the better,' said Juliet. 'I hope the wars stop. The Boer War is awful, all those men dying for no purpose. If I could wish for anything in the new century it would be peace across the world and equality for all.'

'What else do you think will happen, Miss Webster?' asked George.

'I think there will be huge advances in science and medicine,' she replied. 'Travel, too. Father is certain the motor vehicle will become the common choice before the new century is over. Imagine motor cars everywhere. Think how easy it would be to go from one place to another.'

'My hope is that with the advancement of science, more people will come to understand the importance of Theosophy,' said Juliet.

'Theosophy?' asked George, and Alice sipped her Champagne, waiting for her friend to embark on her favourite topic.

'Theosophy is an esoteric movement which was founded in the United States by Russian immigrant, Helena Blavatsky,' said Juliet, delighted to have a new audience. 'Many of its teachings are based on literature, while others draw on Buddhism, Brahmanism and Hinduism. Its intention is to explain that a knowledge of God may be achieved through spiritual ecstasy, direct intuition or even special individual relationships with God. It encourages mystical insight and enlightenment.'

'A religion then?' clarified George.

'We prefer to think of it as a movement,' said Juliet. 'The most radical part, which many find shocking, is that it strives to foster equality within its ranks. Women are given as much opportunity to expound their theories at our meetings as men.'

'A concept with which I agree,' said George.

'How very modern of you,' snapped Alice.

'Alice,' scolded Juliet, but George smiled, making it clear he took no offence.

'Perhaps by the end of the twentieth century we'll all be Theosophists,' George said, 'with equality for all.'

'You may tease,' said Juliet, 'but it would make sense. By the end of the twentieth century the Akashic Record will have grown even broader as it will have had another hundred years of experience added. These positive thoughts will be able to influence everyone for the better.'

'What's the Akashic Record?' asked Alice. In all the discussions she and Juliet had shared about Theosophy, this was a new topic.

'Father was explaining it to Mother and me yesterday,' Juliet said. 'He learned about it at a talk last week when he attended a Theosophy meeting on the outskirts of Paris. Akasha is the Sanskrit word for *æther* or sky and the Akashic Record is a compendium of all universal events, thoughts, words, emotions and intent ever to have occurred in the past, present or future in terms of all entities and life forms, not just human. They are encoded in a non-physical plane of existence known as the mental plane and we all access them subliminally.'

'How extraordinary,' Alice said.

'There are studies being set up to understand these hypotheses,' continued Juliet on a wave of enthusiasm and Champagne. 'Imagine if we were able to harness memories from thousands of years ago. We would be able to prove beyond all doubt that Charles Darwin's theories of evolution are correct. We could contact so many important people and learn from their teachings and wisdom.'

'How could such a thing exist, though?' asked George, topping up their glasses.

'Think logically,' said Juliet, taking a large gulp of Champagne, her cheeks growing pinker with each mouthful, her manner increasingly pugnacious. 'When we speak, where do all the words go?'

'What do you mean?' asked Alice.

'Every thought, word or deed creates minute pulses that cause a vibration in the Akasha, a small burst of energy: where does it go? It must go somewhere. This is the basis of the Akashic Record. A vast pool of energy created by the individual thoughts of every creature on the planet for all eternity.'

A nursery song from *The Only True Mother Goose Melodies* her mother used to sing flashed across Alice's mind:

> *Old woman, old woman, old woman,' said I,*
> *O whither, O whither, O whither so high?'*
> *To sweep the cobwebs from the sky...*

Alice imagined words hanging on the cobwebs, all the words

ever spoken, trapped in shimmering silver webs, swept away by the industrious old woman.

'You should come to a meeting,' Juliet said to George. 'The discussions are fascinating. I'm working on an idea of my own, a connection between the Akashic Record and reincarnation. I believe the two are linked.'

'Reincarnation?' said George, and Alice noticed his tone was incredulous.

'Yes, strange though it may seem, in the Theosophy movement, we believe, as do the Hindus and Buddhists, that Karma dictates the level to which you return on this earth. Helena Blavatsky said, "It is only through these births that the perpetual progress of the countless millions of Egos toward final perfection and final rest can be achieved..."'

Glancing at the clock, Alice realised with some relief that she was running late and would not have to endure one of Juliet's grandiose lectures on Theosophy. The hands of the clock were edging towards five o'clock, the time her aunt had requested she return to the Grand Hôtel d'Angleterre. Wendbury would be waiting outside, fretful and unnerved at her non-appearance at the prescribed meeting time of four thirty. The butler was not adjusting to the fluidity and spontaneity of the life of a traveller.

'My apologies,' said Alice, interrupting Juliet in mid-explanation, picking up her reticule, 'but I promised Aunt Agatha I would return to the hotel by five o'clock and I am dreadfully late.'

'Oh, Alice, really?' said Juliet.

A voice hailed them and Alice saw Juliet's parents striding across the bar, their faces shining and eager.

'Alice, my dear,' said Lady Fraser-Price, 'what a treat.'

In the flurry of greetings and introductions, Alice realised George Perrin, who had stood in order to greet Juliet's parents, was waiting to one side. As Alice explained her need to depart to Juliet's parents, he stepped forward.

'I must also leave,' he said. 'Allow me to escort Miss Webster to her carriage and ensure her safety.'

Before she could complain or insist she needed no chaperone or knight errant to walk her across a hotel lobby, Alice found herself being encouraged away by the Fraser-Prices with promises to see them the next day at the soirée.

As she and George reached the vestibule, she increased her pace, trying to shake him off, but he kept up with her. With relief, Alice saw Wendbury and the carriage waiting outside the doors.

'I will be safe here,' she said, her voice cold.

George considered her for a moment, before speaking, 'Whoever he was, he was a fool to let you go.'

'What?'

'We, the brokenhearted, can always spot another of our tribe,' George said with a small, sad smile, and Alice remembered his stress on the train, his mother's admonishment.

'You, too?' she asked.

'I was recently released from an arrangement of marriage,' he said. 'It was unexpected.'

Alice reached out and placed her gloved hand on his arm.

'I'm so very sorry,' she said, and meant it.

'And you?'

'He was never mine to love,' she replied.

With a look of understanding, George Perrin squeezed her hand before she was claimed by the nervous Wendbury and hurried away to the carriage.

_____

9

'You look beautiful, miss,' said Florence the following evening as she fastened the last in the long line of covered buttons. 'These French styles are very flattering.'

Alice looked at herself in the mirror and could not help but grin. In London, the S-bend corset continued to hold sway, with the desired female silhouette supposed to resemble a Pouter pigeon. Alice found the corset painful and unattractive, particularly as dresses were further embellished with lace collars, ornate ribbons or feathers. The style was too fussy for her; she preferred straight, tailored lines that suited her slim figure.

In Paris, the fashion houses presented a new silhouette with a thicker waist, flatter bust and narrower hips. The embellishments were subtle and the sweeping skirts flowed around the feet as women walked, a contrast to the flute shape preferred in London, which Alice felt made her hobble. Even the fabric of her Parisian dress felt more sumptuous, and she made a mental note to write to her parents in the morning to thank them for these unexpected additions to her already extensive wardrobe. She was going to the Perrins' soirée looking her best.

A letter from her mother had been waiting with Hugo's essay when Alice had arrived in Paris:

Fenella has written with great urgency explaining she and Juliet are updating their wardrobes. I insisted she take charge and order clothes for you, me, Petra and Agatha. You must persuade your aunt into more fashionable attire. It is time she stopped dressing like her mother.

Fenella Fraser-Price had taken Agatha shopping, and Alice was delighted when deliveries of dresses were made for both herself and her aunt. They would be debuting their Parisian styles at the Perrins' soirée.

'Thank you, Florence,' said Alice, who could not bring herself to address Florence by her surname, as was traditional with lady's maids. It felt old-fashioned and impersonal. Before setting out on the journey, they had agreed upon using her first name. 'The colour is wonderful. I was unsure, but it looks remarkable.'

She swirled the cerise-pink skirt of the dress, inspired by her mother's love of that colour, so evocative of the scorching days in the Punjab.

'It should be an exciting evening, miss,' Florence said.

'We won't be too late back,' Alice said, and, picking up her evening bag, went into the drawing room where Wendbury waited.

'Good evening, Miss Alice,' he said, carrying a silver tray towards her. 'Sherry?'

'Thank you, Wendbury,' she replied, accepting the tiny glass.

As she sipped the drink, she wondered what was keeping her aunt. In the past, it was Agatha who would have had to wait for Alice.

'Well, my dear, what do you think?'

Alice spun around and gasped. Her aunt was dressed in a deep blue gown, which showed off her svelte figure. The colour made her eyes shimmer, as did the delicate application of cosmetics. Her usual severe hairstyle had been softened and she looked younger than her forty years. A beaming smile acknowledged how much she was enjoying the effect her appearance was having on Alice.

'Auntie, you look stunning,' said Alice. 'Have you shown the boys?'

'Yes, and the enthusiastic response was, "Top-hole, Mumsy."'

Alice could tell Agatha was delighted and, as they sipped their sherry, she suddenly realised she was looking forward to the soirée. It was a chance to socialise with her aunt as well as have fun with Juliet.

* * *

Several hours later, Alice and Juliet sat on a sofa, watching the guests as they danced. The evening had begun with a performance by a musical quartet. The girls had pronounced this to be charming, causing Agatha to laugh.

'The musicians will, no doubt, be delighted with your assessment,' Agatha had said.

Juliet had grinned and replied with an exaggerated drawl, 'But, Auntie Ag, didn't you know? Alice and I are the height of sophistication,' causing gales of laughter from those gathered around them.

Since then, the Ritz Hotel's band had taken to the small stage and the girls had danced, eaten ices and enjoyed speaking to the eclectic mixture of people invited by the Perrins.

'What did Hugo want in his letter?' asked Juliet. 'Has he sent you another essay?'

'No, thank goodness, but he may have solved our dilemma as to where to travel next. The boys are keen on Greece and Crete, and it seems this is where Hugo's heading too, so tomorrow we shall begin to plan our journey towards Greece and then take a boat to Crete.'

'Why is Hugo going to Crete?'

'He might not enjoy writing essays, but Hugo is passionate about ancient architecture and, it transpires, when Ross was in London for a visit, he told Hugo about one of his friends. He's called Duncan Mackenzie and he will be working with Arthur Evans on his dig in Crete over the summer. Father has spoken to Arthur's father, Sir John Evans, whom he knows through their work connections, and it seems Arthur and his team are confident of discovering a vast site. Father has agreed to fund Hugo's summer on the dig as he believes it'll help him with his studies.'

'All roads lead to Crete,' said Juliet with a knowing look.

'They do seem to at the moment,' said Alice. 'Not to mention the fact that Aunt Agatha is very taken with the Perrin family.'

'George Perrin will be there too?' said Juliet, one eyebrow raised in amusement.

'What has that got to do with anything?' Alice asked. 'You were the one flirting with him.'

'And never have I met a more uninterested man,' grinned Juliet.

'What do you mean?'

'He didn't respond and I realised why the instant he hopped up in order to escort you across the lobby. Even you, with your lovelorn heart, can't deny the beauty of his high cheekbones and mysterious eyes like obsidian rippling beneath deep pools on a winter's night.'

Alice laughed.

'What did he say to you?' Juliet asked.

Alice hesitated, feeling a strange sense of disloyalty to George but under Juliet's eager gaze, she whispered, 'He told me he recognised another of his tribe – the brokenhearted. He has recently been released from an engagement and is another struggling with the grief of loneliness.'

'How very astute of him to spot it in you, too,' Juliet said, her eyes roving the crowd, searching for George. When she located him in the far corner, pointing him out to Alice, she felt the same sting of irritation at Juliet's interest in George as she had the previous day.

'I wonder who he was engaged to?' Juliet pondered. 'Perhaps Ma will be able to discover which mysterious woman chose to forgo the pleasure of gazing on those astonishing looks.'

The conversation ended as they were joined by Juliet's parents, but throughout the remainder of the evening, even though they exchanged fewer than ten words, Alice was aware of George's brown eyes following her around the room. She was unsure whether to feel anger at his presumption or to give way to the unexpected thrill of excitement his attention caused.

* * *

Upon returning to the Grand Hôtel d'Angleterre, Alice readied herself for bed with Florence's help. When she returned to the drawing room, Wendbury was arranging a tray containing a jug of hot chocolate and cups.

'Thank you,' Alice said. 'I'll look after Auntie. Good night, Wendbury.'

'Good night, Miss Alice,' he said, his rugged face crinkling into a smile, as he bowed and hurried from the suite.

Alice tapped on her aunt's door.

'Wendbury has left. Would you like your hot chocolate in your bedroom?'

The door opened and Agatha smiled. Her long hair, once a rich, glossy chestnut, fell past her shoulders. The fire at its heart had been dampened by the slow spread of glittering strands of moon-bright silver, but this did not diminish its beauty. Agatha joined

Alice on the sofa by the wide fireplace, her silk peignoir rustling like autumn leaves, and as she reclined on the cushions, Alice breathed in the soft, rich, floral scent she associated with her aunt, feeling comforted by the smell.

A bottle of L. T. Piver's, Rêve d'Or, in the delicate bottle designed by Baccarat, the French crystal manufacturer, had been one of the last presents given to Agatha by her late husband, the industrialist Sir Barnaby Hope. Her aunt had worn the scent every day since.

'It reminds me of my beloved Barnaby,' she had explained to Alice when she had given her one of the exquisite empty perfume bottles some years earlier. Alice had rushed upstairs to display it on what she called her 'finds shelf'. This sat within a glass-fronted cabinet in Alice's yellow and white bedroom, and housed her collection of prized and important possessions.

'This is divine,' sighed Agatha, now, sipping the hot chocolate. 'How did you find the evening?'

'Quite fun,' Alice replied.

'Perhaps this is a sign your heart is beginning the slow process of healing.'

Alice's head jerked up to see if her aunt was being derogatory, but there was only kindness and understanding on Agatha's face.

'Oh, Alice, I am not unsympathetic to your plight,' she sighed. 'The pain of lost love is the hardest emotion to bear, but you are not the first woman in our family to have loved unwisely and suffered a broken heart.'

It was a few moments before the meaning of her aunt's words permeated Alice's mind.

'You?' she asked in surprise.

'It was a long time ago and my circumstances were very different, but I decided last night that perhaps it was time to reveal some of the family skeletons.'

'What do you mean?'

'Heartbreak is a lonely place, especially when there is no chance of reconciliation. My understanding of this state was one of the reasons I insisted to your parents that you should accompany us on this sojourn,' she continued. 'The tutor did not have measles. I cancelled his employment in order to bring you with me.'

'Do Mother and Father know?'

'Your father may have his suspicions,' she said. 'I believed that removing you from London would allow you the space for your heart to grieve.'

Alice stared at her aunt in astonishment.

'It would also eradicate any possibility of your bumping into Ephraim and spare you from the pain when the birth of his child is announced. These are not easy things to bear when your dreams have been snatched away.' Her aunt paused as she sipped the hot chocolate. 'All these things aside, though, we have always been friends, as well as aunt and niece. I value your company and relish this chance for us to experience this adventure together.'

'Thank you, Auntie,' Alice said, bewildered by this confession. 'We've always been close and it's wonderful spending time with you and the boys.'

'Is there more? I ordered a jug?' asked Agatha as she drained her cup.

Before Alice could reply, Agatha walked over to the tray and returned to top up both their cups while Alice gathered her thoughts. Agatha then sat and pulled a blanket over her legs, while Alice tucked her feet underneath her, sipping her hot chocolate. The fire crackled and Agatha spoke again.

'When I was very young, like you, I fell in love with a man who was unavailable to me,' she said in a quiet voice.

Alice gazed at her aunt, agog.

'However, our ending was rather different. You see, I was not the first Lady Hope to be married to my beloved Barnaby.'

'I beg your pardon?' gasped Alice, and Agatha smiled, her eyes twinkling at the shocked expression on her niece's face.

'Barnaby and I first met at a country house party. I was attending with my parents and your father, Norman. At the time, I was betrothed to another young man, Gerald. He was pleasant, well-meaning, wealthy, but very dull.' Alice laughed. 'Sir Barnaby was older than me but this didn't matter, because from the moment we met it was as though our hearts connected. When I discovered there was already a Lady Hope, I thought I would die from the pain of my broken heart.'

'Who was she, Auntie?'

'Her name was Dominique and they had been married for ten years. The marriage was happy but they had no children. Yet, there was no denying the desire between myself and my darling Barnaby. Our feelings, which we knew to be dangerous and forbidden, were nevertheless real. During that weekend we spent as much time together as possible and it didn't go unnoticed. My mother was horrified and delivered a very stern pronouncement, which, driven to madness by my feelings, I ignored.

'On the final night of our stay, she forbade me from attending dinner, locking me in my bedroom.'

Alice looked at her in surprise. 'What did you do?'

'I climbed out of the window – there was a very useful oak tree nearby, which helped – and I rushed away to meet Barnaby in the Roman temple by the lake. Our behaviour was thoughtless and cruel, but we could not resist.

'At the end of the weekend we parted and I believed we would never see each other again. However, my feelings for Barnaby made me realise it was impossible to continue with my engagement to Gerald. When I told my parents my intention to end the betrothal, they were furious, but I was determined. Even when they sent me away to stay with a great-aunt who lived in a house in the middle of the Yorkshire moors, thinking the solitude would break my spirit, my mind would not be changed.

'Three months later, Dominique Hope died from tuberculosis. The guilt this sent through my heart was even greater than the pain of losing Barnaby. Had our behaviour killed her? Were we murderers by proxy? Whereas before, I had held on to a slim belief we might one day be together, the reality of Dominique's death brought me to my senses and I realised what a romantic and selfish fool I had been. Late one evening, as my elderly aunt retired to bed, leaving me to my thoughts, I resolved to return home, to apologise to my parents and, if Gerald would reconsider, revive our betrothal. This thought broke my heart, but sense told me there was no other way forward.

'To my surprise, the following morning, Barnaby arrived. He was in a terrible state, white-faced and trembling. Welcoming him in, the last thing I expected was to be given a letter from Dominique, a truly remarkable woman. She and Barnaby had long-known about her illness and how it would end. Her words, written after the weekend we had first met, were warm and funny. Her request from beyond the grave was to love her husband as she felt he deserved to be loved. An emotion, she admitted, she had witnessed flowing between us. She confessed that, while she and Barnaby had been friends, and their marriage happy, both knew they were not each other's grand passion.

'Barnaby admitted he hadn't been able to stop thinking about me, and if I was prepared to wait through his time of mourning, he would marry me. I agreed. I loved him. I had loved him from the moment we first met. Our love has never changed. Even after his death my love for Barnaby continues to sustain me.'

Alice realised tears were cascading down her cheeks.

'Why are you telling me this?' she asked, wiping them away. 'There will never be a happy ending for me and Ephraim.'

'Alice, my dear, this is a situation that continues to distress me on your behalf. Barnaby and I were lucky. Our love was one that could have ended in tragedy and, sadly, as you stated, whether your heart belongs to Ephraim Lockwood or not, he will never be yours. To wish otherwise would be cruel beyond belief. Yet, you will survive. You are young and strong and, even if it doesn't feel like it at the moment, you will heal. Perhaps another man will enter your life, one who will help you to love and trust again. If this situation arises, Alice, do not deter him out of a misguided sense of loyalty to Ephraim.'

Alice had felt her aunt's words slice through her heart, knowing everything she said was true.

'Before we retire,' Agatha continued, 'there is another family secret it is high time you knew, especially as it regards your parents.'

'My parents?' Alice echoed.

'Did you know they eloped?'

'Auntie, no, they didn't,' Alice gasped.

'Oh, yes,' Agatha laughed. 'They were impatient to marry and your grandfather Trowbridge, your mother's father, was planning another trip to India, which would have meant delaying the wedding for eight months. Neither believed they could wait, so they took matters into their own hands and, one afternoon, they disappeared.'

'No!' exclaimed Alice, trying to imagine her sensible parents being so reckless.

'They were missing for three days,' Agatha said, 'you can imagine the scandal it caused. Your father is ten years older than me and I remember scurrying about the house, listening at keyholes, trying to discover what was happening. Back then, the family tradition was to have tea every Saturday afternoon with members of our extended family. Anyway, that week, which had been full of upheaval, we gathered as usual in my parents' drawing room and I suspect we were all rather thrilled to have such a shocking topic to discuss. My mother had just suggested we hire a private detective to ascertain their whereabouts, when the doorbell rang and Blighty, my parents' ancient butler, came hobbling in, wheezing with excitement as he announced: "Mr and Mrs Norman Webster". And there they were, as bold as brass, your mother flashing her golden wedding ring and your father waiting for the remonstrations.'

'What happened?'

'The usual apologies and ruffled feathers. Your grandfather Trowbridge was disappointed to have missed the wedding, but your parents agreed to have their marriage blessed when he returned from India. Although, by the time that happened, Benedict had been born, so it was a good thing they did elope. This is why, when you asked to be allowed to attend Newnham, I reminded your father of what it was to be young and impetuous. Alas, none of us expected that your life would follow the path that it did and, for this, I think we are all very saddened.'

'My parents will never forgive me,' Alice said.

'They will. The very fact they have allowed you to accompany me shows they understand. Your situation is one of great difficulty, Alice, because the man you love will always be a part of your life, yet you will never hold his heart. I believe no woman will hold his heart for very long and this is a tragedy for both you and his wife.'

Alice returned to her room with her mind reeling as she viewed her family with new eyes. As she slid into sleep, she realised that throughout the conversation with her aunt, each mention of Ephraim's name had caused her less pain and she wondered if, she was indeed, healing.

10

The roar echoed through the dank corridors. Beneath her feet were bones; white, picked clean, their elegant lengths stark against the crumbling red clay of the earth. Blood ran in rivulets, covering her feet, sticky, warm, the heart-blood of the creature, its life over in a painless ritual representing love and grief. A strip of cord hung on a broken rock, torn and useless. Footsteps behind her. Turning, feeling her way. Soft breath, a murmur, a woman's voice, calling for help. Reaching out, her hands scraping on the rough walls. Shimmering on the glistened stone were words. I love you. Written. I love you. Blood. Written in blood. Her blood...

11

Eloise awoke with a start. The dream, again. Screwing her eyes tight shut, she tried to visualise the scene, to remember its details. A black leather-bound notebook and pen stood on her bedside cabinet. She scrawled the date across the top of the page, then wrote while the images remained fresh. The river of blood was new, with the strange sensation of not being able to feel it against her feet because it matched her own body heat, and witnessing the dark ripples as they flowed around her, staining her skin before sinking into the ground. The words on the wall were new, too, and she shuddered.

Feelings... she thought. What did I feel in the dream, rather than my reactions to it now I'm awake? Concentrating, she waited. What were her emotions telling her? Fear? Disgust? No, neither of these, but the harder she reached for the elusive description, the further it slipped away as her waking brain began to create order with rational explanations.

Snapping the book shut, Eloise leaned back against her white pillows. It was several weeks since she had last experienced the dream. When she was young, it had happened every few days, and

for years it had confused her. In order to try to understand these
night-time wanderings through a subterranean world, her parents
had taken her to a child psychologist. Eloise had explained the
dreams were not frightening. They felt familiar, as though she were
meant to be in the shadowy corridors.

In a family whose businesses dealt with the rituals of death, her
parents had worked hard to ensure their homelife was enriched
with light, colour, laughter and joy. Music, fun and warmth were the
background to Eloise's life. She and Rose had been close friends
since their first day of school, she was doing well in her studies, and
there were no underlying shadows in Eloise's life to explain her
endless excursions into the twisting, turning corridors of her
dreams.

The psychologist suggested she write a dream diary, recording
all she could remember, including her feelings, as it might put her
mind at rest and halt the dream. Intrigued by the idea, Eloise had
mentioned it to her parents and her father had returned home the
following evening with a beautiful leather-bound notebook in dark
purple and a pen that wrote with violet ink. Ever since, she had
kept a notebook beside her bed to capture her sleep-strewn
wanderings. The images were always sharp, clear, and the sense of
familiarity was something she could never explain to her parents.
Although the images should have been horrifying, with the blood,
the dark passages and the roar of a monster, her feelings were of
love, compassion and an unexpected sense of safety.

Over the years, she noted similar themes recurring: the roar in
the distance, the bones, the blood, but, she thought, as she contem-
plated the latest dream, in the majority of her dreams, it was a
puddle, never flowing around her feet. On other occasions, the
blood was in a golden goblet as though it were an offering.
Reaching into the cupboard, she pulled her laptop out, put it onto
the bed and flipped through to her dream diaries. When she

finished each notebook, she would transcribe it, keeping a record of her night-time wanderings, they were all there, from the very first dream diary she had kept.

When she had reached adulthood and she realised the dreams formed a story, she had never shared the images, not even with Rose. The two reasons for this were concern it would worry people about her mental state, and because it was a secret world of her own, a place of sanctuary, and she had hugged it to her, fearing that to share it would ruin her connection with this shadowy place.

Flicking back through the earlier entries to see if the flowing blood had appeared in the past, Eloise put a selection of words in the search function, hoping to discover similar images but, as she had thought upon waking, there was nothing matching her most recent dream. Having made a note of this in the handwritten journal, she closed her laptop and her notebook. Reaching for her cotton robe, she crept out of her room and climbed the spiral staircase to the kitchen to make coffee, awaiting the noise and chaos that would accompany the Hay family when they emerged from their bedrooms.

Rose, Leon and their twelve-year-old twin sons, Sean and Marcus, had arrived late the previous evening and, after a hasty meal, Rose had pushed the boys into their beds. An hour later, she and Leon had followed. Now, as the moka pot came to the boil, filling the kitchen with the fragrant scent of coffee, Eloise heard footsteps and turned to see Rose.

'Coffee?'

'Yes, you angel of divine mercy, coffee and lots of it, please,' Rose said in high drama.

Eloise laughed. 'Go into the living room, I'll bring it in. Do you need anything else?'

'No, not at the moment,' Rose replied.

Eloise watched from the kitchen as her friend wandered around the room, examining the endless curios, reading the spines of the books on the overflowing shelves until she came to a halt, admiring the elaborate wall-hanging, which resided in pride of place over the enormous fireplace. It was made from calico, tough cream fabric resembling the sail of an old ship and, worked in an enormous circle, was an intricate hand-stitched labyrinth. The pattern was picked out in shades of red, from the palest of pinks to the deepest of vermilion. Rose was still staring at it when Eloise entered with the coffee.

'This is astonishing,' said Rose, sitting beside Eloise, who had set the coffee down on a table in front of one of the sofas.

'It was made by a local artists' co-operative,' Eloise said. 'Quinn loved it. When the idea was suggested, each member of the group provided a skein of red thread or wool, the older the better, and they worked on it together to create an image of the labyrinth. It's a potent symbol on the island of Crete.'

Eloise adored the elaborate workmanship in the wall-hanging: the delicate patterns swirling across the canvas, the varying shades of red merging to give the impression of shadows flickering across its surface. A world within the circle, a reflection of life, with its twisting, turning pathways.

'Quinn loved labyrinths,' she said. 'I think it was the story of the Minotaur that first drew him to Crete. Did you know, there's a difference between a labyrinth and a maze?'

'No,' said Rose. 'I thought they were interchangeable words.'

'Me too, until Quinn explained,' Eloise said. 'A labyrinth has one route in and one route out while a maze has multiple pathways, many leading to dead ends. Mazes are about choice and strategy, labyrinths are spaces of continuous flow, like life.'

'And this is a labyrinth?' Rose asked.

'Yes, and mazes and labyrinths each have their own mythology,' Eloise continued. 'The most famous for the labyrinth is the Greek myth of the Minotaur. While in mazes, for centuries it was believed compasses wouldn't work.'

'Why?' asked Rose.

'That was thought to be the magic of the maze. If it was impossible to use man-made devices to negotiate a path, whoever chose to venture in had to rely on their own skill, perseverance and determination to find their way in and out.'

'I had no idea.'

'Did you know King Henry II was supposed to have kept his mistress, The Fair Rosamund Clifford, in a house built like a maze in Woodstock Palace in Oxfordshire?'

'No.'

'According to legend, only the king knew the secret pathway, making it impossible for anyone but him to find Lady Rosamund. Until, one day, his wife, Eleanor of Aquitaine, who was pregnant with what turned out to be her youngest child, the infamous King John, was angry at the thought of her husband having a lover, so she decided to follow him. Unravelling a thread as she went, creeping in his shadow, she waited until she saw her rival, then retraced her footsteps and slipped away. A few days later, she followed the path again to the heart of the maze and, according to the tales, "dealt with Fair Rosamund that she lived not long after".'

'Nasty,' Rose said.

'Although, Quinn said there's no historical evidence to prove Eleanor murdered Rosamund.'

'Which is a relief,' said Rose. 'But please don't mention the idea of a maze inside a house to the boys! They'll want to build one.'

'The palace has long gone, so you're safe,' said Eloise, laughing. 'When Quinn told me the Rosamund story, I was intrigued by the way Eleanor used string to find her.'

'Why?'

'It's a central part of the Minotaur legend and I found it interesting this motif was repeated in an English folktale,' Eloise said. 'Ovid and Homer tell us, when Theseus was sent with the other Athenian tributes to be sacrificed to the Minotaur, Ariadne fell in love with him. To help him to find his way out of the dreaded labyrinth she gave him a ball of string to leave a trail behind him.'

'You're right, it's odd the way they overlap,' said Rose.

'Are you discussing labyrinths?' Leon wandered in, carrying a mug, which he presented to Eloise is the style of Oliver Twist begging for more. 'I followed the smell of coffee,' he added as Eloise passed him the moka pot.

Rose smiled at her husband as he ruffled her hair.

'We are, dearest,' she replied.

'This house is a bit of a labyrinth,' said Leon. 'I was wandering about it last night and I was struck by the unusual layout. It's as though the house is always guiding you downwards to the main garden terrace with the pool as the central point.'

'You're right,' said Eloise. 'I hadn't really thought about that before.'

'It takes an artist to notice such things,' said Rose.

Leon was an artist of some success, although his parents, who believed this was not the career for the son of a peer of the realm, were unimpressed. Despite fashionable galleries clamouring for Leon's work, his parents referred to his painting as a hobby, which infuriated both Leon and Rose. Leon's parents were loath to tell people about Rose's very successful career as a barrister, which they also felt was beneath them. Leon would one day inherit the title of the Earl of Wiston, making Rose a countess, a fact that amused Eloise even while it appalled Rose, the daughter of a builder and a teacher, with staunch working-class roots.

'Where are the monsters?'

'Asleep.'

Eloise returned to the kitchen to prepare more coffee.

'When you think about the violence of the Minotaur story, it's interesting to consider people now use labyrinths as walking meditations,' said Leon.

'As what?' asked Rose.

'It's a way to focus the mind involving movement,' explained Leon. 'You begin with deep breathing, then follow a trail, or specific route, focusing on the steps. The gentleness of the slow walking is supposed to represent a pathway to contemplation.'

'Yet, in the myth, the labyrinth was a place of violence,' said Rose.

'True, but remember, alongside the terror created by the monster, Daedalus crafted a replica of the cosmos,' said Eloise, now leaning on the long worktop that separated the kitchen and living space while she waited for the water to boil up again. 'The intricate pattern of the pathway, with all its beauty and danger is a tool to help us navigate the journey of life. If we stray off the path, the labyrinth will protect us, because within its turns, it will always take us to the same place: home. This circular motion is thought to be soothing, hence the meditative aspect of a labyrinth.'

'Fascinating,' murmured Rose.

Leon took the fresh coffee from Eloise while she arranged a series of pastries on a plate for an impromptu breakfast.

'I'm quite taken with all the maps, too,' he said, gazing around the room at the numerous framed sea charts. 'Was Quinn a keen sailor?'

'Not that I'm aware,' she said.

'I just wondered if that might be the reason he loved maps,' he replied.

'No, it was because of the dragons,' said Eloise with a grin.

'You're wearing one of your smug expressions and I can't bear it,' said Rose. 'Explain or I'll set the boys on you.'

'Around the edge of the old maps, the cartographers always

painted dragons, sea monsters, mermaids and other mythical crea-
tures. They were to mark the dangers of unchartered waters, hence
the phrase: "Here be dragons". Quinn wondered for a long time if
the idea had been inspired by the monsters of myth, including the
Minotaur.'

'Interesting,' said Leon, wandering over to inspect one of the
maps. 'It's a reasonable assumption. After all, these were shadowy
creatures, particularly the Minotaur, as he lurked in the darkness of
the labyrinth.'

'Maybe the ancient writers and cartographers meant for these
to be seen as literal terrifying creatures, to warn sailors to be care-
ful,' said Rose.

'Or perhaps they were supposed to be the dark side of
ourselves. The side we hide, the part of our personalities that
generates anger, violence, murder,' added Leon.

Eloise glanced at Rose, who had sent Leon a furious look. Leon
looked apologetic, returning to sit opposite his wife.

'You're right,' Eloise said, smiling placatingly at Rose. 'Violence
was inherent in ancient cultures, especially against anyone who was
different. When Dad used to recount the stories of the Greek myths
to us as children, he delivered a sanitised version, lots of happy-
ever-afters and good triumphing over evil, but when I was older
and began to read them myself, I realised how much more there
was to the stories. There is beauty in them, but there is terrible
brutality, too.'

'Nothing much has changed,' said Rose. 'I see it in court every
day. We grow up in a world where the pervading emotions
surrounding us each day are violence, anger, hatred and envy. It's
endemic.'

'It's no real surprise when you think about what we're taught in
school,' said Eloise. 'Look at some of the literary classics. Heath-
cliff is deemed to be one of the great romantic heroes, but he's a

violent thug. *The Tenant of Wildfell Hall* is a shocking tale of domestic violence, yet these are seen as great works of literature. Sadly, they were written by women who accepted such treatment as normal. Look at TV, too: the sheer volume of shows that revolve around murder and crime. Have you ever noticed how many of these continue to perpetuate violence against women? We need to reconsider how we view the relationships between men and women. Women should no longer be blamed for being the victims.'

There was silence between the three friends when Eloise had finished, concern showing on both Rose and Leon's faces. Then Rose reached across and hugged Eloise.

'You're right, Lo,' she said, and Eloise could hear tears in her friend's voice. 'It's horrendous.'

Leon squeezed Eloise's shoulder in a gesture of support. Then, reaching for the last pastry, he asked, 'Have you heard from any of the Horsemen?' and Eloise felt relieved that he had changed the subject.

'No,' she replied, 'but then, after my dramatic exit from the funeral, I wasn't expecting them to rush to offer shoulders to cry on.'

'Not even Claud?' asked Rose, in surprise. 'I thought he might have contacted you.'

'How did he react?' Eloise continued, the image of Claud's shocked white face through the car window flashing into her mind.

'What? To you walking out of the funeral and disappearing into the ether?'

Eloise nodded, biting her lip.

'He was furious,' said Rose.

'Understandable,' she murmured.

'Apart from offering condolences to Ethelwyn and Gladys at the funeral, he didn't speak to anyone. The last I saw of him, he was on his phone, then he made his apologies to your parents and left. He was there for about half an hour.'

'He looked quite stressed when he left,' said Leon.

'No doubt one of his many women causing problems,' sighed Eloise, pushing the image of Claud from her mind.

The contemplative silence was shattered by a roar from below. Rose buried her face in a cushion as Leon braced himself.

'The twin Minotaurs are awake,' Eloise sighed, as Sean and Marcus burst into the room.

12

For the first few days, Rose, Leon, Sean and Marcus helped Eloise as she sorted out Quinn's house. The biggest task was to decide what to keep and what to discard.

Quinn's bedroom was an emotional challenge for Eloise as this was the most personal room. It was a relief when Yiannis arrived with one of the winery's trucks and a stack of boxes. He and Leon became immediate friends and they offered to go through Quinn's clothes, which Eloise accepted with relief. Most of Quinn's personal possessions – his watch, his wedding ring and a few other keepsakes – had been left to Josh, who, when the carefully packed box had arrived at their home in west London, had shoved the whole lot in their spare room and refused to look inside. After Josh's death, Eloise had sorted through it and placed the valuables with her husband's effects, which she had passed to his mother, Ethelwyn.

Yiannis took Quinn's clothes and shoes, explaining they would be useful to keep at the vineyard for the casual workers.

'People often underestimate the heat of the day, not to mention, in the autumn and winter – the coolness of the nights,' he explained.

The furniture in Quinn's bedroom was old, but not antique. When they realised the wardrobe door was held on by one hinge and the chest of drawers was warped beyond repair, they loaded it onto the back of Yiannis's flat-bed truck.

'What will you do with it?' Sean asked.

'My sister's an artist, so she'll probably upcycle them,' he replied, intriguing the twins, who then asked if they could try this with their bedroom furniture. Leon wavered, his artist's desire to create new from old skewing his parental judgement, until Rose said a firm 'No', bringing Leon back to his senses.

Each day, Eloise and Rose sorted another part of Sfragida House, replacing furniture, removing photographs, changing the paintings on the walls and deciding on new colour schemes. A few pieces remained, including the vast labyrinth wall-hanging, which Eloise left in pride of place on the chimney breast. Quinn's many framed sea maps were redistributed throughout the house. Eloise, Rose and Leon would often discover the twins sitting beneath one, staring at it while discussing buried treasure.

As Quinn's presence diminished, Eloise felt the old building was turning towards her for warmth, like a sunflower turning towards the sun, embracing her as its new owner.

One afternoon Marina took them to a local pottery and Eloise bought a dinner service with accompanying serving bowls and jugs. Upon returning to Sfragida House, she cleared the kitchen of the bulk of Quinn's chipped, mismatched crockery and when she served dinner on her own plates, she felt the house was becoming her home.

Leon took it upon himself to allow the two women as much time alone together as possible by shouldering the responsibility of the twins. On the days he was not required to help in the house, he piled Sean and Marcus into the car, exploring beaches, local tourist attractions and, to the delight of the boys, helping Yiannis and Marina at the vineyard.

'They're as much his fault as mine,' Rose had said when Eloise asked if she would rather join her family on one of their adventures instead of wandering around the shops buying soft furnishings. 'Let him control them.'

* * *

One morning, after Leon had driven Sean and Marcus off to a nearby water park, with the promise to hire mountain bikes afterwards, Eloise and Rose went on a flying visit to Heraklion town to buy paint. Eloise planned to redecorate Quinn's bedroom and one of the guest rooms, which was a strange shade of mustard, after her friends had returned home. For today, the two women planned to explore Quinn's study.

As they ate lunch by the swimming pool, relishing the freshness of the local olives, bread and *dolmades* bought while they were shopping, they once again discussed the contents of Quinn's letter, as they had several times throughout the week.

'Do you think he meant it?' asked Rose.

'Of course,' Eloise replied. 'He said I may do as I wish with the house as long as I don't sell it until I've had time to consider my future. He suggested I visit Knossos, which will help me decide.'

'What does that mean?'

'No idea. He knew I was interested in Greek mythology, and studying Knossos was his life-long passion. Perhaps he hoped I'd fall so in love with the house, I'd insist Josh and I keep it. How was he to know what was going to happen to his son? Remember,' said Eloise, pouring them each a glass of ice-cold sparkling water, 'Quinn wrote the letter after he discovered Josh intended to sell Sfragida House to a developer. My solicitor has said there's no covenant on the land and nothing to stop me selling it if I choose to. This was simply Quinn's request.'

'Do you think you'll stay?'

'For the summer, yes,' Eloise said. 'I can't go back to the house in London, not after what happened.'

'Will you sell it?'

'Yes, as soon as probate is finished.'

'And then? You're thirty-four, Lo – do you intend to spend the rest of your life here?'

'There are worse places to be,' she said, glancing at the pool and the terraced garden.

'But what about your career?' asked Rose. 'This time last year you were working for a huge promotion, which, incidentally, you achieved. What has your boss at Balin said about your sabbatical?'

'They have a comprehensive wellness policy, which includes up to a year off with pay for sudden bereavement of a spouse. Not to mention the life insurance, which paid out two days ago. The house was such a tie on our finances, Josh insisted we each have a large life-insurance policy.'

'By large, what do you mean?'

Eloise leaned forward and whispered, 'Two million, plus it pays off the house, which has been valued at about the same.'

'What?' Rose squeaked.

'Madness, eh? My life was insured for the same.'

A cold chill fluttered through her as she remembered Josh's words: *You're worth more to me dead.*

'Quinn's other request,' she continued, pushing the thought away, 'was that when I cleared out his study, if I don't want the books in the cupboard beside his desk, they should be offered back to Marina. He bought them from her grandmother many years ago so he wanted her family to have first refusal.'

Eloise sipped her water, hoping her momentary tremor had not shown. There were no secrets between her and Rose, but Eloise continued to struggle with the events surrounding her husband's death.

'Have you been in Quinn's study yet?' asked Rose.

'No. I wanted the other rooms to be sorted out first, then I can take my time over his paperwork,' Eloise said, her fingers moving to the gleaming crystal necklace.

'How's your hand?' Rose asked, and Eloise frowned. She had removed the bandage the day after she arrived in Crete and the livid red scar was not as noticeable.

'It's fine,' she replied. 'As long as I'm careful.'

Rose gave her a long look but did not comment further.

'Even though Quinn's been gone over a year,' Eloise continued, 'going inside his study feels like an intrusion. It's as though we'll be crossing an invisible line into an inner sanctum, trespassing into his secret world where he kept his life's work.'

'Was he precious about it?'

'No, he was the most generous man, and the few occasions we were in there he was enthusiastic about sharing his knowledge. It was a touchy subject around Josh, though. He hated his father's research, so any discussions in the study were short-lived. His book collection is incredible. I imagine a few might be valuable. My plan is to spend the summer reading his research and exploring his discoveries.'

'Did he ever publish his work?' asked Rose as they cleared the table and carried the dirty plates to the kitchen.

'No, it was a hobby, an all-consuming one, but he never believed he had the skills or knowledge to be an historian. Marina would scold him about it, suggesting he had more knowledge than many of the people they employ at the museum.'

'He must have appreciated your interest, though.'

'Why?'

'You knew Quinn for such a short time, yet he gave you Sfragida House.'

'A safe place,' murmured Eloise without thinking.

'Do you think Quinn knew?'

'No,' she replied, although her instinct screamed the opposite. 'Well, I don't think so. I hope not.'

'Shall we make a start?' said Rose, and Eloise nodded, lifting the keys to the study down from the hook in the kitchen.

Another of the quirks of the house Eloise loved were the staircases that ran down the sides, making it possible to reach the central terrace without having to walk through the living room. Leading the way back downstairs, Eloise paused outside the blank-eyed stare of the curtained glass doors leading to the study.

She could not help but think of Josh's frustration with his father, suggesting he was selfish using this room, which opened onto the terrace where the swimming pool was located, as his study, when it would make an ideal living room or even master bedroom. It had the best view in the house but, she thought, as she slotted the key in the lock, perhaps that was why he chose it for his study. This was the place he spent most of his time.

She threw back the heavy red calico curtains and light flooded into the room. Together, she and Rose opened the shutters on the row of small square windows on the side wall, and the heart of Quinn Winter's erstwhile home was illuminated. Eloise and Rose stared around in awe.

More ancient sea maps covered the walls of the large square room. Faded and worn with time, they were a contrast to their cousins in the rest of the house, which were bright and easy to read, obviously copies and restored replicas. As Eloise examined the maps she wondered if they were original.

'The boys and Leon will love them,' said Rose. 'Leon's been so inspired, he told me last night that he's working on a new series called *Maps and Monsters*.'

'The house and I are very honoured to have acted as his muses,' Eloise laughed as she gazed around the room.

Shelves lined two of the walls, heavy with reference books and folders, while the wide desk, with its dark green leather insert, faced the patio doors. Beside it was a knee-high cabinet, with a key in the lock, an elaborate red tassel hanging from the ring. Eloise clicked it open and saw rows of notebooks. Pulling one out, she breathed in the ancient leather, the dust, the age, and a flash of her dream from the previous night caught her as though she had been stung. A woman's voice whispered through the breeze in the lemon tree outside. *I love you.*

'Do you think these are the notebooks he mentioned in the letter?' Rose said, taking out another.

'They must be,' Eloise replied, jolted back to the present, and opening the notebook with careful fingers. 'There are dates inside the cover. "May 1900, Knossos". Oh my goodness, Rose, these are diaries from the Minoan dig.'

'The Palace of Knossos?'

'Yes, it was discovered by Arthur Evans in 1900. Quinn told me Evans was convinced there was a Bronze Age site here and he was sure it would reveal ancient writing. Before the tomb of Tutankhamun was discovered by Howard Carter in 1922, this was one of the biggest and most important archaeological discoveries in the world.'

'Buried treasure?' asked Rose.

'In a way, yes, I suppose it was,' Eloise smiled. 'The boys will be intrigued. Quinn studied the dig for years. He must have been fascinated to discover diaries that could give him an insight into the everyday details. It's the next best thing to being there.'

'I wonder how Marina's grandmother ended up with them,' said Rose.

'Perhaps she was there,' Eloise replied. 'Quinn once told me that local men and women worked at the site...' Her attention had been caught by the red leather journal she had given to Quinn for what had been his last Christmas. It was positioned at the far end of the desk, but what made Eloise's heart skip a beat was a pen nestled inside, as though it were marking a place while Quinn stepped outside. Opening it, she saw it was dated two weeks before he died.

At last, I have found the remainder of Alice's journals. Maybe I'll find out what happened after the wedding...

'The wedding?' Eloise said, intrigued. 'Who was Alice?'

'The author of the diaries, perhaps,' suggested Rose.

'Thanks, Brains. I'd worked out that much,' Eloise laughed.

Rose grinned and turned away. Eloise returned to the diary, vaguely aware of her friend wandering around the room examining the ornaments and trinkets on the shelves. The handwriting in the notebook was beautiful, slanted and elegant, but the ink had faded with age and was a challenge to read. Quinn had told her he was transcribing the journals as he thought they would offer useful insight. Glancing at the shelves full of files, she wondered how far her father-in-law had progressed in his task.

Turning another page, she saw a heading and froze:

My Dream

The unknown Alice had written a brief description and, as Eloise read it, she felt ice cascade through her soul.

... the floor was littered with bones but they had been arranged with care, as though they were offerings. I was at an altar, dressed in a flowing white dress and in front of me were thirteen golden goblets filled with animal blood...

'Lo, look at this,' exclaimed Rose from the corner of the room where she was examining a small wooden box. 'You might want to hide this from the boys in case it's valuable. They won't be able to resist a miniature treasure chest.'

'What?' said Eloise, her heart pounding.

'Are you OK?' Rose asked. 'You look very pale.'

'I'm fine,' said Eloise, pushing the journal back into cupboard with its companions. Hurrying over to Rose, she forced her voice to sound normal rather than shocked. 'Is there anything inside?'

With great care, Rose opened the box to reveal a roll of white fabric, yellowed with age. Eloise took it; there was something hard within the wrappings.

What do you think it is?' asked Eloise.

'Unwrap it and find out,' said Rose.

Eloise felt a strange sense of unease as she unwound the ancient fabric, although she had no idea why. As she peeled away the final layer, she and Rose gasped in surprise. Inside was a tiny carved figurine, and from its weight Eloise guessed it was made from stone or a crystal. It was of a woman with long hair wearing necklaces made of multiple strands of beads. In one hand she held a double-headed axe, in the other a goblet, while on her head were stylised bull horns.

'Who do you think she is?' asked Rose.

'I've no idea, but I bet Marina will know.'

'I wonder if Quinn showed it to her? It looks ancient...'

Outside, they heard a car parking, followed by the shouts of

Leon, Sean and Marcus as they raced into Sfragida House and down the stairs to the pool.

'I'm going to hide this for now,' said Eloise, feeling a sudden fierce protectiveness over the tiny figure.

'Good idea, you don't want it damaged,' said Rose. 'I'll distract the troops.'

Rose hurried away and Eloise replaced the figure in her swaddling before locking it in the cupboard with the journals, wondering if she had imagined the entry she had read. It reminded her of one of her own dreams, uncanny in its similarity.

'No, Dad, no,' Sean screamed from the terrace. 'Don't hurt me…' followed by a gale of laughter, yet the words sent a shudder through her.

This was not the time to dwell on either the strange journal entry or anything else, she told herself. Forcing a wide smile to her face, she hurried outside to join the Hay family. Both boys were stripping off their clothes to jump into the swimming pool. Sean always struggled with his shoe laces, which he insisted on knotting several times, and had been about to dive in wearing his trainers. His shouts of protest were due to his father pinning him to the floor, pulling the shoes, which had been a birthday present, away.

'They cost over a hundred pounds,' Leon said as he wrenched them off Sean's feet. 'You're not swimming in them…'

As Leon released his son, who threw himself into the water, Marcus climbed on an inflatable alligator and began shouting out the events of the day to his mother.

'Mum, Mum, we've had a great day. Dad nearly drowned on the water slide and then he lost his swimming trunks and the security guard wanted to have him arrested and—'

Eloise put her hands over her ears as Rose burst out laughing. Leon grinned at the two women, dropped his son's trainers on the floor and disappeared inside, returning a few moments later, carrying an ice bucket full of beers.

'I hope you don't mind me helping myself, Lo,' he said as he opened one, sank on to a nearby lounger, taking a huge swig as he sighed with relief and closed his eyes.

'Of course not,' she replied, opening a beer each for her and Rose before flopping down on the sunbed beside Leon.

'I love my sons,' he said, 'but, on occasions, I could murder them.'

'Knives or drowning?' Rose asked in a conversational manner, taking the lounger on the other side of Leon.

'Maybe poison,' Leon replied. 'Not so loud.'

'You might want to rethink poison,' said Rose. 'It would be considered premeditated. It would be easier for me to secure an acquittal for a crime of passion: manslaughter due to diminished responsibility. Drowning, which could be deemed accidental—'

'My goodness, this is a fascinating insight into your marriage,' laughed Eloise.

As the boys began an enthusiastic jousting tournament on two lilos, Leon asked, 'How's your day been?'

'Good,' said Eloise, describing their exploration of the study, but excluding the journal entry.

'I might sneak a look later,' said Leon, 'especially if you think the maps might be originals. Would you mind if I photographed them?'

'Help yourself,' Eloise replied.

'Shall we go down to the Brewery Taverna for dinner?' said Rose, who, ever ready to pull either or both out of danger, was watching the twins as they dive-bombed each other.

Eloise was about to agree when an unexpected feeling of panic swamped her and the idea of leaving the house felt terrifying. These attacks had been happening since Josh's death and when she had spoken to a bereavement counsellor, they had explained it was the shock and they would fade away with time.

'Why don't we stay here and have a barbecue?' she suggested.

Looking up, she realised Rose was watching her with concern and Eloise guessed her friend had witnessed the panic flare in her eyes.

'We'll be back later in the summer. We can see John and Steve then,' Rose said, referring to the couple who ran the restaurant. 'Anyway, these two have been busy all day. With luck they'll crash at some point. You're right, Lo, a barbecue would make more sense.'

'Fine with me,' said Leon, reaching for another beer. 'I shall, of course, take responsibility for the barbecue. Man make fire,' he finished, in caveman tones.

* * *

Several hours later, Eloise was sitting in one of the wide chairs on the terrace beside the swimming pool, Sean draped against her, while Marcus was in a similar position leaning on his mother.

Leon was topping up Eloise and Rose's wine glasses when Sean said in a sleepy voice, 'You haven't told us a bedtime story for years, Auntie Lo.'

'Your stories were great because you could tell them without a book,' added Marcus, tired enough not to bat away his mother's fingers as they twirled through his shock of white-blond hair.

'You told me you were too old,' Eloise said.

'We've changed our minds,' replied Sean, and Marcus nodded.

'Do you mind?' asked Rose as Leon settled on her other side and she leaned into him.

As their godmother, Eloise had made a point of being involved in the twins' lives, and telling them bedtime stories had been one of her favourite godmother duties.

'It's my pleasure,' said Eloise. 'As we're in Crete it seems right I should tell you the tale of Ariadne and her brother, Asterion, the Minotaur. How the hero Theseus wreaked havoc, killing the beast, abandoning Ariadne, who was rescued by the lord of wine, Dionysus, before Theseus married her younger sister, Phaedra...'

'And that's before we get to Daedalus and Icarus,' murmured Leon, and Eloise smiled at her friends. She felt relaxed and happy for the first time in months and would be sad to wave them goodbye in a few days' time.

Safe though, too, she thought as she rearranged Sean, who was falling asleep, into a more comfortable position. As she began the ancient story, she wondered again at Rose's question, *Do you think Quinn knew?*, shuddering at the idea he might have guessed the truth about his son.

13

'Ariadne danced, her feet slippery with moonbeams as Hecate, the queen of the night, cast her silver glow. Shadows nestled in her golden curls, painting each perfect strand with the bitterness of betrayal. Below the intricate dancefloor, the creature echoed her steps in his subterranean labyrinth, his howls a lament to the cruelty of his fate.

'"Dance brother," she crooned as his cries reached her, their pain and despair resounding through the stars. "Dance, my sweet Asterion, and let your sorrows fly."

'The strings of crystals around her neck chimed as she moved, joining with the music of the spheres to create the tune for the siblings to weave their magical dance of light and dark. She above, he below. Their blood joined to the cosmos, grandchildren of Helios, the sun god, keys to the mystery of time.

'"You shall be free," she promised. "We shall leave together and never return."

'But her words were an empty promise. They both knew he would die at the hand of the man who had promised to be her lover: Theseus, the son of Aegeus, king of Athens, and the

Troezenian princess, Aethra. The hero of a thousand stories; the rumoured son of the god Poseidon.

'Daedalus, the craftsman, the man who had created the labyrinth and Ariadne's corresponding dancefloor above, had given her the thread. A ball of golden twine for Theseus to unspool as he entered the terrifying depths of the monster's lair. Ariadne knew that with each step he took into the darkness the golden twine would change colour, stained red by the strength of her betrayal. Her blood, his blood, their blood, the lifeblood of the monster, of the universe.

'"Ariadne," whispered her younger sister, Phaedra, and Ariadne opened her arms to welcome her into the dance. With sylph-like grace, they spun together, their souls mingling as their footsteps beat time, as below them, Theseus and their brother, the Minotaur, created their own fatal dance. The thrust and parry, the lunge and spin, a parody of the sisters above, faster, faster their steps wild as the dance in the depths of the earth, ending in the death of their brother, the monster.

'For this is how it had to be, the final brutal outcome. The tales of Crete are as dark as hell, as bitter as any gall, created through family lore and the cruelty of the gods. Asterion, the Minotaur, an aberration, a curse, could not be allowed to live. Nor could his killing of the Athenian children be permitted to continue. You see, in the days before the Minotaur was born, King Minos of Crete, the son of mighty Zeus and Europa, a Phoenician princess, married Pasiphaë, the daughter of the sun god, Helios.

'When Minos acceded to the throne of Crete, he prayed to his uncle, the Olympian, Poseidon, god of the sea, storms, earthquakes and horses, for a sign of his greatness. Poseidon sent a giant white bull from the waves, demanding Minos sacrifice the magnificent animal in his name. When Minos substituted a lesser animal, keeping the white bull hidden in his own herd, Poseidon flew into a rage, but Pasiphaë was the one who was punished. Cursed by the angry god, she went mad, craving the bull above all others. In her mania, she paid the craftsman Daedalus to create a golden cow in which she could hide, until her water-driven madness culminated in a pregnancy.

'The child was born with the head of a bull and the body of a child, with tiny hoofs instead of feet. Asterion, the starry one, bellowed his disbelief and malediction for all who came near him. Due to the sins of his parents and the cruelty of the gods, he must bear the punishment, and as he grew, his power and bloodlust increased until the day he was imprisoned in the labyrinth built by Daedalus.

'Ariadne watched as they led him away, the dance steps she had taught him imprinted on his mind. As she swayed with grace and elegance on the labyrinth painted on the floor above her brother's living tomb, she heard his cries of misery. The sorrow of his broken heart beat through her chest as they danced through the starlit skies. Above. Below. Heartbroken.

'Her father saw the promise of sport with the bull-headed boy and a cruel game was engineered. He declared war on Athens, whom he suspected had murdered his son and heir, Androgeus. When the Athenians begged for mercy, Minos offered a terrible peace: if the Athenians sent a tribute each year of seven young men and seven virgin maidens to be fed to the Minotaur, he would end the devastating war. In desperation, the Athenians agreed. Each year, they bore their punishment and Minos gloried in his tournament of violence; until the day Theseus came to Crete.

'When Ariadne saw him, she was bewitched and there are many who suggest Poseidon cursed her, too. This dutiful princess turned against her father in the flicker of a moonbeam as she promised to help Theseus in his quest to murder her brother. Was the god trying to make amends? To send his son to destroy the creature, half-man, half-bull, who stalked the labyrinth unable to rest, crying for release. Was Poseidon acting in mercy?

'If he was, then his son, Theseus, did not understand; for he was ruthless.

'The door to the labyrinth was left ajar as the tributes walked through on trembling legs and, with each step, Theseus unwound the golden thread. Ariadne danced, her heart beating with her brother's, as the two men met and the Minotaur, with a roar of relief, allowed the dance to end. Bending his head in submission to Theseus, he was released. No more pain, no more humiliation, an end to the bloodlust. The story should have ended there, but Theseus swept Ariadne into his boat. Unbeknown to her, his sport and revenge on Minos were not yet complete.

'To Naxos they fled, where Theseus abandoned the Cretan princess to her fate...'

'What happened to her?' interrupted Robert.

'Did she die?' gasped Andrew.

'No,' said Alice, throwing her cousins an irritated look for interrupting her story, 'she married Dionysus, the god of wine.'

'How did she meet him if she was abandoned on an island?' asked Robert.

'Naxos belonged to Dionysus,' Alice replied.

'Can you own islands?' asked Andrew.

'If you're a god, you can,' replied Robert.

'Alice,' called her aunt, 'time to relax, dear. The boys have had enough lessons for today.'

Robert and Andrew cheered as Alice abandoned her tale of the Minotaur and they ran back to the picnic area, which was being arranged under an orange tree within the citrus grove, a shaded and sheltered area, near the Perrins' impressive villa. Alice stood, stretching her arms above her head as she gazed out across the valley from the rocky promontory where they had been sitting.

The air was sharp with the smell of wild thyme, the tang of the olives and the lingering peaty odour of the brook that tumbled down the hillside. In the distance was the sound of digging, the voices of the workers carrying through the sparkling blue air. The idea of the Akashic Record, which Juliet had spoken of, returned to her, and she imagined the words flying high on silver wings above her head, waiting for the moment to reveal their wisdom.

'When will we be able to visit the archaeological dig?' Andrew called as Alice approached the picnic more slowly.

'Mr Perrin has requested a visit,' Alice replied, 'but it's a serious business and they may not want two rapscallions like yourselves rampaging through the important things they're discovering.'

'We have treasures, though,' said Andrew, but before he could expound on the pile of dusty rocks they had acquired throughout their journey, Elaine Perrin, who was seated beside Aunt Agatha, began to speak.

'Alice is quite correct,' she said, gazing at the boys with a fondness Alice felt would not endure when their veneer of 'best behaviour' slipped. 'Mr Arthur Evans has employed lots of people to help uncover the palace of King Minos and, because of his speed and skill, he is already finding many important artefacts. Why, after two weeks he discovered a magnificent throne room, and he believes he will soon discover even greater treasures.'

* * *

When Agatha and Alice had revealed to Robert and Andrew that they would be travelling to Crete, they had screamed in delight. Wendbury was the only person in their party who was unhappy, wearing a look suggesting he had been sentenced to a lifetime of hard labour. He was struggling with life as a traveller, finding the continuous movement stressful and the increasing heat oppressive.

His consolation was the knowledge they would be staying near the Perrins, whom he hoped would persuade Lady Hope to remain in one place for a considerable period. As plans were made, Alice had felt her excitement growing, and as they had set off on their three-week long journey to Crete, she had thanked her aunt again for including her in their adventures.

'We shall be able to talk about our travels for years to come,' Agatha had exclaimed, as excited as Alice.

The journey had taken them by rail to Cologne, Düsseldorf, Hanover, Magdeburg, Leipzig, Dresden, Prague and, finally, Vienna. Each step of the journey had been monitored by Wendbury and his copy of *Bradshaw's Continental Railway Guide*. From here, they had travelled to Trieste in Italy, where they had caught a steamer to Corfu, remaining on the island for a few days. Alice had taken Robert and Andrew on an evening walk through the orange and olive groves from the village of Castrades to view the One-Gun Battery, where tradition said Odysseus's ship was wrecked. A three-day voyage on the Austrian Lloyd's Mail Steamers, which skirted the Dalmatian coast and ploughed along the eastern shores of the Adriatic, delivered them to Athens, where Hugo was waiting.

They had remained in Athens for a week, exploring the city, wandering the Acropolis and, in the case of Robert and Andrew, questioning people about the Olympiad. They had been delighted to learn about the eternal Olympic flame. When a gentleman staying at their hotel had heard their questions, he had indulged their eagerness and given them as much information as he could remember, because he had attended the games. He had described the Panathenaic Stadium, where the opening ceremony had been held, the Games opened by the King of Greece, George I.

'I've been told that when Arthur Evans was here with his friend John Myres a few years ago,' Hugo had said, 'they found pottery shards that were thousands of years old just lying on the surface around the ruins.'

Robert and Andrew had loaded their pockets with as many lumps of rock and broken pots as they could manage.

Two days later, they had boarded the boat chartered by George Perrin to transport them to Crete. The Perrins had taken a more direct route to Crete, as Gus had been eager to return to the vineyard. When Agatha had asked Elaine for help in finding accommodation for the summer, she had insisted they use a house situated on the outer edges of their land.

'I shall ensure it is ready for your arrival,' Elaine had assured Agatha, 'and I shall hire local staff for Wendbury to oversee.'

* * *

Alice had fallen in love with the house as soon as she had seen it. At its heart was a square, brick-built building that appeared to flow down the hillside. The interior was joined by two staircases and a number of outbuildings were scattered around. Robert and Andrew thought it the most intriguing place they had ever seen, and were delighted with the room they shared in the eaves. Alice and Agatha had a good-sized room each, with a dining room off to one side and a drawing room below, looking out over the Perrins' vines.

A separate cottage housed Nanny Ipswich, Florence, Eagles and Wendbury. Of the servants, Florence alone was enjoying their adventure. Nanny was suffering in the heat, Eagles was angry they would not be visiting Italy, where she had hoped to search for a lost love, and Wendbury would have preferred to be in England. Aunt Agatha, however, was throwing herself into the adventure and Alice thought her aunt looked happier than she had for years.

'Do you think Mr Evans will find the Minotaur's skeleton?'

asked Robert, his voice hushed with awe as he tucked into the picnic.

'How gruesome,' said Mrs Perrin, although her eyes twinkled in amusement. 'Mr Evans has been finding pots, stones and frescoes, but no bones. At least, none that we've heard about.'

Despite the heat of the Cretan sun, an involuntary shudder ran down Alice's spine, raising goosebumps on her arms. Wherever she travelled in Crete, the discussion of Evans and his dig was the main topic of conversation. He was making no secret of his discoveries, each of which convinced him they were uncovering the labyrinth complex: the lair of the fearsome Minotaur. Alice guessed it was the endless debate about the ancient myths that had caused her to have strange dreams. Ever since their arrival in Crete, she had found herself entering an unexpected dreamworld. The previous night, as she wandered passageways lit by flaming torches, she had been suffused with longing to reach the centre of the labyrinth, to comfort the beast. She awoke with the knowledge that if she could reach him, all would be well.

'There are rumours of a strange presence,' continued Elaine as Robert and Andrew gazed at her with round-eyed wonder. 'Old Manoli, one of the Cretan workmen, was guarding the ruins overnight and he claimed he felt something unearthly surrounding him.'

Alice waited for her aunt's exclamation decrying such an idea, but Agatha was quiet, her eyes riveted on Elaine. Despite her dream, which Alice dismissed from her mind as night-time nonsense, she felt a sense of frustration at this superstitious rumour of the supernatural. In her opinion, Mr Evans was carrying out a scientific exploration and, in her university-educated mind, there was no room for suggestions of gods and monsters.

Ever since her aunt had decided on the trip to Crete, Alice had determined to treat the dig as a serious matter rather than a romantic jaunt into the past. In trying to discover all she could about the excavations taking place at Knossos, she had written to a friend, Bernadette, at Newnham and a reply had arrived while they were in Athens. Alice had been amused at her friend's desire to appear intellectual, even in a letter.

> It is believed a Greek gentleman, Minos Kalokairinos, began excavating on Kephála Hill in 1877, but the unrest in Crete made it difficult for him to continue. However, his discovery of large storage jars or pithoi (singular: pithos) suggested a vast and important complex or building, possibly a palace. This is what encouraged Mr Evans to buy that particular piece of land to excavate. There is also a suggestion that Evans has been collecting small sealstones for many years, all of which have their origins in Crete and which demonstrate, or so he believes, evidence of potential writing...

The idea of sealstones intrigued Alice. She had come across descriptions of them during her studies of Ancient Egypt and the Schliemanns' dig of Troy. She knew they were small engraved stones that were used by administrators to mark goods before sale and for identification during import and export. She wondered if discovering such items could reveal information about the day-to-day lives of the people who had lived so many thousands of years ago. It was an amount of time she struggled to comprehend but she was fascinated by the idea of trying to understand them, to imagine their lives.

'Crete is the place for archaeology,' Elaine continued. 'George was explaining it to us this morning over breakfast. There are many rich men who are eager to discover more about the past. In Phaistos, in the Messara lowlands to the south, there is an Italian dig headed by Mr Federico Halbherr, while there is rumour of a

French-led excavation near Malia. Mr David Hogarth has been exploring a cave on Mount Dicte, where Zeus himself was said to have been born. Mr Hogarth claimed he was finding offerings and artefacts at the rate of one a minute. He's joined Mr Evans now at the Knossos site.'

'What sort of things?' asked Alice.

'Bronze blades, pins, tweezers, brooches, rings, needles, all manner of items,' said Elaine. 'There are even rumours that Mr John Myres, who is a very great friend of Mr Evans, is hoping to dig at Petsofas where he believes there might be an ancient temple.'

'Is it true a woman is looking too?' asked Andrew, throwing a goading look at Alice, who scowled back.

'Quite right,' smiled Elaine. 'She visited Arthur while we were away. She's an American who has been studying in Athens at the American School of Classical Studies. Many of the other students have been shocked as she is travelling without a chaperone.'

Alice felt her curiosity piqued.

'And is she here, on Crete?'

'Oh, yes. She's become quite a well-known figure. She's been travelling the countryside by mule, looking for a good site to dig. She's accompanied by a man named Pappadhias, who wears traditional Cretan costume.'

'What's that?' asked Robert.

'It's a kilt made from yards and yards of fabric,' explained Elaine. 'They're very impressive. George has heard she's settled on a site near the village of Kavousi and is hiring workers for the season.'

'Do you not feel uncomfortable with the idea of the Cretans being paid by foreigners to excavate their own historical treasures? It's possible these artefacts will end up in museums in London, Paris or Rome,' said Alice.

'To be honest, my dear, I've never really given it much thought,' admitted Elaine.

'What is this young woman's name?' asked Agatha.

'Harriet Boyd,' replied Mrs Perrin. 'Ah, here are George and Hugo.'

Alice gave a start: the name of Harriet Boyd was one she had overheard when she had been with Ephraim, but, now, as George Perrin's tall figure appeared through the citrus grove, Alice was distracted, allowing the name to slip from her mind. Her hand rose to check her hair, a gesture that earned a giggle from her cousins. Hugo was a few paces behind her, and both men were carrying large cooling jugs containing bottles of wine. As the youngest in her own family, Alice was unused to the endless company of children, and, while she loved her cousins, there were times when their behaviour grated on her nerves.

Wondering if this was how her elder brother, Benedict, and sister, Petronella, had always viewed her and Hugo, she began to understand better why Petra would shoo her out of her bedroom, especially if Alice had been trying on her clothes or playing with her jewellery. The age gap between her and Petra was seven years, nine between herself and Ben; Hugo was eighteen months older than Alice.

'Hello, Mother,' George said as he bent to kiss Elaine Perrin's cheek. 'Lady Hope, Alice, boys,' nodding in turn with each greeting.

'Alice is blushing,' whispered Robert to Andrew, and they fell into a heap of giggles. Hugo gave them a shove and told them to 'Pipe down'. Alice ignored them, but George gave an amused glance in their direction.

'I've been speaking to Duncan Mackenzie, Arthur's assistant,' said George, flopping down in the shade and taking the glass his mother offered. 'Duncan has said we can join the excavation team for as long as we like. Arthur is interested to have new academic blood. I also mentioned you, Alice, and you are very welcome to join us, too.'

'Really?' said Alice, astonished. Despite the tentative offer of being included in the team, she had expected the usual rescindment with the excuse that women would not be able to cope with the heavy workload: a statement she believed to be both untrue and unfair.

'Arthur is happy to employ men and women,' said Hugo.

'Especially when I told him you'd studied at Newnham,' George added.

He paused as his mother requested his help with moving her chair further into the shade, giving Alice time to consider the kindness of his action in ensuring her inclusion in the dig.

'When can we join them?' asked Alice.

'Tomorrow?' suggested Hugo, looking over at his aunt.

'An excellent proposition, my dear,' said Agatha. 'The boys and I can spend some time here with Elaine while you discover ancient civilisations.'

'I shall collect you after breakfast,' said George. 'We have a donkey cart that will be suitable to take us over the rough terrain of the dig.'

Raising a teacup to her lips, Alice glanced at her aunt, who gave her a look of understanding and for the briefest moment, Alice felt a glimmer of hope.

14

Cords hung from the ceiling, twisting, sinuous. No breeze sullied the fetid air of the humid interior — these dripping red ropes moved of their own accord. The hues glimmered from the palest of pinks through to the darkest of reds, a colour of such intensity it gleamed an obsidian black. Reaching out, she touched the darkest sliver, shivering at its unexpected softness, yielding as it reached towards her, winding around her wrists with the gentlest of touches, whispering like a lover, hypnotic, beguiling, her mind lost to its sensuous touch, her breathing shallow as the pleasure increased. His footsteps, his voice, his words: 'I love you.'

15

Eloise put the diary on the desk and moved to the overstuffed bookcases, tracing her fingers along the spines until she found several battered volumes on the theories of Theosophy.

'*Old woman, old woman...*' she murmured, remembering the song from her own childhood, wondering about the evocative vividness of Alice's vision of the Akashic Record. Words hovering, wrapped in webs of light, ready to return with thoughts, inspirations, love. Would the bad return alongside the good, Eloise wondered, and shuddered.

When she had begun reading Quinn's notes, she had not expected to become so involved in the story, but Alice, Juliet, Hugo and George had captured her imagination. As had Aunt Agatha, Robert, Andrew and the cast of characters they had met on their travels. She pondered the amount of time it had taken Alice and her family to travel from Paris to Crete, and wondered whether Juliet and her family had continued to Italy as planned. Eloise had found her ideas surprising, particularly the beliefs of the Theosophy movement about reincarnation.

Returning to the desk, Eloise flicked through each book in turn.

The first two were intense academic studies of the movement, its creators and their beliefs, which she resolved to read over the next few weeks. The third was a recently reprinted version of an original Victorian text. It was written by the founder, Helena Petrovna Blavatsky, and comprised questions and answers concerning every aspect of the Theosophy movement. Running her finger down the index, she stopped at the Theosophists' views on reincarnation and read:

Enq: You mean, then, that we have all lived on earth before, in many past incarnations, and shall go on living?
Theo: I do...
Enq: And we keep incarnating in new personalities all the time?
Theo: Most assuredly so; because this life-cycle or period of incarnation may be best compared to human life...

Reincarnation was a subject that had fascinated Eloise and her siblings ever since they were children, and to be reminded of this in such an unexpected way made goosebumps flourish on her arms. Eloise had assumed this interest in the idea of lives lived repeatedly, the concept of life continuing after death, was because of their family business, in which death ran parallel to life.

The idea of reincarnation was one she, Gareth and Jessica had often wondered about, an interest triggered during their early teens after a visit to a psychic fair when an exhibitor offered to hypnotise them to discover their past lives. The cost had been out of their pocket-money budgets and when they requested help from their parents, Eric and Marissa had gently declined. Not due to the cost, but because each session would have taken an hour and they were required to attend a funeral later in the day.

Upon returning home, the teenagers had tried to hypnotise each other with no success.

Yet, the idea had lodged in Eloise's mind and she had read whatever she could find on the subject. It surprised her she had never discovered the Theosophy movement.

'Eloise?' called a voice.

'Marina, I'm in Quinn's study,' she replied.

There was a side gate into the property that gave access to the garden. Eloise locked it at night, but during the day she left it open, aware either Yiannis, Marina or a member of their extended families would drop by at some point. At first, these visits had felt like an intrusion but after three weeks, she no longer gave them a second thought. She looked forward to the sudden appearance of a friendly face, wondering what piece of gossip, food stuff or alcohol they would choose to ply her with each time. When Rose, Leon and the twins had been staying, a daily visit from the extended Fourakis family had become usual. Now Marina appeared in the doorway.

'It's your study,' she corrected her, hugging Eloise. 'Your house.'

'No matter how long I live here, the room is so quintessentially Quinn, it will always be his in my mind.'

Marina smiled in understanding.

'Are you busy? Am I disturbing you?' she enquired, looking at the piles of books on the desk.

'No, I was reading the diaries and Quinn's notes,' she said, 'but it's nothing that can't wait.'

Marina pulled a bottle from the carrier on her shoulder.

'This is our new prosecco-style sparkling wine. Yiannis wondered if you would be one of our testers.'

'I'll fetch some glasses,' Eloise said with a grin. 'Let's drink it on the terrace.'

When she returned, Marina was uncorking the ice-cold bottle. With a satisfying pop, she poured the fizzing liquid into the two squat glasses Eloise had provided, both made from recycled glass and bought from a local artisan. She placed a pottery wine cooler on the table and Marina slotted the bottle inside.

'*Yamas*,' said Marina, tapping her glass against Eloise's and settling herself on one of the chairs under the umbrella at the large stone oval table.

'*Yamas*,' replied Eloise. 'Oh, this is delicious,' she continued as she took a sip.

'This was my idea,' said Marina, pointing to the bottle. 'A local sparkling wine. We've been developing it for a long time and this one feels right.'

'It tastes right, too,' said Eloise.

The two women sat in companionable silence, sipping the wine.

'How is the decorating going?' asked Marina.

'Slowly. I've almost finished painting the mustard room—'

Since the departure of her friends ten days earlier, Eloise had been dividing her time between decorating, reading the diaries and sleeping. She had never slept so much, and each day she could feel herself healing. The scar on her hand was less prominent and her dreams, while continuing to remain in her familiar shadow realm, were taking on a surprising clarity, which she found thrilling. Her dream diary was full of new details.

'I shall send Paolo and Stefan to help,' interrupted Marina.

'No, it's fine,' began Eloise, but Marina gave her a stern look.

'They redecorated the houses we use for the workers in three days; they will finish your room in a few hours. Then we can hang the curtains, make the bed and it will be another room which is yours, no longer Quinn's. No more sad memories.'

Eloise took another large slug of wine, but did not respond, hoping that if she remained silent, Marina would change the subject and not dwell on what had happened in the mustard room.

Eloise felt a wave of relief when, after contemplating her for a few moments, the other woman said, 'How are you finding the diaries?'

'Fascinating, but, in the original form, slow going,' Eloise admitted. 'They're very faded. Quinn has transcribed them and his typed notes are easier on my eyes.' Then the words of her father-in-law's letters returned and she remembered his instructions, should she ever wish to divest herself of the diaries. 'They belonged to your family, didn't they?'

Marina topped up their glasses before responding.

'My grandmother, Elena, inherited them from her grandmother but she was never interested in the past. When she heard Quinn was looking for information about the Knossos dig, she was happy to sell them to him.'

'Really?' said Eloise in surprise. 'She didn't want to keep them as family heirlooms?'

'It wasn't my grandmother's way. She was very forward-looking, never once looking back.'

'Did you resent it? They're your heritage.'

Marina laughed. 'Not in the least,' she said. 'Quinn paid my grandmother a lot of money, which was needed in the winery. We were trying to modernise and the money helped us on our way. My father, Michaelas, always said Quinn brought us luck, and selling him the diaries marked an upturn in our fortunes. They were good friends and would spend hours discussing the mysteries of life.'

Eloise felt a wave of relief. As Alice's story was unfolding, she was becoming drawn in by Quinn's discoveries. It would have been a wrench to surrender the books, had Marina shown signs of wanting her family possessions returned.

'Quinn developed a number of theories, too,' Eloise continued. 'He was fascinated by the myth of the Minotaur and the labyrinth.'

'He was interested in Crete and the many legends attached to the palace at Knossos,' agreed Marina. 'The Minotaur is the most famous.'

'True,' agreed Eloise, 'but the Minotaur myth was written centuries later than the Minoan civilisation by the classical scholars. Quinn has been comparing the true finds from the Knossos dig with the stories from Homer and Ovid. He's been trying to reconstruct the way the Minoans worshipped. Last night, I was reading *The Mycenaean World* by John Chadwick, which lists the names of the lost gods and goddesses of Knossos.'

'From the Linear B tablets?' asked Marina. These clay tablets had been one of the greatest finds of the Knossos excavation.

'Yes, Quinn's been studying the two languages. I wonder if he was hoping to unravel Linear A.'

Her father-in-law's notebooks on the two languages discovered by Arthur Evans had added another layer to the endless puzzles of his research. He had made extensive notes concerning the solving of Linear B, a process which had taken until the mid-1950s, years after the death of Arthur Evans. The fact Linear A had not yet been translated, and it secrets remained, was tantalising. Linear B had given scholars a wealth of day-to-day information about the Bronze Age civilisation; Eloise wondered what secrets Linear A might one day reveal.

'If anyone was dedicated enough to solving the riddle, Quinn was a contender,' Marina said with a fond smile. 'Did he make any progress?'

'Not that I've discovered,' replied Alice. 'I thought his notes about the Minoan religion were fascinating, although I was surprised to learn about Dionysus being among the gods of the Minoans. From what I'd read before, scholars believed him to be a later addition to the Olympic Pantheon.'

Marina held up the glass of wine. 'It amazes me why anyone

would think he was one of the newer gods. The desire for wine is as old as time.'

Eloise laughed. 'You're right,' she said. 'I stand corrected.'

'In total, Evans and his team discovered over one thousand tablets by the time the dig was complete,' said Marina. 'They gave us a huge amount of information.'

'Why do you think so many of the Minoan gods and goddesses were ignored by Homer and Ovid?' asked Eloise.

'One theory,' said Marina, 'is that by the time the classical Greek scholars were writing, the deities had already faded from the public consciousness. The Minoans lived from 3500 to 1100 $_{BC}$. Homer was writing in the seventh century $_{BC}$ and Ovid in the eighth century $_{AD}$, which is an enormous time span.'

'True,' agreed Eloise. 'There's no surprise things disappeared through the years.'

'However, it doesn't mean we can't revive them,' said Marina.

'You're the expert,' said Eloise, who knew Marina's PhD was a study of lost goddess worship. The bulk of her research centred on the goddesses, both the well known and the lesser deities, from Classical Greek and Roman mythology.

'Thank you,' Marina said with a grin. 'In my thesis I include several of the goddesses listed in the Minoan tablets: Diwia, who was a female equivalent of Zeus; Posidaeia, the female counterpart of Poseidon; and Mater Theia, translated to the Mother Goddess or Mother of the Gods. There are unknown goddesses, too, including Komawenteia – translated as Long-haired Goddess, as well as Pipituna and Manasa, both unknown before the translation of Linear B. It's a shame we'll never know their stories.'

'Perhaps their tales are in Linear A,' said Eloise, 'waiting for you to discover them.'

'A scholar's dream,' said Marina, 'and also unlikely.'

'There's the term *"Potnia",* too,' said Eloise. 'Isn't it supposed to mean Mistress or Lady?'

'Yes, or an important priestess.'

'There were so many: *Potnia* Hippeia – Mistress of the Horses, *Potnia* of Sitos – Mistress of Grain and,' Eloise hesitated because this discovery had caused her to gasp in surprise, *'Potnia* of the Labyrinth.'

'My father, Quinn and I often debated this,' said Marina. 'Quinn believed she was a priestess in charge of sacrifices and possibly a temple that has been lost to time. He thought it could have been a subterranean complex, emulating the labyrinth of the Minotaur legend. My father suggested she was goddess whose name will be rediscovered when the time is right.'

'Do you think one of the goddesses' names could have been attached to the famous Snake Goddess?'

Marina laughed. 'It's possible. She was a popular deity. Many versions of her figurine were discovered.'

The Snake Goddess, whose figurines had been discovered at the Knossos dig in 1903, three years later than the diaries Eloise was reading, was the most famous of the lost goddesses. There were many examples of her in the Heraklion Museum. She stood in bare-breasted magnificence, with snakes winding around her arms, wearing intricately patterned skirts and, in some depictions, with a cat balanced on her head. She was thought to have been the goddess of hearth, home and the purification of water.

'There were other figurines as well,' Marina continued, 'including many in the style of a fertility goddess. It was these images of women that caused Arthur Evans to formulate his theory that Minoans worshipped a Mother Goddess, Mater Theia.'

'Did he think she was the chief deity?' asked Eloise.

'Yes, and remember, this was before the Linear B tablets had been translated and her name was discovered,' said Marina. 'In many ways, Evans was a brilliant man, but he was also a product of his age. He was a wealthy Victorian gentleman who believed he knew better than anyone else. Therefore, when he hypothesised, his opinion was respected even if there was little or no evidence to corroborate his theories. His views influenced beliefs for many years, including his suggestion that at the height of its power, Knossos was ruled by a priest king and his consort a priestess queen, possibly Mater Theia.'

'He must have had some evidence,' said Eloise.

She had worked in research for years – her speciality was the study of parasitic diseases – and while her own explorations had involved rigid scientific detail, the principles of research and the recording of results were similar.

'Evans took his evidence from the frescoes he found. They show a variety of women in elaborate processional robes, men dressed as princes and the famous bull dancers, who appeared to leap over bulls for sport. Evans may have been correct in his hypothesis, but we'll never be able to prove it,' replied Marina. 'Other scholars believe the high priestess was a divine solar figure, which is possibly influenced by Pasiphaë, the Minotaur's mother, who was the daughter of the sun god, Helios. The Hungarian scholar Károly Kerényi believed the most important goddess was Ariadne and that actually it was she who was the Mistress of the Labyrinth referred to in the Linear B tablets.'

Eloise felt a light-headedness envelope her, and for a moment she heard female voices chanting as though in prayer, and the bellow of a bull. The image cleared with such rapidity that she looked at the wine glass in her hand, convinced this was the reason behind her momentary wooziness.

'May I show you what Rose and I found?' asked Eloise, before another thought occurred to her. 'Although, as it was in the study, Quinn might have shown it to you already.'

She hurried inside and returned with the wooden treasure chest.

Marina looked amused. 'What's this?'

'It was tucked at the end of one of the shelves in the study.'

Marina placed her glass on the table and, with careful fingers, opened the box. When she saw the fabric inside, she frowned.

'Ideally, this should be handled with gloves,' she said, and Eloise felt a stab of disappointment. 'However, if I am careful...' Marina murmured, and began unwinding the yellowed cloth. 'Oh my goodness, Eloise,' she said as she revealed the figurine. 'This is astonishing.'

'Why?' asked Eloise.

'It's a goddess figurine,' said Marina.

'Did Quinn never show it to you?'

'No, which is strange.'

Marina gazed at the figure.

'Could it be Ariadne?'

Marina considered this as she stared at the exquisite figure. 'My knowledge is not exhaustive,' she said, 'but I haven't seen another figure like this at the museum, so perhaps it could be a depiction of the Mistress of the Labyrinth. She's holding the double-headed axe of the Minoans – it's called the *"labrys"* and the image occurs everywhere in their art. The bull horns on her head are another icon that repeats throughout the sealstones, the frescoes, the pottery and tablets.'

'And the goblet?' asked Eloise.

'It suggests she's making an offering,' said Marina. 'Did you know, Evans found many vessels with holes in them for delivering libations? What makes this unusual, though, is the detail on her clothes. She appears to be wearing long strands of beads.'

'Quinn has an eye-loupe and magnifying glasses,' offered Eloise, and ran into the study to fetch them.

'This is a stunning piece, Eloise,' Marina said as she examined it in more detail. 'Each of the beads around her neck is engraved with a labyrinth. Do you know where Quinn found this?'

'No idea, but he was meticulous in his notes. There's bound to be something about it in the paperwork. I'll keep an eye out while I'm sorting through. Do you think this is an important piece, then?'

'It's hard to tell. Perhaps I should take it to the museum and let my team assess it. Would you be prepared to trust it to us?'

'Of course,' Eloise replied, although the thought of parting with it felt like a physical pain.

16

Eloise placed the figurine on her white wrappings in the centre of
the table where they could continue to gaze at it, while Marina
topped up their glasses again. As she replaced the bottle in the wine
cooler, Marina gave her a thoughtful look.

'Have you come across Quinn's photographs of the shrine?' she
asked.

Eloise shook her head. 'No, I haven't begun going through the
boxes of pictures yet. Do you think some might be connected to the
figurine?'

'Not exactly,' said Marina. 'I was wondering about the hidden
grove.'

'The what?'

'I haven't thought about the place for years but when we were
discussing the goddesses of the Minoans, the image sprang into my
mind. There's a dell hidden among the trees on the edge of the
vineyard. In the centre, there's a standing stone with markings
about two-thirds of the way up, which has always been said to be a
shrine to an unknown deity.'

'Has it ever been excavated?' Eloise asked.

'Perhaps when it was first discovered, but not in living memory,' Marina replied.

'Not even by Arthur Evans?'

'I don't think he knew about it because it wasn't on his land. My family has owned the land since 1899. Evans owned Kephála, or Squire's Knoll, but the boundary was the olive grove. He didn't ask to excavate because his site was enormous. It never occurred to us that the stone was anything other than an ancient monument and a cave that had suffered a rockfall.'

'What do you mean?' asked Eloise.

'There have been so many earthquakes since the destruction of Knossos in 1600 BCE, an earthquake could have happened at any time. There are always small tremors, but there have been larger events such as the eruption of the volcano on Santorini, or Thera, as it was known. It's thought it caused the huge tsunami that wiped out the Minoan civilisation. In 1303, there was a massive earthquake on Crete that caused a tsunami, which damaged the Lighthouse of Alexandria. Since then, there have been any number of the small quakes that could have caused a rockfall.

'My family rediscovered the grove in the 1950s,' she went on. 'When my father told us about it when we were children, me, my brother and our friends used to visit it, daring each other to go further and further inside.'

'How large is it?' Eloise asked in surprise. She had been imagining a tiny area but the more Marina described it, the more she adjusted her expectations.

'The grove is small, but my brother, Christos, and his friends said the cave was the beginning of a passageway leading underground. Quite how they knew this, I'm not sure.'

'Perhaps they went down there.'

'No, at some point in history the passageway or cave, or whatever it is, was blocked. There have been solid boulders in the entrance for as long as anyone can remember. It does appear to slope downwards, though, so perhaps that's why they formed the idea.'

Eloise sipped her wine, staring at the tiny statue as she glinted in the sun.

'Would you mind if I visited the shrine?' she asked.

'Of course not,' said Marina. 'If you're reading the diaries and Quinn's research, I think it might be helpful. Yiannis and I tried to work out a way to help Quinn to see it but the terrain is steep and he wasn't mobile enough. So instead I took the photographs.'

'Was that recently?'

'A year or so before he died,' replied Marina. 'It was around the time he had the barn to the side converted. One day, he suddenly began asking about the goddesses in Minoan culture. Until then, he'd been more interested in the dig itself but, for some reason, he began researching the religions.'

'Maybe he felt he'd exhausted his other ideas,' suggested Eloise.

'Perhaps,' said Marina. 'Let me draw you a map so you can find the grove. There are two entrances. The one from the vineyard side is reached via a large rock, which you have to slither down. It's a bit precarious. The path near Knossos takes you through the edge of our olive grove. It's steep but far easier than clambering over a boulder.'

Marina finished her drawing and wrote the combination code to the padlock on the gate to the land around the olive grove.

'Since the popularity of Knossos has increased over the years, we've had to fence the olive grove off as there are old well shafts and we couldn't risk an accident. Don't worry, they're all covered and the lids are locked, but it was easier to protect it. People do the strangest things when confronted with a challenge like a hole in the ground.'

Eloise laughed and studied the piece of paper Marina had pushed towards her.

'It's near the Knossos complex,' she said. 'I've been considering going.'

'Have you never been?' asked Marina in surprise.

'No. On the few occasions Josh and I visited Quinn, Josh refused to go and because we were here to see his father, I didn't push things.'

Marina stared at Eloise, a curious expression on her face.

'What?' asked Eloise. 'Do I have something on my nose?'

'No,' replied Marina, her face softening. 'It's good to see you smiling. You don't have to answer but I've often wondered: your marriage to Josh, was it happy?'

'Why do you ask?' asked Eloise, a cold lump forming in her stomach, the thrill of the archaeological discussion dissolving with the speed of a snowflake on a child's mitten.

Marina gave an expressive shrug. 'The time you became ill when you were visiting Quinn, Josh seemed angry with you, as though it was a deliberate ploy to spoil his holiday,' she said, and Eloise swallowed, the fear rising in her throat. 'His reaction was strange, especially when it transpired you were having a miscarriage.'

Taking a deep breath, Eloise's instinct was to shut down, deny it, pretend all was well, but as it had been Marina who had sat with her in the hospital while Josh had been out drinking, that terrible night had forged their friendship. Eloise closed her eyes, wondering whether to reveal the truth about the loss of her child but she could not face the other woman's sympathy or horror.

'We were happy at the beginning,' she said, her voice cautious.

'How did you meet?' asked Marina.

'Through Rose,' replied Eloise. 'Josh was new to her legal chambers and there was a drinks party to welcome him. Rose invited me along.'

'Was it love at first sight?'

'No, perhaps second sight,' she said, sipping her wine, the cold glass soothing against the scar on her palm, which continued to twinge.

'What happened?'

She remembered Rose begging her to attend: 'Please, Lo, your moral support is vital; without your charming company I will be forced to endure an evening trapped in a windowless room full of sexist, racist old men. They will expect me to laugh at their off-colour jokes, not mind when they peer down my top or oh-so-accidentally touch my bottom, treating me as though I am mentally sub-normal because I am a woman, forgetting I am one of their most successful barristers, and when I flip and commit mass murder using a stapler, a letter opener and a battered copy of Hansard, it will be you whom I hold responsible.'

Her voice had taken on the authoritative ring she adopted when she was in court delivering a determined summing-up to a jury.

'Put like that,' Eloise had said, 'how can I resist? I expect my amoebas can cope alone for one night. Although how I'm going to break it to Petri dish number four I'm not sure; it's their birthday today.'

'Josh made a speech,' said Eloise, now, gazing back across time. 'I thought he was attractive but I was wary of becoming involved with anyone. The long-term relationship I'd been in since university had ended six months earlier and I was happy being single.'

Eloise paused as she considered her first sight of Josh. It had been unremarkable. Josh Winter was a man who blended into the crowd. His grey suit, his conservative tie and traditional shoes made him just another man earning a living and then returning home to an anonymous life, day after day after day. Yet, when he had laughed, Eloise became aware of his ice-blue eyes, chips of pale sapphire, adding a hint of menace to an otherwise cherubic choirboy face. And when he had begun to speak, Eloise had been hypnotised.

'Then Rose collapsed and I realised she'd gone into a diabetic coma,' said Eloise. 'Rose had been feeling strange for a while but kept putting off going to the doctor, even though Leon and I kept trying to persuade her. Josh waited with me for the ambulance, and the following day, when I was visiting Rose at the hospital, he turned up too.'

'How thoughtful,' said Marina, although her tone suggested otherwise.

Eloise remembered the horror of the night, the relief at Rose's recovery and her friend's despair at being told her condition was chronic and would involve insulin for the rest of her life. To cheer her up, Eloise had arrived at her hospital bedside the next day with a bag full of treats suitable for a diabetic to prove to Rose she would not have to give up everything she loved.

'It's lucky my best friend's a doctor,' Rose had said, squeezing Eloise's hand and the unspoken understanding of years had flowed between them.

'Let's hope I never have to use your special skills,' Eloise had replied. 'Although, if I'm ever accused of murder, you'll be my first phone call.'

They had been laughing at the ridiculousness of this thought when Josh had appeared in the doorway, clutching a bunch of flowers. Afterwards, Rose had teased Eloise that when he saw her, Josh had blushed scarlet.

'Leon and the boys arrived not long after, which is always a bit of a shock for people who aren't expecting such an increase in volume,' she said, 'and Josh invited me for a drink. Our relationship grew from there.'

'And his friends?'

'Were very much part of our lives,' she said, forcing a smile. 'I met them that night in the pub.'

'Quite as much of a shock as the twins,' said Marina.

'The difference is, I love the twins,' said Eloise.

'Not his friends?'

'Oh, Marina,' Eloise sighed, 'perhaps under different circumstances we might have found common ground, but I found their presence a constant intrusion.'

'Have you heard from them since you've been here?'

Eloise internalised a shudder at the thought of Claud, Nahjib or Martin swooping down on her, and shook her head.

'No, but they were very much in evidence when Josh died,' she said as Marina gave her a knowing look.

'In what way?'

'Once the ambulance arrived, I called my parents. Dad called Claud and Rose. He decided we needed another doctor and a legal representative. As Josh was being declared dead, Claud arrived with Nahjib and Martin. It was without doubt the worst night of my life.'

Eloise did not need to close her eyes to visualise the procession of police officers, her own medical examination and, when her mother rang Ethelwyn Winter with the news, the accusations that came thick and fast, accusing Eloise of everything from witchcraft to murder.

And Claud. Always Claud. Phoning, texting, even arriving a few days later, asking for details, his eyes blank, shocked.

'Isn't Claud the one you told me about? The one who had a puppy with him in the pub?' asked Marina, and Eloise grimaced.

'That was the night I first met him,' she said. 'When Josh and I arrived, I went to the Ladies and when I opened the door to leave, this terrified puppy came scrambling inside, trailing her lead. I love dogs – we've always had pets – so I scooped her up to comfort her.'

Eloise remembered walking outside, the puppy snuggled into

the warmth of her cashmere jumper, the dog's tail fluttering with nerves. It was then she had seen Claud for the first time.

Tall, dark-haired, standing in the doorway to the pub car park, shining the torch from his phone, he was frantically calling, 'Pippin, Pippin, come here, baby girl. Come on, sweetheart.'

His voice was at once tender and scared, and Eloise had felt her heart quicken at the compassion in his tone.

'Is this Pippin?' she had called, and as he had swung round, his handsome face, stark with fear, had broken into a smile of intense relief and happiness.

'Oh, thank goodness,' he had said, rushing towards her. 'Her lead slipped out of my hand when I bent down to pick her up and she bolted. Where did you find her?'

'In the ladies' loos.'

'The one place I didn't think to search.' He had gazed down at Eloise and their eyes had met, his a deep and unusual amber-brown. Eloise had felt her breath catch in her throat...

Then, 'There you are,' a voice had hailed them from behind, and Josh had appeared, halting the infinitesimal moment they shared and breaking the spell. 'Eloise, this is Claud.'

'Oh, you're Eloise,' Claud uttered, a look of disappointment clouding his face.

Josh had led the way back into the crowded pub, while Claud held Pippin in his arms and was immediately surrounded by cooing women.

A few days later, on their second date in an expensive Italian restaurant, Josh had been charming and funny. When he had explained that Claud had borrowed the puppy in order to make himself more attractive to women, Eloise had laughed, even though she felt this did not quite tally with the sound of panic she had heard in Claud's voice. However, as her relationship with Josh had grown, she had found Claud's presence unnerving, until the day

Josh had explained that Claud did not like her and she had retreated, tolerating him for Josh's sake, but always wary and, although she refused to admit it, saddened by this revelation.

'And is Rose healthy now?' asked Marina, pulling Eloise back to the present.

'She manages her condition well,' replied Eloise, relieved to push aside the thoughts of Josh and his confusing friends.

'It's a relief. It must have been a shock for you all,' said Marina.

'It was awful at the time,' agreed Eloise, 'but we come through these things together, supporting each other.'

Marina smiled. Then, having drunk the last mouthful of her wine, she asked, 'What are you doing this evening?'

'Nothing,' replied Eloise.

'We're having a birthday dinner for Yiannis's brother, Nikos, at the Brewery Taverna,' she said. 'We'd like you to come. The tables are booked for a quarter to seven, and,' Marina gave a grin, 'Nikos is recently single.'

Before Eloise could protest, Marina had gathered the figurine and stowed it in her bag, before heading towards the exterior staircase. She paused at the gate.

'You're a young woman, Eloise. Do not die waiting. Live each day with love.'

17

'Eloise!' exclaimed John Lowdon in his Scottish accent as he hugged her. 'You're looking better. Crete is working her magic.'

John's partner, Steve Lester, hurried over to greet her.

'We've missed you,' he said in his clipped London tones. 'How's your lot doing?'

'Good. They miss you, though.'

Despite their eclectic origins, Eloise had known John and Steve for years as, prior to their move to Crete three years earlier, they had run a pub and restaurant in the village of Cosheston in Pembrokeshire. The Brewery Inn had been a popular place and was not far from where Eloise's maternal aunt, uncle and cousins lived and ran the Orwell Hotel.

The two men had fallen in love with Crete and, having decided to up sticks, they had bought the taverna in the village of Archanes, rebuilding its clientele as well as the crumbling building. When Eloise had begun dating Josh and discovered Quinn's proximity to the newly opened Brewery Taverna, she had introduced the men. Although her late father-in-law's health made travelling too far prohibitive, he had struck up a friendship with John and Steve, who with Yiannis and Marina's families had taken it upon themselves to care for Quinn.

The taverna was a two-storey building with a smaller annexe on each end. These had both originally been barns, but the two men had converted them with such sympathy it was impossible to tell that they had not been part of the original building. The exterior was painted white with a roof of bright red locally made tiles, and a flight of three steps led up to a covered terrace. A vine crawled up one side of the building, old and gnarled, with bunches of grapes glistening under the shimmering leaves, their dark red skins blushed with sunlight.

The top floor provided spacious accommodation for John, Steve and their three pugs. A hairdressing salon was in the larger of the two annexes, which was Steve's domain, providing another useful meeting place in the small village of Archanes. John ran the taverna, with Steve working there in the evenings. A large, two-bedroomed apartment was in the second annexe. It had once been a hay loft and was rented out on a long-term basis, as the men had found the upheaval of the endless changeovers of the holiday trade too exhausting. Until two weeks earlier, a retired musician had been staying there, but he had returned home to France.

* * *

John ushered Eloise towards the corner of the taverna where the Fourakis family was making itself at home. Marina waved as she helped her parents, Michaelas and Donna, to their seats, while from across the room, Yiannis's father, Darius, called to his sons to help him at the bar. Yiannis's mother, Calliope, chatted to Nikos, while trying to stop Marina's two children, Tobias and Thea, from fighting over the huge basket of bread. Eloise was reminded of the chaos of her own family whenever they dined out en masse, as well as Rose and her family, and she felt a twinge of homesickness.

'We've got a new chap staying,' said John, reappearing with a stack of menus, distracting her from her sadness. 'Very good-looking but angry. He's taken the place for two months. It's not ideal but Jean-Pierre didn't give us much notice and it's better than it standing empty. My goodness, though, this fella – I've never met anyone who's so brooding. Mr Darcy has nothing on him.'

Eloise laughed.

'Shame you're taken,' she teased.

'No good for me, lassie. It's a pity you're not ready to move on. He's tall, dark and handsome. He'd be ideal for you.'

Eloise swallowed the wave of revulsion that enveloped her at the thought of beginning another relationship. Forcing a smile, she took the menu John proffered.

'Not you as well. I think Marina's trying to push me into Nikos's well-muscled arms.'

'You could do worse,' laughed John, but then his face fell and Eloise realised some of her horror must have shown.

'Eloise, sit here, beside me,' called Marina as John hurried away. 'You OK?' she whispered, squeezing Eloise's hand. 'Was John match-making?'

'Yes, but he meant nothing by it. People forget,' she said, and Marina arched an eyebrow.

'I don't forget,' she said. 'Nikos is a kind man. When I explained he was single, it was so you would be able to enjoy his company with no obligation. My intention was friendship, should you need it, nothing more.'

'Here you are, my lovelies,' said Steve, placing a selection of wine bottles on the table. 'Apologies for John,' he whispered to Eloise. 'He's worried he upset you.'

'Really, he hasn't,' she assured him.

'He gets a bit carried away, but I reminded him, you're a widow and...' his voice faded away. 'Anyway, John eventually got our touchy new guest chatting, you know how he is, John can put anyone at their ease, and he regaled us with a tale of a funeral he attended where the widow stalked out in a red dress while Judy Garland belted out "Get Happy." She'd planned it with the funeral directors apparently, then she climbed in a cab and disappeared abroad. Yikes, better go, crisis at the bar.'

Eloise felt a wave of nausea envelope her.

'Marina, I'm sorry, perhaps I should leave...'

'What's wrong?' asked Yiannis, who had returned from the bar with his father. Taking her hand, he stared at her in concern. 'Are you sick? Nikos will drive you back to Sfragida House.'

Yiannis beckoned Nikos, a younger version of himself with the same thick dark hair, high cheekbones and dark eyes. Eloise had always thought Nikos was the better looking of the two brothers, but she had never been attracted to him. Nikos leaned forward, taking her hand from Yiannis, his arm curling around her waist as though to support her, ready to escort her to the car should she faint.

'Nikos, it's unnecessary...' she began.

There was a footstep behind them.

'You didn't waste any time,' said a cold voice, loud enough for all those at the table to hear. 'Your husband isn't even cold in his grave and you're playing the Merry Widow with the locals.'

Eloise felt bile rise in her throat. Yiannis and Nikos spun around, squaring up to the man.

'Who are you?' demanded Nikos.

'She knows who I am.'

Eloise placed a hand on Yiannis's arm, shaking her head at Nikos as she moved away from his well-intentioned support. Nikos clenched his fists. Silence was gathering over the Fourakis table like a curse as they stared at the man. Even Tobias and Thea, young as they were, stopped squabbling and gazed over.

'What are you doing here?' Eloise asked, turning to the glowering man. 'You can't leave me alone for a moment, can you? What's the matter, Claud, run out of women to torment at home?'

Claud Willoughby gave a derisive laugh.

'Do you think I want to be here?'

'Why are you then?'

'Looking for you and trying to stop you from doing anything stupid,' he replied.

'Meaning?'

Claud gestured towards Nikos and the Fourakis family, who were staring at him with varying levels of dislike.

'Josh is dead and you're here, living it up on holiday. Not to mention the fact you're all over someone else and look like you're very much part of the family. It didn't take you long to move on, or was this something you had in the pipeline before you let your husband die on your kitchen floor?'

There was a collective gasp and, as the room tipped and swayed, the floor buckling beneath her feet, Eloise gripped the edge of the table, trying to steady herself.

'You came all this way to check I wasn't having a holiday romance?' she said, her nerves stretched to breaking point. 'That's low, Claud, even for you.'

'No, I came to discuss your house. I'm executor of the will but it's lucky I arrived when I did—'

'What? Are you insane?' Eloise cut across him. 'You could have phoned me. The house is being put on the market as soon as possible.'

'But—'

'But nothing,' Eloise shouted, near to tears. 'I never want to set foot in there again.'

'Your parents have cleared your belongings and they asked me, Nahjib and Martin to help Josh's mum do the same for his,' Claud continued as though she had not spoken. 'We thought we should discuss it with you first, in case—'

'What? I'd changed my mind? The last time I went to that house was the day of the funeral. I swore never to cross the threshold again and I meant it. Why do you think I came here?'

Claud hesitated, then said, 'It wasn't only to discuss the house.'

Eloise narrowed her eyes. 'Go on,' she said, her voice ominous, aware everyone around the table was listening.

'Nahjib wondered if you were having a breakdown, brought about by grief. We thought it might be the reason you behaved the way you did at the funeral. We wanted to help.'

Eloise stared at him in disbelief. Would they never leave her alone? Throughout her marriage to Josh, despite her best efforts to distance herself, his friends – Claud in particular – had been intrusive and suffocating. It seemed even in death they would not release their oppressive grip.

'And yet, you felt able to tell John and Steve all about the funeral as though it was an hilarious anecdote. Wow, Claud, that shows real concern for my mental health,' she said. 'Please, tell Nahjib I'm appreciative of his concern but, no, I'm not having a breakdown and, if I were, there are other people who would support me before I reached out to the three of you.'

Claud recoiled as though Eloise had slapped him. She felt a flash of contrition. He looked devastated and she realised he was suffering, too, coping with the loss of his friend.

'Claud, this is difficult for us all,' she said, forcing calm into her voice, 'but Josh died in that house and I could never sleep there again. It's why I moved in with my parents afterwards. It's going to be put up for sale.'

Eloise turned to leave and had taken a few steps away from him, when he asked, his voice harsh again, 'And is that the only reason?'

Eloise felt a flush rise up her neck. Involuntarily, she curled her fingers over the scar on her palm, her breath catching in her throat.

'Go home, Claud,' she said, continuing to walk away from him, tears in her eyes. 'Leave me in peace.'

'From the moment he introduced you to us, I knew—' he shouted across the restaurant.

'You knew what?' she hissed, stopping, turning to face him as all the loathing and disgust for Josh's friends she had felt throughout her marriage rose in her like a snake.

'I knew you were wrong for him.'

'We should take this somewhere else,' said Nikos, stepping between Eloise and Claud, his expression cold, his knuckles white. He, Yiannis and Marina had been hovering behind Eloise and Claud, their expressions growing increasingly anxious.

'Why?' snarled Claud.

'Because you are causing a scene in the restaurant of our friends and it is unacceptable,' said Marina's calm voice, as she, in turn, stepped between the men.

'Enough,' said Eloise, glaring at Claud. 'Throughout my marriage, you tried to destroy it; turning Josh against me, causing problems, yet you have no concept of the real person. Your best buddy, the mate you could always rely on...'

'At least he understood loyalty.'

'Really?' snarled Eloise. 'So, why was he having an affair with your girlfriend?'

A stunned silence filled the restaurant. Eloise strode towards the door, desperate to reach fresh air and the village square. Her legs were trembling with such intensity she was amazed they would respond when she commanded them to move, but she was determined to remove herself and avoid this scene.

Stumbling down the steps, she heard footsteps behind her as

Nikos, Yiannis and Marina caught up with her.

'I'm sorry,' Eloise said, fighting back tears. 'This is so embarrassing for you...'

Marina held up her hand to halt Eloise. 'It's nothing – it's a typical Greek night out – shouting, accusations, revelations – but this is unimportant. It's you I'm concerned about.'

She spoke to Yiannis in rapid Greek, and he fished the car keys from his pocket and opened the doors for them. But before they could climb into the winery's Jeep, Claud appeared.

'No more,' said Marina standing in front of Eloise, who could not stop herself shaking. 'If you have something to say, you will discuss it tomorrow when you are calm. Eloise has been through enough.'

'She's been through...?' Claud spluttered. 'Did she tell you?'

'Tell us what?'

'What she did at Josh's funeral?'

Eloise swallowed hard, resisting the urge to defend herself. Claud's lip curled with contempt at the silence.

'The fact she wore a red dress and stalked out while a showtune played. "Get Happy", wasn't it, Eloise? Josh was laying in his coffin, the church was full to bursting with people there to pay their respects, to mourn his loss and she danced out.'

Yiannis and Nikos exchanged a startled look, but Marina's eyes narrowed as she contemplated Claud.

'Perhaps you should ask yourself why!' she snapped, and Eloise placed a hand on Marina's arm, trying to stop her.

'Meaning?' asked Claud.

'If their marriage had been happy, she would have stayed.'

Eloise saw Claud falter.

'Take me home, please, Marina,' she said, and climbed into the Jeep. Marina glared at Claud and followed, gunning the engine and hurtling away in a shower of dust.

18

As they wound their way up the twisting mountain road to Sfragida House, Eloise stared out of the window in horror, unable to believe Claud had followed her to Crete. Above her, the first stars of evening rippled across the purpling sky and, as Marina whizzed the Jeep around the steep bends, Eloise found herself wondering again about Alice's idea of the words floating into the sky. Wherever the exchange between her and Claud had floated, she hoped they would not cause thunder and lightning.

A noise from Marina caught her attention and, at first, she thought her friend was crying, then she realised Marina's shoulders were shaking.

'Are you laughing?' she asked in astonishment.

'Did you really wear a red dress to Josh's funeral?'

Eloise hesitated, not wishing to lose Marina's good opinion, but deciding on honesty, she replied, 'Yes, with matching shoes. His mother was disgusted until I lied and said Josh had bought me the shoes before he died. After that, she thought they were wonderful.'

Marina snorted with laughter.

'Did he buy them?'

'No. Rose and I did the day the police released his body and we could organise the funeral.'

'The police?'

'Yes, he was a young man, it was an unexpected death, so there was an investigation and an inquest. Ethelwyn had also reported me, suggesting I'd murdered Josh. Accusations like that require paperwork before they go away. Rose always says it's good her best friend is a doctor now she has a chronic condition. Well, let's just say I was relieved my friend was a top barrister.'

For the remainder of the journey they were silent, but as they came to a halt in the courtyard outside Sfragida House, Marina turned to Eloise, her face serious.

'The time you stayed here, the day you miscarried,' said Marina. 'Did Josh push you down the stairs? Is that what caused your fall?'

Eloise felt her breath catch in her throat, a denial sprang to her lips, then her eyes filled with tears and she nodded.

'He wanted to go out drinking and I told him my suspicions that I was pregnant,' she admitted. 'It wasn't planned but I thought he'd be delighted; we were engaged. Instead he accused me of ruining the holiday and as we were going down the steps to the terrace he shoved me in the back.'

'He could have killed you!' Marina exclaimed. 'Those steps are steep and they're stone.'

'Yes,' said Eloise. It was a thought that had occurred to her on more than one occasion. Josh's furious words echoed around her head: *You're worth more to me dead...* Pushing them aside, she continued, 'I landed with a thump as he turned away to ring Martin. I remember him describing the house and asking if he thought it was valuable. The next thing I knew I was in the car with you and Quinn as you took me to hospital.'

Marina's face was white with fury.

'Why did you marry him?'

'He apologised, sobbed all over me, told me he loved me and nothing like that would ever happen again. Like a fool, I believed him.'

'And his affair with Claud's girlfriend?'

'Davina?' Yes, she was one of many...' Eloise said, her voice cracking.

'We're going inside and you will tell me,' said Marina. 'Josh is the one who should have felt ashamed of his behaviour, not you, but if you keep it inside, a bitter secret, it can be corrosive.'

Half an hour later, after Eloise had changed into cotton pyjamas, and with the doors open to allow the cool night breeze to flow through the house, Marina handed Eloise a plate of steaming *skioufichta*, a local dish of macaroni with a hot sauce before sitting opposite Eloise with her own plate. Marina took up a fork, then paused before eating.

'When did you discover Josh's treachery?' she asked.

'On a weekend away in the Lake District,' Eloise sighed. 'We'd been married less than two years...'

* * *

The Lake District

Claud pulled off his shirt to a roar of applause. Martin put two fingers in his mouth and wolf-whistled, Nahjib cheered, Marcella gave a nervous laugh, Davina rolled her eyes and Josh put a hand across Eloise's face, blocking her vision.

'Not in front of my wife,' he said, a comment that was greeted with more laughter.

Claud bowed to the crowd.

'It's because of your wife I am in my present state of undress,' he replied, 'but, please do try to control yourselves.'

He smirked as he sat back on the floor, shuffling the cards and dealing. Eloise grinned, delighted to have taken Claud by surprise.

'What I want to know,' Claud continued, 'is where she learned her card-sharp skills? Do you have a secret past, Lo?'

Eloise made herself more comfortable on the large cushion where she sat cross-legged, gathered her cards, glanced through them, selected two and discarded them onto the floor in front of her. They were all lounging on various cushions, beanbags and sofas. Josh sat in a wing-backed armchair behind Eloise, and before her attention had been caught by the card game, she had been leaning on his legs. Now alert to the fun of strip poker, as suggested by Martin, she had broken physical contact with her husband.

'My mother worked as a croupier during her university days. She taught us all how to play cards when she was teaching us how to count.'

'Do you mean count as in one, two, three? Or count cards?' asked Marcella, flicking her dark hair out of her eyes and settling her cool gaze on Eloise. She, alone, had chosen to watch rather than play. Davina and Josh, as the two least interested players, had subsequently played a few hands before Davina had arranged herself on the sofa and Josh had settled in the chair opposite, watching Davina as she watched Claud, laughter brimming in her eyes as he lost to Eloise. Martin and Nahjib, like Eloise and Claud, sat on cushions on the floor.

'Both,' Eloise replied. 'Mum was trying to teach us to count to one hundred but as she said, old habits die hard. I'm better at stacking the deck when I shuffle. Gareth was the card counter. Jessica was never good at the card counting but she does make an amazing fan with the deck and her shuffling is off the scale.'

'You can count cards?' Martin asked.

'Yes, but not very well,' she conceded.

Josh beamed with pride as he added, 'Eloise can work out when a fruit machine is going to pay out, too.'

'There's a certain amount of guess work involved,' she admitted, 'but yes, if you watch a machine long enough, it's possible to decipher it's payment cycle.'

Nahjib laughed. 'I wish I'd trained at the same medical school as you. I bet you were a demon in the student bar.'

'I had my moments.'

Marcella gave her a cold smile, glancing from Nahjib to Eloise, but did not join in the conversation again, turning instead to her phone and beginning to scroll. Josh leaned over Eloise's shoulder to study her cards but she placed a hand over them.

'Why can't I look?' he asked, affronted.

'Your face is far too beguiling and innocent – you'll give my hand away in a moment,' she said, reaching up to kiss his cheek. 'Remember, we're aiming for Claud's trousers next.'

'Interested in the content of my best friend's trousers, are you?'

Eloise looked up in frustration. The underlying threat of temper was present again in her husband's voice and she felt a surge of irritation. As far as he was concerned, he could flirt with and make outrageous comments about any woman he chose, yet he displayed petulant jealousy if Eloise so much as glanced towards another man.

'Should I be?' she asked, ice trickling through her words.

'You're married,' he hissed.

'We both are, to each other, but it doesn't seem to be hindering you,' she replied, before turning her back on him and focusing on the game, even more determined than ever to beat Claud and force him to remove his trousers. Her motivation was not to view Claud in his boxer shorts but to annoy Josh.

The marriage was less than two years old and Eloise was startled at the change that had come over Josh since the return from their disastrous honeymoon. When the June wedding had been arranged, Josh had suggested a fortnight in Las Vegas for their honeymoon with 'the gang' joining them for the second week. Eloise had refused, having had enough of Josh's overbearing friends in their everyday lives. Instead, she had organised and paid for the trip. It began with a week in Venice, after which they would travel to Crete to see Quinn, who was too weak to fly to London for the wedding, before finishing with a tour of the Greek islands on a private yacht.

After a great deal of sulking, Josh came round to Eloise's idea, but to her horror, two days after their arrival in Venice, she had returned from a trip to the Basilica in St Mark's Square to discover Claud, Martin and Nahjib with Josh, waiting to surprise her. For the rest of the honeymoon, the three men had stayed at nearby hotels and there were many evenings when the four would go out drinking, leaving Eloise alone. The only time the men had retreated was during the few days when Eloise and Josh had stayed with Quinn. Instead, they had waited on the private yacht. When the bride and groom joined them, they had set sail. Each day, Eloise would retire to one of the decks and read, while they drank.

She had returned from the honeymoon devastated and made it clear to Josh this was not how she intended their marriage to continue.

'I married you,' she had said, her voice low and sad. 'Your friends are a huge part of your life and I understand that, but you're my husband, I'm your wife, we're a partnership. I love you, Josh, but we'll both have to make changes, and sharing our honeymoon with your friends was disappointing, to say the least.'

'I invited Rose and Leon too,' he had blustered in return, 'but Rose refused.'

Of course she did, thought Eloise. As any sane person would.

'Shall we put it behind us and begin again?' she suggested, and for a few moments she had wondered if Josh would continue to obfuscate around the point, but his face changed and he smiled.

'I'm such a fool,' he said, his lopsided smile making him look years younger. 'How do you put up with me?'

Pulling her into his arms, he had kissed her and promised to be faithful and tender for the rest of their lives. Bursting with love for her new husband, Eloise had believed him. However, as the months passed, she began to notice a creeping change. It had remained unacknowledged, but the day before their trip to the Lake District she had returned from work early in order to pack, only to discover the bed had been remade with the pillows the wrong way up. The pattern was distinct, with a precise up and down, the mismatch was startling, and it made Eloise stop in surprise. Before leaving for work that morning, she had smoothed the bed to perfection and she wondered why it had been altered.

Picking up Josh's pillow, she felt her heart contract in horror. There was a lingering breath of perfume. Opium. A heavy, recognisable scent and one Eloise avoided as it made her sneeze. A sick swooping feeling filled her and she found herself sitting on the bed. When the same thing had happened before but with a lighter scent, lily of the valley, she had explained it away to herself as the new fabric softener she had bought. But this scent was unmistakable. It was definitely Opium. Aware Josh was on the phone to Nahjib and would be distracted, she searched the room to see if any more clues remained but there was nothing, although, she noticed the rubbish bin had been emptied.

During the long drive to the house in the Lake District the following day she had pondered Josh's roving eye, wondering whether it was a trait she had failed to notice when they first met or if it was a new development. Feigning sleep in the back of the car, Eloise decided her husband's philandering was a state brought about by Josh's new-found confidence in having secured a wife. His self-assurance in his looks had been boosted and was making him flirt – and more – in a way Eloise had not witnessed before, and it was disquieting.

'How many cards?' Claud's voice broke through her thoughts.

'Two.'

They were placed face down in front of her and, bending back the corners to assess her hand, she forced herself not to react. If her calculations were correct he would have a hand worth less than her own royal flush. She would win again, unless Claud folded first but she doubted he would give in. He was enjoying the challenge as much as she was. Gradually, the others dropped out, leaving Eloise and Claud bartering over which pieces of clothing the loser would remove and, when they had no more to bargain with, dares.

Josh sat behind Eloise, sullen, brooding. She could sense his bubbling jealousy and, in her annoyance at her husband, a demon rose in her. Long buried flirtatiousness surfaced as she made her final wager.

'Dance naked on the table to the song of my choice,' she challenged.

Claud held up his hands in surrender while the others howled with laughter, suggesting songs.

'Those stakes are too high. I'll see you.'

With a smug smirk he put two pairs on the floor in front of her. With an equally triumphant gesture, she fanned her royal flush and placed them next to his, smiling with all the sweetness she could muster, fluttering her long eyelashes and giving him the full benefit of her dimpled green-eyed gaze.

'The rest of your clothes, please,' she laughed, amidst cheering and clapping from the others. Even Josh, who seemed to have thawed, shouted encouragement to Claud.

With good grace, Claud began his striptease, flinging the

remaining pieces of his clothing around the room while the others watched agog, wondering how far he would go. Eloise stared in fascination, hiding her eyes in embarrassment as he struggled out of his jeans. Martin's mouth hung open, Nahjib was wolf-whistling, Josh, to Eloise's surprise, was shouting for a complete strip. Davina, Claud's on-off girlfriend, was hiding her eyes behind a cushion. Marcella sat in silence, her eyes flashing around the room from one face to the next, unsure how to react to the banter and the noise between the friends.

Finally Claud stopped, clad in his boxer shorts and took a theatrical bow.

'The next performance will be at seven o'clock this evening,' he said, amid huge laughter and cheers.

Josh slid his arm around Eloise, leading her into the kitchen, as Claud gathered his clothes. As Davina threw him a blanket from the sofa, with a 'Cover yourself up, man', Eloise caught a waft of the distinctive perfume and she sneezed.

'Sorry,' Josh whispered. 'I didn't mean it. I do love you.'

'Oh, Josh,' she sighed. 'I love you, too.'

They hugged, but Eloise could not shift her feeling of unease.

'It's stopped raining, do you fancy a walk?' Behind her back she crossed her fingers, hoping he would refuse.

The card game had been a way to fill time until the football began; an international match of huge importance, an event Claud, Josh and Nahjib had been hinting they would like to watch from the moment they had arrived two days earlier. Josh hesitated and Eloise continued, 'You can watch the football, I don't mind.'

'Would you rather I came with you?' he asked, and Eloise could hear his reluctance.

'No,' she replied. Experience told her if he was made to abandon his friends and an England game, she would never hear the end of it. 'It's your holiday too. You have fun with your friends.'

She appreciated his offer to accompany her, even though it had been half-hearted, and was relieved to have earned herself some solitude away from the enforced friendship of Marcella and Davina.

'I'll be fine.'

With both feeling they had secured the better part of the deal, they separated for the afternoon on good terms, Eloise slipping away before anyone else could ask to join her. She walked for an hour, finding a space high enough to get a signal on her mobile phone. Then she called Rose, who was enduring a weekend with her in-laws.

'Lo, thank god,' came Rose's voice, rich with unnecessary drama. 'I want to kill them all.'

'An awfully messy idea,' Eloise replied. 'Any particular reason?'

'The shits want us to move here and look after Aged Parent Female. After all, I am a woman and therefore my career is a mere hobby, dispensable when others need me to administer to their needs...'

'But you and Leon wouldn't survive without your money. He's doing well, but the money hasn't quite reached what you would need for you to give up work. *We* know he'll be appreciated soon and the financial security will follow, but until the rest of the world catches up, you've got bills to pay.'

'They have a solution to their son's poverty. They've been in discussions with their solicitor to try and pass over the inheritance with immediate effect. Heaven forbid they should ask me for legal advice.'

'What, even the title?'

'No. Only when Aged Parent Male dies does dearest hubby become Lord Arsewipe.'

'Are you being rude about the landed gentry, you upstart wench? Flogging's too good for the likes of you.'

'I hate them all!' Rose screamed in frustration, and they both laughed. 'Anyway, how's your weekend with the Horsemen of the Apocalypse?'

'Delightful. I saw Claud in his pants.'

'Good or bad?'

'Surprisingly good. I beat him at strip poker.'

'How did dear Josh react to his pure wife being sullied by such behaviour?'

'He had a minor strop.'

'Jesus, Lo, what is wrong with the guy?'

'I have my suspicions.'

'Sounds ominous.'

'Perhaps, maybe I'm overreacting.' Eloise could not bring herself to voice her fears on the phone; she wanted to be face-to-face with her friend. And there was another reason. Saying it aloud would make it real, and she continued to hope, if she ignored it, the problem might dissolve. A mist vanishing with the morning light.

'I'll tell you something, though,' Eloise continued, forcing lightness into her tone. 'Marcella is a weird one.'

'Have you only just noticed?'

'I found her counting the knives in the kitchen last night.'

'Freak! Make sure you lock your bedroom door.'

'You're going crackly...'

The connection broke and the phone refused to work again. After several minutes, Eloise abandoned the idea of resuming her conversation with Rose and set off for the house they were renting, aware the usual argument of the evening meal would be brewing. Should they go out or cook, and if so, who should be in charge and what should they eat?

'Oh, the joys of married life and a holiday with my husband's friends,' she sighed, burying her hands in her pockets and marching back to the old farmhouse.

Martin appeared to be alone when she let herself in. He was

absorbed in throwing himself around the room to very loud pop music.

'Hi,' he said without missing a beat. 'The others have gone for a walk, they thought they'd try to find you.'

'I'll start dinner, then,' Eloise said, finding herself unable to say more without giggling.

Martin embraced dancing with more enthusiasm than talent and as he closed his eyes, to really *feel* the beat, Eloise walked away, keen to hide her mirth. Her mother had insisted all three of her children learn to dance: ballroom, Latin American and tap from an early age. Jessica, however, had gone further, taking up ballet too. Gareth had protested until his father had assured him that learning to dance was a great way to attract girls later in life.

'It's how I persuaded your mother to go out with me,' he had confessed to his sulky son.

Eloise had continued dancing into her twenties, only abandoning it when she left university, but it was something she loved. On another of their weekends away, she had taken pity on Martin and taught him some basic steps, and ever since, he had been angling for more lessons. On occasions Eloise would oblige, but today she was too tired and in desperate need of a hot drink.

Sitting on the stairs, she removed her wellies and jacket, then padded on silent feet into the darkening kitchen. She had no real intention of starting dinner, but making coffee was high on her list of priorities. Humming along to Martin's twangy music, she filled the kettle, feeling her way through the purple dusk, avoiding the moment when yellow electric light would shatter the gentle shadows of the damp spring day and bring another evening of bickering upon them.

She gazed out of the window, soothed by the craggy, haunting hills, watching the colours drain away with the twilight. It was hard to believe in two days' time she would be back in the heart of the city, London beating all around her like a pulse, while she watched with gathering concern as her new husband metamorphosed into a belligerent stranger.

'Too soon,' she murmured.

As she contemplated her uncomfortable thoughts, a movement caught her eye and Davina clambered over the stile at the bottom of the garden. She must have heard someone calling behind her, because she paused, peering through the gloom, a smile lighting her pretty face. Presuming it was Claud, Eloise stepped back into the shadows of the kitchen, watching the woman whom she feared was her rival, standing in a position where she could see but not be seen, wanting to gauge Davina's reaction to Claud, to see if there was genuine affection between them. But, the person who followed her over the stile was too short to be Claud. It was Josh.

One small action can change everything. Eloise, frozen in the kitchen, watched as Josh kissed Davina. No mere peck on the cheek but a kiss of passion, longing and desire. Her stomach tightening, Eloise turned away, her brain refusing to acknowledge what she had witnessed. Then adrenaline flooded her and she took flight, hurrying to the bedroom she shared with Josh, slamming the door, throwing herself on the bed as she tried to rationalise what she had seen. But she knew no amount of calm evaluation could explain the curl of his arm, the curve of her spine and the intensity of their desire. Opium.

19

The thirteen golden cups gleamed on the altar. Candles flickered in the twilight world of the labyrinth. Strings of crystals created their own tunes around her neck as she prepared the tinctures for the sacrifices. The soothing herbs to ease their path to the next world, taking them to the place where they would all end their days. As she worked, the footsteps began, each dragging, clawing movement bringing him closer. Smiling, she continued to work, knowing he would never hurt her. The pungent smell of his breath and the shuffling footsteps heralded his arrival, and as she turned to look at the disfigured beast hidden in the subterranean hell, the words floated through the air. A woman's voice. 'I love you.'

20

'I look like an explorer.'

Alice stared at her reflection in the mirror and, despite the undercurrent of sadness that continued to permeate her days, she could not help but grin. Her pale cream skirt and matching blouse were light enough to keep her cool, but covered her arms and legs to protect them from the heat of the sun, which was gaining strength with each new morning. A lightweight pith helmet with a wide length of gauzy fabric attached to the rim would protect her face from flies and sand, the soft leather gloves would be ideal for both assisting and guarding her hands as she dug in the hard Cretan soil.

'It suits you,' Florence said. 'Mrs Perrin sent this over, too. It's her own recipe, one passed down through her family. It's a cream to repel insects and to protect your skin against the sun.'

Alice opened the glass jar and breathed in the scents of lavender and lemon balm. Rubbing a small amount on her hand, she was surprised at its softness.

'Thank you, Florence,' she said, placing the jar in her canvas bag, which was full of all she would need for a day at the Knossos dig.

She hurried from the room and down the spiral staircase.

'What do you think?' she asked as she entered the drawing room, spinning around for her aunt, brother and cousins to admire. Hugo was already waiting, dressed in a lightweight suit and with his own pith helmet. He had added some dashing dark-lensed glasses.

'Quite the adventurer,' he exclaimed.

Aunt Agatha beamed. 'Alice, you look wonderful. I'm quite envious. Perhaps I shall order myself similar attire and join you.'

'Mother, yes!' exclaimed Andrew. 'What a top-hole idea.'

'Mr Evans would be delighted to show you around, Auntie,' said Hugo.

'Perhaps later in the week,' said Agatha. 'Ah, sounds like George is here. Run along and enjoy yourselves. Robert, Andrew and I shall be studying the stories of Crete while you are uncovering their origins, then we'll have lunch at the vineyard.'

From outside came the sound of the donkey cart.

'Good morning,' George called as Wendbury threw open the front door, while the cook, Gaia, whom Mrs Perrin had hired to look after the family, passed him boxes of food and water canteens. Alice dropped her own bag into the back, where it clanked as her trowels and the small hand axe she and Hugo had bought in Heraklion, hit the wooden floor.

'Impressive,' said George.

'Don't underestimate my sister,' said Hugo, helping Alice on to the narrow seat next to George and climbing up beside her. 'She's the cleverest person I've ever met, and that includes all the chaps at Peterhouse. She'll be having very deep discussions with Mr Evans, you can be sure of it.'

Alice blushed. 'It's true, I do enjoy learning,' she agreed.

'Arthur will be delighted to add you to the team,' said George.

'The number of people involved in this site grows with each day. When they began, they employed fifty local workmen to help, along with Evans's assistant, Duncan Mackenzie.

'He's the chap who knows Ross,' said Hugo. 'From the highlands of Scotland, isn't he?'

'Yes. There's also Theodore Fyfe from the British School of Archaeology at Athens. He's an architect.'

'Marvellous,' said Hugo. 'Architecture fascinates me. I shall very much look forward to hearing what he has to say about the buildings that are being uncovered.'

'He and Arthur believe at least part of the palace was destroyed by fire as they've discovered blackened walls. Arthur has suggested this could have been caused by smoke from a "great conflagration",' said George as he guided the well-fed donkey down the narrow lane beside the house and out on to the wider track.

Upon their arrival on Crete, Alice had been surprised to discover there were few roads, only tracks, making travel a bumpy and often hazardous experience.

'There are also large quantities of broken pottery,' George continued as they lurched over a pothole and Alice made a grab to steady herself, snatching her hand away as she realised she had grasped George's leg. Instead, she leaned towards her brother, who tucked her arm into his, squeezing her hand. 'But the most exciting thing is that the team has discovered nothing Greek or Roman,' George continued, ignoring Alice's mistake.

'Why is that a good thing?' queried Hugo.

'It means this is an ancient site,' explained George. 'Everything in it dates from a period that goes back to the era now known as pre-Mycenaean, although some people refer to the people as the Minoans and the Minoan period.'

'Which is what?'

'Prehistoric,' replied George. 'Evans has estimated it's between 3500 and 3600 BC.'

'Bronze Age, then,' added Alice.

Alice was aware of George's surprised glance in her direction. Hugo grinned in appreciation.

'This means the writing system Evans believes he's discovered is prehistoric,' said George. 'The diggers have uncovered up to a hundred writing tablets and they believe there are more. Arthur is confident these are the oldest documents yet to be found on the doorstep of Europe He's named them Linear A and Linear B.'

'How unromantic,' said Alice. 'He's discovered an entire new writing system and he's chosen such a utilitarian name.'

Hugo laughed. 'What would you have named it?' he asked.

'Mycenaeans, at least, but why has he given it two names?'

'There are two distinct styles,' replied George, guiding the sturdy donkey down the steep slope towards the bustling archaeological dig. 'One is linear, formed of lines and outlines, making it akin to European languages, while the other is pictographic, resembling Egyptian hieroglyphics.'

'How fascinating,' said Alice. 'The question is, will we be lucky enough to discover our own version of the Rosetta Stone to help us decipher its meaning?'

'We can but dream,' laughed George, his spirits higher than Alice had yet witnessed. His dark hair was ruffled by the breeze, which brought the smell of wild basil into the air. 'I saw the Rosetta Stone in the British Museum and it is a truly remarkable object.'

'It is a wonder,' agreed Alice. 'When I stood in front of it, staring at all those letters and pictures, it made me dizzy with the idea they were written thousands and thousands of years ago.'

'What did you think of it, Hugo? Did you visit with Alice?'

'No, not my thing at all, old chap. She went with our elder sister, Petra, and her husband.'

'Here we are,' said George, and as they rounded the corner, Alice gasped in wonder at the vast archaeological dig spread out before her.

As George had explained, Evans had hired more people. Over one hundred and fifty men, women and children filled the site, pickaxes ringing against the stony ground, children running to and fro as women washed and cleaned the piles of finds. Not far from where they had stopped, the diminutive figure of Arthur Evans, with his walking stick, was speaking animatedly to a man who towered above him.

'There's Duncan,' said George, helping Alice to jump down from the cart.

'Is that Arthur Evans?' she whispered to Hugo as George hurried to greet Duncan Mackenzie.

'I think so,' replied Hugo, and they gripped each other's hands in excitement.

A moment later, George and Duncan turned away from Evans and began striding towards them. Alice stared at the Scotsman with interest. At over six foot three inches, he had a thatch of red hair and an exuberant moustache, turning heads as he cut a swathe through the crowd. Duncan called to one of the workers in a local dialect, switching to French to answer another man's shouted question. Alice could feel the waves of respect washing towards Mackenzie. He was obviously well-liked, and from his easy-going, charming smile, she could understand why.

'Theo,' he called to another man, who was bending over a trench, discussing a shard of pottery that caught the light and glimmered with blues and yellows.

The man, who was not as tall as Mackenzie, but exuded a similar attitude of confidence and command, fell into step beside George and the Scotsman.

'Miss Alice Webster and Mr Hugo Webster, may I present

Duncan Mackenzie, assistant to Mr Evans, and Theodore Fyfe, our resident architect,' said George.

A wave of shyness washed over Alice, but she reminded herself she had completed two of her three years at Newnham. She had written every single one of both her own and Hugo's essays, receiving top grades and guiding Hugo towards a distinguished degree; there was no need to be nervous of these men.

There were a flurry of 'hellos' and, within moments, Fyfe was called away to examine a dubious-looking wall. When Hugo requested the honour of accompanying him, Fyfe accepted with alacrity and they marched away, deep in discussion.

'What would you like to see, Miss Webster?' asked Mackenzie in his clipped Scottish accent. 'I would be happy to give you a tour of the site, then arrange some refreshments.'

'I'm here to work, Mr Mackenzie,' she replied, holding up her canvas bag and showing him her tools, 'not sip tea.'

For a moment Mackenzie glared at her, then a smile spread across his rugged face.

'You too, George?' he asked. 'Are you prepared to leap into the dust?'

'Of course,' he replied. 'When I contacted Mr Evans and reminded him of our previous acquaintance at the Ashmolean Museum, he was delighted to invite me to take part.'

'You'd better come and say hello, then,' said Mackenzie, and set off across the labyrinthine pathways of the dig.

* * *

As they followed, Alice's leather boots tapped along the wooden boards that led to the heart of the archaeological dig and she wished they would slow down. Scurrying through the red dust, she felt as though she had fallen into the pages of the Bible and she wanted the chance to stop and absorb all the activity around her. This vast site exuded antiquity and as dogs barked, donkeys brayed and a cacophony of languages melded in the sparkling blue air, she felt a rush of exhilaration roaring through her. Breathing in the heady scent of dust, sunshine and discovery, Alice felt truly alive for the first time in months.

'Mr Evans, some new recruits,' said Mackenzie.

Despite standing at just a few inches over five foot tall, Arthur Evans was an imposing figure. Wearing a starched Victorian collar on his shirt, and holding his stick, which Alice had heard was named Prodger, he peered at her and George. All his life, Arthur had suffered from myopia, although he refused to wear glasses. Yet those eyes sparkled with intelligence and enthusiasm, his dashing moustache was neat and combed; his elegant clothes were crisp and clean. Even if Alice had not known he was the man at the centre of this excavation, the energy and calm control he exuded would have drawn her to him.

'Mr Perrin, a pleasure to be reacquainted with you. I must ask you to thank your father for the very acceptable wine he organised to be delivered to my house. The Champagne was a particular treat.'

'Our pleasure, Mr Evans,' George replied. 'Father is the expert when it comes to wine.'

'You should try the *raki*,' said Mackenzie, his eyes twinkling as Arthur cringed. 'A glass of the local beverage to wash down the *koukiá* is the perfect end to the day here in Crete.'

'*Koukiá?*' asked Alice.

'A Cretan dish of boiled beans mashed down with olive oil,' supplied Evans. 'It does well enough, but my tastes are not quite the same as the Cretans' when it comes to food.'

'Which reminds me,' said George. 'My parents have invited you and your team to dinner at the weekend.'

As the men discussed the arrangements, Alice turned away, gazing out over the bustling dig. In the distance she could see Hugo with Fyfe, pointing to the precarious-looking wall, surrounded by local Cretans as they discussed its safety. All around her, the sounds of shovels and axes against stones, cries of delight as treasures were unearthed and the excited laughter of the children as they acted as messengers and errand runners, made her desperate to throw herself into the mêlée.

'We've discovered more fragments of the fresco depicting a life-size figure in a skirt,' she heard Evans explaining as she turned back to the men. 'It's holding a *rhyton* – a funnel-shaped vase – and I found the clay impression of a Mycenaean signet ring, too.' Turning to Alice, he continued, 'Come and see the carved gypsum chair we discovered a few weeks ago. It's in what we're calling the throne room. It's a vast, grand room, which, to my mind, proves this was a palace. In fact, I believe we have discovered the seat of King Minos himself.'

Despite trying not to behave like a gauche schoolgirl, Alice stared at Evans in wonder at this pronouncement. Having picked their way across channels and trenches, they rounded a corner and another man hailed the small group, hurrying over to join them. He was of average height and wore a battered pith helmet.

'This is David Hogarth, director of the British School of Archae-ology at Athens,' Mackenzie said. 'Arthur's constant companion in his quest to discover Knossos.'

Alice smiled at Hogarth, who beamed in response and fell into step beside her as they headed for the throne room. George and Evans were discussing the Ashmolean Museum in Oxford, of which Arthur Evans was the Keeper and had spent a great deal of his own personal fortune in updating the building and the collection.

'How are you finding Knossos, Miss Webster?' asked Hogarth.

'It's huge,' she replied. 'How did Mr Evans know this was the place to excavate?'

'This dig is the fruition of many years of research and study by Arthur, me and Arthur's friend, John Myres,' said David Hogarth, guiding Alice over an uneven piece of ground. 'After the Turks left Crete in November 1898, Arthur, having already identified this area as one of interest, thanks to Minos Kalokairinos, bought a Bey's part share of the site.'

'What's a Bey's part?'

'A Bey is a courtesy title formerly used in Turkey and Egypt. It refers to the governor of a district or province in the Ottoman Empire,' explained Hogarth. 'The land was owned by the Bey, who had built his country house near the stream. After the Kalokairinos discoveries—'

'Of *pithoi*?' interjected Alice, remembering Bernadette's letter, and Hogarth's smile widened further.

'Exactly, the area became of interest to many scholars. It has always been known locally as Knossos, with the attached rumours that it was the ancient site of the palace of King Minos. However, its real name was *Kephála*, which translates as "Squire's Knoll". It was a large rounded mound that had been absorbed into the surrounding terrain on two sides, but fell steeply downwards in deep gullies to the south and east where the Kairatos stream ran. There was nothing visible above the surface except a few minor relics, until the discovery of the *pithoi*.

'Arthur was able to persuade the Bey to sell him the land but, unfortunately, not long after, unrest began again in Crete and he was forced to abandon his plans to dig. With the Turks invading and blood running like rivers in the street, all Arthur could do was try to negotiate help, as he had done before in the Balkans.'

Alice was aware of Arthur Evans's many years of travelling; how he had lived in the Balkans and worked to highlight the plight of the war-torn and impoverished people.

'In the aftermath of the war with the Turks, Arthur helped to bring relief to Crete,' continued Hogarth, 'including going on board British Navy ships himself to ensure the food was delivered to those most in need. It was quite a feat, as Arthur suffers terribly from seasickness. He also brought the difficulties of the islanders to the notice of the world, particularly the British government.'

'He's remarkable,' said Alice, shading her eyes against the sun as she watched Arthur and George marching through the ancient site.

'This was a popular spot to dig and Arthur faced some fierce competition, even though he owned the land. Other wealthy claimants tried to suggest it was morally wrong to allow a foreigner to excavate on such an historical site and they kept trying to find reasons to halt him. However, Arthur's plans were supported by the Cretan authorities. It was their way of thanking him when he'd helped them so much in their hour of danger.'

'It was a huge risk to take, based only on the discovery of a few *pithoi*,' said Alice.

'That wasn't the only reason,' said Hogarth. 'You know about Troy?'

'Heinrich Schliemann and his wife, Sophia, discovered it in June 1873,' she said.

'They found a huge array of artefacts but there was no trace of the written word among them. But a city as rich and powerful as Troy didn't happen by mistake. It was a vast administrative base and you need writing to make such a system work. It bemused Arthur as he believed there should have been the remains of records.'

'Did he begin looking?'

'Not directly, but he was curious and made a point of observing any items he felt were contemporary to the discovery.'

'And he found something?'

'Oh, yes. It was hiding in plain sight all along,' said Hogarth. 'When Arthur and John Myres were grubbing about, turning up shards of pre-Mycenaean vases near the Acropolis one day, Arthur noticed scratchings. Not damage but deliberate marks. A short while later when he was in Athens, in Shoe Lane, poking around in the antiquity shops, he found more evidence. He might not be able to see very far in front of him, but when Arthur brings things close to his eyes, he can spot details most people miss.'

'What did he find?' asked Alice intrigued.

'Strange three- and four-sided sealstones engraved with symbols. He gathered as many as possible, examining them closely, and with each one he became convinced the symbols were not random images but, like the scratches on the vases, deliberate and methodical. They were hieroglyphs, but different from those in Egypt. When he asked the man where the sealstones were from, he was told Crete. It was then he remembered the sealstones in his own collection that he had found at various locations around the island. These were also engraved. When he discovered there were sealstones with similar markings in the Berlin Museum he believed this was the clue to the existence of a system of picture writing.'

'George said you've already found clay tablets bearing marks. Are they the same?'

Hogarth could barely contain his glee and he grinned as he continued.

'Yes, and once Arthur had made these connections, he realised this was the only place to dig. In our hearts, we knew Minos was waiting beneath this hill, which, when you see it in the landscape, is quite patently man-made. I believe Minos himself guided Arthur to this place. We began digging on 23 March on the mound of Kephála, and soon discovered layer upon layer of houses, temples and tombs. As we were interested in the original occupants of the land, those who had lived at ground level, there was a lot to clear before we could meet the Minoans. But they were there, waiting for us.'

As he spoke, he threw his arms wide to encompass the entire site. Alice was sure tears glistened in the man's eyes, but before she could respond, she heard George calling her name. Hogarth swept round again and together they hurried over.

'In here,' Hogarth said, and as she and George followed him into the ruins of the room, Alice gasped. In front of her was an ornate throne. Around it were crumbling frescoes, hints of colour remaining after their lengthy incarceration.

'It's stunning,' she said. The chair, tall and austere in its beauty, was positioned against a wall, with low benches on either side. Alice stared at it in wonder, imagining how it would feel to sit on it, to shiver at the touch of the cool stone beneath her. The rigidity of the throne, running straight against the wall, was softened by a broad back, with curved sides. Staring at it, Alice was reminded of the shape of an oak leaf, each bend a work of art. The image of the oak tree outside her bedroom window in Hampshire flashed across her mind and she felt a stab of homesickness. Then Evans's voice brought her from her reverie.

'King Minos himself might have sat on this throne,' he said to George, and for a moment Alice was going to correct him, to explain the seat had belonged to a woman, then she stopped herself, bemused by her own audacity, yet convinced she was correct.

'Have you found the labyrinth yet?' asked George, and Arthur swept his hand around in an expansive gesture.

'The entire palace is a labyrinth, my dear boy. Minos administered his mighty empire within a living replica of the subterranean world. It seems right the creature below was in a similar arrangement. However, I'm not here to prove Homer or Ovid correct. I'm here to discover the people and their way of life. If we happen to find the Minotaur, then so much the better.'

* * *

The rest of the day passed in a blur of excitement, dust and shouting. After their tour of the site, Evans was called away and Duncan Mackenzie guided Alice and George to the mound of earth near the wall Hugo and Theo had been examining earlier.

'We need a delicate touch as we don't want to miss anything,' Mackenzie said. 'Pottery shards over there, figurines in the basket, and anything you're unsure about, give me a shout.'

Having emptied her canvas bag into a small basket she found on the edge of the trench, Alice folded it in half, placed it on the ground and knelt on it. A shiver ran down her spine as she peeled off her leather gloves and touched the crumbling ground of ancient Crete for the first time. It was cool, clumped with moisture as old as the mountains. Picking up a clod of earth, she breathed in the smell of soil, decay, water and time, and, with a grin, she began to dig.

An hour later, Alice had discovered several small pot shards, a thrill of delight jolting through her with each find. Pausing to drink from her water canteen, she looked around, brimming with excitement.

Then she resumed digging until the blade of her trowel scraped against something hard. She peeled off her gloves and probed further, eventually scooping up the lump of earth to examine it in more closely. As her hand tightened around the soil, crumbling it through her fingers, she felt a sting as a sharp-edged object grazed her palm.

Brushing away the dirt, expecting to see a pebble, she felt her heart rate quicken as the light caught the oblong stone. For a moment Alice was transported to the past, seeing a young woman walking along the path in front of her, laughter ringing, confident of her future and the love in her heart. Her feet were clad in embroidered slippers, her long hair flowed in silken coils down the back of her tunic, and around her neck were strands of sparkling beads making their own music in the breeze, while a shimmer of iridescent light shone around her head.

The image cleared and Alice reached for her water canteen, pouring it over the stone, clearing away the detritus of millennia with trembling hands to reveal a sparkling crystal.

'George,' she called. 'Look!'

George and Mackenzie, who were a few feet away, rushed to her side and, as she held up her find, they stared at it in as much wonder as Alice.

'Is it a sealstone?' she asked.

Light fractured through it throwing rainbows around them.

'If it is, I've never seen one like it,' said Mackenzie.

'Is it a diamond?' asked George.

'Perhaps,' grinned Mackenzie as he helped Alice to her feet. 'Where did you find this, Alice?'

She pointed to the red earth and was surprised when Mackenzie squatted down beside her and began shovelling earth into a wide sieve, which had been discarded a few feet away.

'What are you doing?' she asked.

'It's a new technique Arthur is using. We sieve the soil to ensure we can find even the smallest of artefacts.'

'Let me,' said Alice, protective of her discovery. Mackenzie relinquished the sieve and Alice began the painstaking ritual of checking the soil, while George and Duncan watched in anticipation. 'Look,' she gasped after sieving three more trowelfuls. 'What is it?'

She handed the dirt-clogged find to Mackenzie and he began to clean it using the water from the canteen Alice had placed beside her.

'It's a figurine,' Duncan exclaimed. 'Let's show Arthur.'

Alice scrambled to her feet and, with George grinning at her in shared glee, they followed Mackenzie across the site.

21

They waited – pale, beautiful – the sons and daughters of Athens, gazing with sorrowful eyes upon the perfect blue of the Cretan sky for the final time. The Games were won, the bull dancing finished, these annual tributes to celebrate the wisdom of the Minotaur were complete. The Minoans waited, aware the time was upon them, all eyes gazing towards the girl who would begin the ceremony. Potnia of the Labyrinth, priestess, princess, Ariadne, rose from the ethereal white of the gypsum throne followed by her robed handmaidens. Hers was the dance they dreaded, the jingle of her crystal necklaces as with gentle steps, she led the way across the elaborate floor to the heavy doors of death...

22

The air was golden. Eloise breathed in the silence of the dawn, cherishing her solitude. She pulled the hand-drawn map from her pocket, placed the compass she had found in Quinn's study on top and, having ascertained east, hitched her small rucksack onto her back and headed down the gentle slope.

The grand palace of Knossos hovered in the early morning mist, distant, mysterious and other-worldly. It would not open for several hours, and she intended to enjoy as much of the extraordinary site as possible before coachloads of tourists swamped the attraction. Until then, she was on a mission of discovery. Edging down the narrow pathway, she peered through the olive trees and vast clumps of wild rosemary, searching for the grove Marina had described.

Whether it was the conversation with Marina that had led Eloise back to her night-time world of labyrinths and mysterious rites, she did not know. Her search through Quinn's box of photographs had been unsuccessful, and when she had awoken with the dawn, she had felt compelled to search out the ancient site. It was time, she had decided, to stop worrying about Claud and live her life.

Since her encounter with him the previous week, Eloise had remained in Sfragida House. This retreat had been for more than the simple expedience of avoiding an unexpected encounter with Claud. Her reasoning was that if he wished to speak to her, he would be able to find her. Any confrontation would take place in private. It would also give her the advantage of being in her own space. His reasons for being on the island rankled. The sale of the house could have been dealt with by a call to her solicitor, and the supposed concern about her mental health felt contrived, so why was he here? Eloise could think of no acceptable answer.

To her relief, Claud had not reappeared. Instead, word had come from the Brewery Taverna in the shape of a visit from John: Claud had apologised to him and Steve the following morning and had offered to leave. They had declined, instead helping him to arrange hampers for Marina's family to express his apologies. After this, according to John, who had dropped by with a loaf of the delicious bread he made, Claud had taken to his room.

If he thinks I'm going to him, he's in for a long wait, thought Eloise as she slithered down the incline, the stones skittering away from her feet in a giddy rush.

She paused to check her map and take a sip from her water container. If she was on the correct path, the shrine was situated on her left. A pile of stones, similar to a cairn, and a number of bushes were marked on Marina's map. Taking a few more steps, she saw the cairn. It was surrounded by a tangle of wild thyme, juniper and rosemary bushes, glistening with morning dew. As Eloise pushed past the clawing branches, their scent filled the air. Three steps cut into the side of the hillside were her next landmark and, having scuffed away the dry earth and fallen leaves, Eloise gave a cry of triumph as they emerged from the undergrowth. Each step was a vast piece of natural stone, set one on top of another. Easing down them with care, she saw the bushes give way so that with a final step onto cool soil, she arrived in the shaded grove Marina had described.

Eloise stared around in wonder at the wide and peaceful space. The grove was wrapped in an eerie silver-green light as the early morning sunshine filtered through the covering leaves of the surrounding olive and lemon trees. Now she could understand why this area had never been discovered by Arthur Evans. It was impossible to see unless you stumbled upon it.

At the centre stood a large stone, reaching out of the ground as though it had grown there. It was mottled with age and, in the shimmering light, the tiny quartz particles within it glowed like hidden diamonds. It exuded age and a strange sense of calm, reminding Eloise of the bluestones within the circles of Stonehenge.

Eloise's hand slid to the necklace given to her by Quinn. Since her arrival in Crete she had worn it every day, only removing it at night or when she swam in the pool. Her fingers closed around the smooth clear crystal and a sense of being connected to this land wrapped itself around her.

Walking around the stone, she felt herself relax. She breathed in the scents of the wild herbs, the ancient soil and the hint of grapes from the rows and rows of vines, and a smile spread across her face as she leaned on the stone and closed her eyes.

In the distance, she heard laughter, but she did not open her eyes; it was too far away to disturb her. There was a sigh, then what could have been the jingle of bells, before the words floated around her: *I love you.* Her eyes flew open in panic and she stared around, her breath coming in short, painful bursts as the scar on her hand throbbed, causing her to cry out. The intensity of the feeling swamped her and a sob escaped, her face crumpling as tears rose in her, hot and fearful. But within seconds, the pain had passed, as though drawn from her like poison, to be replaced by a feeling of

pure happiness. Eloise took long, deep breaths, trying to under-
stand this confusing conflict of emotions.

She stepped away from the stone and a breeze moved the
branches overhead, changing the light and drawing her eyes
upward. As the sunlight fell across the stone, she saw the markings.
In the gloom, they would have been easy to miss but the unex-
pected burst of iridescence illuminated them like a spotlight and
she wondered whether this was part of the secret of the grove.
Neolithic monuments across the world were positioned on celestial
curves, designed to welcome either a solstice or an equinox. She
wondered if perhaps this stone had been positioned to celebrate an
ancient rite: had pure good fortune brought her here on the day of
the year the writing would appear?

* * *

Eloise's mind strayed again to Stonehenge, a monument she had
visited with Josh. The trip was his birthday present to her as he
tried to make up for inviting his friends on their honeymoon, but
his boredom had been evident from the moment they arrived.
Eloise had suggested they walk to the stones from the visitor centre,
but Josh had insisted they take the shuttle bus, and he had spent
the five-minute journey on his phone. When they disembarked,
Eloise had gazed at the ancient stones, entranced by their age,
absorbing the wisdom in the air around them.

As she had breathed in the stillness, she had experienced a
similar sense of time slowing down, of being suspended between
each second as though it had elongated. Voices had reached
towards her, the chatter of excitement, love, celebration, shadows of
lives lived, promises made and eternity worshipped, when she had
been aware of a man standing beside her.

'They're beautiful, aren't they?' Claud had said, and Eloise's heart had sunk.

Was it impossible for her and Josh to go anywhere alone?

'From your expression,' Claud had said, 'Josh didn't tell you he'd invited us.'

Eloise had looked up at Claud and been shocked by his appearance. Although usually groomed to perfection, he looked exhausted. Dark rings circled his eyes, his skin was pale and stubble prickled on his chin.

'No, this was supposed to be a trip to apologise for the fact he invited you all on our honeymoon.'

Claud had looked uncomfortable.

'I'm sorry, Lo,' he had said, and a ripple of irritation had coursed through her as he used the familiar name of her close friends and family. On their lips, it was affectionate, but whenever Claud used this nickname, it felt like an intrusion.

From behind them came a gale of cheering from Josh, Nahjib and Martin, who were bent over Josh's phone, watching the football.

'Shall we?' Claud had asked and, with reluctance, Eloise had fallen into step beside him, realising she would get no more sense from Josh.

Despite finding Claud overbearing, Eloise's natural empathy at his altered appearance led her to ask, 'Are you feeling all right?'

'Yes, why do you ask?'

'You look pale and I was concerned.'

Claud had paused, running his hand over his rough chin.

'I was away for work and it was full on,' he had replied, 'but thank you for your enquiry.'

There was a strange finality about the response and Eloise decided not to pry any further; Claud was allowed his privacy. However, she knew he was a successful Harley Street gynaecologist, and she wondered what kind of conference he could have attended to leave him looking so exhausted.

As they had circled the stones, Claud had begun to tell her the story of the henge and, as Eloise had once been drawn to Josh's perfect prose, she felt the passion in Claud's voice. It was a shock when he used an expression she remembered from the first speech she had heard Josh make. It felt like a ghost, an unexpected spectre, but, she reasoned, they were friends; it was natural they would use similar phrases. She and Rose often did the same thing. Unable to help herself, she had mentioned it and Claud had looked unsurprised.

'When we first met, I coached him,' he had admitted. 'Josh struggled with giving his final verdicts and public speaking, whereas I'd learned oratory from an early age. It's amusing he used one of my expressions to woo you, though.'

Eloise had brushed the comment away but, once again, Claud's version of events seemed at odds with Josh's, who had claimed he was the one who had coached Claud.

'Did you know one of the first excavations that took place here in 1901 was by a man called William Gowland?' Claud had said, drawing her attention back to Stonehenge.

'No,' she had replied.

'There had been a storm, and a stone and its lintel fell over in 1900. This prompted a project to restore the monument,' he said. 'Gowland had been working in Japan as a metallurgist for the Osaka mint, but in his spare time he'd excavated a tomb at Shibayama in Osaka. While he was there, he had adopted one of the techniques used by another wealthy archaeologist, Arthur Evans, who had pioneered the use of sieves to ensure nothing was missed from all the discarded soil. His work was so impressive he was invited to come here and try to unlock Stonehenge's secrets.'

'How do you know all this?' Eloise had asked.

'The Neolithic era fascinates me. It was thanks to Gowland's work that this site was considered Neolithic. He was also one of the first people to suggest the theory that they transported the stones using large numbers of people with ropes and rollers.'

Claud's enjoyment of the monument had overtaken Eloise's anger at the intrusion of Josh's friends. Despite herself, she found him good company as they discussed the history and myths of Stonehenge, the science and the possibilities of all it might once have represented.

By the time they had found Josh, Martin and Nahjib in the visitor centre, discussing which was the closest pub, Eloise had been glad Claud had accompanied her, otherwise, she suspected Josh would have grown petulant and wanted to leave far earlier. Instead, he grinned at her, slipped his arm around her waist and they had decided to travel to Salisbury for dinner. Relieved to have avoided another sulking session, Eloise had forgiven Josh for inviting his friends.

* * *

Forgiveness, she thought now, as she extracted her camera and began taking pictures of the writing carved into the stone. We say the word without thinking but it isn't a word, it's an action, one that is very difficult to do. Looking at the scar on her palm, she shuddered, wondering, would she ever be able to forgive Josh?

Eloise had never identified as a victim. The word, she knew, was from the Latin and its earliest meaning was a sacrifice. Discovering this had filled her with a sense of irrational shame she was loath to share with anyone, even Rose. In the days after his death, she had thought that if she forgave him, Josh would win. It was only now, with distance, that Eloise was beginning to understand forgiveness was the thing that could save her. Letting go of her fear and bitterness, absolving Josh, would give her strength, make her the victor, yet the thought of it continued to cause her ripples of fear.

Circling the stone, drawing strength from the peaceful atmosphere in the grove where centuries of people had worshipped the unknown goddess, Eloise remembered the day she had sat in a coffee shop during her lunchbreak from work and taken a quiz in the magazine on her lap.

On this particular day, as she waited for her toasted sandwich to cool, she had been reading a feature on successful women. The main double-page spread featured Faye Mostin, the founder of multiple refuges across the country for people fleeing abusive relationships. Faye's story was heart-breaking, but her resolve and courage to help others was inspirational. At the bottom of the feature was a box containing a list of questions and, having had another row with Josh the previous night, Eloise decided to answer them.

The argument had concerned money. Josh had challenged her about the items she had bought from their joint account, demanding to see receipts, suggesting that in future she should check with him before making such decisions. His suspicions had felt wrong and Eloise did not understand why he was questioning her. At first, she had thought he was teasing, but when she realised his eyes were dilated, she suspected he had been drinking, or worse, and as he could be a spiteful and violent drunk, she had complied.

As Josh leafed through the receipts, checking them against the balance on their online account, she had waited by the kitchen island. When he had finished, he turned to her and smiled, as though she were a child, accused of naughtiness who had subsequently been cleared of wrongdoing. He had ruffled her hair, kissing her on the forehead and told her he would join her in bed soon. Eloise had felt diminished by his actions but did not dare refuse him when he had sprawled on the bed an hour later, demanding sex.

The questionnaire in the magazine was from the refuge's website and was to help people to establish whether they were in an abusive relationship. Eloise had read the questions, answering them in her mind – yes, no, yes, yes, no, yes – horrified when one created a similar financial scenario to the one she had experienced with Josh. When she reached the bottom, she read the shocking words: 'If you have answered yes to one or more of the above questions, this indicates that you may be experiencing domestic abuse.'

She had pushed the magazine away, leaving it on the table where she had been eating her lunch, returning to her desk, refusing to believe what the feature was suggesting. She was an intelligent woman with a good job and a top salary. Her husband was a barrister, they had a beautiful home and yet...

Pushing the memory aside, she pulled a torch from her backpack and began exploring further into the grove, searching for the cave Marina had mentioned. A few steps away from the monolith, she saw the darkened space and as she moved towards it, she felt a wave of déjà vu of such strength that it made her dizzy. This place was familiar. Again she heard bells, except she realised it was not bells, it was the jangle of beads. As she turned, she saw them: the parade of young women and men, creeping through the cave, guided by the priestess with the golden hair from her dreams. The woman turned, gave a deep curtsy and then vanished. Eloise snapped back to the present.

Having pulled a small bottle filled with wine from Marina's vineyard from her rucksack, she poured half into the ground at the entrance to the cave and half at the base of the standing stone, before placing a small posy of flowers she had brought with her beside the stone. Thanking the goddess, as Marina had instructed, she pushed her way back through the foliage and on to the path that led to the vast expanse of Knossos. A question she had been asking since her childhood had been unexpectedly answered.

* * *

Eloise was the first person to enter Knossos that morning. A small tour and a few other independent visitors arrived in the car park as she wandered down the pathways and away from the vast arena that dominated the site. As she disappeared into the cool rooms, her trainers making soft shushing sounds on the stone floors, it felt as though the palace was hers alone. Reading the signs, she decided to avoid the House of Sacrificed Oxen in favour of the Throne Room, directing her steps into the heart of the complex.

Having searched through Quinn's books, Eloise had found a number of photographs of the original dig and could visualise Arthur Evans, Duncan Mackenzie and the many Cretan workers whose skills had helped to bring the Minoans out of the rich soil and into the modern world. However, despite searching, she had not found an image of Alice, Hugo or George, and she felt as though part of the story was missing until she could picture their faces.

Stepping into the impressive Throne Room, with its recon-structed and reimagined frescoes, Eloise was struck by the hints of Art Deco in the swirls and flounces on the pillars. The beauty of the gypsum throne was staggering. As she stared at it, she felt as though she were standing beside Alice on her first day at the dig, absorbing the detail, wondering about its origins. Subsequent generations of archaeologists had suggested the throne had been designed for a woman, and now Eloise knew in her heart who had been permitted to sit here.

Next, she wandered through the other exotic rooms, each offering images and insights into the Minoan people and their lives, in frescoes adorned with their faces, their beliefs, their ideologies and rituals. Eloise understood why Arthur Evans had spent so many years of his life rebuilding this extraordinary structure. Searching the walls, she tried to find an image matching the tiny figurine from Quinn's study, but, as Marina had explained, there was nothing similar.

As she doubled back, Eloise heard the clatter of an increasing number of footsteps and the babble of voices as Knossos welcomed its visitors. Turning away from the oncoming crowd, she followed a path to a courtyard with a seating area, but as she rounded the corner, she halted. A wooden seat was built around a shady tree but it was occupied. Eloise was about to flee, when she heard the sob.

'Claud?' she whispered, and when he looked up, she gasped in horror. His face was blotchy with tears, his eyes swollen, and he reached out to her.

'What's happened?' she asked, rushing forward, taking his hand, sitting beside him.

'It's Nahjib,' he sobbed. 'He's in intensive care. Marcella attacked him.'

23

'How did I miss the signs?' he wept, unashamed of his tears, turning his head to rest on Eloise's shoulder.

Eloise felt a chill run down her spine.

'What do you mean?'

'Nahjib and Marcella. How did I miss it? I'm supposed to be trained to spot these things and I missed it in my best friend.'

'What do you mean, trained?' Eloise repeated, her heart pounding. She was thankful that at the angle Claud's head rested, she could not meet his eye, but he did not seem to hear her question.

'Martin said she's been arrested,' he continued, his tone as far from his usual confidence as Eloise had ever heard. 'She's confessed to abusing him throughout their relationship.'

'She admitted it?' exclaimed Eloise, horrified.

Although she had never warmed to Marcella, thinking her cold and humourless, Eloise had never imagined she could be violent.

'Not at first, but we've since discovered she has two previous convictions.'

'How?'

'Auntie Faye recognised her. I sent her a photograph,' he said, his voice breaking again.

Claud's hands, which she had taken when he reached out, remained entwined in hers; he squeezed them as though searching for reassurance. In an unconscious gesture, Eloise returned the pressure, stroking the back of his hand with her thumb. His head remained on her shoulder, and she adjusted her position to make it more comfortable and to enable her to hear his muffled voice.

'Who's Auntie Faye?' said Eloise.

'She's my godmother,' he said. 'She was the one who trained me. She and my grandma Elinor, two amazing, strong women, saved me from a very bleak and lonely childhood.'

Eloise stared at him. In all the years she had known him, apart from the occasional comment about not being close to his parents, he had never mentioned his personal life. Whenever his past was mentioned, he always deflected the attention elsewhere, so to have this sudden confession was unnerving.

'Claud, I don't understand,' said Eloise. 'What has this to do with Nahjib? What happened? What do you mean, "trained to spot this"?'

'For the refuges,' he said, leaving Eloise in further confusion. 'Nahjib's mother rang Martin late last night. She was in hysterics and begged him to go to the hospital to intervene. Nahjib's father was threatening to remove Nahjib because he was convinced his son would be attacked in hospital.'

'What? Why?' asked Eloise, but either Claud chose to ignore her or was so engrossed in his grief that he did not hear.

'When Martin arrived, he discovered the police were there and Marcella was bordering on the hysterical,' he continued as though she had not spoken. 'Every time the police asked her what had happened, she changed her story. First she said Nahjib had attacked her and she had stabbed him in self-defence. Then she said she thought there was a burglar in the house, but it had been Nahjib, and she stabbed him by mistake.'

'Stabbed him?' said Eloise in horror as Claud's words sunk in.

'Thankfully, she missed all his major organs,' he said, 'but I was suspicious because nothing she was saying made sense. There's natural confusion after a violent event, but there was something off about her constant story changing. To be on the safe side, I emailed her picture to Auntie Faye, who's in touch with vast numbers of people. She messaged back within minutes, confirming Marcella was known at one of the refuges. She has two previous convictions for violence and coercion against men. I sent this information to Martin, and she was arrested.'

'Claud, this is awful,' Eloise gasped.

'Nahjib's lost a huge amount of blood, and he's still in intensive care. It's possible he may not pull through. His head wound means that he might even have some brain damage. When the doctors examined him, they discovered he had bruises around his kidneys and cigarette burns all over his back.'

'Claud, no,' gasped Eloise.

An image of the first night she had met Nahjib came back to her: tall, handsome, charming, funny, confident in his role as an orthopaedic surgeon, while pale-faced Marcella sat in the corner on her phone. Eloise had put the woman's reticence down to disinterest. It was difficult to comprehend she had spent months coercing and abusing Nahjib.

'I should have known,' Claud muttered. 'Two of my friends and I did nothing to save them.'

'What do you mean?' asked Eloise.

'Auntie Faye would have seen it,' Claud said, his eyes glazed.

'Claud, who *is* Auntie Faye and what does she have to do with Nahjib?' Eloise asked again. The sharpness of her voice seemed to bring his mind back into focus.

'Auntie Faye and my mother were friends at university, but they grew apart when my parents' politics became more extreme,' said Claud, wiping his eyes, his voice stronger. 'Auntie Faye felt they'd lost their compassion. She drifted away from the friendship with my mother, but stayed in touch with me, offering me a home with her and Uncle Reuben if ever I needed it. I'd spend my summers between them and Grandma, and it was because of what happened at Auntie Faye's that I decided to specialise in gynaecology.'

'What happened?'

'Auntie Faye runs a number of women's refuges,' he explained, lifting his head from Eloise's shoulder and staring across the small courtyard while continuing to grip her hands. 'Her father used to beat her mother and Faye swore, when she was old enough, she would find a way to help her mother and any other woman she was able to save.'

'Claud, I'm sorry, that's awful,' said Eloise, her heart racing.

'Faye's father died in his sleep one night from a massive stroke. She thinks if he hadn't, her mother, Bridget, wouldn't have survived much longer. When Faye graduated from university with a degree in business management, she persuaded her mother to turn their home into a refuge. It was a rambling old house that had once belonged to her grandparents and had some land with outbuildings, so it was private and, as it was at the end of a lane with one entrance, it was easy to make it secure.'

'Did her mother agree?'

'Yes, and the refuge was a success,' said Claud. Eloise could hear the pride in his voice. 'From there, Faye and Bridget raised funds and awareness. Faye has six centres around the country now, and we hope to open more soon.'

'More?' echoed Eloise.

'It's an endless struggle to find safe places, and Auntie Faye is determined to make sure there is always somewhere for people to go to escape an abusive relationship, no matter their sexuality or gender.

'Anyway, this particular summer, I was staying with Auntie Faye and Uncle Reuben, doing odd jobs when one of the women had a miscarriage. I already knew I wanted to be a doctor and had taken plenty of first aid courses, so I offered to help. Faye's friend, Trudi, who's a midwife, was there and she got me to drive the woman to hospital. All the way there, Trudi raged about how difficult it was to find doctors who would give dedicated time to refuges, to build relationships with the women and offer advice. She said women's services were already pushed to breaking point on the NHS and they needed a dedicated gynaecologist, a doctor they could rely on to drop everything and come to them if there was an emergency.'

'But you have a swanky private practice in Harley Street...' spluttered Eloise.

'Which pays for me to work at Auntie Faye's refuges as often as I'm needed,' he interrupted his temper flaring. 'It's where I go for the occasional week.'

'Josh always said you were away with your married mistress,' said Eloise, thinking of the occasions when Claud would be inexplicably absent, remembering the exhaustion on his face at Stonehenge.

'Did he really?' Claud's voice rang with disgust.

'When you weren't able to make the boating weekend on the River Avon, Josh told me you had a long-term mistress and that was why you would never commit to Davina.'

'He said that, did he?' said Claud, and a look of loathing flashed across his face. Eloise recoiled, shocked at the cold anger rippling through his words as he continued, 'He wasn't in a position to criticise people having affairs.'

For a moment the words hung between them, then the image returned to Eloise, the two shadows in the gathering twilight, the intensity of their kiss. The accusation she had shouted at Claud at the Brewery Taverna, which he had not denied.

'You knew?' said Eloise.

'Yes.'

Eloise snatched her hands away.

'Why didn't you say anything? She's your girlfriend, or do you have an open relationship?'

'Davina isn't my girlfriend, she's my flatmate, and I did say something. She stopped seeing him after the weekend in the Lake District.'

Eloise swallowed the bile rising in her throat and realised Claud was right. The Opium had not been discernible after that, but the other perfume had returned: lily of the valley.

'Your flatmate?' Eloise said in disbelief. 'Why do you always bring her to parties, then? You shared a bedroom when we went to the Lake District and in Cornwall, when we went for Martin's birthday.'

'If you remember, we would always volunteer to take the room with the twin beds. In fact, it was bunk beds in Cornwall.'

'I never noticed. But why bring her?' said Eloise, confused.

'Davina came to Auntie Faye for help when she was sixteen and, because she was so young, Auntie Faye and Uncle Reuben insisted she live in their house with them,' he replied. 'Over the years, she became like a daughter to Auntie Faye and Uncle Reuben. She's a few years younger than me and we were like brother and sister. When I returned from university and bought the London flat, things were tight. Shelley and I needed a lodger in the first few years before either of us began to earn decent money. Auntie Faye suggested Davina. We'd always been close, so I agreed. When I bought the penthouse, she moved with me. We were used to each other.'

Eloise stared at Claud in bemusement.

'First, who's Shelley? And, second, why did you let me assume Davina was your girlfriend?'

'Around the time you began dating Josh, I'd broken up with Shelley Longbury, my long-term girlfriend since sixth form. Davina had been in a string of relationships, none of which had worked out. One weekend when we were both moping around the flat, we made a pact to accompany each other to social events, weekends away, and we would never explain but allow people to jump to their own conclusions.'

'Why go to such lengths?'

'I'd fallen in love with someone who was unavailable,' he said, his eyes focused on the group of people entering their courtyard.

Eloise surveyed Claud, unsure whether to believe him and, despite herself, her mind wandered back to Josh's scathing comments about Claud's married lover. Was this the woman who had stolen his heart?

'Lo, I'm sorry about the other night, in the restaurant,' Claud said, turning to face her. 'I should never have said those things. It was unfair. I didn't mean it. My stupid temper and pride got the better of me.'

'Why didn't you just ring me about the house?' she asked.

'It would have been the most sensible thing,' he agreed, 'but I wanted to see you. To check you were coping.'

Eloise did not respond – she could not fully comprehend his reasoning – so instead she said, 'Have you apologised to John and Steve?'

'Yes, you know I have: John told you. I said sorry the next morning and offered to leave, but they were very good about it and insisted I stay.'

'And Marina's family?'

'I wrote them a letter and sent them a hamper. Steve and John helped me put it together. Your chap, Nikos, came over and we had a drink. He accepted my apology on behalf of the two families, his and Marina's.'

'Nikos isn't "my chap",' said Eloise. 'He's Yiannis's brother and we've met twice.'

Quite why she felt she owed Claud an explanation, she was unsure, but, as he had been honest with her, she wondered if maybe she had a certain obligation to reciprocate.

'Did you drive here?' she asked, watching the visitors as they milled in their direction.

Claud shook his head. 'John dropped me off.'

'I've got Quinn's car... my car,' she corrected herself. 'Come on, let's go to the taverna for lunch, then back to mine to see if there are any updates on Nahjib. Will you fly home?'

They stood, both brushing away a few fallen olive leaves from their clothing.

'If I have to, Martin will sort out the flights,' he said as Eloise moved aside for a crocodile of visitors to pass. 'Having a friend who runs a high-class travel agency in Mayfair does have its perks. Will you come home too?'

'Why?' she asked. 'Nahjib doesn't need me there. It's his family, you and Martin who are important.'

'If I asked you?' said Claud. 'If it was necessary?'

Eloise stared up at him, uncertain what to say, but there was such sadness in his eyes, she found herself nodding.

'Yes, if you think my presence will help. I like Nahjib; he's a good person.'

Eloise did not see the pained expression on Claud's face as she turned to lead the way out of the labyrinth of Knossos.

24

'This place is stunning,' said Claud, staring out of the window as Eloise drove down the winding mountain roads towards the Brewery Taverna. 'What brought Josh's father here?'

'His health,' said Eloise. 'He'd always suffered from asthma, and years of smoking made it worse. When Josh was eighteen, Quinn had a heart attack. After he'd recovered, he decided it was time for a dramatic change of lifestyle and he bought Sfragida House from Marina's father. He'd travelled here many times because of his interest in Knossos and had known Marina's family from staying at the guesthouse on the vineyard. The climate suited him better than in the UK and he loved it here.'

'What about Josh's mother?'

Eloise glanced at Claud, who continued to gaze out of the window, his eyes roving across the towering slopes of Mount Juktas. Eloise wondered how, as Josh's friend, he did not know the story of Ethelwyn and Quinn Winter. It was one Josh liked to tell, siding with his mother and scorning his father, although they had always been happy to accept his financial support throughout his life.

'Josh's parents separated because she refused to leave England,' said Eloise. 'From what Josh told me, and the few bitter stories I've heard from Ethelwyn and her younger sister, Gladys, Quinn and Ethelwyn met at a Rotary Club drinks' party in the 1960s and bonded over their love of reading. Ethelwyn thought he seemed a sensible sort because he worked at the Home Office.'

'But he wasn't?' asked Claud, turning his startlingly amber eyes to her.

'No, he was a dreamer, wanting to be an archaeologist and travel the world. After the wedding, when he suggested going to university to study, Ethelwyn was appalled and refused to support his ambitions, even telling him he had lured her into marriage under false pretences.'

'Harsh,' said Claud, and Eloise, once again quashed her curiosity as to how Claud did not know this story. Josh would recount it regularly, with extra recriminations if he were drunk.

'Ethelwyn wanted two children and a pretty house in Surrey, so the idea of following Quinn around the world to various dusty dig sites was anathema to her. Quinn capitulated and spent years working his way up through the ranks of the Civil Service, providing the house and lifestyle his wife dreamed about. Sadly, Ethelwyn had a string of miscarriages and, after years of disappointment, pushed Quinn away.

'Quinn told me he'd been planning to leave Ethelwyn for a woman he worked with, Joan, but on the night he was going to tell her, Ethelwyn stunned him with the news she was four months pregnant. This time she carried the baby to term.'

'This was Josh?' Claud asked.

'Yes, but as soon as Josh was born, Ethelwyn went out of her way to drive a wedge between him and his father.'

'Why?' asked Claud, and Eloise shrugged.

'I've no idea.'

The car tipped to the left as Eloise took a tight bend, and Claud reached to grab the door handle for support.

'How do you drive this car?' he asked. 'It practically falls over every time you go around a bend.'

Eloise laughed. She adored the quirkiness of Quinn's 2CV.

'It's a challenge, I admit, but it suits this place, this house.'

'How did Josh's mother react when you inherited Sfragida House?'

'It's difficult to say who was angrier, Josh or his mother, at the will reading. She called me a gold-digging slut, who had seduced both her husband and her son...'

'What?' Claud's voice was sharp with anger and disbelief.

'Thank you for being upset on my behalf. Josh called me a few choice names, too.'

Eloise took the next steep bend with care, following the signs for Archanes, the closest village to Sfragida House.

'Claud, why didn't you know all this about Josh?' she asked.

'We rarely discussed our families.'

The Brewery Taverna came into view where John was serving a family on the terrace, and he waved when he saw them. As Eloise parked, John wandered over to the short flight of stairs that led to the entrance of the restaurant, watching as they climbed out of the ancient red Citroën 2CV into the sunshine.

'Well, hello, you two!' he exclaimed, grinning. 'Have you stopped fighting?'

'I've apologised, and Eloise has forgiven me with all graciousness,' said Claud.

'Good,' said John, hugging Eloise. 'Grief does strange things to people and it would be a shame for you to lose each other in the aftermath of Josh's death. Grief and love, the two most powerful emotions. Grief is the price we pay for love. Are you eating with us?'

'If you can fit us in,' said Eloise.

'Always for you, my love.'

John ushered them to a corner table beside the ancient vine that climbed up the building in an arc of the most voluptuous nature. Then he furnished them with menus and they ordered a bottle of wine.

'I suppose John is right about love and grief being the two most powerful emotions,' said Claud.

'Well, grief comes from love,' said Eloise. 'Grief wells up in us when we have nowhere to place the love we feel for the person who has died.'

'I've never really considered they were linked before,' said Claud.

'Why do you think death rituals began in the first place?' asked Eloise, perusing the menu. 'Humans have always needed a way to stay connected to the loved ones they've lost. Whether it was the ancient Egyptians sending their pharaohs into the afterlife with a wealth of grave goods, or the Vikings and their ship funerals; the rituals we've evolved around death are to help the living deal with their pain.'

'You know a great deal about it,' said Claud, but there was no challenge in his voice, just interest.

John arrived to take their orders and deliver their bottle of ice-cold wine. Filling their glasses, he winked at Eloise and hurried away.

'Of course I do,' she said. 'My father is the third generation of undertakers to run our family business and my brother, Gareth, will be the fourth. We've grown up around death and its customs.'

'Such as?' asked Claud, and again she realised there was no aggression in his question, just genuine curiosity.

Eloise swallowed her instinct to change the subject and allow him to lead the conversation. When she had once tried to explain these things to Josh, he had listened for a few moments, then his attention had wandered and he had talked across her, telling her about a funeral he had once attended where everyone had been asked to wear red as it was the deceased favourite colour. After this anecdote he had flipped on their enormous television and fallen asleep in front of the Tottenham Hotspur and Arsenal match. Eloise had never mentioned the subject again.

'There are hundreds of rituals around the world,' she said with a hint of cautiousness, ready to change the subject if Claud looked bored. 'One of the most well known is the Mexican festival of *El Día de los Muertos* – the Day of the Dead – where parades celebrate those who have passed away. It takes place in November and has similarities to traditional Hallowe'en celebrations. Both nights are said to be when the veil is the thinnest between the worlds of the living and the dead and it's possible for our loved ones to visit. That's why candles and lights play such a huge part in the rituals. They're the lights guiding those we've lost home.'

Claud topped up their glasses and, under his encouraging smile, Eloise continued.

'The Malagasy people of Madagascar practise *"Famadihana"*, or "the turning of the bones". Every five to seven years, they bring the bodies of their relations out of their crypts, wrap them in fresh cloth, spray them with perfume and dance with them. It's seen as a chance to share stories with the beloved deceased and ask for their blessings. In the Northern Philippines, the Igorot Tribe place coffins on stilts, high up on the cliffs. They believe that the higher up the body is resting, the easier their passage to heaven will be.' Eloise sipped her wine. 'There are hundreds more, and that's before we begin discussing the symbolism of flowers at funerals. Mum and Jessica have encyclopaedic knowledge of that, from all around the world.

'My favourite description of grief, though, came from a woman whose great-grandmother's funeral was with us,' said Eloise. 'She was beautiful, tall, radiant and had blonde hair that shone like a halo. She was accompanied by her son who was upset about losing his great-great-grandmother. The woman explained to the boy that grief was like glitter. When a sad event took place, grief would cover everything in glitter, then as the process of dealing with the loss of the person, the ritual of the funeral, of the chance to say goodbye, each of these things cleared away the glitter until the day came to move on. But glitter gets everywhere. Every now and then, we come across a piece of leftover glitter and it reminds us of the person. If it falls in our eye, we might cry, or we might see it shimmering in an unexpected shaft of sunlight and we smile, remembering the person in the pure light of love.'

'What a beautiful way to describe grief,' said Claud. 'Was it odd? Always being surrounded by death, especially with your surname?'

'Why do think my great-grandfather began the business? De'Ath's Fine Funeral Services – it was tailor-made.' Claud laughed and Eloise continued, 'It was always my world, which made it feel normal. If I'm honest, when I reached my teens, I enjoyed the noto-riety. Especially as, from the age of seventeen onwards, I learned how to lay out the corpses.'

'You must have been streets ahead in anatomy when you were presented with a cadaver to dissect for the first time during your training to be a doctor,' he said, causing the couple at the table behind them to glance over.

Eloise grinned, pausing as John delivered two large Greek salads and Claud's side order of fries.

'It was witnessing people's grief that made me want to go into research once I was qualified,' she said.

'Why?'

'I wanted to find new ways to stop disease, to help people survive longer, to allow them to remain with the people who loved them and whom they loved.'

'Love and grief,' said Claud. 'Eternally entwined.'

'I have a theory on love too,' said Eloise, then hesitated.

'You're willing to discuss your theory on love with me? Your sworn enemy?'

Eloise stared at Claud is surprise.

'You're not my sworn enemy,' she said.

'I'm not?'

'No, you're...' She drained her glass, which Claud refilled. 'I don't know what you are, Claud,' she admitted. 'I want to say "friend", but from the first night we met, once I'd rescued Pippin, you seemed to despise me.'

'I didn't—' he began but she could not bear to hear excuses, so she cut across him.

'What happened to Pippin?'

'She belonged to a family who Auntie Faye was rehoming. I'd rescued her from the house of the woman's abusive husband a few hours before you and I met. That's why I was so stressed that night and why I had multiple phones with me. One was mine, one was Auntie Faye's. The bloke had come home when I was leaving with Pippin and two suitcases of clothes, and I had to run for it. The situation was a mess, but the family was rehomed and Pippin was reunited with them after a few days staying with me and Davina. I've got a picture somewhere.'

He flicked through his phone and turned it to Eloise, showing her a fully grown fox-red Labrador grinning at the camera with a girl of approximately eight years old on one side and a younger boy on the other. Eloise remembered Josh telling her a few days later that Claud had borrowed the puppy to enhance his ability to attract women and the reason for the two phones was because he gave one number to women, so he could avoid them more easily, while the other was his usual phone for his friends.

Lies, thought Eloise. Why the endless lies?

'Despised you, though?' Claud said, forcing her away from her confusing thoughts. 'Why would you say such a thing? I've never despised you.'

'It doesn't matter...'

For a moment, they stared at each other across the table and an image flashed across Eloise's mind, a memory: Claud in a morning suit, she in a wedding dress, Josh and Rose sharing a swig of brandy from his hip flask, while her parents laughed and Ethelwyn Winter scowled. The scent of spring flowers and her sister, Jessica, tripping over a misplaced piece of photography equipment.

'We're married,' Josh had whispered

'I know,' she had grinned back as he bent to kiss her, causing catcalls and cheers from the congregation.

To ringing applause, the vicar had led the way to the vestry for the signing of the register. Eloise had been so immersed in her own happiness she had missed the opportunity to giggle at Rose, who, as matron of honour, had been forced to take Claud's arm in his duties as best man. She knew neither would give an inch in the battle of seething charm.

As they gathered in the small square room, the nervous tension of the service had dissipated. Eloise had begun to laugh as she took the pen she had given to the vicar two days earlier. Signing her name, she moved to allow Josh to sign.

'No going back now, darling,' he had said, and Eloise had beamed, glowing with happiness and love.

Her father had been next, signing as a witness, followed by Claud. For a moment Eloise's smile had faded, but she pushed her feelings aside. Nothing was going to spoil her day.

'After all,' Rose had muttered at her elbow, 'how many times does a girl get married? Two? Three at the most. The first one's always the big one.'

Giggling, Eloise had been delighted to see Claud shoot them a reproving glance. The photographer appeared and the rigmarole of taking the posed photographs had begun. Eloise had smiled and smiled until her face ached.

'How about a picture of the bride and the best man?' Josh had suggested.

'Why?' asked Rose in surprise.

'Well, then I thought we could have one of you and me,' Josh had replied with slight reticence. 'If it hadn't been for you, Rose, Eloise and I might never have met.'

Mollified, Rose had acquiesced, and Eloise had returned to her place behind the table, posing as though she were signing, while Claud had been told to shuffle closer, closer, closer until the wool of his suit brushed her arm. She had steeled herself not to recoil, then Jessica had sneezed, taking a step backwards and knocking the tripod, so the photographer missed his shot.

'Don't move a muscle,' he had called, grinning at Jessica. 'These things happen. Let me frame it again. Not that I want to cause a scandal, but you do look very handsome together.'

Despite the photographer's request to remain motionless, Eloise pulled away.

'What's the matter?' Claud had asked.

'Nothing.'

'Are you sure?'

For a fleeting second their eyes had locked, and she recoiled at the unexpected tenderness of his expression.

'Claud,' she had gasped.

'Don't start crying,' he had hissed.

'Now the pose again!' said the photographer, and this time, as Claud leaned towards her, Eloise felt a turmoil different from her usual hatred.

Now, outside the Brewery Taverna, Claud broke their eye contact and emptied the last of the bottle into their glasses. Eloise wondered if he too was remembering the wedding day. The scorching look they had shared, which Eloise had pushed from her mind ever since, believing she had been mistaken. But there had been another unexpected intimacy on her wedding day.

After the first waltz, which had been more of a slow shuffle around in a circle as Josh had refused to allow Eloise to teach him even the most basic of steps, Josh had insisted on dancing with Rose, forcing Eloise and Claud together. As an old Wham! tune, 'Wake Me Up Before You Go-Go', had blared across the dance floor, they had moved towards each other, and Claud had whispered, 'Do you still remember how to jive?'

Eloise, who loved to dance, and found Josh's refusal to learn frustrating, had grinned.

'Of course.'

'Follow my lead,' he had replied, and before she knew it, she was being spun across the floor.

As their proficiency became obvious, couples moved aside until the three remaining pairs of Eloise and Claud, Eloise's parents, Eric and Marissa, and her brother, Gareth, with his wife, Nadine, were left, each whizzing like tops. Eloise's dress streamed out like a banner before the finale when Claud's hands encircled her waist and, to huge applause, he hoisted her on to his shoulder. Afterwards, Claud had lowered her with care, holding her hand as he steadied her and, in the briefest heartbeat, his touch had felt more welcome, more natural than Josh's...

'How's the food?' John asked, pulling her from her reverie.

'Wonderful,' Claud replied. 'Shall we make an afternoon of it? Order a second bottle?'

'What about Nahjib?' asked Eloise, glancing towards Claud's phone, which lay on the table.

'Nothing yet. I doubt we'll hear anything until later, maybe not even until tomorrow, unless...'

For a moment, they stared at the empty bottle.

'Should we be enjoying ourselves while he's in danger? It seems...' Eloise searched for the correct word, wanting to say 'heartless', but that wasn't right, '... disrespectful?'

'We have no reason to feel guilty about enjoying ourselves,' Claud said. 'Nahjib is in safe hands. If nothing else, this proves we should grab every moment of joy.'

'Yes,' said Eloise. 'Death could be waiting around every corner. Look at Josh. And we should eat more chips. Salad is lovely, but chips are the best. Perhaps if we drink enough, we can demonstrate our jiving techniques later.'

Claud laughed, his own mood tinged with a recklessness she had never seen before.

'As long as I'm not going to have to break up any fights?' said John, amused.

'We'll give you ample warning if it's heading that way,' promised Claud, ordering bread, olives and chips. 'We're more likely to dance, though.'

'Either's fine with me,' said John laughing, as he went off with the order.

* * *

'Tell me your theory on love,' said Claud, leaning forward, his voice velvety with wine and sunshine.

Eloise wondered whether this was the right time, but then she considered his words. Josh was gone, and no amount of wailing and grieving could bring her husband back; Nahjib was in the safest place and receiving the best treatment. They were allowed to enjoy this moment in the sun.

'Very well,' said Eloise, 'this is a theory I've worked on for a number of years. When I was at university, I met and fell in love with Pete Dolohov. He was a chemistry student in the year above me. We were together throughout our degrees and my medical training. We rented a flat and I thought he was "The One",' she put air quotes around the phrase and Claud raised his eyebrows. 'Until the day he told me he was moving to America to marry his fiancée, whom he'd failed to mention before. Apparently, our relationship was fun but nothing more.'

'You were living together when he was engaged to someone else and he hadn't told you?' said Claud in astonishment.

'Yes, he didn't seem to understand why I was upset. Then he spent half an hour telling me why he could never have married me because I was awkward, argumentative, selfish, so many things. It was then I realised how mistaken I had been about love.'

'What do you mean?'

'Love,' she said, sipping her wine, self-conscious in his attention. 'The day Pete left, I looked it up in the dictionary.'

'Really? What does it say?'

'There are multiple definitions, but the one I remember was "A strong feeling of affection and sexual attraction", which seemed underwhelming. Another was "A formula for ending an affectionate letter". It also divided it up into nouns and verbs.'

'Not very inspiring,' said Claud.

'I tried a Thesaurus next and discovered there are something like two hundred words for love, which is significantly more than there are for hate, which is encouraging. Love is from the old English *lufu*, and Latin *lubere* – to please.'

'And your theory grew from here?'

'Yes, and from years of researching parasitic diseases. As far as we're concerned, love's an emotion, a magical experience of joy and desire, a state we all crave. Am I correct?' Claud nodded and Eloise continued, 'We read poems about it, listen to songs, but nearly all of them focus on the pain and the despair of lost love rather than the beauty of lasting love.'

'True,' said Claud, 'but you have to experience love with all its crazy wonderfulness in the first place or you wouldn't be able to write about it, lost or otherwise.'

'Maybe so, but this proves love always ends in sadness,' said Eloise.

'Does it? What about happy marriages of fifty years or more?'

'One partner will always die first. It's the nature of life: there will always be one left behind. Alone. With nothing but their memories to warm them. You might smile at the nostalgia of photographs, but when you put them away, you're still alone.'

'True, but happy memories can bring their own joy,' said Claud.

'But no matter how great the love, it will always hurt you in the end. It's like John said: grief is the price we pay for love. When Pete left, I realised the truth: love isn't an emotion, it's an illness.'

Claud stared at her aghast. 'Love is an illness?'

'Yes, and having studied the causes of numerous illnesses in my research, love fits the profile of a parasitic disease.'

John brought more food to the table and topped up their glasses, and Eloise paused until he hurried away to seat new customers.

'Explain,' said Claud, dipping a chunk of fresh bread into the olive oil before piling chips on top.

'OK. So love begins with the host. An unprepared creature going about its daily duties, minding its own business, when the love-parasite appears in the air. A killer waiting to strike…'

'What does love look like?'

'Like a mosquito, but meaner and impossible to swat.'

'In theory then, if the host was quick enough, love could be splattered with a newspaper or well-placed shoe…'

Eloise shot Claud a stern look and he held up his hands in a motion of mock surrender.

'The host, meanwhile, continues with his, her or its daily business, until the parasite, spying its targets, bites and burrows inside, waiting to destroy them from within. This is the contradictory nature of a parasite: it will kill the very thing that offers it shelter.'

'You are very bleak.'

'Yes, I know,' agreed Eloise.

'Then what happens?'

'There are two possible outcomes. Love burrows into our hearts, it destroys our equilibrium and our peace with being alone. When you meet someone, when the L-word is said out loud, a sense of ownership descends on couples – *my* boyfriend, *my* girlfriend, *my* wife, *my* husband – mine. "I" transforms into "we", and in order to accommodate this new connection, a portion of ourselves is forced to retreat.

'We do this voluntarily, we do it with "love", yet, in allowing this, we diminish. The relationship advances and love worms its way further into our soul. We adapt, we compromise and then, it seems the very thing that drew the lovers together, the joy, the happiness, is revealed to be the first, ecstatic stage of the illness, a stage that vanishes when the parasite is embedded in its host.

'As this first stage fades, the parasite begins to feast on the joy until it has devoured all happiness. The relationship ends, whether through death or a separation. With nothing remaining to live on, the parasite flees and the lovers, now parted, recover.'

'And the second possibility?'

'This occurs when the host meets a person carrying the cure.'

'The cure?'

'The one who has the power to overwhelm the parasite.'

'How?'

'With friendship, respect and companionship. These drive the negative emotions away.'

'But those things are the basis of a good relationship. They're what most people consider to be the real secret of love,' said Claud, his voice low and sad. Eloise did not respond. 'And you developed this theory after you split from your first long-term boyfriend?'

'Yes, it was six months before I met Josh and I had to find some way to justify Pete's hold over me,' said Eloise, blinking to hide the tears that welled in her sparkling green eyes.

'And where did Josh fit?'

'I thought Josh was the cure.'

'Was he?'

'No.'

Claud reached across the table and took her hand, for a moment his brow puckered into a frown as he ran a gentle thumb over the scar on her palm.

'What you've described isn't love, Eloise,' he said. 'It's destruction.'

'Which in my experience, is the same thing,' she replied.

'Then you've never been in love and, more importantly, you've never been loved.'

25

The passageway turned, its sinuous corners dizzying the minds of the uninitiated as they were taken first one way, then another. The flames guttered in the lanterns of her handmaidens, the shadows eerie on the walls with their shimmering flecks of ancient quartz, drawing them deeper into the heart of the earth. Every bend was familiar to her feet as she traversed the age-old paths of the labyrinth. At its centre lay the temple, the place of sacrifice, and it was to here she led the tributes.

26

Alice pulled off her leather gloves and wiped her hand across her brow, relieved to be in the shade of one of the canvas tents erected at various points around the Knossos site. A table, chairs, rugs and cushions furnished the small space and Alice sank into one of the chairs, fanning herself with her gloves. Although the heat of the day was receding, the Cretan air never entirely cooled.

Alice was tired and thirsty after a long day. Folding her gloves in half, she slipped them into the pockets of her breeches, discovering her handkerchief, shaking it out and smiling on seeing the red marks of earth streaked across it from a day of wiping away grit and dust. As she dabbed herself with the smallest of remaining virgin squares, she wondered at the adventure of her summer. When she had been fleeing with Ephraim, she had believed her future lay in America, the New World, but instead fate had led to the discovery of one of the oldest worlds on the planet.

For the past two weeks, she, Hugo and George had spent their days at Knossos helping with every task imaginable, from trundling the iron wheelbarrows, imported from England, backwards and forwards to the large piles of discarded spoil, to using brushes and cloths to wipe dirt from delicate frescoes or helping to dig the relics from the dusty ground itself.

As the time at the dig had passed, friendships had been forged. With Duncan Mackenzie's help, Alice had learned basic words of the local Cretan dialect and when she had offered to help with the careful cleaning of ancient potsherds, clay tablets and other tiny finds from the dig, she had befriended two women of a similar age to herself, Angeliki and Maria. Although halting at first, they had developed a *patois* of their own, a combination of English, Greek and the local Cretan dialect.

The two young women had been friends since childhood and their friendship reminded Alice of her own relationship with Juliet. Angeliki's cousin, Mani, was marrying a cousin of Maria's, Elena, and the discussion about the wedding was one of their favourite topics, second in popularity to the young men they found attractive and whom they would like to marry.

At first, Alice listened rather than joined in as Angeliki and Maria giggled, watching the young men flexing their muscles when they swung axes or heaved barrowloads of soil to the spoil heap. Until the day when Angeliki nudged Alice as George paused nearby, his shirtsleeves rolled up, his muscular arms revealed, laughter on his face as he shared a drinking skin with Vassilis, the young man who had stolen Angeliki's heart.

'George is good-looking, do you not think, Alice?' Angeliki laughed.

'Very,' Alice agreed, because to deny such an obvious fact would have been ludicrous.

'You like him?' Maria asked, her eyebrows raised in fun, her brown eyes sparkling.

'I...' she had begun as the other two collapsed into well-meaning giggles.

'He will help to heal your broken heart, Alice,' said Angeliki, 'and,' she continued, her voice taking a more serious tone, 'he likes you.'

'We're friends,' Alice replied, uncomfortable at the turn of the conversation.

'I think he would like to be more than friends,' said Maria. 'He was jealous when you were talking to Vassilis this morning.'

Alice forced a laugh but brushed the comment away.

'You must be careful, Alice,' Angeliki concluded. 'Men like George are never single for long. The American woman who is hoping to dig in Gournia visits again soon – perhaps she will steal him.'

'She's very welcome to him,' Alice laughed, but the irritation that had risen in her when Juliet had flirted with George in Paris snaked its way around her heart again.

After this, Alice had become aware of George and the number of times he appeared at her side during the day. The laughter as they worked together, their shared delight in the ancient antiquities they were discovering, a passion for the works of Shakespeare and a love of a little-known American poet called Emily Dickinson.

'One day she will be regarded as one of the most important poets of our age,' Alice had said one evening as she and her friends sat under the vine-draped pergola at the Perrins' villa.

'Your man's clothes make him smile,' Maria grinned, nodding towards Alice's breeches. 'He watches you, always.'

Alice gathered the potsherds they had finished drying with soft cloths and transported them to Duncan's centre of operations in a tent nearby, ready for the Scotsman to add them to his meticulous daily records. As she returned to her friends, she watched George in the distance and wondered if Angeliki and Maria were correct. As if in answer, he looked up and waved. She responded and saw his face crease into a smile.

When a parcel had arrived from Juliet the previous week, Alice had been unable to fathom what gift her friend could be sending. It was not her birthday until later in the summer, but when she had unwrapped two pairs of lightweight breeches, similar to those Hugo wore when he went riding, but cut to fit her, she had squealed in delight, scrambling to open the accompanying letter.

Juliet had scrawled in her exuberant hand,

> Dearest A,
>
> These are a gift which I hope doesn't shock Auntie Ag too much. If she is horrified, explain to her that Jane Dieulafoy, a famous archaeologist, who with her husband, Marcel, has uncovered endless relics in Persia, always wears a suit. I thought you would be rather hot in a Worsted three-piece, so Tybalt and I conspired to have these made and we send them with our love. We are heading to Venice tomorrow and hope to travel to Greece in a few weeks. If we can persuade Ma and Pa, we'd love to come and join you at your fascinating dig. Speaking of which, how is the equally as fascinating Mr G. Perrin? I hope we do see each other soon, as I have exciting news. We may have exited our début without marital incumbent but this situation will be changing for me soon.
>
> Toodle-pip for now, J

Alice had gaped at the letter, rereading it three times to ensure she had not mistaken her friend's words. As she traced her fingers across Juliet's handwriting, it seemed the prospect of marriage was no longer an estate her friend wished to avoid. The laughter of their débutante balls floated across time and her heart contracted in pain as her mind flew towards Ephraim, standing at the altar, marrying another woman. Yet, even as Alice had pulled on the new breeches, she realised the pain, while piercing in its arrival, fled with the same quick-silver speed, and she wondered if perhaps she was recovering from her love affair with Ephraim.

As one recovers from the measles, she had thought, surprising herself with her flippancy.

Mere weeks ago, the thought of Ephraim's marriage would have reduced her to heartbroken tears. But now, despite his having been an all-consuming obsession, Ephraim Lockwood was no longer the waking beat of her heart and this puzzled, as well as saddened, Alice. Examining her reflection in the short mirror on the inside of her wardrobe, she wondered when her love for Ephraim had changed from its charged and passionate desperation to a subject that fluttered through her mind, leaving a sting rather than a death blow.

The image of herself in the breeches pushed him even further from her mind and, grinning, she had raced down the stairs, excited to show her aunt the contents of the package. Ever since the evening when Agatha had told her the full story of her marriage to Barnaby, a new understanding had grown between them. Alice smiled at Juliet's presumption that Aunt Agatha would be shocked by her new attire; from what she was learning about the older woman, Agatha would be ordering a pair of breeches for herself to enable her to stride among the hills and valleys of Crete, which she was beginning to love.

When she had erupted into the room and spun around for her aunt and cousins to admire her outfit, Robert and Andrew had gasped in surprise.

'Alice is dressed as a boy,' Robert had exclaimed, as Andrew sniggered.

Agatha had looked up from her book of poetry and given Alice an appraising look.

'Far more sensible, dear,' she had said. 'Don't forget to wear your hat, though.'

Hugo had been shocked when Alice had presented herself in her new garb the following morning and felt sure she would be ravaged by local men unable to keep their hands to themselves. As they climbed off their cart, Hugo had tried to stand in front of her, making Alice laugh, but apart from a few curious glances and a look of appreciation from George, her new clothes had garnered very little response. As Alice fanned herself, she wondered how she had coped in her voluminous skirt.

'Ah, there you are,' came Duncan Mackenzie's quiet Scottish vowels. 'Hugo said you might be over here in the shade.'

'It's been much hotter today,' she said. 'The coolness of the tent seemed a good idea.'

Duncan removed his water skin from his belt and passed it to her.

'I refilled it a few minutes ago,' he said. 'Drink. We don't want you fainting.'

Alice grinned and gulped down the water, fresh and cool from one of the fast-flowing mountain streams.

'Theo and Arthur have finished examining the stone you found on your first day,' Duncan said, sitting beside her and stretching out his long limbs.

'When I unearthed it, I had a momentary hope it might be a diamond, but it's vast, which makes it unlikely,' Alice admitted.

'Alas, you're correct. It isn't a diamond but it has similar properties. It's a zircon, which is thought to be one of the oldest minerals on earth. On first examination, the suggestion that it was a sealstone seemed the most obvious hypothesis, but the more Arthur has considered it, the less sure he and Theo have become. Part of the reason is because it's made of zircon.'

'Is this unusual?' asked Alice.

'So far we've haven't found any others made of zircon. We have plenty made from beryls of multiple colours, citrines, amethysts, but none of zircon. It's not to say we won't discover more, but it's certainly intriguing. The pattern is one Arthur claims he has not seen before either.'

'The labyrinth?'

'Indeed,' replied Duncan, and a shiver ran down Alice's spine, 'as well as some pictorial characters in Linear B.'

'How extraordinary,' she said.

'The shape is fascinating, too,' continued Duncan. 'It's an octagon, whereas the others are all squares and oblongs. The stone has been drilled as though it was once a pendant or part of a necklace.'

'Isn't that quite common?' asked Alice, who had shared a long discussion with Arthur Evans concerning the sealstones in his own collection. He had explained many Cretan women used them as charms and amulets, stringing them on thin strips of leather to wear around their necks during childbirth, believing they could ease the pain. The women also claimed they helped the mother's milk to come in abundance afterwards to feed the baby.

'Quite right, but the sealstones Arthur has bought from antiquity dealers have been adapted in the modern era. Any we've dug from the earth here at Knossos are intact. This is the first we've discovered with the potential for it to have been made to be jewellery.'

'Meaning it could be a bead rather than a sealstone?' suggested Alice.

'It's not something we can rule out,' Duncan replied. Alice passed him the water skin and he took a hearty swig.

'What about the figurine?' she asked.

'She's very interesting and the first find to give us clues towards the nature of Minoan worship. It's possible she was used for home worship, perhaps a depiction of a household goddess or a votive offering for a temple. With luck, we'll find more and might be able to piece together the nature of their religion.'

Duncan passed the water skin back to Alice.

'This place is incredible,' sighed Alice, gazing out over the site. 'There's history everywhere, even in the everyday. It's magical.'

'And with each sunrise and sunset we discover more treasures,' replied Duncan.

'Do you have much trouble with theft?' she asked. 'Surely the Cretans must feel a sense of ownership over the items.'

'Not really,' replied Duncan. 'At the end of each week, we pay each person extra for the objects they've found as a reward for their vigilance. It's part of the reason we keep such detailed records. Arthur believes this reward system helps induce honesty. He turns a blind eye to the occasional pocketed potsherd or small items, what he calls "the permissible limit of peculation", but if bigger or more valuable items are stolen he'll sack the person involved. Aristides, our first foreman, lost his job when inscribed tablets from Knossos turned up on the Athens market and were traced to him. Most of our workers were horrified at this breach of trust. They're loyal and proud Cretans, and because of Arthur's respect for them and their heritage they are devoted members of our team. As essential as Arthur himself, in fact.'

Alice smiled. Her fondness for the Scot had grown over the weeks. She respected his integrity, his work ethic, and his fiery temper, which often flared when he and Arthur disagreed over some point of history or archaeology.

'The Cretans are delighted by the new skills they're learning too,' Duncan continued. 'Arthur and I decided we needed to be thorough, which is why we began sieving the spoil as it was removed from the ground. Even the tiniest artefact has a tale to tell. *The Times* has written about Arthur's methods, and I believe other archaeologists are employing his methods. I had a letter from an old colleague, William Gowland, who told me he's decided to try the same at his excavations in Japan.'

'Japan? How incredible,' said Alice, awestruck by the vastness of this new science. 'The sealstones are important, aren't they?'

'As important as the many clay tablets we're unearthing, which are revealing the writing of the Minoans.'

'Do you think you'll be able to decipher the languages?'

'Keep your fingers crossed that we find the equivalent of the Rosetta Stone,' he said, taking the water skin back from Alice. 'I understand from Hugo you've been invited to attend the wedding party tomorrow evening between young Mani and Elena. We're all invited; it should be a spectacular night.'

'Arthur, too?' Alice found it difficult to imagine Arthur Evans dancing at a local wedding. Despite his boundless energy, enthusiasm and respect for the Cretans, Evans tended to keep a polite distance from his local workers, not joining them socially or becoming involved in their lives away from the site.

'No, it isn't Arthur's thing,' said Duncan, 'and what would he drink? Despite my best efforts he's never taken to the local *raki*. It's made from fermented raisins, which I keep telling him is only one step away from his beloved wine and Champagne.'

Alice laughed.

'Does the Perrin Vineyard supply him?'

'He's sampled a few bottles of their wine but, at the moment, a great deal is imported. Gus Perrin made his money as a wine importer. The family is from Plymouth and for years Gus was a seaman in the Merchant Navy, but as his family grew – George has an older brother and a younger sister – Gus wanted to spend more time at home. He knew one of the most lucrative cargoes was wine, so he made it his business to learn more about it. Within three years, he'd retired from the sea and was running a thriving wine importers in Plymouth. He even supplies the Queen and has a royal warrant from Prince Bertie, too.'

Alice listened to this explanation, her eyes fixed on the view through the pinned-back entrance to the tented area, wondering why she did not know this about the Perrins. In the past few weeks, Aunt Agatha and Elaine Perrin had become good friends, and the visitors had dined at the vineyard on numerous occasions. She, George and Hugo would often spend evenings discussing a variety of topics, yet, for some reason George had never shared his family history.

'The wedding should be fun,' Duncan continued. 'The Cretans have dances similar to Scottish reels. I could teach you a few, if you're unfamiliar with them. The music is played on the lyra rather than the bagpipes. It's the musical instrument of Crete and is a descendant of the ancient seven-stringed cithara or lyre, which we believe was played by the Minoans.'

'We've been to Scotland numerous times,' Alice replied. 'My friend Juliet has links to one of the Scottish baronies, so we've been to many a party. Hugo is very fond of a reel.'

'Are you waiting for Hugo?' he asked.

'Yes, he's probably engrossed in a conversation with Theo about architecture...' Alice halted as a shadow loomed outside the tent and she looked up in anticipation, wondering if her brother was about to appear, summoned by her saying his name aloud, which was a game they would play when they were children. Instead, George entered, a frown between his eyes as he took in Alice and Duncan.

'This looks cosy,' he said, but his tone sounded forced, clipped.

'A moment's respite before we face our journeys home,' said Duncan. 'See you tomorrow, Alice.'

Duncan raised a hand of farewell and, taking his water skin from Alice, ducked out of the tent into the late afternoon sunshine.

'What was that about?' asked George.

'We were discussing the stone I found.'

George's look was so full of such suspicion that Alice could not help but laugh.

'Did you think Mr Mackenzie was making improper suggestions, driven wild by my unconventional garb?' she teased, and a faint hint of pink stained George's cheeks.

'Of course not,' he snapped. 'He's a gentleman. Although, you do cause quite a stir as you traverse the site. I've often observed more than one man trailing his eyes behind you. When you're bending over the spoil heap, it's most distracting.'

This time, it was Alice's turn to blush.

'Why, Mr Perrin, how forward,' she said, but there was humour as well as an unexpected thrill of excitement in her voice.

George took Duncan's seat, staring out at the dusty vista, before he spoke again.

'Has your aunt given you permission to attend the wedding?'

'When we discussed it last night, Aunt Agatha declared that with both you and Hugo to chaperone me, even I wouldn't be able to find any trouble,' she replied.

'Do you tend to attract trouble?' he asked.

'I do my best to avoid it, but am not always successful,' she replied. 'Did you see Hugo?'

'Talking to Theo,' he replied. 'We might have a long wait.'

Having made himself more comfortable on one of the large cushions on the ground beside Alice's chair, George looked up at her and smiled. Unable to resist, and with Angeliki's words floating into her mind – *He wants to be more than friends* – Alice smiled in response. As they watched the site being cleared for the night, the valuables taken back to Arthur's property for safe-keeping, Duncan's words about the Perrin family's origins in Plymouth came back to her.

'Why did you never tell me you were from Plymouth?' she

asked. 'Aunt Agatha has friends near Tavistock, who we visit. They're not far apart.'

George looked at her in surprise. 'Why do you ask?'

'Duncan was telling me about your father's wine importing business – we were discussing *raki* and Arthur's preference for wine,' she explained, not wishing George to think they had been gossiping about him. 'It came up in conversation that your family originated in Plymouth and you have an older brother and younger sister. Why did you never tell me? I thought we were becoming friends.'

George shifted on the cushions, his expression closed. A rush of empathy overwhelmed her and Alice berated herself, suddenly realising why he had kept this part of himself private. As she did not discuss Ephraim, George had given no hint to the world where his heart had been shattered.

'What happened, George?' she asked, her voice gentle. 'When we were in Paris, you said I was one of your people, a person living with a broken heart. Who broke your heart, George? Is this why you won't talk about your family beyond your parents and the vineyard?'

Alice was wise enough to realise her recovery was due to the life she was living under the heat of the Cretan sun. It was so far removed from her normal existence, she could dwell in a bubble of make-believe where it was easy to forget Ephraim. Should she be faced with him again, she wondered whether she would fling herself into his waiting arms, not caring about the hurt they would cause, as long as they were together. Was George also distracting himself from pain, allowing a new life to wash away the old?

'It's not a pleasant story,' George's voice seemed to come from far away. 'You would think me appalling.'

On impulse, Alice reached for his hand, making him start in surprise but he did not disentangle himself from her grip.

'I would never think you appalling,' she said. 'Believe me, what-ever you have done, my tale is far worse.'

George gave her a curious look. 'What could you have done?' he murmured, but Alice shook her head, not yet ready to discuss Ephraim.

'My story is shocking,' he reiterated.

'If you would like to tell it, I will listen without judgement,' she said.

'And you will tell me who broke your heart?'

Aware, she could not ask him to reveal his darkest secrets without reciprocation, Alice nodded.

George took a deep breath and, continuing to hold her hand, he began.

'Millicent Fanshawe and I had been childhood sweethearts,' he said. 'We both grew up in Plymouth and we were ambitious. I loved her, and there wasn't a time I could remember when she wasn't part of my life. We had an agreement we would marry, although, because we were young, it was never a formal arrangement, more an understanding between the two us, a knowledge of our destiny. We would chart our own course, away from Plymouth, and we would be the happiest and most successful couple who had ever lived and loved.

'My brother, William, followed Father into the Merchant Navy. He married Eliza Judd and they have two children, Irene and Charles. My sister, Clara, is married to a clerk at the port, Timothy Thorsson, who has Swedish origins. She is expecting their first child later this year. When I went to Brasenose College at Oxford, Millicent was delighted. We both believed this was the start of our ambitious plan to become intellectuals. She was fiercely intelligent and bought all the same books as my course demanded, so we could learn together. Then, one weekend, she came to Oxford to attend a ball and she met Edward Balstead, the third son of Percy Balstead, Viscount Brook.

'Edward wasn't part of my circle. I knew of him and he'd always seemed a decent chap, but he and Millicent fell head over heels in love. It was shocking to watch. She and I had been dancing and I'd retired to collect our ices, and when I returned it was as though I'd entered another world. Millicent and Edward were dancing and the expressions on their faces suggested they were the only two people in the room.'

Alice could hear the bitterness in his voice.

'When the music ended, he walked her back to me and had the grace to look shame-faced, but the damage was done. I escorted Millicent back to her lodgings but the next morning when I returned to collect her, she'd fled, leaving me a note, breaking off our agreement. She stated that there was no formal engagement between us, she felt no obligation ever to see me again. This was the woman who had been my constant companion since childhood, my love, and she had thrown me aside as though I were worthless. The line in the letter which drove me to madness stated: "When I saw him, I realised how love was supposed feel and this is not how I have ever felt about you."'

'Oh, George, how awful for you,' gasped Alice, squeezing his hand at the brutal revelation from a woman he had trusted. 'What happened?'

'Balstead dropped out of the course the following week and no matter how many letters I sent to Millicent, there was no reply. My brother, Will, and Father came to see me to break the news that Millicent had left Plymouth and was living with a chaperone at the Balstead family seat in Lincolnshire, where she would soon be marrying Edward. I was weeks away from my final exams and they stayed with me throughout, encouraging me not to waste my years at Oxford. Thanks to them, I achieved my First but it felt like ashes in my mouth. What did any of it matter if the future I'd planned with Millicent had been ripped away?

'By then, Father had bought the vineyard and was planning to move here to oversee the building of the new villa and the planting of the extra vines. He insisted I accompany him and, for a few months, we worked together, but as the summer drew to an end and we were due to return to Plymouth for Father to make the plans to move his business and my mother to Crete on a permanent basis, I saw an announcement of the pending marriage of Millicent and Balstead in *The Times*. I continued to struggle to comprehend how our life together had meant nothing to her and I convinced myself he had duped her and was holding her against her will.'

'Was he?' asked Alice.

'Of course not, but I set off for Lincolnshire, determined to "save her" and stop the wedding,' he said, breaking free from Alice's grasp, dropping his head into his hands.

'What happened?'

'I arrived early on the morning of the wedding and hid outside the church. When she arrived, it was clear she was alight with happiness and that my thoughts of her being forced into this union were my imagination, which was when anger took over and my behaviour... Are you sure you want to hear this?'

'Believe me,' she said, 'there is nothing you could have done that is worse than the awful things I did in the guise of love.'

Giving her a curious look, George nevertheless continued.

'I slipped into the back of the church and waited for the moment when the vicar asks if there was any known impediment to their being joined in holy matrimony,' he said, his voice flat and Alice tried not to inhale with shock. 'I leapt up, waving a piece of paper, which was actually my hotel bill, claiming it was a marriage certificate and Millicent was married to me.'

'Oh, George, no!' gasped Alice. 'How did they react?'

'As you can imagine, there was a shocked silence, followed by pandemonium. Balstead flew at me, threatening me with all manner of legal and physical threats. His family was scandalised, and her family, people who I have known and loved all my life, looked at me as though I were less than the dirt beneath their feet. It was my fault, of course, but my heart was bleeding with the pain of her betrayal. And as much as I loathe myself for saying this, I wanted to hurt her and ruin her life, as I felt she had ruined mine.'

'You poor soul,' said Alice, understanding this terrible pain of rejection, the self-loathing it brought and the recriminations. These were emotions she had lived with for months.

'Balstead's two older brothers dragged me into the vestry, followed by the vicar and Millicent's parents. They wrenched the supposed marriage certificate from my hand and discovered it was nothing of the sort. The vicar made me swear on the Bible that Millicent and I were not married.'

'Did you?'

'I was tempted to refuse but sense and shame were gathering in my mind and I realised that even if the situation were salvaged enough for the couple to marry, I had ruined their wedding day. It seemed churlish not to admit my claims were a lie.'

'And did they marry?'

'Yes. They threw me out of the church and I skulked in the graveyard. An hour later, they came out, the bells ringing, smiling as best they could but looking shaken. It was then the full impact of what I'd done hit me and I realised what a terrible cad I'd been, ruining Millicent's wedding day through my own spite and pain. This wasn't me. I'd always prided myself on my sense of fair play and gentlemanly behaviour, yet I had behaved in the most abominable manner.'

'Love and its loss can make us do terrible things,' Alice sighed. 'I imagine you tried to repair the damage, even if it was at great emotional cost to yourself?'

'Of course. I returned to the hotel and spent the rest of my day writing letters of apology and regret, which I addressed to Millicent and Edward, her parents, his parents and their wider family. I posted them all that evening, then in the early hours of the morning, I left Lincolnshire and returned to Plymouth.'

'Was it Millicent you were telegramming on the day we met you?' asked Alice, and George looked at her in surprise.

'How did you know?'

'A guess, from one broken heart to another.'

'Yes, she had returned from her honeymoon and sent back my letter unopened. I telegrammed an apology and begged her to read the letter, which I had re-posted. It felt essential to me that she at least understand the depth of my remorse that I had hurt her.'

'How do you feel now?' Alice asked.

'Less angry with her, but furious with myself for behaving in such an appalling manner,' he said, his tone rueful. 'Although, since we've been here and I've been dividing my time between the dig and the vineyard, the pain, which I thought would never leave me, has eased. Laughter has entered my life again, a tentative sense of healing and joy.'

His eyes were hopeful as he looked at her and she smiled with understanding.

'I still don't understand why you didn't tell me all this or about your family.'

'You come from a wealthy family. Your father is a successful businessman with contacts throughout the government and the higher echelons of society. Your best friend is the daughter of a baronet. I was nervous you might know Edward Balstead, or worse, know Millicent. I suppose it was shame, self-preservation, that made me hide my background in case you deduced I was the cad who broke up their wedding. The foolish, lovelorn man who was thrown unceremoniously from the church.'

Alice reached over and hugged him, an involuntary reaction and one she would have used to comfort her brothers.

'Neither Juliet nor I have ever met Edward Balstead,' she assured him. 'Even if we had, I like to think we are understanding enough to know there are two sides to every love affair. My experiences have taught me this and, like you, my love story does not reflect me in a good light.'

In that split second she decided she would tell George about Ephraim, but as she opened her mouth to begin, Hugo bounded into the tent.

'Sorry, chaps,' he beamed. 'Have I kept you waiting?'

Alice gathered her belongings as George rose, following Hugo. When they reached their trusty donkey and cart, she took George's hand.

'Thank you for trusting me,' she said, gazing up into his startling eyes. 'Tomorrow, I shall tell you my tale and hope you won't think too badly of me.'

'If you promise not to think badly of me in return.'

'Never,' she said. 'Love is madness, a malady, and we have both suffered severe cases.'

With an understanding smile, George helped Alice onto the cart and the three rode home in contemplative quiet.

27

'Do you think there was a Minotaur?' Hugo asked Alice as they walked down the slope into the village of Archanes for the wedding party.

'It would be wonderful to think the Greek myths had their origins in real people,' she replied.

A huge cry of excitement had erupted the previous day when the remains of a painted stucco bull had been discovered in the north-east *propylaea*. The details of the image had astounded Alice and she had abandoned washing finds to assist with the removal of the rubble around it, helping Evans, Theo and Duncan to reveal the ancient image. Since then, the discussions surrounding it and the possible meaning had been rife.

'Arthur believes the painting of the bull we found is a representation of either the animal with whom Pasiphae was supposed to have created the Minotaur, or an image of the monster itself,' continued Alice.

'He always claimed not to be trying to prove Ovid and Homer were correct,' said Hugo. 'It's rather wonderful to think a scientist and scholar with the intelligence of Arthur believes the Minotaur existed.'

'Every day we uncover more treasures,' said Alice, 'including hundreds and hundreds of clay tablets containing our unknown languages, Linear A and Linear B. Arthur told me he believes that if we are ever to translate these, it will tell us a story more extraordinary than even the most outlandish tales written by the classical scholars.'

'Do you agree?'

'We've discovered images of bulls throughout the site, and myths are always said to have their origins in fact. Perhaps the stories told centuries later evolve from the frescoes.'

'Robert and Andrew keep asking whether we've discovered any disfigured skeletons. They're such little ghouls,' said Hugo. 'As if such a creature could have existed.'

'It could have been possible,' said Alice.

'How?' asked Hugo.

'What about Joseph Merrick?'

'Who?'

Alice gave him a withering look. 'The Elephant Man,' she replied. 'He suffered from a disease that made his bones grow differently, giving him a large, misshapen head. Perhaps the poor man who was known as the Minotaur had a similar condition.'

'What an interesting idea,' said Hugo. 'You know, Alice, you might be correct. Thousands of years ago, the Minoans might not have understood such a man was ill and instead thought he was part beast, hence the legend of the Minotaur.'

'If tales came down through the centuries of a monstrous crea-ture, part man, part beast, the Roman writers must have used it as inspiration,' Alice answered.

'Thank goodness we live in enlightened times,' said Hugo, tucking Alice's hand under his arm, before changing the subject.

The idea had come to Alice after another night of intense dreams. Each night she traversed the labyrinth of myth, with ritual and blood at every turn. In some dreams she was alone, in others, she was accompanied by handmaidens and always shadowed by shuffling footsteps. She knew somehow that these belonged to the monster who dwelled at the centre of the labyrinth but she had not yet seen him. Despite the occasional *frisson* of fear, her heart understood that when they met, all would be well as he wished her no harm.

Each night as she went to sleep, she prayed she would learn more about this midnight world and, to her delight, the images were becoming sharper with every passing slumber. A few days earlier she had woken in the early hours, compelled to pick up a pencil as a poem flooded from her, which she scribbled on the back page of the journal she had set aside to record her dreams.

> *Forget sorrows, allow grief to heal*
> *Hold your head high and do not let fear weaken your*
>   *resolve*
> *Every step is a complete journey*
> *A moment in time, in truth*
> *Where love is perfect and your heart is strong...*

The poem echoed words she had used before in her failed attempts at writing love poems, all of which she had abandoned after the jibe made by Andrew on the train: *Or will you be wasting away here, writing bad love poetry in desolate isolation? A bit like the Lady of Shalott.*

Alice had known they were not good, yet this poem came from somewhere unbidden and she was bemused by its meaning. A conversation with Juliet had replayed itself in her sleep-strewn mind.

'Theosophists understand we have lived before,' she had informed Alice. 'Dreams often give us clues to our previous existences.'

Was this what she was experiencing? Alice had stated in her journal she was confident these dreams came from her daily discussions about mythology and history at the archaeological dig. Yet, part of her would not commit to this attempt at rational scientific theory.

Instead, she found herself staring at the palace of Knossos as it emerged from its resting place deep in the Cretan soil, wondering whether the latent thoughts and dreams of its people were rising with the walls. Arthur Evans had discovered the ancient writing of the Minoans: were their words, freed from the tomb of the Cretan soil, circling, offering clues to the stories they had hidden for centuries?

'Do you remember the first term we returned from Cambridge, when Mother and Father had converted our old schoolroom into a study area and salon for us?' said Hugo, dragging Alice from her thoughts.

'Yes, it was a wonderful surprise,' she said, remembering how her parents, brimming with excitement, had commanded Alice and Hugo to close their eyes while they had led them up the narrow staircase to the top of the house.

'Your father and I thought you'd need a room to study, to read, to relax,' her mother had said. 'A place that is not always infested with dour adults.'

Her mother was the furthest from dour that Alice could imagine and, as they gazed around at the old schoolroom, which had been converted into the perfect den for them to relax or study, they had stammered their thanks. Bookcases lined the walls, there were several tables for working, as well as sofas arranged around the fireplace. In one corner was an upright piano, but the most exciting item was the brand-new phonogram with its pile of records.

'I chose it,' their elder brother, Ben, had said, bounding through the door with equal enthusiasm as their parents. 'We're having one delivered for downstairs tomorrow, too.'

'We live in a truly modern age,' their sister, Petra, had laughed, hurrying in behind Ben.

Alice had shrieked in delight and, when Ben had placed one of the shellac records on the turntable, the entire family had danced to the jaunty hornpipe as the music filled the room.

'Are you thinking of the hornpipe?' asked Alice, now.

'Yes, this afternoon when we were dancing with the cousins and Auntie Ag reminded me of it. Petra was married not long after, and Ben, who had recently married Anna, moved into their house on the Strand the following week; life changed.'

'We had fun growing up, didn't we?' said Alice, remembering the laughter, the sunlit holidays at the seaside, the games on long winter evenings, but with these flashes of joy came the awareness it was her fault such light-heartedness and spontaneity were unlikely to happen again.

'We did,' said Hugo, before adding, 'You look better.' His round, friendly face gazed at her with a serious expression as he squeezed her hand. 'I'm glad.'

'After everything I did, you don't think I should continue to suffer?' Alice's question was genuine.

'Alice, you weren't to blame...' he began, and Alice stared at him, aghast.

'It was my fault...' she snapped.

'No, it wasn't,' replied Hugo with a forcefulness Alice had never heard him use before. 'There were two of you involved and he was older and more experienced. He should never have taken advantage of you.'

'I should have refused.'

'Did you try?'

Alice halted on the dusty track, looking at her brother in confusion, unable to comprehend why he was exonerating her from her terrible behaviour.

'Yes,' she said, 'the first time we met, it was by accident. I was at the British Museum. Father was taking me for lunch and I'd arrived early in order to see the Rosetta Stone. I was in the Egyptian room when he appeared. We strolled around the exhibits together and bumped into some of his friends. Then he escorted me downstairs to meet Father. Petra was with him and we went for lunch together.'

'And the second time?'

'I was shopping in Bloomsbury with my maid and he was walking down the road. He took me to tea.'

Alice remembered the incident well. It had seemed so innocent, Ephraim asking about her studies, their laughing together over stories of shared friends and acquaintances, until he had reached across the table and whispered, 'You're beautiful, I wish I was married to you.'

A thrill of illicit pleasure had rippled through her and she had blushed. It was the first time a man had paid her such a compliment and compared to the sweaty-palmed youths she and Juliet had encountered during their début, his sophistication had been intoxicating. The fact he was forbidden to her made her desire him with more intensity.

'Do you still think about him?' asked Hugo.

Alice hesitated, then said, 'George and I had a long talk yesterday. He told me something of the sadness he has suffered in his life. It occurred to me that...' she hesitated over the name, '... Ephraim no longer brings me the terrible pain he once did. My feelings are changing and I'm beginning to realise love will not destroy me. Being away from home, talking to Auntie and experiencing the dig has made me realise what a sheltered creature I have been.'

'It's not surprising,' said Hugo, whose eyes had narrowed at the mention of Ephraim Lockwood. 'You're the baby of the family. We all went out of our way to protect you from the harshness of life.'

'You did?' There was surprise in Alice's voice and Hugo smiled.

'Of course,' he laughed. 'Whenever you were naughty, we all thought it was adorable. You were excused from more bad behaviour than the rest of us put together, especially where Father was concerned.'

'I had no idea,' she said in bemusement.

'It's why Petra would sulk; you were allowed far more freedom than she'd ever been given when she was your age.'

Alice did not know how to reply. This casual revelation by her brother had set her mind racing, and not in a way that was comfortable. As she examined her memories, she realised it was true and, if this was the case, then she, the adored youngest child, had repaid her doting family with an enormous betrayal of trust.

A fresh wave of remorse and humiliation washed over her as she faced the full impact of her behaviour. Until this moment, her reactions had been driven by loss, grief and, reluctant though she was to admit it, self-pity at the demise of her 'great love'. Yet, Hugo's words had brought her clarity, and she understood the full impact of her subterfuge for the first time. Tears of shame sprang to her eyes and she turned away from Hugo, who was continuing to chat about the bull frescoes, unaware his throwaway comment had caused her waves of emotional turmoil.

Wondering how she could have been such a fool, Alice wiped away her tears with an impatient hand. Anger with herself was growing as they walked towards the wedding. Why had she done it? Was it because she was used to everyone making excuses for her? What an untenable brat I have been, she thought.

Self-loathing and humiliation wound around her like the tendrils of a vine and for the first time, she realised how widespread and humble her apologies needed to be if her family were to forgive her. Thinking of George writing his letters requesting forgiveness, she realised she should have done the same thing weeks ago.

* * *

'Alice, look.' Hugo's joyful voice dragged her away from her growing anger at herself. 'Isn't it delightful?'

The village of Archanes opened up before them. In the background was the brooding shape of Mount Juktas and, below, the winding, narrow streets were lined with rows of houses painted in shades of pink, pale blue, soft green, yellow and traditional white. Rows of flaming torches and strings of candlelit lanterns led them through the twisting, turning roads to the village square where a bonfire flared against the starlit sky. Music and laughter filled the air, then delighted shouts of welcome.

Alice found herself drawn forward by Angeliki and Maria, while in the distance, towering over the crowd, she could see Duncan throwing himself into the dancing with enthusiasm. Hugo was borne away by several of the young Cretan men whom he had befriended, a glass of *raki* being placed into his hand. In the centre of the square were Mani and Elena in their wedding finery, surrounded by family and friends. Alice hurried over, placing an envelope of money on the table beside them, a traditional gift, which Duncan had advised her and Hugo to present. Spread across the remainder of the table were the elaborately decorated loaves of traditional Cretan bread. Elena's parents smiled their thanks at Alice, who bobbed a curtsy, before being whisked away by Angeliki and Maria.

'Here, try this,' said Maria, pushing a glass of *raki* into Alice's hand.

Alice stared at the shimmering liquid. Taking a tentative sip, she gasped as the alcohol hit the back of her throat. Angeliki burst out laughing, patting her on the back.

'Don't worry, Alice,' she said. 'The first sip of *raki* is always a curse.'

It was stronger than anything Alice had ever tasted, but once she was over the shock, she enjoyed the spiky sensation of the warmth that spread through her body.

'Come and dance,' called Angeliki, catching Alice's hand and dragging her towards the musicians.

Throwing the rest of the *raki* down her throat, Alice placed the glass on the table and allowed herself to be led to the mass of whooping dancers. The revelations of her conversation with Hugo coursed through her. Whether it was the *raki*, their relaxed way of life in Crete or a sense of anger at herself, at Ephraim and at their behaviour, Alice was in no mood for calm, rational thought. A recklessness had overcome her, and with it came a burst of angry energy.

The music filled her and she realised she had never wanted to dance more in her life, to lose herself in the heady whirl, in the music and the silken night sky of this magical island.

Duncan greeted her with a delighted roar and, before she knew it, he was leading her through a fast Cretan reel. As he spun her away, another hand reached out and grabbed her arm and Alice found herself staring up at George Perrin.

'Shall we?' he asked, his eyes sparkling with an intensity she understood.

'Yes,' she replied, her eyes locked to his, their gaze breaking when they were drawn into the next dance. His arms snaked around her and, pushing all thoughts from her mind except the music, the joy of dancing with her new friends and the feel of George's arms around her, Alice spun and spun, laughing, dancing, drinking *raki* as it was passed among the younger Cretans, while above, a timeless velvet sky, alive with a million glittering stars, watched over them.

Several hours later, Alice and George tripped from the dancefloor, Alice clinging unsteadily to George's arm. Sighing, she settled herself on a pile of cushions arranged under one of the olive trees in the square, while George disappeared to find them refreshments. He returned with a plate containing two large slices of *melachino* and glasses of local lemon cordial.

'This is a traditional wedding cake made with raisins and walnuts,' said George, feeding Alice a few morsels.

'It's divine,' she replied, dropping a few crumbs into his mouth in return. 'It tastes like treacle.'

Leaning back against the trunk of the tree, Alice smiled up at George, who after the briefest of hesitations, moved in closer to her side. Alice sipped the cool drink, its vibrancy energising her after the revels. With a smile, she fed George a few more mouthfuls of cake. Once again, their eyes locked and Alice felt a thrill of heat run through her, followed by a stab of confusion. Where were her feelings of undying love for Ephraim?

Waiting to feel guilt or the familiar sense of loss, she felt nothing other than the joy of the moment, sitting under the olive tree, sharing the heady, aromatic cake with George and watching as Hugo whirled Angeliki across the dancefloor. Sighing with happiness, she looked up through the silvery leaves, and as the flawless stars glittered in the night sky, she felt anything was possible.

'Imagine if we lived our lives over and over again,' she said, leaning back into the crook of George's arm, 'think what tales we could tell. What secrets we would be able to impart? We would all be linked, one soul for ever.'

George curled his arm around her waist and Alice waited for memories of Ephraim to claim her, but none appeared.

'It's a wonderful concept,' he said, 'and there is proof we are all connected.'

Alice laughed. 'What proof?'

'Well, did you know we're all Trojans?' asked George.

'What do you mean?' said Alice. 'We're British. Britain's thousands of miles from Troy.'

'This is the secret of our past,' said George. 'Or, so says the ancient monk, Gerald of Wales. He claims the Britons were originally from the hot Trojan plains and our dark colouring and warm personalities are reminders of our origins.'

Alice raised an eyebrow before saying, 'Tell me about the Trojans.'

'On 14 June 1873, after searching for three years, Heinrich Schliemann and his wife, Sophia, discovered the ancient city of Troy,' said George, his voice hypnotic in the moonlight. 'He was determined to prove *The Iliad* had been based on truth. After a great deal of searching, he settled on a site at Hisarlik and here they unearthed staggering amounts of gold, which he claimed was the treasure of Troy. Whether Achilles and Hector had actually fought, or Helen was the face that launched a thousand ships, we shall never know, but Schliemann proved there had been a city of great wealth and power.'

'What a love story it was,' said Alice. 'The courage to risk everything for your true love.'

'Do you mean Paris and Helen?' asked George.

'Yes, he fell in love and carried her away, despite the consequences...' Alice broke off, realising her words, the rush of disgust at her own behaviour returning.

'Do you think it was love?' mused George. 'Or infatuation? Love should be gentle and kind. There should be understanding and the sense of rightness, of knowing you have found your match, not abduction and war.'

'Do you mean the idea of soul mates?' said Alice.

'Perhaps.'

'Plato wrote about soul mates in *Symposium*,' she continued. 'Aristophanes tells the story of Zeus: how, fearful of the powerful and physical perfection of the human race, he splits them in two, creating men and women, leaving us forever searching for our other half.'

'He did,' said George. 'Except Plato himself later refuted the idea. He suggested there can never be perfection in love. In the end, he came to believe we should strive for independence within love. Our perfect match should love us for us and not try to change our souls or our hearts.'

In the background, the music continued, the feet of the dancers beating out the rhythm of the spheres. Alice leaned back against George, closing her eyes, breathing in the scent of his cologne, the hint of sweat from the dancing, wondering what it would be like to be loved by him.

'Tell me a story,' she said, 'one as old as time.'

Alice could feel the thud, thud, thud of the drums echoed in George's heartbeat and for a moment she wondered if he thought her too forward. But then he began to speak and she allowed his words to flow around her.

'Long, long ago, when countries were new,' he said, his voice soft, measured, 'there was a land in the far west, perched on the edge of the world. Rumours abounded of this wondrous place, inhabited by giants, with jewels as big as boulders, gold, silver and copper running in rich veins through its mountains. It was a land of promise and hope, of opportunity and safety. In due course, this land became known as Britain, the name taken from the tale of Brutus, the Trojan prince who tamed this barbaric island.

'Brutus was the great-grandson of the Trojan Aeneas and, some say, he was the son of Venus. He was banished from his homeland, Troy, after killing his father, Silvius, in a hunting accident. A magician had prophesied he would have great strength, power enough to be created the first king of a land that was once inhabited by giants—'

'Your story doesn't start at the beginning,' Alice interrupted but, like George, her voice was soft, her tone dreamlike. 'Men may choose to idolise Brutus, they may believe the stories of Geoffrey of Monmouth and Gerald of Wales, but there is another tale to be told first: the legend of how Britain was given its original name, Albion.'

George smiled, his face in the moonlight a series of plains and shadows, his eyes gleaming like stars.

'Tell me the story of Albion,' he murmured, and Alice felt her heart quicken.

'Albina and her sisters were born in Syria,' she said. 'There were thirty of them and they were all tall, strong and beautiful. Each believed herself to be her father's favourite until the day he began planning their weddings. All the sisters wanted the same power as their father, but they knew, if they were married, they would become mere chattels of their husbands.

'In a whirl of fury they plotted to kill their proposed husbands and take over their homeland but the youngest sister could not bear the guilt of such violence and ran to her father. In punishment, the sisters were banished. Set upon the ocean in a hardy craft, they drifted for weeks across the seas, collecting water in their sails, eating fish from the sea, angry with their father but determined to survive. A storm blew up and, for three days and three nights, the boat was tossed on waves as high as mountains, until the sisters, exhausted from fighting the unforgiving water, fell into unconsciousness.

'When they awoke, the air was calm and cool, and the boat was crunching on the sand of a beach. Albina, the eldest, the most beautiful, scooped up a handful of sand and let it fall through her fingers, declaring, 'This is our country and I name it Albion.' Her sisters cheered and Albina became the first queen. They were alone in this realm, but they learned to gather food, to hunt and to build shelters. They changed from pampered princesses to survivors and warriors. But they were lonely and one night the devil responded to their desire. Into the darkness he delivered a host of spirits and as they crept into the sisters' beds, their voices laced with honey, the sisters gave in to their lust.

'The children, when they were born, were monstrous. Giants, the terrible offspring of princesses and demons, who prowled the hills and valleys, fighting and squabbling. With their mothers they mined the earth, creating idols from gold, worshipping bulls and swans and dragons. Until the day the last of their mothers died and the giants inhabited Albion alone.'

'And this is where Brutus arrived,' said George, tightening his arms around Alice. 'Brutus and the Trojans he had gathered during his exile were searching for the home of the giants. He had been staying at the court of the Greek king, Pandrasus, where he discovered Trojans who were being kept as slaves. He freed his fellow people, sacked the city and married Pandrasus's daughter, Ignoge. Gathering around him men who were willing to fight, including Corineus the Giant Killer, they sailed away from their homeland, through the Pillars of Hercules, defeating pirates near Africa and sacking Gaul in search of their promised land.

'For months, they sailed, gathering displaced Trojans as they travelled, until they reached an island on the edge of the earth. "This is my kingdom," claimed Brutus, "and I shall name it Britain, after me. From this moment forward, we shall be Britons." The new Britons cheered but the giants who called it Albion glowered with rage.

'The giants gathered their treasures and hid in the shadows of caves and mountains, watching in fury as the new Britons spread far and wide. Brutus and his men knew they had found their home, but to make it perfect, they intended to kill the giants and steal their gold, their treasure and the precious metals that ran in the veins of the mountains and streams. In fury, the giants fought back, determined to protect their beloved Albion and live in peace again.

'One night, as the Trojans danced and sang to their gods, the giants crept along the cliffs. Skulking through shadows, until they could feel the sand between their toes, they launched themselves at the invaders. Screams filled the night air and blood ran in sinuous trails across the beach as the old fought the new.

'Although the giants were stronger, the Britons were faster, better organised and carried brutal weapons. The giants fell one by one until the last remained; the largest, Gog Magog, but as he was overpowered, tied up and questioned, the land of Albion began to fade. In a final battle, Gog Magog and Corineus the Giant Killer wrestled for supremacy. Gog Magog found his strength ebbing, and as Corineus felt rage flow, a strength he had never known he possessed exploded through his body and with a roar of triumph, he flung the last giant into the sea.

'The Britons spread throughout the nation, settling at Llud, which became known as London, Corineus was given the western tip, which he named Cornwall and Brutus became the father of three sons. When Brutus died, he gave each of his sons a portion of Britain to rule. To Camber, went Kambria, now Wales, to Loegria was appointed the place now known as Scotland, and to Albany was what we call England. Yet, deep down, despite our differing accents, our national pride, we are all Trojans at heart.'

Alice did not want to speak, to break the spell the magical tale had woven around them.

Then George whispered, 'What happened, Alice? Why were you so sad when you arrived this evening?'

'How did you know?' she asked.

'You were ashen, as though you'd experienced a shock.'

She gave a low humourless laugh.

'Yes,' she murmured. 'The shock came from Hugo.'

'He upset you?'

'No, he would never hurt me. It was a realisation I had from the simplest of his comments, and it meant that the true awfulness of my actions was revealed to me in stark and terrible clarity.'

She had not noticed the tear sliding down her cheek until George wiped it away.

'Tell me,' he urged. 'It can't be worse than my behaviour.'

'It was,' whispered Alice, 'it was far worse.'

'The man you fell in love with, was he married?'

'Yes,' she replied. 'He was married with a child, and his wife was expecting another, and yet I agreed to flee with him to America to enter into a bigamous marriage of our own.' When George did not reply, she looked at him, 'You're shocked?'

'I'd guessed some of it, and you're not entirely to blame...'

'Hugo said the same thing, but I *am* to blame. It was my responsibility to say no.'

'It was his responsibility to behave with more respect towards his wife and children, and towards you.'

'There is more,' she said, bracing herself to see the disgust in his eyes, to watch as he walked away, never to speak to her again.

'Tell me,' he said. 'Nothing you could say would shock me.'

Alice sighed. George was perfect. Her heart, which she had thought would never recover, was pounding with an intensity she had never felt even for Ephraim, yet she knew her words were about to destroy their burgeoning affection.

'His name was Ephraim Lockwood,' she said, and George's eyebrows raised in surprise, 'and the reason I am such an appalling person is because Ephraim is married to my elder sister, Petronella. I was a bridesmaid at their wedding, I am godmother to their son. She is my sister, yet I did not refuse her husband's advances. No matter what anyone says, I should have said no, but I didn't, and there may never be a way to repair the damage and pain I have inflicted upon my family.'

29

Heat radiated off the walls; this far into the earth, no soft ocean breeze cooled the air. Incense burned, disguising the scent of blood, sweat and fear, but it would never eradicate it. The smell was as ingrained as the secrets she protected. Alone, she waited, knowing it would not be long and their pact would be made. Each heartbeat drew him closer, each dragging step, until, without turning, she knew he was waiting, his shadow huge and monstrous in the torchlight.

'What have you brought me, sister?' he rasped, his voice broken with sadness and despair.

As she turned, her golden hair shone in the gloom, a beacon of hope.

'If you wish it, brother, I have brought you freedom. A way to end your misery.'

Tears welled in his eyes and as the siblings embraced, he whispered, 'Yes, Ariadne, let it be the end. No more of this torture. I am ready to leave.'

30

Marina swung the Jeep into the staff car park and Eloise picked up her handbag.

'We'll use the front entrance,' Marina said, 'then you can see the museum in all its glory.'

It was three days since Eloise had heard the news about Nahjib. By the time John and Steve had begun laying the tables around them for the early evening diners, her afternoon with Claud at the Brewery Taverna had come to a natural end. After the second bottle of wine, they had switched to fizzy water and coffee. When Marina and Yiannis arrived with a wine delivery, they had offered to drive Eloise home, Marina with Eloise in the 2CV while Yiannis followed in their 4x4. Claud returned to his apartment with the promise he would call her the moment he heard anything.

Since then the news about Nahjib had been growing more positive with each day. Eloise and Claud chatted on the phone but they had not seen each other since. The question of whether Claud would return to the UK continued to hang in the balance. Eloise was surprised when she discovered the thought of him leaving made her feel disgruntled. It was a relief when Marina had popped in one morning and, after seeing the photographs Eloise had taken of the standing stone, suggested a trip to her usual workplace, the Heraklion Museum.

'These are the clearest images I've ever seen,' she had said. 'The printer and enhancement software at the museum will be far superior to Quinn's.'

Marina led Eloise along the front of the low sand-coloured building, the tall central section giving the impression of a medieval tower. Ornate grilles opened on to a bustling courtyard, but what caused Eloise to pause and stare was the banner. Advertising the Minoan galleries and their treasures, it bore the image of the magnificent snake goddess. Bare-breasted, with snakes in either hand, she wore a multi-layered patterned skirt. Her gaze, staring across the millennia, had lost none of its power. Balanced on her head was the figure of a cat. Whether it was a hat or supposed to be a real feline, Eloise was unsure, but it was imposing rather than amusing.

'Come, there's more inside,' said Marina, and Eloise could tell her friend was enjoying being the person to introduce her to the true spectacle of the Minoans.

Waving her staff security pass, Marina led Eloise through a side door and they walked down the corridor to the offices.

'We can leave our things in my office,' said Marina, 'and Cosmo, my assistant, has said he'll print out the images. I want to see how well the writing can be enhanced before we run off multiple copies.'

'Are you going to tell your team where they were taken?' asked Eloise.

'Of course,' said Marina. 'If the markings prove to be significant, we might be able to raise funds to excavate.'

Eloise felt a shiver of fear at the thought, and for a moment she wondered if showing Marina the photos had been a good idea. But she knew she was being silly. Marina had known about the markings for years, and the excitement Eloise's images had caused was thanks to the unexpected clarity from the shaft of sunlight. Perhaps it was meant to be, she thought, and the fear dissipated.

'Come on, let's go and see the treasure,' Marina said, and Eloise followed her into the Minoan galleries.

* * *

For an hour, they wandered through the relics of the past. Eloise was spellbound. Cabinets of intricate gold jewellery glittered in serried ranks, vast storage jars almost as big as Eloise were lined along the walls, statues of people, animals and mythical creatures were everywhere she looked. Another gallery displayed ornately carved marble furniture, while nearby was a vast section of a wall with images of men and women dressed in sweeping elegant robes, their expressions haughty, and although Eloise found it odd the men seemed each to be carrying a reclining leopard. Ceramic vases decorated with sinuous octopi, frescoes of sea creatures, images of bulls and the acrobatic bull dancers allowed Eloise to imagine the colour and spectacle of this lost civilisation and its vibrant people.

Women predominated, represented in positions of power, but whether they were being depicted as priestesses, queens, princesses or goddesses was impossible to tell. The cabinet containing the effigy of the bare-breasted Snake Goddess that Arthur Evans discovered in his third digging season in June 1903 made Eloise gasp in surprise.

'I completely understand your interest in female power within the Minoan religion,' Eloise said as she and Marina peered at the bewitching figurines.

'The women are certainly difficult to ignore,' Marina grinned, pointing Eloise towards another vast display showing the upper bodies, bare breasts and raised arms of larger female figures. 'There were so many depictions found representing goddess worship.'

'No wonder this became Arthur Evans's life's work,' said Eloise. 'The number of finds is staggering.'

'These days, modern archaeologists look at the methods Arthur Evans used and cringe,' Marina said as they wandered through the galleries. 'He hacked through layers and layers of archaeology to reach the Minoans. Who knows what other history was lost along the way? Despite this, he did discover and preserve a huge amount of information, so we have to forgive him the ignorance of his time. It was not intentional destruction and, while his rebuilding of the palace is dubious, he did create a version of how the Minoans might have lived. Who are we to argue with it? He may have been correct.'

Marina's phone pinged and as she read the message, she smiled.

'We'll head back to the office. Ezio and Selene have an update on your figurine.'

Weaving their way through the hushed and awed crowds of tourists, Marina let them through a discreet side door, leading the way back to her office. After introducing her colleagues, Ezio and Selene, Marina stepped back, her eyes sparkling, and Eloise wondered what information they were about to share.

'Your figurine,' said Ezio, not quite able to suppress his grin, 'is, as far as we can tell, unique.'

'Really?' said Eloise.

'We've searched the records and, while there are a vast number of female statuettes, there is only one record suggesting a smaller stone depiction of a woman but the piece has vanished,' said Selene. 'From this we assume it was either lost, stolen or disintegrated, as many of the pieces did when they were exposed to the air.'

'If your figure is this missing artefact,' said Ezio, 'her appearance, which is so different from the other goddess statues, suggests her origins might not be Minoan Knossos.'

'What do you mean?' asked Eloise.

'Assuming she was found at the Minoan dig, this would point to her either being contemporary – which we doubt – or, more likely, pre-dating the Minoans. And as she's carved from greenschist, which is part of the volcanic bedrock of the island, this makes me think she's older than the rest of the finds from Arthur Evans's site.'

'Earlier than Bronze Age?'

'We think so,' he replied. 'It would have taken a skilled artisan to carve such a delicate piece and the work in your sculpture is exquisite. Greenschist tends to flake and can split, but whoever made this knew how to work with the natural grain. We think she may have been baked in some sort of primitive kiln, too, to ensure the pigments remained on the porous rock.'

'The question is,' said Selene, 'where did she come from and where did your father-in-law find her?'

'I've no idea, but I'm hoping there might be information about her in his paperwork, which I'm still sorting out. Would you be able to date her?'

'It might be possible,' said Ezio, 'but it could damage her. However, our best guess at an age is that she might be older than the Minoans by five hundred to a thousand years.'

'This is astonishing,' said Eloise, then she realised Ezio was staring at her.

'Your necklace,' he said, 'where did you get it?'

'Another present from my father-in-law,' she replied. 'Why?'

'It reminds me of a description of a piece that was in the records of the first year of the Knossos dig but, again, we've never found it. During the intervening years, it disappeared.'

'What are you suggesting?' asked Eloise, a sense of unease creeping across her.

'If your father-in-law found these in his house or garden, it's possible you're sitting on an unexplored, ancient site, which could have been the original source of these pieces. They could easily have been taken to Knossos or the area around it from elsewhere on the island, or even been washed down there in the flood that destroyed Knossos.'

Eloise stared at them in confusion.

'You think Quinn found these?' she said. 'I had assumed he'd bought them at an antique stall.'

'It's possible he bought them but remember, Quinn had difficulty with his mobility. My first thought was that he might have discovered them at Sfragida House,' said Marina. 'When did Quinn give you the necklace?'

'As a wedding present, four years ago.'

'He was having building work done around then,' said Marina. 'I remember because Thea was toddling and Quinn would come to our place to avoid the noise. He taught her to play hopscotch and once she'd mastered it, she forced us all to play.'

'Marina said your father-in-law was a collector,' said Ezio. 'Have you found any other unusual items?'

'No, nothing yet,' said Eloise. 'The bulk of his collection is contemporary. He loved supporting local artists and craftspeople.'

The door opened and Cosmo entered, a stack of fresh printouts under his arm, a grin on his face.

'These images are stunning,' he said, laying them out in front of Eloise, Marina, Ezio and Selene. 'Look at what it says.'

He pointed to the close-up of the hieroglyphics and, as Marina examined them, she gasped, her eyes wide with surprise.

ᛏᛞᛉᛏᚲ,ᛌᚾᛉᛂ,

'What does it mean?' asked Eloise, but Marina had skirted around them, pulled a large book off the shelf and was flicking through it with urgency. Ezio and Selene leaned over her shoulder and, with a flurry of excited Greek between them, they began examining line after line of the unusual writing.

'This one,' said Marina, pointing to an image halfway down the page. 'It's definitely this inscription.'

Eloise could feel her frustration growing and was about to ask again when Marina spun the book round for her to see, pointing at an image identical to the carvings from the standing stone in the grove. Eloise read its translation.

'*Potnia* of the Labyrinth,' she said, and her eyes widened in surprise.

'The stone is a tribute to the priestess of the labyrinth,' said Marina. 'Eloise, this is a huge discovery.'

31

On the journey home, Eloise and Marina discussed the multiple meanings of all they had found out, their excitement growing.

'Do you think I might be able to tempt you away from medical research into becoming an historian?' Marina asked.

'Perhaps,' Eloise said. The idea did not seem preposterous.

'Is there anything in Alice's diaries that might elucidate things further?' asked Marina, as they let themselves into Sfragida House.

'Actually, yes,' said Eloise. 'Have you ever read the transcripts?'

Marina shook her head. 'Quinn offered them to me but I've never found the time to actually look at them.'

'I think you should,' said Eloise. 'Alice Webster was a fascinating woman. In her journal she records finding a large clear crystal and a figurine on the first day she spent at the dig with Arthur Evans.'

'My great-great-grandmother found similar items?' said Marina in surprise.

'Your... what?' said Eloise in astonishment. 'Alice Webster was your great-great-grandmother?'

'Yes,' said Marina. 'Did Quinn never tell you? It's the reason we had the diaries, but, as I told you, my grandmother, Elena, didn't want them. She was a very forward-looking woman, but she had her superstitious side and she believed they were cursed.'

'Cursed. Why?'

'She claimed they gave her bad dreams,' said Marina, but before Eloise could question her further about this, she continued, 'Anyway, when she discovered Quinn was interested in the dig, she mentioned them to him. He was offering a great deal of money and she knew he would respect the journals, so she sold them. I'm sorry, Eloise, I thought you knew.'

'You're related to Alice,' gasped Eloise, her mind whirring. 'Then you might be able to tell me the end of the story.'

'What do you mean?' asked Marina.

'The final entry in Quinn's diary says, "At last, I have found the remainder of Alice's journals. Maybe I'll find out what happened after the wedding…" but he died a week later and I've no idea what he discovered.'

Marina squeezed Eloise's hand. 'There are two more diaries. Quinn found them with another box of books he had bought from Grandma. We discussed it not long before he died.'

Eloise stared at her in astonishment. 'Where are they?' she asked, her voice urgent.

'In the study, I believe,' said Marina, but Eloise was already running down the spiral staircase.

'Here,' said Marina, following Eloise inside. She pointed to a small cupboard beside one of the bookcases where a cardboard storage box stood. It was a little battered, a marked contrast to the other neat ranks of boxes and files. Written on the top, with the date that Quinn had bought them, were the words:

Books from the vineyard

'He put them back in here for safekeeping,' said Marina,

opening the box and sorting through the assortment of leather-bound books.

The majority were written in Greek, but at the bottom was a *Complete Works of Shakespeare*, in English, a copy of Charles Dickens's *Great Expectations* in French, and two more journals, one with a red leather binding matching Alice's journals, while the other was in green. Marina grinned as she handed them to Eloise.

'This is like finding buried treasure,' Eloise said.

'I shall leave you to explore,' said Marina. 'I have to get back. Call me if you need anything.'

'Thank you,' said Eloise, tearing her eyes away from the two notebooks. 'You're a life saver. Perhaps, when I've read these, if I have any queries about Alice…?'

She left the question hanging and Marina nodded.

'Someone in my family will be able to help,' she said. 'They might be able to shed some light on the figurine, too.'

'One more thing. Do you know if there are any photographs of Alice?' Eloise asked.

Marina paused. 'I'll ask Mama,' she replied, then with a cheery '*Ta léme*' she let herself out through the side door.

* * *

Eloise ran upstairs to fetch herself a drink, then returned to the table where she gathered her own notebook, laptop and Quinn's red journal. Beside these she laid the two new journals, a thrill of anticipation running though her. Checking Quinn's notebook again, in the margin on the previous page to his final comment was the faint, pencil-written message:

Two more journals discovered in the box of miscellaneous books. What a relief!

Eloise could have cheered. Quinn must have read the diaries but had passed away before he could transcribe them.

Staring at the battered books, Eloise wondered what these final journals might reveal. When she had read Alice's heart-breaking confession, she had felt the other woman's pain reaching across time. While in her journal Alice berated herself, placing the entire blame for the affair on her own shoulders, Eloise could not help feeling she had been targeted and groomed by her unpleasant brother-in-law. Eloise found it easy to imagine how Ephraim's behaviour must have torn the Webster family apart and wondered whether his marriage to Petronella, Alice's older sister, had survived.

Forcing herself to curb her imagination, she placed the red journal to one side and opened the green book to ascertain whether the different colour signified a different sort of memoir, perhaps a more scientific record of the dig. A cold shiver ran down her spine, when on the first page, she saw the heading:

My Dreams

Throughout the other journals, Alice had captured snippets of her dreams but it had never occurred to Eloise that she would have a dedicated journal for them. Eloise stared at it, her hands trembling as she wondered for the first time if the two transcripts, hers and Alice's, would fit together. The book fell open, the spine at the back broken with age and overuse, and Eloise glanced at the page it revealed.

'How is that possible?' she gasped.

On the final page there was a poem. Pulling her laptop towards her, Eloise opened her own dream diary and typed a few words into the search bar at the top of the document. A page appeared and Eloise began comparing them. Word by word, line by line, her sense of unease grew as she checked again and again. As a child, Eloise had loved to write poetry, all of which had been overblown and grandiose, until one morning she had awoken from one of her dreams with words running around her head. The dream diary was still a new and exciting game and, feeling very grown-up, the twelve-year-old Eloise had scribbled out a poem.

This rush of words had never happened before or since, and now, staring at the page in the journal, Eloise was unsure how to react. In Alice Webster's notebook, the date beside the poem was 23 May 1900. Exactly one hundred years later, to the day, Eloise had written the identical poem in her own diary.

Eloise's hand went to the crystal around her neck and she yelped, as though it had burned her fingers. The connections were becoming too strong: the crystal that matched the description of the one Alice had found, the uncanny appearance of the figurine, the increasing similarity of their dreams. Even the fact that fate had conspired to deliver her to this island, the home to a myth she had dreamed about since childhood. Through these various twists of destiny, she was the owner of a property beside the fabled labyrinth. The house, she was beginning to suspect, was the same property described in Alice's journals. And now the poem: the strangest coincidence yet.

Her mind flew to the idea of the Akashic Record, the repository of consciousness of the whole of humankind since the beginning of time. Could it be real? Was this the source of these bizarre connections? Had traces of the Minoans been left behind on their belongings, as Alice had suggested? Tiny fragments of their lives unearthed after centuries in the ground, links from another time, joining her to a woman who had lived over one hundred years earlier? The thought made Eloise shiver.

Then she thought of her dream of the previous night. She had returned to the shadowy labyrinth, experiencing the hug between siblings, the promise of release, and for the first time since her dreams had begun there was the bewitching name: Ariadne. For as long as she could remember, these dreams had spoken to her but this was new and she could not help but feel a small *frisson* of fear with the discovery of the identity of her dream-self.

Eloise had finally realised that the obvious truth lay in front of her: she needed to weave the dreams together and they would reveal the story of the Minotaur and his sister, Ariadne. The woman Eloise believed was the fabled *Potnia* of the Labyrinth.

For the next few hours, Eloise worked, moving between her own dreams and Alice's, finding the spaces in her own tale, discovering with each turn of the page of the green journal the remains of the story. When her phone rang, she was so engrossed she physically jumped.

Claud's name flashed on the screen.

'Hi,' she said, 'what's up?'

'Nahjib's awake,' Claud replied, his voice resonating with relief.

'Thank goodness,' gasped Eloise. 'How is he? Does he remember anything?'

'Yes, all of it, but she's done such a good job on him his first question was to ask how Marcella was coping without him,' said Claud, and Eloise closed her eyes to push away the familiar feeling of anxiety.

'Where is Marcella?'

'She's been charged and remanded in custody. The judge felt she was a flight risk.'

'How did Nahjib react?'

'At first, horrified, but according to Martin, he's coming to terms with the situation. His parents are with him but his father is shattered to think what Nahjib has suffered. I spoke to the consultant and Nahjib's physical recovery is good, but his mental health is fragile. Just between us, Lo, he's all over the place. Martin has asked if I could go home for a few days as he thinks we could help. I know how happy you are here, so I won't ask you to come back too, but will you be all right?'

Eloise was half gratified that he should care enough to ask and half infuriated at his assumption she needed to be looked after. She and Claud had not spent much time together and she could not understand why he would even ask.

'Of course,' she replied. 'You have to do what's best for Nahjib. Have you spoken to your auntie Faye?'

'Yes, this morning, she's going to find him some specialist help, too.'

Relief swept through Eloise. Of all Josh's friends, she had liked Nahjib the most, and the thought that he had been suffering such trauma at the hands of Marcella, and that she hadn't noticed, devastated her.

'Will you be coming back?' she asked when Claud had finished explaining he would be leaving the following day.

'Do you want me to?' he asked, and where she had expected to hear his usual teasing, swaggering bravado, instead, his tone was hesitant.

'It's your choice,' she replied, her defences in place, then she softened, remembering Claud's distress over Nahjib, his tales of his past and the afternoon they had spent together in the sunshine 'But, yes, it would be good to have you back again. Perhaps, if he's well enough to travel, you could bring Nahjib. A complete break might do him good. You'd both be welcome to stay here. Do you want to come here for dinner this evening? We could work out the logistics.'

The invitation had come from nowhere and as soon as it was out, she wondered what demon had possessed her.

'Thank you,' he said, 'I'd love to come to dinner, and I'll discuss things with Nahjib when I'm home. What time?'

'Whenever you feel like coming. I can cook for us.'

There was a pause and Eloise wondered if he would prefer not to come. She was about to withdraw the invitation when he said, 'I need to pack but I can be with you in an hour. Is that too soon?'

An unexpected thrill of excitement fluttered through her.

'Sounds good to me. See you later.'

Hanging up, she looked at the phone and wondered again what had possessed her to invite Claud to Sfragida House. She turned back to the diaries and tried to concentrate, but her mind wandered towards what food she could serve.

A barbecue, she thought, then Claud will insist on cooking, as what man can resist the lure of the coals?

Her mind went back to the night with Rose, Leon and their sons, as she remembered the storytelling around the firepit. They would be returning soon to spend two weeks during the school holidays, and she was excited at the thought, calculating the space in the house, which she realised would accommodate the Hay family, even if Claud and Nahjib were staying. Her parents were considering a few days in the sun, too, as were her siblings and their families. A happy glow suffused her at the thought of being able to share this treasured space with those she loved.

'Although first,' she muttered to herself, 'there's Claud.'

To her surprise, she realised she was impatient to see him again.

32

'What an intriguing story,' said Claud as Eloise talked him through all she had learned from the transcribed journals. 'Alice's reasoning about the Minotaur suffering from the same condition as Joseph Merrick is an interesting hypothesis.'

'That's the answer of a doctor,' said Eloise. 'Although, I've been thinking along similar lines. The condition was discovered by Michael Cohen in 1979 but it wasn't named until 1983 when Hans-Rudolf Wiedemann called it Proteus Syndrome. He took his inspiration from the shape-shifting Greek god of the sea. In the list of deities from the Linear B tablets, Proteus is one of the early pantheon of gods.'

'As is Dionysus, isn't he?' Claud asked. 'The god of wine. Strange that there was a vineyard at the heart of Alice's story.'

They were on the cushioned seats at the large table by the side of the swimming pool. Behind them, the barbecue was cooling in the sultry evening heat and Eloise reached across the table to take another olive. Although she had discussed the details of Alice's life with Claud, Eloise had not mentioned the dreams. They felt like a private matter between her and the woman who was long dead, and she wasn't ready to trust him with anything so personal.

'It's odd that she discovered a stone similar to the one Quinn gave you,' said Claud. 'Do you think it's the same one?'

'For a while, I wondered, but if that was the case, how would Alice have acquired it?'

'She could have bought it,' suggested Claud.

'True, but I don't think Arthur Evans was interested in selling the items. He either shipped them back to the Ashmolean or donated them to the museum he helped to set up here.'

'Perhaps Evans made an exception for Alice,' suggested Claud.

'It's possible,' Eloise agreed. 'If Josh hadn't insisted on having this valued,' her hand went to her pendant, 'I would have assumed it was a copy, but it was confirmed as zircon and ancient.'

'The mystery might be solved in the final book,' said Claud, sipping his brandy.

The starlight glimmered in the honey-coloured liquid and Eloise picked up her own balloon glass, swirling it around in her hands, lost in thought. Claud had arrived in under an hour, with a bottle of Metaxa brandy, and a fresh loaf of Cretan bread and olives donated by John and Steve. They had settled at the table where Eloise had told him about her day with Marina and he had asked to see the carvings in the photograph.

'They remind me of Neolithic rock carvings from Roughting Linn in Northumberland,' he had said.

'You're a mine of information,' Eloise had laughed. 'Tell me more.'

'It's one of the largest known decorated outcrops in the UK,' he had continued with a shy grin. 'There are all sorts of patterns and a few are similar to these letters. Is this a solo project or could we puzzle it out together?'

'Would you be interested?'

'I love the Neolithic era,' he'd said. 'It's fascinating because it was the time when tribes evolved from hunter gatherers to farming and raising livestock. These people built Stonehenge and hundreds of other monuments, too. As it cuts across the timeline of Knossos, I thought I might be able to help, but only if it isn't an intrusion.'

'Perhaps you should have studied history rather than medicine,' Eloise had said as he had pulled the chair up beside her and they both began examining Quinn's papers.

'I wanted to help people, and medicine was the best option. The history is a hobby that helps to keep me grounded when I have troubling issues to deal with at work or home.'

Eloise had wanted to ask what these were, hoping this could be a place where he was able to discuss his problems, but he'd changed the subject, riffling through Quinn's books and asking her about Linear B. For the rest of the afternoon, they had pored over the Linear B pictograms, hypothesising about Linear A and how to go about decoding the unknown language.

'What do you think about the idea of the Akashic Record?' Eloise asked now. She had explained it to Claud while they were discussing the diaries and she hoped his love of the Neolithic might make him open to her theories.

Claud mirrored Eloise's mesmeric swirling of her brandy, considering the question before he replied.

'It's a wonderful thought and I'd love to believe it – the idea that the knowledge of all time is floating somewhere above us,' he said.

'Imagine being able to tap into it, a bit like a cosmic internet.'

Claud grinned in response and Eloise sipped her brandy, happy to have amused him. Staring up at the stars, she thought about Alice and George, Ariadne and Theseus, all the lovers who had ever danced under the beauty of the sparkling night sky.

'Is there something else?' Claud's voice was soft and as she looked up, their eyes locked.

'What do you mean?' she asked.

'I feel as though you're testing me,' he said. 'Seeing whether I trust your reasoning. Whatever you're not telling me, I wish you would; I'll never hurt you, Lo.'

Eloise swallowed, her breath catching in her throat as the prolonged look deepened. There was honesty in Claud's eyes and compassion, both of which unsettled her as she wondered again whether her interpretation of his behaviour over the years had been accurate. It was, after all, Josh who had told her Claud did not like her.

'He can be odd,' Josh had said. 'You have to win him over, a bit like a spoiled child.'

Eloise, finding Josh's easy-going manner attractive, had believed this comment, wondering how two such different men could be friends. After their marriage and the alteration in Josh's behaviour, it had never occurred to her to question his earlier descriptions of people but, as Claud gazed at her, she wondered about their relationship and whether this, too, had been a victim of Josh's violent and controlling nature. Claud had travelled all this way to be near her; this was not the action of someone who despised her.

'Anything you tell me, no matter how outlandish, I won't laugh.'

Eloise continued to stare at him and, suddenly, she knew she could trust him. Where this conviction came from, she could not explain, but it was soul-deep and she realised she wanted to share her discoveries, to tell him everything. She needed to take him into her twilight world because she knew he would listen without judgement and he might help her to make sense of the dreams.

'May I show you something?' she asked.

'Of course,' he replied, and she hurried into the study to collect the printout she had made earlier in the day.

'These,' she said, as she handed him the pages, 'are records of a dream I've been having since childhood.'

'The same dream?' he asked.

'Yes, well, it's the same setting, but the dreams vary,' she said. 'I don't expect you to read it all but what's been so unnerving is that it's clear from Alice's journals that she was having similar dreams.'

Claud looked up in surprise.

'Alice was alive over a hundred years ago.'

'I know, which is why this is so strange,' Eloise said. 'Even more bizarre is the fact that the content of the dream seems to be the story of the Minotaur, and where there are gaps in my version of the story, Alice's fills them in.'

Claud gave her a curious look and, despite his promises, she braced herself for ridicule or disbelief. But, to her relief, neither came. Instead, he gave a thoughtful nod and turned to the dream diary.

'Let me read a few pages, then perhaps it would be better for you to tell me the story.'

'This version is different from the myth we know, but it feels more authentic. Do you think I'm insane?' she asked, her voice trembling.

'You are the sanest person I've ever met,' said Claud, reaching out to take her hand. His thumb found the scar and he frowned but he did not comment. 'Tell me the story, Lo, and we'll work this out together.'

Taking a deep breath, Eloise began to speak, her voice drifting to a timbre she did not recognise, as Ariadne's words began to flow across time.

* * *

* * *

There are many who call me the Goddess of the Labyrinth, and perhaps this is how the tales of the gods and goddesses began, with human folly. I am Ariadne the daughter of Minos and Pasiphae, who claims to be the child of Helios, the sun god. My father is said to be the son of Zeus, and he has the cruelty required to sit within the pantheon of gods, but I wish to be human. I wish to return to dust when my work here is complete, to feel, to love, to cry and to laugh. To be free of my burdens and to release those I love of their prisons, both real and imagined.

Each night, I walk the paths created by the architect Daedalus; the labyrinth beneath the palace, the lair of my brother, Asterion. But he is no monster. He is gentle and there are many who revere him and would make use of his wisdom. But my father is wicked and he uses the strangeness of my brother's appearance to seek revenge on those he believed have wronged him. King Minos has created a cult of religion around our bull-headed boy, and as the daughter who delivered the deformed child, it is my duty to act as his priestess.

Once a year, they arrive, the tributes demanded by my father to provide payment and retribution for the death of my brother, the heir, Androgeus. My father believes the Athenians, ordered by Aegeus, king of Athens, killed Androgeus out of jealousy and spite. After waging war on the Athenians, my father offered a terrible peace: seven boys and seven girls were to be provided as a tribute to Crete each year as food for the vicious Minotaur. Aegeus felt he had no choice but to capitulate. How could he justify the deaths of thousands more if the war were to continue, when instead a mere fourteen could be sacrificed each year? With a heavy heart, he agreed to my father's terms.

Each year King Minos insists on an Olympiad for the tributes to show their skills, in bull dancing – the speciality of my people – and in the parade of the tributes through the streets. When this macabre procession is finished, I lead them through the double doors of the labyrinth; the opening to death, a pathway more shadowy and fearful than the journey across the Rivers Styx and Acheron to Hades, with Charon the ferryman.

They cry and I harden my heart, pausing at the first altar to sacrifice the white bull, the blood pouring in rivulets at our feet. My handmaidens collect the liquid in our thirteen golden goblets, and carry it aloft to the second altar where the libations to the Minotaur are made by candlelight. The blood, sticky with the life of the animal is poured into a channel, where it flickers in a cloying pool, a reminder of the poor beast's sacrifice.

A rope leads the way to the heart of the labyrinth, a cord stained with guilt and betrayal, red, rusty, black with the blood of the bulls. The tributes have no idea what will happen next. Some cry, some scream, a few try to run, but whether they choose to flee or to follow, the paths lead in one direction. One way in. One way out. All lead to the centre where he waits.

And this is where I look back through time and try to mend the tale. My brother was no monster. He was a man, not a beast. He had no desire to partake in the sacrifice of human flesh. His features were strange, his voice rasping, his feet deformed, clawed with pain, making him stumble and shuffle as he walked, but he was kind. When the pain ripped through him, he would roar in misery and despair, but he had no desire to hurt another human, and neither did his fragile bones have the strength.

At the centre was his home, a bed, soft with feather cushions and silken throws, donated by those who believed he could grant their wishes. Food was delivered by my handmaidens and, when he was well, he would play the lyre. We would dance and he would ask me to sing. The tributes expected a violent death but this, like so much else created by the tongues of men, was a lie. For the sake of their lives, we would shelter the tributes for forty days and forty nights, then I would lead them through the labyrinth and release them into my sacred grove, away from the palace of my father.

Boats would deliver them to wherever they chose to travel, and it was no surprise to me that few would request to return to Athens, the city who had sold them into death. When they were free we would go back to the labyrinth and, with my handmaidens, I would nurse my brother and keep him safe. This was the secret of the labyrinth: there is one way in and one way out. Nobody but Daedalus, Asterion and I knew the path that was the way out.

Until the summer Theseus the Boaster arrived. A man who wished to slay a beast, his bloody desire disguised as a quest to free his people. He tricked us with threats and lies, but we did not know this until the blow fell. He offered us freedom on the island of Naxos, for me and my brother, and seduced by his beauty, I placed my trust in a handsome face and a shiver of deceits.

I told him about the grove, the freedom of his people, and he promised to wait, to transport us all to safety. But that night, as Hecate the moon goddess shone her beauty on the stone at the exit of my labyrinth, he waited with his sword and as each person reached their freedom, he cut them down in cold blood. I was the last to leave, stepping into the moonlight, onto a floor that was red with betrayal. Pools of blood, the screams of the dying and Theseus's armour glinting with malice as he held up my brother's head.

When I awoke, I was stranded on the island of Naxos, the home of Dionysus, the god of wine. It was in his arms I found love despite my grief. There are dark tales about my husband, but he was kind, he cared, and when I died he wept.

My myth has been retold so many times but it has always been wrong. It was not a tale of death and violence, it was a story of love. We must trust our hearts and know that love is always the answer, as it will save us from the darkness of our foes. Tread soft through my dreams of love and remember me.

* * *

As Eloise finished, she wiped tears from her eyes. Claud continued to hold her hand and as his thumb stroked the scar he whispered,

'Tell me another story, Eloise. Your scar, when did it happen? Was it the night Josh died? Did you kill him to save yourself?'

33

'You think I was involved in Josh's death?' she said, her whole body shaking as she tried to free herself from Claud's grip, but he wrapped her damaged hand in his grasp with his other hand, his tone imploring.

'Were you?'

Eloise stared at Claud but did not reply.

'This scar, it's fresh,' he said. 'I noticed it the day Nahjib was admitted to hospital, when we were having lunch. What happened, Lo? Josh was a difficult man; we were never close friends. He and Nahjib had been at school together. Nahjib and I were university friends and Martin was my neighbour. We clicked and before we knew it, we were this foursome, but the cracks in the friendships were wide...'

'But you were Josh's best man...' said Eloise.

'He asked me and there were reasons I didn't want to refuse. He said he wouldn't invite me to the wedding if I said no and it was important for me to attend.'

'Why?' she asked, and a pained look crossed Claud's face.

'Did you kill Josh?'

'No,' she whispered.

'The police questioned you...'

An expression of intense compassion and love flickered across Claud's face and Eloise felt the last inch of her reserve vanish.

'I didn't want to show you because he was your friend,' she said, her voice low. 'Despite everything he did, I wanted you to remember him as you saw him. Good old Josh, your best mate, the life and soul of the party, always there for the boys...'

'How do you know I saw him that way?' asked Claud, and his voice too had an edge that made it almost unrecognisable. 'How do you know?'

'How do I know?' gasped Eloise, stopping a burst of sardonic laughter. 'You never left him alone. From the moment he and I met, you were there at his side. Meddling, spying, turning him against me. Perhaps I should have paid attention.'

'Perhaps you should,' agreed Claud. 'I never tried to turn him against you, I love...'

'Loved him?'

'No, not him.'

Josh's crude jokes about Claud having a married lover and Claud's own confession, *I was in love with someone who was unavailable*, the photograph, the dance, the weekends away. Eloise's mind was whirring. She stood and her legs were shaking. Then she ran inside and up the spiral staircase. She had never wanted to show anyone this, but Claud would accept nothing less than the truth and if she did not let him see it for himself, he would never believe her. The police hadn't when they had arrived to question her, but Rose had discovered the tiny camera, Eloise had shown it to the police and then they had understood.

Her suitcase was stored in the spare bedroom. Retrieving the key from her bedside table, she unlocked it and pulled out the laptop, the seal on the police evidence bag unbroken. Grabbing the charger, she returned to the patio where Claud waited. He had not moved, his face bloodless in the setting sun, and when she ripped open the tape and handed him the MacBook, he looked confused.

'Why was it in an evidence bag?' he asked.

'The police took it, but after they had seen the content and dropped the charges, it was returned to me. I don't know why I brought the laptop with me – perhaps because I didn't want anyone else to have it. Like you, the police thought I'd murdered Josh. Although in their imaginations, they thought it was a sex game gone wrong.'

'What?' Claud's voice was like a thunderclap.

'The day after Josh died, the police became suspicious, but unwittingly, Josh provided me with a cast-iron alibi.'

'What do you mean?'

'Josh had bugged the house,' she said, her voice low, shaking with anger and the residue of fear she had not yet managed to overcome when she discussed her late husband. 'Our own house. He'd installed hidden cameras in every room so he could watch me. The police also discovered a tracker on my phone, which I had no idea about.'

'He... what?' Claud's face was ashen.

'Josh liked filming himself, too,' she continued, trying not to cry. 'There are hours and hours of footage of Josh talking to the camera, describing his fantasies in vivid detail. There are also files showing his sexual exploits with numerous women, including Davina.'

At this, Eloise looked up and saw Claud's devastated face.

'I'm sorry,' she said. 'He was so high on coke on the night of his death, he must have forgotten about the camera in the kitchen. Either that or he was going to delete the footage, afterwards. Rose found the first bug after the police invited me down to the station to question me. She then demanded Josh's laptop was examined and they found the files. I have to plug this in. You should watch it in the study. I can't sit through it again.'

Eloise walked inside and plugged in Josh's laptop, waiting as it whirred into life. As she keyed in her late husband's password, Claud joined her, his face hidden in shadow as she searched the files; relieved they were intact after the police investigation. Opening the file dated the night of Josh's death, she gave Claud one last chance.

'When Rose saw this, in her capacity as my legal representative the day after Josh's death, she vomited. Are you sure you want to see it?'

'Yes,' he replied, taking his place beside her like an automaton.

'Press play whenever you're ready,' she said. 'I'll be waiting for you upstairs in the living room, if you want to speak afterwards.'

Eloise collected her brandy glass from the table and, leaving the French doors ajar, she walked away, up the spiral staircase to the living room, where she lit the lamps and, despite the warmth of the night, pulled a blanket over her legs. Topping up her brandy glass, Eloise stared at the livid scar on her palm, then hearing her own voice float up from the study like a warning, she began to sob as she relived the night she thought she was going to die.

* * *

Three Months Earlier

'Josh, are you home?' Eloise called as she opened the door, praying there would be no response. For a moment, hope soared. Then he appeared in the kitchen doorway, a large glass of red wine in his hand.

'Where have you been?' he snarled.

'Having a drink with the people from work,' she replied, unbelting her raincoat and hanging it on one of the hooks in the hallway.

'Why didn't you let me know?'

'I did. I texted, telling you where I was and inviting you to join us.'

Josh gave a snort of derision, stumbling as he took a step towards her, and Eloise realised he was more than drunk, he was high. Fear quivered through her.

'As if I'd want to spend my night with you and the nerds from the lab,' he sneered. 'Bunch of posh, loser twats.'

Eloise did not respond. There was no reasoning with Josh when he was in this mood. Her safest option was to remove herself from his vicinity until he either passed out or found another distraction, usually hard-core porn, which revolted her.

'I've a migraine coming on,' she said. 'I'm going to bed.'

'No, you're not,' he growled. 'Not until I give you permission.'

Eloise hesitated, taking a small step backwards, wondering whether to make a run for it into the rainy April night. Her handbag was by the front door, she could grab it as she left and head for Rose's house in a cab. Thankful she had changed into flat shoes before her journey home, she knew she would be able to outrun Josh in his present condition. Whether her flight instinct flashed across her face, she had no idea, but the second she had considered the plan, Josh moved. He darted forward with an almost super-human speed and grasped her wrist, dragging her down the hallway and into their large open-plan kitchen-living room.

'Oh, no, you don't,' he hissed as he flung her against the kitchen island causing her to wince as her side caught the edge of the marble worktop. 'No running away for you, Mrs Winter. It's time we shared some family time. You and me, husband and wife. There were things you agreed to when we took our vows, rules you promised to follow in the eyes of God and in front of over one hundred witnesses. To honour and obey...'

'No, I didn't,' whispered Eloise, her eyes darting around, looking for a weapon. But, as usual, the worktops were empty, pristine. Josh had always claimed he hated clutter and she had agreed to stowing everything in drawers, throwing away the antique knife block she had bought when they had first moved in together. Josh stood between her and the knife drawer.

'What do you mean?' he asked, stepping forward, too close, invading her personal space.

'I said "honour and cherish",' she replied, adrenaline giving her the courage to stare him in the eye.

'Well, I must have been distracted by your cute arse to allow you to leave out the word "obey",' he hissed, his fingers kneading into her flesh, pinching her. Eloise didn't react to that, knowing this would increase his enjoyment and not wishing to give him any excuse to escalate the violence.

'Allow?' she said, but a feeling of hatred and anger rose up. Despite her fear, she could not quash her instinct to fight and she snapped, 'You aren't in a position to "allow" me to do anything. I make my own decisions.'

'You're my wife.'

'Yes, your wife, not your sex slave.'

The blow across her face made her ears ring and white lights pop before her eyes.

'Do you love me?' he snarled, his face so close to hers she could smell the wine on his breath, see the residue of cocaine on his nostrils as his bloodshot eyes glared into hers.

'No,' she gasped, her breathing ragged as the pain from his blow resonated through her body. She groaned as a well-aimed punch to her kidneys made her double up.

'Let's try again, darling wife. Do you love me?'

His hands were in her hair, pulling her back into a standing position.

'No,' she said.

'Oh dear, I hoped it wouldn't come to this...' and to Eloise's horror, he reached across and pulled a large knife from the drawer.

Lifting her right hand, he held the blade to her palm.

'Do you love me?' he asked, and she was sickened to see the glee and excitement in his eyes, how he revelled in her fear and pain. Forcing away her momentary spark of self-defence, she realised, with Josh brandishing a knife, it would be safer to play along, so she nodded. 'Say it,' he commanded, pushing the blade harder on to her hand.

'I love you,' she whispered.

'Do you?' he asked, his head on one side, like a demented child. 'Do you really, though? What will you do to prove it?'

'Josh, please, stop,' she gasped.

'Not until I'm satisfied you love me. I have an idea. If you write, "I love you" and sign it with kisses, I'll know you're telling the truth.'

'Yes, I will...' she agreed, hoping this would be enough to satisfy him and then he would release her.

'Good girl,' he murmured, bringing his mouth to hers, forcing his tongue inside as he kissed her. Eloise tried to respond but tears were running down her face and terror filled her.

'Where shall I write it?' she asked, praying if she played along, he would leave her alone.

'On the floor,' he whispered, running his finger down her cheek in the parody of a lover's touch, 'in blood.'

'What?'

'And then I'm going to take what's rightfully mine, whether you want to give it or not Mrs Winter.'

The blade flashed across her palm and blood spurted from the cut. Josh knocked Eloise's knees from under her, forcing her onto the floor.

'Write "I love you" in your own blood on the floor,' he laughed, his eyes wild. 'Then I'll believe you love me and I might not slit your throat.'

He threw her forward, pushing her face down on the white marble floor, his foot in her back.

'Write it, you bitch. Persuade me to let you live. After all, you're worth more to me dead,' and Eloise, in terror for her life, tears blotching the drops of blood, did as he commanded. Josh kicked her in the side, then turned away and chopped out two more lines of cocaine, which he snorted before pouring himself a glass of red wine, watching her efforts with amusement.

Ten minutes later, she sat back on her heels, wondering if she had the strength to fight Josh off and make a bid for freedom through the front door. He was drunk, high, unstable and she was sober and pumping with adrenaline. The jagged words were sprawled across the white floor.

I love you

'Aww, wifey, you're so sweet,' laughed Josh. 'Do you? I love you.'

As he stood, he stumbled again, this time knocking over the wine glass, sending it skittering across the kitchen island and into the air, falling as though in slow motion, landing on the marble floor beside Eloise, exploding in a shower of glass and red wine. Eloise screamed, throwing herself out of the way, her reactions instinctive. Behind her, she heard the click of his belt as he unbuckled it and slid it from his trousers.

'You've been a very naughty girl,' he said, whipping the belt around his head like a lasso, the sinister whooshing sound of the leather sending more tremors of fear through Eloise. 'Unless you're undressed and lying naked on the floor, waiting for me by the time I've counted to ten, you know the consequences.'

Eloise could not bear it. How was this happening? How had her marriage dissolved into this violence?

'One,' he began, in a childish sing-song voice as though they were playing hide and seek. 'And after each number, I want you to say, "I love you."'

Eloise shuddered. She knew his threats were not empty. He would rape, then beat her and, the mood he was in, she feared he would not stop until she was dead. Defiance roared through her misery and despair. Who was he to treat her this way? The will to survive flickered through her like a flame. He would not prevail, so Eloise turned and, despite the heart-stopping fear that he would kill her at any moment, gave him her most seductive smile as she began to unbutton her shirt.

'Say it, bitch,' he screamed, with a total and shocking loss of control.

'I love you,' she managed, her throat constricting with fear again, all pretence at enjoyment in order to try to appease him slipping from her face.

'Good girl,' he said, his voice cold with malice. 'Two, you'd better hurry, my darling. I don't want to have to punish you but you know I will. After all, it's for your own good.'

'I love you.'

'Three,' said Josh, grinning. 'There, it isn't difficult to please me, is it?'

'I love you...'

'Four, five, six...'

He had increased the pace and Eloise's fingers scrambled with her remaining buttons. He faltered and his arm spasmed, there was a clatter as the belt hit the marble floor.

'I love you. I love you. I love you...'

'Seven,' he gasped. 'Say it again, Eloise, this time like you mean it, I love you...' but Eloise was staring at him in horror. The colour was leeching from his skin, turning it a putrid grey, his arm fell to his side.

'I love you,' she whispered.

Before he could say the next number, his knees buckled underneath him and he reached out, beseeching, unable to form words as he struggled to breathe. Eloise was frozen to the spot as Josh fell forwards, his eyes rolling, his tongue lolling, face down in the wine, blood and glass. *I love you*: their final words to each other.

Eloise stared at his unmoving form, not comprehending, wondering if he was about to leap back up, whether this was part of the torture. Several minutes passed and her ragged, fearful breathing was the only noise in the ice-white kitchen.

'Josh,' she whispered, nudging him with a toe but there was no response. 'Josh,' she said, her voice louder, stronger. 'Josh, stop this, it isn't funny.'

Dropping to her knees, ignoring the pain in her hand, she crawled through the mess on the floor and grabbed Josh by the shoulders.

'Josh,' she shouted, shaking him as though trying to wake him, but as she stared at his parted lips, edged with blue, his half-closed eyes, his grey skin, she knew the combination of drink, drugs and whatever else he might have imbibed that night had wreaked havoc on his body. For a moment she stared at him, a wave of relief sweeping through her, followed by the hysterical urge to laugh. Then her medical training kicked in. Taking a deep breath, she rolled him on to his back and began checking for signs of life: lifting his eyelids, searching for a pulse.

'Come on, Josh, breathe,' she muttered. Despite everything, she had never wanted him dead.

She scrambled to her feet, ran to the hallway, retrieved her phone from her handbag and, putting it on speaker, dialled 999. Placing it on the floor beside her, she began compressions on Josh's unresponsive chest as she requested an ambulance and the police, telling them she was a doctor and instructing them what to bring as she tried to bring her husband back from the dead, even though she knew it was too late. Josh Winter was dead and despite her shock, Eloise had to force herself to stop the smile spreading across her face. She was free.

* * *

From somewhere downstairs in Sfragida House, Eloise heard the side door slam. Taking measured steps, she followed the curve of the spiral staircase and entered the study. It was empty. Claud had gone. Burying her face in her hands, Eloise began to cry.

34

A soft scraping of bone on rock guided her footsteps. Pausing in the entrance to his lair, she waited for him to notice her presence.

'Is it another necklace?' she asked, her fingers sweeping through the glistening crystals adorning her neck, each carved by him with images of their childhood and their darkened lives below ground. When he looked towards her, his grotesque features creased into a smile, a sweet, gentle smile, revealing the man he could have been if fate had not played such a cruel game.

'No, a statue.'

'Of Father?'

His snort of laughter made her smile too.

'It's you,' he said, and held out the delicate carving in his scarred and deformed hands.

35

'As the Paris Olympiad doesn't finish until the end of October, I've promised the boys we could attend during the last week. Robert is obsessed with the idea of winning medals. He's requested that Alice help him to write a letter of admiration to the weight-lifter, Launceston Elliot, who won a gold medal in the 1896 Olympiad.

'Elliot? Is he connected to the Mintos? They're a very well-established branch of the Scottish aristocracy. I believe there's a rumour Earl Minto is being considered as the next Viceroy of India,' said Lady Fraser-Price as she and Agatha relaxed under the pergola on the terrace of Villa Perrin.

In the golden light of early evening, a young vine offered glimmering patches of dappled shade, its branches green and supple, strung with miniature bunches of grapes as tiny as if they had been grown by fairies.

'I believe there is a familial connection,' agreed Agatha. Beside her, Alice stifled a giggle and Juliet rolled her eyes.

'Will they be invited to the wedding?' asked Elaine Perrin.

'Probably,' sighed Juliet. 'Ma is intent on inviting most of the world.'

'Darling, you're exaggerating,' her mother laughed, but the indulgent smile showed relief, and Alice wondered if her own parents would ever be in such a position, planning her wedding with delight.

Juliet and her family had arrived a few days earlier and the two girls had flung themselves into each other's arms.

'Congratulations!' Alice had exclaimed.

'Thank you,' replied Juliet. 'Who would have expected it?'

'And you love him?'

Juliet's cheeks had tinged pink. 'More than I could ever have imagined,' she had sighed. 'To think, he was there all along and we hadn't noticed each other. Then one morning, as Ma and I were enjoying a coffee at one of the cafés, he appeared. He and his uncle were staying with a friend near the Ritz. Ma wished to visit the dressmaker for a fitting but he invited me to accompany them to visit the Louvre. Ma agreed and it was the most wonderful day. Since then, we've been inseparable.'

'Your dream of marrying a duke has come true,' Alice had laughed. 'I never imagined it would be Ross Montrose, though, the heir to the dukedom of Arkaig. We've all grown up together. What changed?'

Alice had been bemused when the secret fiancé was revealed to be her brother's best friend.

'Love,' Juliet had sighed. 'Love changed us.'

The two girls laughed and hugged each other again, but when she had retired to bed later that evening, delighted though she was for Juliet, Alice could not stop a small part of her feeling grief at the impending nuptials. Even as Juliet had promised things would remain the same between them, it was inevitable their friendship was about to change for ever.

Juliet was embracing her future as the Duchess of Arkaig, a position with status and power. It was the end of their carefree girlhood, and as Alice realised this, a parade of images passed through her mind, each one showing her and Juliet laughing, their arms linked as they waltzed through their lives, sharing jokes, building dreams and making plans. They would no longer share their secrets first, as Ross would be Juliet's confidant. Alice wished her friend all happiness, but there was a sadness in her heart, too, as she saw a part of her life would change.

'Do you have a wedding date?' Alice heard her aunt ask, as she sipped the small glass of sweet wine they each had been given upon their arrival.

'We're hoping for Christmas,' said Fenella.

'How romantic it would be if it snowed,' said Juliet, 'with a honeymoon touring the estates Ross will inherit in Africa. His uncle owns game reserves and Ross is keen to ensure the wildlife is cared for rather than hunted. It will be such an adventure. You will attend, won't you, Alice?'

'Of course,' she said, reaching over to squeeze her friend's hand. 'It'll be strange, though, seeing you as a married woman, while I continue to tread the path of the spinster.'

Juliet let out a peal of laughter. 'You're not a spinster. There's plenty of time to meet the right man.'

'What if I don't want to marry?' Alice asked. 'To follow the line of duty and run a household.'

'But, Alice, what would you do instead?'

'There are worse things than remaining alone. There are lady archaeologists who travel the world, so perhaps I shall join their ranks. A pioneer, developing new ways to discover the past.'

'It's an exciting thought,' Juliet agreed, 'but it doesn't mean you have to dispense with matrimony. Jane Dieulafoy is married to Marcel Dieulafoy, and Zelia Nuttall is married to Alphonse Pinart.'

'Gertrude Bell remains unmarried as she explores Persia, although there are rumours she has taken a civil servant named

Harry Cadogan as a lover,' Alice responded, extending the word 'lover' with a dramatic roll of her tongue, making Juliet giggle, 'and, before she died, Amelia Edwards travelled the Nile with her companion, Lucy Renshaw. Not far from here, Harriet Boyd is running a dig alone. There is no requirement for me to marry. We are modern women, in a new age.'

'What about the delectable Mr G. Perrin?' Juliet murmured, leaning forward to avoid being overheard by Elaine, who was seated beside Agatha. 'He's been following you around the dig all summer, according to Hugo. Perhaps he can be persuaded to whisk you away to foreign climes for you to explore together.' Alice knew her face had frozen because Juliet's had changed from teasing to horrified. 'Alice, my dear, I'm sorry, I didn't mean to upset you...'

'You haven't,' she reassured her friend.

'Does it continue to hurt?' Juliet whispered, squeezing Alice's hand. 'Ephraim?'

Alice swallowed the unexpected lump in her throat.

'No,' she admitted. 'At present, my struggle is with the selfishness of my behaviour and the pain I have inflicted upon my family. Last week, I wrote letters of apology to them all, particularly Petra, who I fear will never forgive me.'

'Oh, Alice,' Juliet sighed. 'You were not to blame—'

'I was,' she snapped. 'Petra is my sister and I betrayed her out of childishness, jealousy and spite. My behaviour was despicable.'

'And George?'

Alice was desperate to discuss George. The day after the wedding celebrations in Archanes, when she had revealed to him the true scale of her betrayal, a note had arrived from the vineyard addressed to her. It was from George, explaining his father had sprained his ankle tripping over a vine and was unable to travel. A large shipment of wine was due in Athens, which Gus should have been overseeing. George had no choice but to deal with the issue on his father's behalf.

I shall write again as soon as I am able,

George had scrawled to Alice.

Don't despair, your revelation makes no difference to my feelings. When I return, we shall talk.

Since then, there had been silence and Alice wondered if George's words and the fortuitous trip were his way of putting a gentle distance between them. He knew Alice and Hugo would be leaving with Aunt Agatha and the boys when the dig ended, and she wondered if he would delay his return until then, in order to avoid her.

'We shared our stories,' she admitted to Juliet.

'What did he say?'

'The same as you and Hugo. It was not all my fault, and Ephraim was the one who manipulated me into an impossible situation.'

'Then you should listen to us,' Juliet said. She hesitated before continuing, 'Did he tell you about Edward Balstead and...?'

The end of the question hung in the air until Alice responded, 'Yes, he explained his behaviour.'

'Tell me your views.'

Alice considered this before replying, 'He was brokenhearted and he acted without thought and in a state of despair. However, he realised his mistake and has been trying to make amends ever since. I admire him for his honesty and his desire to put things right rather than deny responsibility. Love is a dangerous force that can drive even the sanest, most sensible people to madness.'

'Do you not think, my dearest Alice, that perhaps he might feel the same way about you and all you suffered at the hands of that unscrupulous cad? Why would he berate you, when he too has made mistakes in love?'

Alice stared at Juliet is astonishment. Throughout her endless turmoil, this view had never occurred to her, and she wondered at the revelation. After his confession, her forgiveness of George had been unconditional. Yet she could not forgive herself. Before Alice could reply, Fenella interrupted them.

'Girls, Elaine has made a wonderful suggestion. They will provide the wines for your wedding, Juliet. Gus imports wine for the Queen and Prince Bertie – he will know the right varieties to choose. If they are as delectable as these,' Fenella continued holding up her glass, 'then the wedding will be the toast of society.'

Elaine smiled as Fenella raised her glass.

'Wine is a very important part of life,' said Elaine. 'It's the very soul of happiness. Gus and I have always believed we are bottling sunshine and love with every grape we press. Now, if you will excuse me, our other guests are here.'

The Perrins' butler, Fletcher, had materialised by her side, announcing the arrival of Arthur Evans and Duncan Mackenzie. Evans had agreed to give a short talk about the dig and had brought a collection of smaller finds to display in the Perrins' library.

'Agatha, you and Elaine have become friends?' said Fenella, phrasing it as a question, as Mrs Perrin walked across the terrace. Alice knew her aunt had never had a close female friend before and was glad she had discovered the support good confidantes could share.

'This summer has been a revelation,' said Agatha. 'We have learned to relax, to dispense with convention and, yes, in the midst of these discoveries, I have found a dear friend in Elaine Perrin. The boys and I will be returning to Crete on a regular basis as I have decided to buy the property that we are renting on the edge of the Perrins' land. Andrew and Robert have already decided on a name, Sfragida House, which is named after the sealstones Mr Mackenzie showed the boys when they visited the dig. The air is healthy for us all and it'll be fascinating to watch as Mr Evans continues to draw the ancient world from the dusty soil.'

'Auntie, is this true?' asked Alice in astonishment. She and Juliet exchanged excited glances.

'Indeed,' replied Agatha. 'Crete has worked its magic on me. It is my intention to embark on a programme of rebuilding and extending to create a perfect home for us all. However, while the purchase is negotiated and the works planned, we shall continue with our tour.'

'Where do you intend to travel next?' asked Fenella, accepting a glass of Champagne from one of the Perrins' footmen.

'Alice and Hugo wish to remain here until the beginning of June, when the digging season will end, which is not long. As I've mentioned, the boys would like to return to Paris for the Olympiad. I have suggested we travel from here to Egypt and sail along the Nile before returning to Europe, where we will wend our way to Paris before returning to England for Christmas and then to Scotland for Juliet's nuptials.'

Alice listened as her aunt laid out the plans for the next few months. Christmas seemed an age away and she felt a strange sense of claustrophobia at the thought of having her days organised with such efficiency. The dig would end on the third of June, which was very soon. Arthur and Duncan had invited the hundreds of dedicated workers to a *glendi*, which would be held to celebrate all they had achieved. Arthur believed he was less than halfway through his recovery of Knossos and intended to return the following year. Duncan had explained this to Alice when she had delivered the days' pottery shards earlier that afternoon.

'Will George be back for the *glendi*?' he had asked, and Alice had felt an unexpected slice of pain as she contemplated his continuing absence.

'You'll have to check with his parents,' she had replied, walking away with heavy footsteps.

For the remainder of the day, Alice had worked hard to push thoughts of George from her mind, but with her aunt's unexpected revelation about the purchase of the newly named, Sfragida House, Alice felt a glimmer of hope. If she were to return next year to stay with her aunt, George would be at the Perrin Winery with his parents and possibly helping at the dig. A year was a long time and, perhaps, they would be able to try again and at least forge a friendship. These were small comforts but, she felt, they were better than nothing and were perhaps all she deserved after her conduct with Ephraim.

* * *

Beside Alice, Juliet and her mother were discussing the evergrowing list of potential wedding guests, with the occasional suggestion from Agatha, when Hugo's joyous voice interrupted her thoughts.

'More bubbles?' he asked, holding aloft a bottle of Champagne. 'Gus suggested we could act as your footmen and top up the glasses.'

He was followed by Juliet's brother, Tybalt, carrying spare glasses and Ross, who was armed with a second bottle. Beaming with happiness, he poured the foaming liquid into Juliet's glass. Alice watched as her friend smiled up at him, the radiance on her face reflecting the wonder and happiness in Ross's eyes. Hugo finished refilling their glasses and raised his in a toast.

'To the island of Crete and this golden summer,' he declared, 'and congratulations to my dearest friend, Ross, and my adopted younger sister, Juliet. May you be as happy as Mama and Papa.'

Congratulations rang out from the group, before Hugo grinned and continued, 'Champagne reminds me of Peterhouse and the chaps on my floor. Wainwright Minor is a demon for this stuff. No matter the time of day, there's always a bottle on the go in his rooms.'

'I hope you don't indulge before midday,' said Agatha, giving her nephew a mock-glare.

'Never, Auntie,' he replied, 'because I am rarely awake before midday.'

'You scoundrel,' she pretended to scold as Alice, Juliet, Ross and Tybalt laughed.

'Don't worry, Alice, you'll be next,' Lady Fenella said, her voice sympathetic. 'You're too beautiful to be a spinster.'

Alice smiled, understanding the comment was well meaning, but she was relieved to see Elaine, Gus and Juliet's father, Jolyon Fraser-Price, heading towards them, diverting the conversation away from her single status. Gus retained a slight limp from his sprained ankle but he was recovering his strength each day. To avoid a repeat of the incident he had decided to follow Arthur Evans's lead and had begun using a stick. It had been hand-carved by one of their workers, made from wood from a fallen olive tree, which had been polished to a glistening sheen.

'Boys and their salad days...' said Fenella as her husband sat beside her and Elaine helped Gus into his chair. 'The enjoyment of youth is invigorating, don't you think, Agatha?'

'Indeed, although these boys don't need extra encouragement. I should lock away your stocks of Champagne, Gus,' said Agatha to general merriment.

Duncan Mackenzie and Arthur Evans appeared in the doorway of the villa and Gus waved them over.

'Are the exhibits ready?' he asked as the two men joined the group under the pergola.

'Indeed, they are,' replied Arthur, placing his walking stick, Prodger, beside him before taking the proffered glass. 'It was considerate of you to suggest a small display in order to show your guests what we've discovered. Although, these two,' he pointed towards Alice and Hugo, 'have been a great asset all summer. They've witnessed the rebirth of a nation.'

'It's been fascinating,' agreed Hugo.

'We're waiting for one more guest, Harriet Boyd, who is digging in Gournia,' said Elaine. 'Then perhaps you would like to give your speech, Arthur, and allow us all to view your finds before we eat. No doubt Miss Boyd will be interested to hear about your discoveries. I believe she is making her own mark in the world of archaeology.'

'Harriet is doing an excellent job...' began Arthur, halting as the Perrins' butler, Fletcher, appeared and murmured something to Elaine.

Alice watched Elaine excuse herself and go, and she wondered why the expression on Elaine's face had changed to one of curiosity. Then, turning her attention back to Evans, Mackenzie and Hugo, Alice was drawn into a discussion about the gypsum throne and the possibility it could have been designed for a woman. Her mind flashed to her strange dream from the night before when she herself had been seated on it.

Behind her, she heard Elaine Perrin and the voice of an American woman, who she assumed was Harriet Boyd. Alice, however, was engrossed in a debate with Duncan about the role of women within the temples of the Minoans and she did not turn around. When Hugo gripped her hand, she jumped in surprise.

'What's the matter?' she asked in alarm, seeing all the colour had drained from Hugo's face.

'Agatha, Hugo, Alice, I have a wonderful surprise for you,'

Elaine's voice, guileless and full of excitement, floated down to them. 'By chance, Harriet was hosting her cousin, who has been helping to fund her dig. They are connected through the American side of his family. Oh, this is such a wonderful coincidence, an impromptu family reunion.'

Alice stared at Hugo, whose eyes were wide with fury, his face blanched white. Across from her, Agatha had risen, the disgust evident on her face as she stared over Alice's shoulder. A shadow fell across her, a whisper of scent, the familiar Hammas Bouquet from Penhaligon's, its woody fragrance as familiar to her as the scent of her own skin, and with a pounding heart she turned to stare up into the face of Ephraim Lockwood.

36

'Hugo, old man, Aunt Agatha, what a perfect time for a family reunion and to celebrate the birth of my second son,' exclaimed the new and unexpected heir to the earldom of Bentree, Alice and Hugo's brother-in-law and Agatha's nephew-by-marriage.

Alice felt sick as he took her hand and kissed it.

'My darling girl,' he whispered, 'I've missed you most of all.'

'Isn't this wonderful?' exclaimed Elaine, although her smile faltered as Juliet, Fenella, Jolyon, Ross and Tybalt glared at Ephraim. 'Harriet is enjoying a preview of the artefacts... Ah, here she is, my dear, do join us.'

As the introductions were made, Alice could see her family and friends were making every effort to welcome the woman who had, without doubt, been duped into bringing Ephraim to this gathering. Of medium height, with dark brown hair and eyes, Harriet was dressed in head-to-foot white, a dark cameo brooch at her neck. She brimmed with enthusiasm and, under different circumstances, Alice felt they would have been immediate friends. As it was, the woman was tainted by her association with Ephraim, and Alice struggled to offer anything more than the politeness that had been drilled into her since childhood.

'The items you've found are exquisite, Arthur,' said Harriet, taking a glass of Champagne. 'Over in Gournia, we've found an abundance of treasures but they're all small: bronze arrowheads, jewellery, iron swords, gold leaf and a thin bronze plate engraved with sphinxes, griffins, lions and human figures. There's nothing as spectacular as your palace.'

Harriet's voice had a soft American twang and Alice shuddered. The idea of running away to America no longer held any appeal. Looking up, she realised Ephraim was watching her and, as their eyes met, he gave her the smallest of winks. Alice turned away in disgust. It was a relief when Elaine and Gus summoned their guests into the library to hear Arthur and Duncan's talk, and Ephraim offered his arm to Harriet, while Hugo escorted Alice, with Tybalt accompanying Aunt Agatha.

As the group made its way inside, Alice whispered to Aunt Agatha, who was a few paces in front of her, 'Shall I pretend to have a headache? Too much sun. Hugo could take me home...'

'Let's not give him the satisfaction,' Agatha replied. 'Leave him to Hugo, Ross, Tybalt and Jolyon,' she said, receiving grim nods from the men around them. 'We ladies shall form a wall around you, my dear, and you will leave with your dignity and reputation intact, which is what we have all been striving for since we whisked you away to the Continent.'

Alice did not hear much of Arthur's talk about Knossos and it took Hugo's nudge to make her realise Arthur had mentioned her name as he held up the zircon crystal and figurine she had discovered.

The talk was followed by a five-course dinner and when, after what seemed like an eternity to Alice, Elaine suggested the women withdraw, Agatha made excuses for herself, Alice and Hugo to leave, while the Fraser-Price family and Ross hemmed in Ephraim before he could try to tag along.

Upon returning home, Florence helped Alice to undress, before Alice fled to her aunt's room where Agatha held out her arms to her niece. She rocked Alice as though she were one of her boys, stroking her hair, comforting her until her tears ceased.

'The man is a cad of the highest order,' Agatha said. 'Poor Miss Boyd and poor Elaine – they have no idea about our family rift. Elaine suspected there was a problem and could not have been more apologetic or charming.'

'Did you tell her?' asked Alice.

'Of course not, my dear,' replied Agatha. 'This terrible situation was Ephraim's doing. Alice, please do not allow yourself to feel as though this was your fault.' Then, handing Alice a clean handkerchief, she continued, 'My dear, I'm sorry to ask, but how do you feel about him? Would it better if we left Crete in the morning?'

A wave of horror rippled through Alice at the thought of departing before the end of the dig and leaving the place to which George would return. The idea of never seeing him again shot through her with an intensity of pain far greater than the self-indulgent grief and embarrassment she had felt when she had lost Ephraim.

In that moment, she understood that during the weeks of hard work and friendship in the sunshine of Crete, her heart had recovered from her brother-in-law's dubious affections, and real love had found her, with a man she feared she might never see again.

'I am not in love with Ephraim,' she said. 'You were right, Auntie. I don't think my feelings for him were ever love. My tears are from the shock of seeing him and sorrow for all the pain I've caused to you all.'

'Nonsense, dear, we love you,' Aunt Agatha said. 'That man is not a gentleman and it's a shame we were all duped by his shallow charm. Your sister is the one we must support because her future as his wife will be forever difficult.'

Alice went to bed thinking of Petra. Her letter to her sister had been heartfelt and genuine, and she hoped one day Petra would be able to find a way towards forgiveness.

Alice slipped into an uneasy sleep and, as was becoming usual, her dreams took her to the labyrinth and she found herself staring down at a figurine similar to the one she had found on the first day of the dig...

* * *

A movement behind her caused her to turn. He was there: tall, fearsome, his face imbued with a craggy handsomeness.

'It is very pretty,' he said, pointing to the figurine in her hand. 'Is it you?'

'Yes, it was carved by my brother,' she said, her heart beating in excitement as Theseus smiled, his eyes twinkling.

'He's very talented.'

'He deserves better than being locked away in the dark.'

'Perhaps I could help.'

His smile was sweet, his eyes sad and she believed his intentions were good.

'Perhaps...' she replied, but as she turned away, one of the trailing necklaces caught on the short sword he carried by his side. The blade sliced through the string, causing the beads to cascade around her, a rainfall of sparkling crystals.

Laughing, he hurried to and fro, gathering the zircons, until they were piled in her hands.

'They are the labyrinth,' he said, inspecting the carving on the final bead.

'Yes, they are a gift of love, the words on the bottom say "I love you."'

'Then I shall keep one,' he said, raising the stone to his lips, 'and the figure of you, although she will never be as beautiful as the real woman.'

With her hands full of the beads, she was unable to stop him from taking the small statue from her pocket.

'Until tonight, my love,' he whispered, and disappeared around the corner of the palace.

Ariadne sighed in delight. A true hero, ready to free them all.

She did not see, as he threw the two trinkets into the midden, a look of distaste on his handsome face.

37

'Last day,' said Duncan Mackenzie as Alice collected the basket of pottery shards for her, Angeliki and Maria to wash. 'Will you and Hugo be attending the *glendi*?'

'We hope to,' she replied. 'Juliet, Ross and Tybalt would like to join us. Would that be possible?'

'The more the merrier,' Duncan replied. 'What about your brother-in-law?'

'We believe he returned to Gournia with Harriet,' she said, trying to keep her voice calm.

'Everyone is welcome,' said Duncan, and disappeared into one of the trenches.

Alice returned to the table and the young women began to divide up the potsherds.

'Have you heard the rumours?' asked Angeliki as Alice picked up a soft brush, dipping it in the water. She stroked it over the jagged fragment, watching as the mud melted away to reveal a flash of brilliant blue.

'No, what?' asked Maria, leaning forward, her eyes aglow with excitement.

She adored gossip and enjoyed being able to impart informa-tion to other people. Alice did not comment, instead focusing on the ceramic in her hand, hoping the pattern would reveal itself to be another of the stylised sea creatures that had begun to appear regularly on the pottery.

'After the dinner last night, a few of the items Arthur used as exhibits have vanished,' she whispered.

'How do you know?' asked Maria.

'This morning, I overheard Duncan and Theo discussing it. Duncan thinks they've been mislaid and will turn up, but Theo is less sure.'

'Does he think they were stolen?' asked Maria.

'Perhaps.'

'But who would have stolen them?' asked Alice.

'Who knows? Someone at the party or someone who works there. The vineyard employs a number of people and not all of them are local,' said Angeliki, exchanging a knowing look with Maria.

'What does Arthur plan to do?' Alice said, wondering if he would investigate.

'Nothing yet, according to Duncan, especially as the American woman is arriving later.'

'Harriet Boyd?'

'Yes, the one who is in Gournia. When she was here before, she and Arthur had long discussions about the finds.' Angeliki waved her hand across the table to encompass the mass of relics they were sorting and cleaning. 'Perhaps she borrowed the items to examine them.'

'Maybe,' murmured Alice, but there was an uneasiness to her tone. 'Did Duncan say which items were missing?'

'Sealstones and the jewel you found, along with the figure,' said

Angeliki, and Alice felt another wave of bitter fury swirl around her heart.

In the distance, she could see Hugo and Theo clambering aboard a small donkey cart to take them to a local quarry to study the rock formations. The idea had been Hugo's. He suggested that by examining the old quarry, they might be able to establish the source of the stones used to build the palace of Knossos. Alice looked down at the potsherd and wondered whether she should shout to her brother to wait while she washed her hands and accompanied them. The idea of Harriet Boyd visiting the site unnerved her.

Alice was not concerned about meeting Harriet again; it was the thought of Ephraim accompanying her, using Harriet's presence as an excuse to infringe upon this new world Alice had created. This was her place, these were her friends. She would not be driven away by him. He had ruined enough things in her life, she decided; she would not allow him to spoil the last day of the dig with her friends.

The morning passed and, with no visitors, Alice began to relax. All around her there was evidence that the site was being closed up. Holes were back-filled, large tarpaulins were secured over the emerging walls, while fences were raised around the areas of highest importance.

Evans would be returning to England to write his first report on his finds, establish his theories and, once again, pick up the reigns at the Ashmolean. He had told Alice he was looking forward to settling back into his home, Youlbury, the vast house he had built at Boars Hill, a few miles from Oxford. It had been intended for his wife, Margaret, but ill health had stolen her from Arthur in 1893. His writing paper had borne a black border to indicate mourning ever since; a quiet tribute Alice felt showed a true devotion to the love they had shared.

Above them, the sun climbed higher, Helios driving his chariot across the skies. Alice listened as Angeliki and Maria discussed the merits of the young men on the dig and who would prove good dance partners at the *glendi*. As the conversation moved on to their plans for the rest of the summer, Alice heard Duncan calling her name.

'Someone to see you,' he boomed.

Angeliki and Maria squinted into the dazzling sunshine and with, trepidation, Alice turned. Duncan was approaching, accompanied by Harriet Boyd, Arthur and, with a sinking feeling Alice saw, Ephraim. His crisp linen suit looked out of place and she took a vindictive pleasure in noticing the dust clinging to his trouser hems.

'There you are, my dear,' said Arthur, feeling his way over the uneven ground with Prodger. 'We thought you might like to join our tour. Mr Lockwood has explained the family connection to you and Hugo. What a coincidence your brother-in-law should be here sponsoring his cousin, Harriet, on her endeavours.'

Alice looked up at Ephraim and thought, how did I ever find his smile attractive? He looks untrustworthy and sly. Her heart contracted with pity for her sister. The whole family had been deceived by this man and she wondered whether her parents would be able to rescue Petra from Ephraim as they had saved her.

Duncan Mackenzie stepped forward, as though offering his protection, and Alice suspected he could sense her discomfort. However, as Harriet Boyd and Arthur were staring at her in anticipation, Alice realised she could not snub Ephraim. To do so would cause embarrassment to those around her and could lead to unpleasant explanations.

Handing the potsherd she was cleaning to Maria, Alice washed her hands and joined the group. Harriet smiled, holding out her hand to shake Alice's.

'Hello, Alice. It's wonderful to meet you properly. We didn't get a chance to speak at the dinner last night. Cousin Ephraim talks about your family with such warmth. If I'm ever lucky enough to travel to England, it would be wonderful to visit you all.'

Alice smiled with as much politeness as she could muster.

'How are you and Ephraim related?' she asked.

Ahead of her, Arthur and Duncan were explaining the palace of Knossos to Ephraim, who appeared to be interested, yet Alice could not quash her rising unease. He feigned an interest in archaeology because it was a fashionable pastime for wealthy gentlemen but he had once confessed to Alice that it bored him rigid.

'But one has to follow fashion,' he had laughed, and, in thrall to him as she had been, Alice had thought this comment the height of sophistication.

Ephraim, she remembered, would often denigrate men of science behind their backs and, she was ashamed to admit, she had laughed at his cruel comments, on occasion adding spiteful remarks of her own. With all her heart she hoped he would not say anything insulting to Arthur or Duncan, two men whom she admired and respected.

'Distantly, through our mothers,' Harriet was saying as they made their way across the baked earth. 'My mother died when I was a child and I was raised in Boston, Massachusetts by my father and four elder brothers. It was a riotous upbringing. Ephraim's grandfather, Deuteronomy Pepworth, was my mother's second cousin.'

Alice knew the history of Ephraim's maternal side. Esther Pepworth was the only child of Deuteronomy Pepworth, a Texan oil billionaire. She, like many wealthy Americans, had come to England to marry into the aristocracy. It was said the marriage between Esther and Ephraim's father, the Earl of Bentree, had been a love match.

Whether this was the case or not, Alice had always found the idea romantic. Their elder son, Patrick, was born a year after the wedding, with Ephraim following a few years later. Ephraim had never expected to inherit the title, and the trip to America had been the beginning of a new life for him and, supposedly Petronella, where he would have been trained to run his grandfather's vast oil holdings. However, the unexpected death of Patrick in a riding accident had changed everything.

Patrick's wife, Flora, had not been blessed with children and, therefore, upon his elder brother's death, Ephraim had assumed the role of heir. Alice wondered if the new child, whose name Aunt Agatha had informed her was Ernest, would one day be given the position in the oil business instead. The thought of their awful plan to embark on a bigamous marriage, to abandon Petra and the children, made Alice cold with shame.

His pale hair, she noticed now, was combed in such a way as to hide the fact he was thinning on top, and his grey eyes, which she had once thought attractive, looked small and mean, over a nose that was thin and beaky. Heartfelt sympathy for her sister filled her, as did the desire to laugh in ridicule at her own preposterous behaviour. Why, she had been a child. No wonder her family had tried to remove her from the situation in order to save her from her own naïvety.

Foolish man, she thought.

Harriet continued to chat about her own excavations in Gournia.

'You should visit,' she suggested to Alice, who gave a polite smile, wondering how soon she could think of a reason to leave.

'Perhaps Alice could give me a tour of the areas she's worked in,' said Ephraim, and before Alice could protest, Arthur had agreed, pointing towards the path Alice had followed on her first day.

'Take Mr Lockwood to the gypsum throne,' said Arthur, beaming. This was one of his most prized exhibits and Alice realised the honour Arthur was bestowing upon her in suggesting she accompany Ephraim.

'Are you sure?' she asked, hoping Arthur would not be able to resist doing the unveiling himself, but he and Harriet were already turning away and heading to the north-east *propylaea*, where the remains of the stucco bull had been discovered.

Shooting Ephraim a look of contempt, Alice marched away, hoping to spray as much dust over his trousers as possible.

'Slow down, Alice,' he called, but she continued at the same pace until she reached the broken walls of the throne room, where the gypsum throne stood in all its glory. 'You're as eager as me to be on our own, are you?' he laughed as he caught up with her, grasping her hand and drawing her towards him.

'What are you doing?' she spluttered, wrenching herself free from his grip.

'Don't pretend you haven't missed me,' he said, trying to pull her back into an embrace, which she resisted, pushing him away, revolted by smell of his cologne.

'I'm not pretending,' she snapped. 'At first I missed you. Then, thankfully, with the love and understanding of my family, I came to my senses.'

'Meaning?'

'We did a terrible thing. You're married to my sister.'

'But I love you...'

'No, you don't.'

Ephraim stared at her, and she watched as first surprise, then anger registered across his face.

'How do you know what I feel?'

'If you loved me, truly loved me, you wouldn't have followed me here. You would have realised the appalling thing we did and let me go for ever.'

Ephraim glared at her. 'You're such a child, Alice,' he said, his voice ringing with disappointment.

It was a taunt he had used before, and it was this desire for him to see her as sophisticated and elegant that had made her agree to their diabolical plan to elope. But as she stood before him in her breeches and her grubby blouse, she did not care if he thought her childish.

'Perhaps so,' she said, 'but at least I'm trying to make amends rather than pretend it didn't happen.'

He considered her for a moment, then he reached into his pocket and withdrew a handkerchief.

'You're very ungrateful, especially as I went to the trouble of acquiring these for you,' he said, pushing it into her hand.

There was a hardness at the centre, and Alice guessed the contents before she opened it. With hands trembling with anger, she unfolded the fabric and stared down at the two items she had discovered on the first day: the zircon and the figurine.

'Did you persuade Arthur to sell you these?' she asked.

'Of course not,' he laughed. 'I took them from the table last night. When Arthur mentioned in his lecture – which was remarkably dull, by the way – that you were the one to discover them, I decided to take them. After all, my love, you found them. In my book, that makes them yours.'

Alice stared at him in disgust. 'I'm not your "love" and what you did is stealing.'

'How dare you accuse me of theft?' he barked.

'I shall return these to Arthur,' she said, and turned to leave.

'No, you won't,' he said. 'Because, if you do, I'll tell him that one of your Cretan peasant friends stole them.'

'What would be the point?'

'Arthur told me last night his policy on theft. I should think being accused of stealing these artefacts in this backwater would be a scandal that would be remembered for generations. Who were those girls you were laughing with when I arrived? I might accuse one of them.'

'You petty, pointless man.'

'If you don't want to see your friends shamed, you should keep the gift.'

'Why are you so determined I should have them?' she asked. 'Do you think if I keep them they will give you leverage over me?'

An unattractive blush rose up his face. Alice stared at him, horrified he could be so vindictive. Shaking her head in wonder at his childishness, she said in her most formal manner, 'Thank you for the gift, Ephraim. I shall deal with it in my own way but, trust me, you have no power over me, not any more.'

With a final glance at the man she had once thought she loved, Alice turned on her heel and walked back towards her friends and her new life in the teeming walkways of the palace of Knossos, gripping the ancient stone and the figurine in her hand.

38

The house was quiet. Alice, along with a number of the other young women, had left the site earlier than usual in order to prepare for the *glendi*. She had shared a ride home with Angeliki, who had spent the entire journey describing her outfit, words that had floated past Alice unheard as thoughts of Ephraim and his perfidy had raced around her mind. The slow ride home, however, had given Alice time to consider her next course of action and, as she waved goodbye to Angeliki, a plan was forming in her mind.

'See you this evening,' she called as Wendbury let her into the house and the cart eased away down the rutted track.

'Tea, Miss Alice?' he asked.

'Wonderful, thank you, Wendbury,' she said. 'In the parlour in fifteen minutes, please. Where is my aunt?'

'Resting,' he said. 'She has asked to be awoken at four o'clock.'

'Thank you,' said Alice, hurrying down the spiral staircase to her bedroom on the floor below.

Rummaging through her chest of drawers, she found a small wooden box shaped like a treasure chest. She had bought it at a market in Paris, intending to fill it with sweets in order to give it to one of her young cousins as a Christmas present. Then she drew the handkerchief Ephraim had given her from her canvas bag and opened it. Inside nestled the crystal and the figurine.

'Thank you for sharing your story,' she whispered, 'but it's time you returned to the earth. If I'm able, one day, I'll take you back to Knossos. I promise.'

The small bundle fitted inside the box, which she then wrapped in a scarf, and, knowing with certainty this was the correct course of action, she crept to the side door. Alice paused, running a mental inventory of where each member of the household would be at this time of day. Her aunt was resting. The boys would either be out with Nanny Ipswich or confined to their rooms, reading. Although, Alice thought, reading was doubtful; a spirited game of Racing Demon with their battered playing cards would be more probable. With her request for tea, she was assured Wendbury and the cook, Gaia, would be occupied in the drawing room and kitchen respectively. Nancy Eagles, her aunt's lady's maid, would be resting, too, as would Nanny Ipswich if she were not out with the boys. The one person who might scupper her plan was Florence, who loved to wander the lanes around Sfragida House.

Peering outside, Alice saw no one. The garden around the house was steep. Her aunt planned to terrace it but, at present, it was sheer and littered with stones. Alice hurried over the uneven ground, determined in her mission. Glancing over her shoulder, she slipped unobserved into the barn attached to one side of the house. It was a tumbledown building and Agatha planned to demolish it in order to build a more sturdy structure to use as storage or stabling.

Taking her small trowel from her canvas bag, Alice moved an old storage jar from its position in the corner. The boys had discovered the stone beneath it was loose and had asked Alice to help them lift it to see if it marked the opening to a secret passage. To their great disappointment, it had revealed only damp earth and a few worms. Levering the stone out of the way, Alice bent down and, using the skills she had acquired over the summer, she dug a neat square hole and placed the box in it.

'When Arthur has finished his excavations, I'll take you home to the site,' she said as she filled in the hole. 'In the meantime, you'll be safe here.'

Replacing the stone, then the storage jar, Alice crept back into the house.

* * *

The stars spun in the heavens and Alice sipped the *raki*, savouring the fire as it hit her throat, eager to return to the dancing. Hugo grabbed her hand and whirled her into a reel with Ross, Juliet, Tybalt, Angeliki, Maria and Duncan. Around them, exuberance and joy filled the night air and Alice imagined the words flying upwards, cheering the cosmos with their delight, colouring an exultant place in the sky above.

Change was upon them and the atmosphere at the *glendi* was bittersweet. In three days' time, she and Hugo would be setting out with Aunt Agatha on for their journey to Egypt. They would travel via Athens, where Robert and Andrew had requested to see the Acropolis again, before visiting the pyramids in Giza, followed by a trip up the Nile to Luxor and the Valley of the Kings. Alice was excited, but her thrill at visiting this ancient world was tempered by the fact George had not returned.

Despite his note and the news from his parents that he was awaiting the final part of the wine shipment, hence his delay, she felt sure he had been shocked and disgusted by her behaviour, removing himself from her company rather than hurt her further by dismissing her. She did not blame him. Before leaving for the *glendi*, she had written him a letter, which she intended to have delivered to Villa Perrin after they had set sail for Athens, explaining how she understood his decision and hoped he might one day be able to forgive her. Tempting though it had been to dissolve into sadness, Alice refused to let self-pity overwhelm her again. George's rejection was due to her own shoddy behaviour.

'Come on, Alice,' called Tybalt. 'I'll be your partner for the next one.'

Alice was considering a polite refusal because she had danced with Tybalt before and, despite his best efforts, he had no sense of rhythm and tended to flatten the feet of his partner. It did not help that he was shorter than her, but as Hugo was partnering Maria, Angeliki was dancing with Vassilis, Duncan had vanished and Juliet was hand in hand with Ross, she had no choice.

'I'll do my best not to trample your feet,' he whispered as he spun her across the dancefloor. 'I promise.'

The music increased in pace and Alice thought of the last time she had danced so happily. It had been at the wedding, with George, when they had told each other tales in the moonlight before her confession. Perhaps this is my penance, she thought, to find a man who is worthy of loving but to lose him because of my past behaviour. Perhaps this is the karmic balance described by the Theosophists.

Tybalt spun her away again and she laughed as he lost his balance and collapsed into a heap. Alice stepped forward to help him to his feet when a firmer hand took her waist, a more sure-footed partner. Peering up through the torchlight, her heart began to pound.

'George,' she gasped.

'Alice!' he exclaimed. 'I was so worried I was going to miss the end of the dig, to miss seeing you.'

'No, you didn't,' she said, cursing herself for stumbling over her words.

'If you'd left, I was planning to chase you down the Nile,' he laughed, his brown eyes boring into hers.

'You would have done that?' she asked in surprise. 'For me?'

'Of course,' he said, and, taking her hand, he led her away from the dancefloor and the grinning Tybalt.

The noise of the *glendi* faded. George stopped near one of the tents they had used for shade and, in the distance, Alice saw Maria sweep Tybalt up and spin him around.

'Alice,' George said, and she realised his hands were trembling. 'I know this may seem forward but ever since I saw you on the train, my heart has been telling me you were special. You were unlike any woman I had ever met, but my brain continued to doubt my heart.'

He paused and she squeezed his hand, smiling.

'Hearts and brains are often in discord,' she agreed. 'Mine have been waging a similar battle.'

Hope flared in his eyes.

'They have?' he asked, and she nodded. Under her encouraging gaze, he continued, 'It seemed to me my heart had led me to disaster in the past and I feared causing more pain. I knew you were unhappy although why any man in his right mind would have left you, I couldn't fathom. For weeks, I refused to allow myself to feel anything other than friendship for you as I felt sure, whoever he was, he would come to his senses and return to claim your affections.

'When I told you about my behaviour towards Millicent, it was a gamble, yet because you too had suffered a broken heart, you understood these things are never simple. Love is a recalcitrant emotion, a will-o'-the-wisp, a moonbeam on the water, until we meet our true soul mate. As Plato said, there are two halves to every person and I believe you are mine: the part of my soul that was taken away when Zeus was angry with the human race. When Father sent me away, I was worried you would think I was avoiding you, but I wasn't. The story you told made me realise how extraordinary you really are...'

He ground to a halt and Alice stared at him in amazement.

'I'm not extraordinary,' she said. 'My actions were those of a spoiled brat who believed she could take whatever she chose with no thought for the consequences. I hurt the people I love, my sister most of all, but their love has protected and saved me. This summer has taught me humility and the strength of real love. When I told you my story, I, too, thought you would be disgusted by my actions. They were abominable but, my wise friend, Juliet, pointed out that as I could forgive you, then hopefully you could forgive me.'

Alice reached for George's hand and stared up into his brown eyes, the moonlight dancing over his face, washing it with an ethereal silver light.

'Do you?' she asked.

'My darling Alice, there is nothing to forgive,' he exclaimed. 'We were both fools in love and, perhaps these were the lessons our untrained and arrogant hearts needed to learn, so when we found our soul mates, we would understand.'

They stared at each other, the pipes, drums and the voices in the background sounding as old as time.

'Oh, George,' she said. 'Would you really have followed me down the Nile?'

'Yes, I would follow you anywhere.'

A silence grew between them and she knew there was one final obstacle to overcome.

'Ephraim is in Crete,' she said, and George's arms loosened around her. 'He arrived at your parents' dinner party with Harriet Boyd.'

'Yes, my mother told me. She was devastated when Agatha

explained there was a family rift – your aunt was discreet enough not to say what, however – but, I wondered, how did you feel, seeing him again?'

'Anger, disgust, contempt at the arrogance of the man,' she replied. 'After you told me about writing the letters, I did the same, with a particular mind on the one to Petra and, perhaps one day, she'll forgive me.'

'Mother said your aunt has bought the house on the edge of the vineyard.'

'Yes, Auntie Ag has fallen in love with Crete. She intends to return every summer.'

'And will you accompany her?'

'Would you like me too?'

'Yes, although, I would prefer it if you would stay.'

'Stay? With you and your parents?'

'Yes,' he said, and to her amazement he bent down on one knee.

'Alice Webster, will you marry me?'

Her eyes brimmed with tears and a smile illuminated her face as she reached out to him.

'Yes, George, yes, I will.'

With a whoop of joy, he swept her into his arms as, behind them, the moon shone and the ancient music played.

39

The waves hissed and sighed across the sand. Eloise shaded her eyes to watch as Leon, Sean, Marcus, Yiannis and Tobias continued their beach volleyball tournament with far too much seriousness. Tobias, Marina and Yiannis's nine-year-old son, was delighted to be on a team with the twins, whom he idolised. As Leon and Yiannis discussed tactics, the three boys danced on the sand, taunting their fathers.

Thea, Marina and Yiannis's daughter, was building a complicated sandcastle complex nearby, aided by her uncle, Nikos. He managed the beach umbrellas and, in Eloise's view, took it upon himself to command his area of beach, too. It had been useful, though, because with the school summer holidays upon them, Crete was bursting with visitors. When he was not occupied with the loungers and beach umbrellas, Nikos was busy digging tunnels beside his niece.

Marina lay on a sunlounger to Eloise's left, Rose to her right, watching the volleyball game and shouting the occasional cheer of encouragement or word of warning as the action became too fast and furious.

Rose had suggested the day on the beach and Leon had requested a visit to Malia, a village with a long sandy beach renowned for its nightlife.

'I came here on holiday before I met Rose,' he had said, raising his eyebrows, when they had been unloading the beach bags. 'What happened in Malia, stays in Malia.'

'Well, you're in Malia again,' Rose had replied. 'Want to tell us about your terrible antics?'

'No, I don't think I shall,' Leon had replied, walking away with a wicked grin on his face to set up the volleyball net.

'We haven't been to this beach for years,' sighed Marina, reaching for the cool box and pulling out a bright pink water bottle. 'Thank you for inviting us.'

'It wouldn't have been the same without you,' Eloise replied, and Rose smiled.

Marina reached over and squeezed Eloise's hand. A few days earlier, Eloise had finally told Marina the full story of Josh's death. Marina had been shocked and devastated for all Eloise had suffered but unsurprised at Josh's behaviour.

'I suspected he was not a good man,' she had said.

'Do you think Quinn knew?' Eloise had asked. 'You knew him better than me.'

'Quinn was very wise,' Marina had replied. 'Perhaps he suspected, even if he didn't know. This was probably the real reason he left you Sfragida House: it gave you a place of safety.'

Rose interrupted the volleyball match to suggest refreshments, and ten minutes later, as the two teams returned to the net and Thea persuaded her uncle to buy her an enormous chocolate ice cream, Rose delved into her vast beach bag and produced a stack of magazines.

'How about some intellectual stimulation?' she said, waving

them in the scorching sunshine. 'It's been years since we've had time to do the quizzes.'

'Do we have to?' asked Eloise, wondering why Rose had suggested this when she knew about the last quiz Eloise had taken.

'Yes,' replied Rose, 'because I don't want every area of your life to be tainted by Josh. You did a quiz about domestic violence and it was terrible. We used to answer questions about daft things and I want you to begin to understand the fun and gentleness that remains in the world. Not everything has to be about him and what happened.'

Eloise felt tears prick her eyes at the look of hope and love on her friend's face.

'You're right,' she said. 'What's the topic?'

Rose brandished a copy of *It's Fate*, a magazine that celebrated the psychic side of life.

'Reincarnation,' said Rose with glee.

Marina grinned and Eloise rolled her eyes, 'Go on then,' she said. 'Ask the questions.'

As Rose posed each dilemma, the three women discussed the various options for the answers and, despite bursting into gales of laughter at a few of the questions, neither Marina nor Rose balked at the possibility of reincarnation.

When they had finished, with Rose concluding from their results that Marina had lived at least twenty-six times before, she had lived fourteen times and Eloise appeared to have resurfaced on one hundred and thirty-two occasions, Eloise asked, 'So do you actually believe in reincarnation?'

'Yes,' replied Marina in a matter-of-fact voice.

'And you, Rose?'

Rose considered the question and, echoing Eloise's more serious tone, said, 'Yes, I suppose I do. It isn't a subject that occupies a huge amount of my time but I remember when we were growing up and you wanted to be hypnotised at the psychic fair.'

'And my parents were reluctant because we had to be home for a funeral.'

'We tried to hypnotise each other a few weeks later.'

'I'd forgotten all about that,' said Eloise, surprised at this lapse in her memory.

'I haven't,' said Rose, 'you were obsessed with the idea. We went to the library to see if there were any books on hypnosis.'

'You're right, we did.'

'Were you successful?' asked Marina.

'No, I fell asleep whenever Eloise tried to hypnotise me, and when I attempted the same on Eloise, she spouted a made-up language, then said she couldn't remember anything.'

'Did I?' said Eloise.

Rose nodded, taking a swig from her bright green water container.

'Why did you ask, Eloise?' said Marina.

Eloise hesitated, before taking a deep breath and saying, 'The diaries, the ones belonging to Alice Webster...'

'My great-great grandmother,' confirmed Marina.

'Yes. I've reached the end and I wondered what happened next.'

Eloise had told Rose, Leon and the boys the story of Alice, George and Hugo as they had wandered around Knossos at the beginning of their holiday. Sean and Marcus had been fascinated.

'I asked Mama and Grandma about Alice,' said Marina, leaning over to riffle through her beach bag, 'and they gave me these.' She handed Eloise a plastic wallet. Inside were enlarged copies of four aged photographs. 'Grandma thinks these were taken after the dig ended in June 1900. Cristos printed them for me – these are for you.'

'For me? Thank you, Marina.'

Eloise wiped her hands on her towel, not wanting to spoil the images, even though they were copies, with sand or suncream. She moved off her sunlounger, kneeling on the floor before pulling out the photographs and placing them side by side, unable to tear her eyes away. In the first, a middle-aged couple smiled from outside a large villa.

'Is this Gus and Elaine Perrin?' asked Eloise in delight.

'Yes, and we think the young couple in front of the Sphinx are Alice and George.'

Both were beaming at the camera and Eloise felt a strong connection to the young woman.

'They must have accompanied Aunt Agatha on the rest of the trip,' said Rose, leaning over Eloise's shoulder.

'In the other one, by the pyramid, we think it's Hugo with Aunt Agatha and the two boys...'

'Must be Robert and Andrew,' finished Eloise.

'The other is a wedding photograph,' said Marina, pointing to one of rows of well-dressed guests with the bride and groom at the centre. 'After the trip, the family returned to England where Alice and George were married at the Webster family home in Hampshire in 1901. I wonder whether Ephraim is skulking in the background. Beyond that, apart from the fact I'm descended through a line of sons who are related to Alice and George, I know very little.'

'What was your maiden name?' asked Rose.

'Perrin,' she replied. 'We're half-British.'

Eloise grinned as she stared at the photographs. She did not know why seeing their faces made her so happy.

'And you don't know what happened to the rest of Alice's family, her brothers, Hugo and Benedict, or her sister, Petronella?' she asked, trying to work out who might be who in the wedding picture.

'All we know about Benedict was that he inherited the family business. I believe Hugo married a Cretan girl,' she said. 'Angeliki, I think. They met again on the second year of the dig and fell in love. They moved to Africa.'

Eloise and Rose exchanged surprised looks.

'What about the villain of the piece?' asked Rose. 'Ephraim Lockwood.'

'Quinn discovered what happened to him through a genealogy website,' said Eloise. 'It was in his notes. Ephraim died aboard the Titanic.'

'What a release for Petronella,' said Marina.

'There's something else, too,' said Eloise, and against the background shouts of the volleyball, the noise of Thea and Nikos digging holes to bury each other and the general holiday mayhem of Malia, Eloise told Rose and Marina about the dreams she and Alice had shared. Rose knew about Eloise's night-time wandering, but it had been many years since they had discussed her dreams.

'The last two journals,' she said, turning to Marina, 'the ones in the box, one was a dream diary and there was a poem at the back which Alice had written in 1900. I went back through my diaries because when I was a child I'd once woken up with a poem going around my head. It was the same poem, written exactly one hundred years later.'

Rose gasped but Eloise continued, explaining how her dreams had never been a complete story but, by combining them with Alice's dreams, she had pieced together a different version of the Minotaur myth.

'This is extraordinary,' said Marina, who had listened in silence. 'And you say that in the dreams, the exit to the labyrinth is by the standing stone in our grove?'

'Yes,' replied Eloise, 'it would explain why the engraving reads "*Potnia* of the Labyrinth".'

'Are you suggesting you and Alice shared a reincarnation?' said Rose.

'Would it be impossible?' asked Eloise, even though she knew the conversation was taking a strange turn. 'We lived over a hundred years apart and, while I don't believe I'm the reincarnation of your great-great-grandmother, Marina, perhaps she and I did share another connection.'

'There could be another reason you share memories,' suggested Marina. 'The crystal in the necklace Quinn gave you.'

'I've been wondering about that, too,' said Eloise. She reached for her throat in an automatic gesture but, not wanting to risk losing it, she had left the necklace at home.

'Where did Quinn get the crystal and the figurine?' asked Marina. 'If these are the items Alice found, why aren't they in the museum?'

'Ephraim Lockwood stole them,' said Eloise, and explained what she had read.

'What an awful man,' said Rose. 'Sorry, Marina. He was distant relative of yours, too.'

'Not by blood,' said Marina. 'I'm descended from Alice, who was related to Petronella, not the scoundrel Ephraim.'

'In her diary, Alice said she intended to return the artefacts, but it seems this never happened. When Quinn was refurbishing and rebuilding the old barn where Alice had hidden them, he must have rediscovered them and had the crystal made into a wedding present for me.'

'So, there isn't another ancient site under the house,' said Marina with a hint of disappointment in her voice.

'Alice's dreams began when she arrived in Crete,' said Eloise, 'and my dreams have been with me since childhood, so they're not caused by the crystal, but perhaps the many twists and turns of fate brought me to the stone. Maybe Alice was brought here for the same reason, to uncover the crystal and begin the dream cycle. I think I'm meant to finish it.'

'What do you think you're supposed to do?' asked Marina, and suddenly, as the hot Cretan sun beat down, Eloise understood.

40

They returned to Sfragida House, hot, tired and slightly sunburned, with Marina and Yiannis's invitation to join them at the Brewery Taverna later ringing in their ears.

Sean and Marcus were revived after a feast of Cretan *kalitsounia* – the local delicacy of sweet mini cheese pies – that they had discovered during their first visit. Marina's mother, Donna, had sent over a huge box when she had heard how much Sean and Marcus enjoyed them. They threw themselves into the pool with Leon watching, his legs dangling in the water as he taught the boys how to count in Latin while they swam.

'Have you heard anything from Claud?' asked Rose, as she and Eloise sorted out the wet beach towels and swimming costumes, piling them into the washing machine.

'A text, apologising for walking out on the day I showed him the footage,' she replied.

'Did he offer any explanation?'

'No. Was he so repulsed by what happened that he can't speak to me?'

Tears sparkled in Eloise's eyes and Rose hugged her.

'There's more to this, Lo,' she said.

'Are you defending Claud?' asked Eloise in astonishment.

'Perhaps, for the first time, I am,' she said leaning against the kitchen worktop.

'Why? You hate him.'

'After what we've learned about Claud – and I see no reason for him to lie – I've revised my views on his behaviour. He's already admitted Josh wasn't above emotional blackmail between his friends, including coercing Claud into being best man, when the obvious choice was Nahjib. Yet, he chose the man that he delighted in telling you disliked you. Who was he punishing? You or Claud?'

'Why did Claud agree, though?'

'Honestly, Lo, have you not worked it out yet?'

'What?'

Rose pretended to bang her head against the fridge.

'It's the same reason he used those weak excuses to fly out here. He could have rung you about the house and, at the same time, asked how you were coping, but he chose to fly all the way to Crete.'

'Which is what?'

'Claud never hated you, Lo. He's in love with you. He wanted to be at the wedding because he couldn't bear being apart from you...'

'No, you're wrong,' said Eloise, her voice harsh.

'I think it's the same reason he agreed to the madness of coming on your honeymoon, and every other weird scenario Josh set up to throw the two of you together. Claud couldn't resist being near you, so Josh continued to force you together to torture you both.'

'If you're right, which I'm not sure you are, do you think Josh knew?'

'Guessed, perhaps, but even so, he liked to manipulate people and, I think, Claud played into his hands.'

'Why did you never say anything at the time?' asked Eloise.

'It didn't occur to me,' said Rose. 'I'm ashamed to say, I fell for

Josh's manipulation of the situation and became the first to line up to bitch about Claud. Josh and I would often spend our lunch hours having a go at Claud and, honestly, he didn't deserve it, I understand that now. Josh was very clever, he could be charming when necessary, and as a barrister, a supposed man of honour and truth, his integrity was not to be questioned.'

Eloise allowed Rose's words to sink in and realised there was truth in them. Josh had blinded her with his charm and, even after his behaviour had become violent towards her, he had continued to manipulate her. There was no reason to believe he hadn't done the same in all his relationships.

'Why hasn't Claud contacted me, then?' asked Eloise.

'What you showed to Claud was a huge shock, especially if he's supposed to be trained to spot these situations. He's dealing with the loss of Josh, who, it seems was not the close friend we'd always been led to believe,' said Rose, her voice gentle.

'What do you mean?'

'No one should feel glad someone is dead, but maybe a small part of Claud does and he's having to come to terms with these unpleasant feelings,' said Rose. 'Nahjib's attack was another shock, again involving abuse, and again Claud missed the signs. I suspect he was so busy trying to intercept you and Josh, he missed Marcella's odd behaviour.'

'Do you think he suspected Josh, then?'

'You said yourself he would often turn up unannounced. It was one of the things that irritated you, but one night—'

'He arrived halfway through the England match,' remembered Eloise, her hands shaking as she thought how close Josh had come to raping her when the doorbell had rung, forcing him to stop. 'England were two nil down, Josh was drunk, and losing matches always made him worse. He was badgering me to have sex in front of the television while he watched the football and I refused. He was furious and had me pinned to the floor when the doorbell rang. Josh said to ignore it, then his phone buzzed and Claud said he was outside with a takeaway.'

'Why do you think Claud turned up then?'

'I was never sure, but a few days before there had been a feature in one of the newspapers saying that a study had shown there was an increase in domestic violence when there were international football matches. Apparently, it went up by twenty-six per cent on the days England won or drew, and thirty-eight per cent if England lost. Perhaps Claud had read it and decided to make sure Josh was distracted.'

'You survived, though, Lo,' said Rose. 'Despite Josh's terrible behaviour, you're alive. You have this beautiful house and people who love you.'

'Because he died,' Eloise said, anguish in her voice. 'I survived because Josh took so many drugs, his heart stopped working. Otherwise, I could have been a statistic. Yet, even with all he'd done, I didn't leave.'

'People like Josh, abusers, are skilled manipulators and when they have the charm Josh was able to switch on and off, they're even more dangerous,' said Rose.

'I began to believe his behaviour was normal,' Eloise said, 'possibly even my own fault. It was a gradual build up, a "funny" comment here, referred to as "banter", "I'm teasing you because I love you", "Can't you take a joke?", but I allowed myself to believe the problem was mine and I was overreacting, being too sensitive, when really he was the one who needed help.'

'Josh is gone,' said Rose, tears in her eyes. 'Don't let him win from beyond the grave. If you think you have feelings for Claud, and I suspect you do, reach out to him. Claud may be scared to make the first move but, if you're ready at least to talk to him, you have to be brave. You're allowed to be happy, Lo. You're allowed to live and love again.'

A blood-curdling scream from outside interrupted their conversation as both women ran outside to discover Leon being tickled by his two sons.

'Fools,' said Rose with huge fondness. 'Sorry, shall we go back inside? We can continue our discussion.'

'No, I'm going to have a shower. We'll need to leave soon to meet Marina and Yiannis.'

As Eloise entered her bedroom, she pondered Rose's words. Was this the reason Claud had walked away? He was overburdened with a form of survivor's guilt concerning the attack? Determined no longer to hide behind her fears, Eloise stared at her phone. When they returned from the Brewery Taverna, when she had time to talk, she would ring Claud. Rose is right, she thought as she stepped under the hot water, it was time to reach out to him and offer him support. Claud was as much a victim of Josh's manipulations as she was.

41

'Your usual table awaits,' announced John grandly as Eloise led the way up the short flight of steps into the Brewery Taverna. Rose, Leon, Sean and Marcus followed, the boys running off to speak to Steve and try to persuade him to allow them to play with the three pugs.

'Thank you,' Eloise said, accepting the hug John offered. 'We're starving after a day on the beach.'

'I'll send over bread and olives,' he said. 'Marina rang ahead and asked for wine to be waiting.'

Eloise laughed, but before she could follow the others to the end of the terrace where John had laid a long table under the vine, he beckoned her aside.

'What's the matter?'

'Nothing,' he responded but his smile had slipped. 'Did you know Claud was back?'

'What?' Eloise felt a strange jolt, followed by a spurt of unease that he had not been in touch. 'No. When?'

'About an hour ago and with his friend Nahjib. He was going to call you but I told him you were all coming here this evening and he asked if I'd divert you away for a few minutes. Did I do the right thing?'

Eloise reached out and squeezed John's hand.

'Yes,' she said. 'Where is he?'

'Upstairs in the apartment,' said John as he ushered Eloise through the bar so she could use the private entrance.

'Will you let Rose know where I am, please?' she said as she ran up the stone staircase and knocked on the door.

When Claud answered, Eloise felt as though the air had left her lungs. Claud had always been good-looking but over the years she had denied the effect his appearance had on her. Josh would taunt him and Eloise would agree, he was too good-looking and deserved to be mocked. She had never acknowledged how breath-taking she found him until now. As she stared up into his wary eyes, she was transported back in time to the night in the pub, when she had seen him for the first time, as she cradled the lost puppy.

'I'm sorry...' they said together.

'You first,' he said.

'I'm sorry for not realising what Josh did to us,' she said. 'From the moment, I met you, there was a connection, but I never understood.'

'I'm sorry too,' Claud said, reaching out to take her hands, his thumb once again stroking the livid scar, 'for not helping when I suspected what Josh was doing. It was in the weeks before he died it dawned on me what was happening, but I didn't act fast enough to spare you...'

'It wasn't your fault,' said Eloise. 'Only one person was to blame.'

'But he didn't deserve to die...' Claud's voice broke with suppressed emotion.

'No, he didn't deserve to die,' she agreed, 'and I tried all I could to save him.'

'I know,' he said.

'And us, Claud?' she asked. 'What about us? I understand now, Josh did everything he could to make me dislike you.'

'Do you think he loved you and that was why?' asked Claud.

'No,' she said, realising at last that this was true. 'He never loved me, he never loved anyone. I think Josh must have seen something between us that first night in the pub and played with us for his own twisted reasons. It was you and I who should have been together.'

Eloise had used every ounce of courage she possessed to deliver these words and her whole body shook with fear of his rejection. Claud was looking at her in astonishment.

'Do you mean that?' he whispered, pulling her towards him.

'Yes,' she replied, but as he opened his mouth to say the words she longed to hear, she put her finger to his lips. 'Not here,' she said. 'It has to be the right place.'

'What do you mean?' he asked in bewilderment.

'Trust me?' she asked.

'Forever.'

42

Wrapped in shadows, they crept through the tunnel, the cord guiding them towards the glimmer of hope in the darkness, to the standing stone in the grove.

'You shall soon be free,' she assured them. 'The boats will take you wherever you choose to travel. There will be no more fear.'

Each carried the small purse of gold, the last gift from the Potnia of the Labyrinth. The money was from the donations made by the people of the island, the good and the bad, a way to ease their own sins by paying tithes to the creature created by the gods as a terrible warning.

'This way,' her handmaidens urged, and they fled, borne again from the darkness of the labyrinth into the night.

'Sister,' he wheezed, his voice full of wonder and excitement, 'we shall be safe.'

'And we shall be together,' Ariadne replied as the corridor turned and the yawning mouth of the cave stood before them.

'We are free,' he said, smiling. 'I love you.'

She stroked the side of his face, watching as he walked in his ungainly way towards their new beginning. Looking behind her for one last time, she said a final farewell to the labyrinth that had been their home, then turned as her brother disappeared into the night.

With swift footsteps, she followed, her voice soft with moonlight as she said, 'Wait for me, Asterion. I love you.'

43

The sun was a misty ball of fire in the distance as Eloise, Claud, Rose, Leon, Sean, Marcus and Nahjib met on the hillside. Marina and Yiannis arrived moments later and together they walked the steep path to the hidden grove with the standing stone.

Eloise was sure-footed, feeling as though she was being guided through the Cretan countryside, a path laid out that she had been traversing her entire life. A story that was about to end.

'It's here,' she said, pushing aside the wild rosemary and thyme, leading the way down the three steps into the hidden grove.

'Wow,' whispered Sean, and Eloise smiled. 'This is awesome. Do you think we might find the skeleton of the Minotaur?'

'No,' replied Eloise, hugging her godson, 'and even if we did, we would leave him in peace.'

'I'd forgotten about the tranquillity of this place,' said Marina, her hand in Yiannis's as they walked around the standing stone. 'You would never know the vineyard is a few metres away.'

'It's magic,' said Marcus, in the same hushed tone as his brother.

'You're right,' said Claud. 'Ancient magic, linked to us all.'

'A lost moment in time,' said Nahjib.

'Let's find the right spot,' said Leon. 'Any thoughts, Lo?'

'Here,' she replied, stopping at a small dip in the ground halfway between the stone and the blocked entrance to the cave. 'This is the place.'

Leon, Claud, Yiannis and Nahjib pulled out trowels provided by Marina, and together they dug a deep, square hole. Eloise, Rose and Marina, meanwhile, prepared what Eloise thought of as the tribute to the goddess, to Ariadne, the *Potnia* of the Labyrinth, the woman about whom a thousand tales had been told.

Perhaps, thought Eloise, as she laid out the silken scarf and placed the flask of wine on it, followed by her necklace and the figurine, she was a real woman and by doing this, she will finally be able to rest.

Sean and Marcus inspected the blocked-up cave, discussing in whispered tones how many bodies might be buried on the other side of the rockfall.

When the hole was big enough, the men stepped behind the women. Rose called the twins and they gathered in silence. Eloise picked up her crystal necklace and kissed it.

'Thank you, Quinn,' she said as she placed the stone in the wooden treasure chest she had discovered in his library. 'You helped bring the story together.' The figurine followed and Eloise closed the box, wrapping it in the silk scarf. Placing it in the hole, she added rose petals before pouring a libation, encircling it with a ring of red wine, as a representation of blood.

'Thank you, Ariadne,' she whispered. 'Thank you, Alice. The story has been told.'

With great care, the group of friends refilled the hole and, when it was done, they each took a white stone from Eloise and placed it on the mound of fresh earth. 'Say goodbye to someone or something you have loved and lost,' she said as she handed out each stone.

She and Claud waited until the end. Then, together, hand in hand, they placed their stones on the earth.

'Goodbye, Josh,' Eloise whispered. 'I forgive you.'

'Goodbye, Josh,' Claud repeated. 'I forgive you.'

Then Eloise turned to Claud, squeezing his hand, and together they whispered,

'I love you.'

ACKNOWLEDGEMENTS

Thank you for reading *The Forgotten Palace*. I hope you enjoyed meeting Eloise, Alice and their friends and families. A book is never the work of one person – there are many people involved. First, thank you to my wonderful agent, Sara Keane, who is generous with her experience, wisdom and laughter. Thank you to Sarah Ritherdon, my editor, who has made this process fun and enjoyable. Thank you also to the wider team at Boldwood Books for the cover, copy-editing, proofreading and marketing. You're all wonderful.

Thank you to Carol McGrath for reading an early copy and being such a good friend and strong supporter of my work. Also to Jane Cable, who offered endless encouragement, Deborah Black, who listened to me rant, and to the wonderful Gemma Turner, who allowed me to use her description of grief as glitter. Thank you to you all.

One last, more random acknowledgement. Thank you to Abby, Colin, JB, Martin (Mad-Dog), Steve, Rob and Naomi (Lady Lowe) for the fun we had on the official *London 2012 Olympic magazines* all those years ago. Who knew our office poster boy, Launceston Elliot, would one day appear in a novel? Love you guys.

Most importantly, thank you to you for reading this book. Without you, none of this would be possible.

If you would like to know more about Arthur Evans and the dig at the Palace of Knossos, then please read on.

THE FORGOTTEN PALACE – THE HISTORY

Alice's story features the real-life excavation at Knossos in Crete. While I have taken a few liberties with the finds discovered by Alice, I have tried to place the rest of the dig and its personnel in the correct historical content. Here's a bit more information.

In 1900, Arthur Evans (1851–1941) began digging in Crete. He was looking for the palace of King Minos and remains of the lost Cretan civilisation of the Minoans. As his team split the earth apart with pickaxes and shovels, Arthur dreamed not only of finding this lost world but, more importantly to him, a form of early writing, which he believed was waiting in the soil beneath his feet.

But who were the Minoans and what happened to them?

Very, very briefly, the Minoans were a Bronze Age civilisation who enjoyed a thriving, wealthy way of life, trading widely and worshipping on a grand scale. However, in approximately 1600 BCE, there was a catastrophic volcanic eruption on the island of Thera (better known as Santorini) not far from their shores. This caused a huge tsunami, which engulfed the surrounding islands, including the Minoans on Crete, destroying their cities. Although many survived, the Minoans never again achieved such a wealthy and powerful existence. Arthur Evans wanted to rediscover the Minoans and tell their story.

The Forgotten Palace positions my fictional Victorian heroine, Alice Webster, at this real-life dig. She is in disgrace and searching for a way to move forward with her life. I liked the idea of her trying to find her way out of a symbolic labyrinth of despair and lost love by helping to physically dig the winding palace of Knossos from the soil.

Arthur Evans, however, was very real. The son of the wealthy industrialist Sir John Evans of Nash Mills, and his first wife, Harriet, Arthur was the eldest of a large family. He had two brothers, Lewis (b. 1853) and Philip Norman (b. 1854) and two sisters, Harriet (b. 1857) and Alice (b. 1858). Arthur was seven when his mother died in 1858.

His father remarried and the Evans siblings were raised by their stepmother, Fanny (Frances) née Phelps. Arthur and his siblings remained close to each other throughout their lives and were also close to Fanny. She predeceased Arthur's father and in 1892, Sir John Evans married the classical scholar Maria Millington Lathbury, who was many years his junior. When John was seventy, they had a daughter, Joan.

Throughout his life, John, who was also a fanatical geologist and archaeologist, offered support and financial help to Arthur as he excavated Crete and the incredible complex of Knossos. John died in 1908 when Arthur was aged fifty-seven.

Arthur was not only an archaeologist. For many years he travelled, writing for the *Manchester Guardian* (the forerunner of the *Guardian*) highlighting the plight of people in war-torn nations. His particular love was the Baltic states and he had many adventures, including being incorrectly arrested as a spy. He became Keeper of the Ashmolean Museum in Oxford in January 1884 and spent a great deal of his own fortune rebuilding it and donating artefacts.

He married Margaret Freeman in September 1878 and she

followed him on his adventures. After her death in 1893, Arthur continued to use black-edged stationery until his death. He never remarried.

Along the way, Arthur became friends with most of the renowned archaeologists of the day and together they discovered ancient civilisations, including the Schliemanns, Heinrich and Sophia, who found what they believed to be the Troy that featured in both *The Iliad* (Homer) and *The Odyssey* (Homer). Many years later, archaeologists proved this to be incorrect. Arthur, however, was inspired by this find and was determined to find a source of writing, which he believed was a missing but vital part of the Bronze Age.

Although Arthur claimed, unlike Schliemann, he was not hoping to prove Homer and Ovid correct and was not looking for the source of Greek mythology, as the Palace of Knossos emerged before his eyes, with its winding corridors and endless rooms, even he could not deny the grandeur of the unusual layout. Evans came to believe it was this complex that could have inspired the myth of King Minos the Minotaur and the labyrinth.

This belief was further enhanced by the discoveries of images of bulls throughout the palace. Endless depictions of goddesses also caused Arthur to suggest the Minoans worshipped a Mother Goddess. He did indeed discover evidence of writing, which he named Linear A and Linear B. However, he died before Linear B was finally deciphered in the 1950s, giving details of day-to-day life and a pantheon of gods and goddesses. Linear A continues to remain untranslated, its secrets a tantalising mystery.

His other close friends included David Hogarth, director of the British School of Archaeology at Athens; Duncan Mackenzie, who had been educated in Vienna and Edinburgh and came to Knossos after many years of field experience with the British School of Archaeology, Athens; the architect Theodore Fyfe, also from the

British School of Archaeology at Athens; and the artists, Emile Gilliéron, who helped Evans to reproduce the frescoes with help from his son, Edouard Gilliéron.

Sadly, their methods were haphazard and a huge amount of the archaeology following the Minoans was lost along the way.

One of the most interesting things I discovered during my research were the number of female archaeologists who were making their presence felt at this time. These included Amelia Edwards (1831–1892), Jane Dieulafoy (1851– 1916), Zelia Nuttall (1857–1933), Gertrude Bell (1868–1926) and Harriet Boyd Hawes (1871–1945). Many others followed but these intrepid women fitted my timeline and would have been an inspiration to Alice.

The Theosophy Movement was also gaining popularity at the turn of the century and, as it had beliefs that fitted with elements of the story, I decided Alice's friend Juliet could be the conduit for her discovering the Akashic Record and more details about the idea of reincarnation.

Arthur Evans returned to Knossos for many years, unearthing a staggering amount of information. The palace of King Minos was once the most important discovery of all time. However, when Howard Carter and Lord Carnarvon discovered Tutankhamun's tomb in the Valley of the Kings in November 1922, the glamour of the boy-king's golden death mask stole the limelight from Minos and the labyrinth.

While Arthur Evans, Duncan Mackenzie, David Hogarth, Theo Fyfe and Harriet Boyd were real people, Alice, Hugo, Aunt Agatha, Robert, Andrew, Ephraim et al. are entirely from my imagination, but they proved to be true adventurers and were fun to meet.

If you're interested in discovering more about the Knossos dig, then some of the books I found useful were:

Sylvia L. Horwitz, *The Find of a Lifetime, Sir Arthur Evans and the Discovery of Knossos* (The Viking Press, New York, 1981)

Anne Brown, *Arthur Evans and the Palace of Knossos* (Ashmolean Museum Publications, Oxford, 1983)

Margalit Fox, *The Riddle of the Labyrinth* (Profile Books, 2013)

John Chadwick, *The Mycenaean World* (Cambridge University Press, 1976)

Helena Petrovna Blavatsky, *The Key to Theosophy* (Amazon, first published 1889)

Amanda Adams, *Ladies of the Field, Early Women Archaeologists and their Search for Adventure* (Greystone Books, 2010)

Bradshaw's Continental Railway Guide, 1853 (Collins, 2016)

David Turner, *Victorian and Edwardian Railway Travel* (Shire Publications, 2013)

Walter Shewring (translator), *Homer, The Odyssey* (Oxford University Press, 1980)

Robert Fitzgerald (translator), *Homer, The Iliad* (Oxford University Press, 1974)

Elaine Fantham, *Ovid's Metamorphoses* (Oxford University Press, 2004)

A. D. Melville, *A new translation, Ovid, The Love Poems* (Oxford University Press, 1998)

A. D. Melville, *A new translation, Ovid, Metamorphoses,* (Oxford University Press, 1986)

ABOUT THE AUTHOR

Alexandra Walsh is the bestselling author of dual timeline historical mysteries, including *The Secrets of Crestwell Hall*. Her books range from the fifteenth century to the Victorian era and are inspired by the hidden voices of women that have been lost over the centuries. She was formerly a journalist, writing for national newspapers, magazines and TV.

Sign up to Alexandra Walsh's mailing list here for news, competitions and updates on future books.

Visit Alexandra's website: http://www.alexandrawalsh.com/

Follow Alexandra on social media:

X x.com/purplemermaid25
f facebook.com/themarquesshousetrilogy
○ instagram.com/purplemermaid25
♪ tiktok.com/@alexandracwalsh

ALSO BY ALEXANDRA WALSH

The Forgotten Palace

The Secrets of Crestwell Hall

Letters from
the past

Discover page-turning
historical novels from
your favourite authors
and be transported
back in time

*Join our book club
Facebook group*

https://bit.ly/SixpenceGroup

*Sign up to our
newsletter*

https://bit.ly/LettersFrom
PastNews

Boldwood

Boldwood Books is an award-winning fiction publishing company seeking out the best stories from around the world.

Find out more at www.boldwoodbooks.com

Join our reader community for brilliant books, competitions and offers!

Follow us
@BoldwoodBooks
@TheBoldBookClub

Sign up to our weekly deals newsletter

https://bit.ly/BoldwoodBNewsletter